iGoli
City of Gold

Kelvin Robertson

Published by Keldaviain Publishing

A CIP catalogue record for this book is available from
The British Library.

ISBN 978-0-9928599-7-8

Chapter 1

The man pushed open the heavy steel and glass door, stepped over the cill and emerged onto the deserted deck of the *Armadale Castle*. It was early, not long after the sun had risen and the orange rays bouncing off the still waters of the South Atlantic excited his senses. Inhaling the fresh morning air, he stepped forward, strolling across the gently vibrating deck as he had done every morning since leaving Southampton, and made his way towards the ship's side to pause and rest his hands on the teak rail. He looked across the wide expanse of ocean, at first seeing nothing but the unbroken line of the horizon and then his heart skipped a beat. His eyes narrowed as he noticed a dark disfigurement on the horizon, he blinked several times to clear them, to make sure it was indeed his first sight of land and he remembered why he was here.

It was a month since he had left Edinburgh, the result of a chance encounter with his Cousin Angus and he would still be there, languishing in the estate agent's office if it had not been for that meeting. His father, a successful tailor in the city had mapped out for him a professional path ever since he had won the scholarship to the city's James Watts College. His father expected his second son to follow a profession, to become a lawyer, a banker or perhaps a stockbroker, but it had all come to nought, Norman had been a disappointment.

Of above average intelligence and with a physical presence he had made a good rugby player and been an asset to the school team. However, He was argumentative and at times self-opinionated and he did not get on well with the games master, an ex-soldier who was a stickler for discipline. In the end it became a case of the irresistible force meeting the immovable object. After a disastrous first half in the final of the Scottish Schools Cup the games master heaped most of the blame onto Norman and it came to blows. The result leaving the games master nursing a bruised jaw and Norman expelled from the school.

He could see his father now, furious but pragmatic, reasoning that if the professions were out of reach then his son should at least try for some form of apprenticeship and learn a skill. He would speak with a customer of his for whom he was fashioning a top of the range suit in the finest Harris Tweed and two days later, after a drastic price reduction, Norman began his working life as the tea boy at a firm of estate agents in the city.

Pursing his lips at the memory of this humiliating end to his education Norman took a cigarette from his silver case, struck a match and rested his elbows on the rail. Drawing in the smoke he felt he had not been a complete disaster: after all, he had managed to work his way up in the sales department and things had seemed to be going well until one wet September night when he bumped into his cousin Angus in a Princes Street bar..

2

'Norman Campbell, how are you, I haven't seen you since your wedding day. How's Lucy?' asked Angus.

'She's well, very well and we have two children now, a boy and a girl.'

'Goodness, how old are they?'

'My daughter is four and young Alistair is just a year younger.'

'Ye didna waste much time Norman,' said Angus with a laugh.

Norman did not reply, instead he looked at Angus's empty glass and made a tilting motion with his hand indicating that he was due for a fill-up.

'Och Aye,' said Angus pushing his glass along the bar, 'and what are you doing with yourself these days, you were working in an estate agents office weren't you?'

'Yes, and I still am. What are you doing for a living, still in shipping?'

'Yes, pushing a pen for old Gregor McNiven. He must be a wealthy bastard with all those ships. Do you know we've carried tons and tons of ostrich feathers out of South Africa during the last couple of years and I know the freight charges, why when I was in the Cape Town office we . . .'

'The what, the Cape Town office? Is that where you've been hiding?'

'Aye, ah did three years out there and I'll tell you what Norman, the weather beats Scotland's hands down.'

Norman smiled to himself as he lit a second cigarette, remembering the conversation and how upset his half-drunk cousin had become. The poor chap had only been home a few weeks, not yet acclimatized to the Scottish weather and now all he wanted to do was to get back to that warmer climate.

'Another beer Angus, tell me a bit more about the country,' That seemed do the trick, Angus began to relax and then Norman could not stop him talking, astonished at his tales of gold and diamond mines, the wealth of the country.

'An educated chap like you could make his fortune over there in no time,' he had said and in Norman's head, a light had come on.

He smiled to himself as he drew on his cigarette and looked around the deck to see several more passengers come to take their morning exercise and to watch the ship's final approach to land. It was January 1912, the height of the southern summer and he understood now his cousin's concerns, guessing that he must be suffering back home in the Scottish winter. He took one last drag of the cigarette and flicked the glowing stub in an arc towards the sea, his gaze lingering on the distant landscape for a little longer.

'I hope you're not smoking too much,' said a voice behind him, and before he could turn round, another voice called out 'Daddy, daddy . . .' and he felt a tug at his trouser leg.

'Lucy, hello,' he said to his wife and placed a hand on the head of his small son whose arms were now firmly wrapped about his leg. 'I've been out here an hour or more already and I think I'm entitled to a cigarette or two. Look, I do believe that is Table Mountain.' He said, pointing to the lump on the horizon. 'It won't be long before we're there I think.'

Lucy paused for a few moments to look and then she reached down to take hold of Alistair's hand. 'We have had breakfast Norman, and I think we ought to pack the rest of our things before we dock, don't you? I will see you back in our cabin, come Rosemary,' she said to her daughter, waiting patiently beside her and led both children back into the ship's interior.

Norman and Lucy had not seen eye to eye for some time. He had been eager to move to South Africa, captivated by Angus's description of the country and its opportunities. Initially it had been a pipe dream and he had not mentioned it to Lucy, but he could not get the idea out of his head. Then, a few weeks after coming across Angus, a chance encounter changed things. He had become something of a star salesman, often looking after well to do clients and today his boss had entrusted him with a Mrs. Bingham, recently come from South Africa. Married to a wealthy businessman who yearned to return to the mother country, at least for the season, she had come to look for a suitable property and when the subject of South Africa surfaced, she became very enthusiastic.

'I went out there in 1900 after reading about the plight of the Boer women and children, I felt it my duty to help. My first husband was an officer in the Coldstream Guards and I saw it as an opportunity for us to be reunited. Alas, we were together for only a very short time before he was killed and when the war ended I decided to stay.'

Norman was intrigued and remembering his cousin's words, could not help asking questions, probing to find out if it were possible for him to go there, possible perhaps to make money.

'I must say the opportunities for someone who is prepared to take a few risks and work hard are endless. My present husband became interested in diamonds, bought a small claim and then another and, as he struck lucky, another and in no time at all he had made a fortune.'

Fascinated, Norman hung onto every word as he showed her round the house. His job was to talk her into buying the property but instead his curiosity got the better of him and all he seemed able to do was ask about this fascinating country.

'You seem very interested in South Africa. If you are serious then perhaps I could put in a word for you with some real estate people I know at my tennis club.'

Norman had nodded his head with obvious pleasure, realising that it was a perfect opportunity for him to better himself, a chance to make his fortune and enthusiastically he related his encounter to his wife.

'This woman, who is she?' asked Lucy when he told her the good news.

'The wife of a wealthy businessman.'

'What do you know about her Norman? You cannot go chasing half the way round the world on this woman's say-so. What about us, how will you look after us?'

She was less than impressed, evaporating his euphoria in no time, leaving him in a state of mild depression and for several days he sulked. Gradually he overcame his disappointment, then a letter arrived at the office from Mrs. Bingham advising him to write to Williamson and Williamson of Cape Town, a firm of land agents, enquire about a position with them and he did, straight away. Six weeks later, he received a reply offering him a position with a starting salary almost twice as much as he was earning in Edinburgh. Here was concrete evidence of a job and after much persuasion, Lucy had agreed to come and at last, they were here.

Disembarkation was a tedious, haphazard affair; passengers were ushered down the gangplanks and guided towards a large corrugated shed where the authorities checked them for entry into the country. An official asked Norman a few cursory questions and once he produced the letter of the job offer, he waved them through. Leaving the shed and back out in the sunshine, they made their way towards a crane swinging luggage from the ship's hold, landing its load next to a line of black porters. Norman was unsure of what to do; he had expected someone from his new employer to meet them, his final letter of engagement had advised that a Company representative would meet him off the ship but there was no one. Anxiously, he began to look around and then a voice from behind him quietly asked.

'Mr. Norman Campbell?'

Norman spun round, '. . . yes?'

'Pleased to meet you! My name is James, Arthur James, and I have come from Williamson and Williamson to take you to the house the Company is providing and help you settle in.

'Thank you; er . . . this is my wife Lucy, and my son and daughter.'

The man was dressed in a lightweight grey suit, he was shorter than Norman, his most prominent facial feature a thin moustache and he seemed completely at ease as he raised his trilby hat in greeting. Norman, felt reassured and raised his own Homburg in reply. Beside him, Lucy smiled a little nervously, her doubts about living in a new country tempered by the news that they were to have their own house.

'Come boy,' said Arthur, clicking his fingers at a porter. 'Show him your luggage mister Campbell.'

7

Norman searched amongst the pile of bags and trunks to locate his effects and Arthur instructed the porter to load his barrow and follow to a car parked a few yards along the road. After the man had loaded the bags everyone climbed into the car and Arthur began the drive towards the town and as they passed old colonial buildings Arthur gave a running commentary saying, 'They are the old British army barracks, or that one is the original protestant church'.

'You can see table mountain ahead, look, there.'

Norman and Lucy looked out of the car windows, taking in their first real sights of the country and soon the car was heading into Cape Town proper. Norman was surprised by the size and grandeur of some of the buildings and wide streets filled with both motorised and horse drawn vehicles.

'Adderley street, it's one of the busiest streets in the city,' said Arthur. 'What do you think, what are your first impressions?'

Norman and Lucy were pleasantly surprised and said so before settling back to enjoy the rest of their short journey and before long the car turned off the main road to make its way along a quiet street filled with pretty, whitewashed wooden houses.

'Your new home,' said Arthur bringing the car to a halt and jumping out to open the rear door for Lucy.

Impressed, Lucy stood for a few moments to look at their new home, sighing with pleasure at this very different prospect to the tenement they had left behind. It was a two story wooden structure standing on its own plot with a well-kept garden to the front and she could not wait to have a closer look.

'Come children, our new home, isn't it exciting?'

The children emerged from the back seat to stand next to their mother and taking hold of their hands, she stood a while longer to gaze at their home. Norman joined them and put his arm around his wife, pleased things were working out, happy that Lucy no longer saw him as a villain. Arthur beckoned them to follow him and as they reached the front door, it opened to reveal a native man and a native woman.

'Marsha, go and make a pot of tea will you' Arthur said to the girl. 'Mabutu, the car, bring the luggage into the house.'

The man bowed slightly and stood to one side, allowing them into the house before he walked towards the car. By now Lucy and Norman were perspiring freely in the heat of the day and Norman was forced to remove his jacket but Lucy soon forgot her discomfort, overcome by an inquisitiveness to look around the house. It was a little shabby, simply furnished but straight away, she could see ways of improving things. The chairs and a settee fashioned from cane would look better with some brightly coloured cushions. The place needed some decent curtains and her mind was elsewhere when Arthur took his leave.

'Settle in for the rest of the day Campbell. I will call round tomorrow at eight thirty to drive you to work and in the meantime, Marsha and Mabutu will look after your needs. Don't be afraid to ask them to do any job around the house – that's why they are here. You will take to the life once you have settled in I am sure. I'll see you in the morning,' he said, giving a short wave goodbye.

Norman waved back and turned to see Lucy and the children opening doors, peering into rooms and soon they were at the foot of the stairs ready to explore the bedrooms. It had not taken Lucy long to realise what a wonderful home the house would make and she felt happy watching the children explore, laughing as they ran around and when she told them they would have a bedroom each they clapped their little hands. Then she said, 'look here, out of the window.'

Alistair and Rosemary ran to the window to stand on tip toe and peer over the sill but little Alistair wasn't quite tall enough and so Lucy had to lift him up to look out at the small garden.

'Look it's a garden where you can play.'

'Oh yes mummy,' said Rosemary, pleasure written all over her face.

In the kitchen Norman was with the servants taking charge of a situation he was unprepared for and found difficult to come to terms with. Haltingly to begin with, he asked questions.

'Mabutu what are your normal duties here?'

'I clean outside the house, I fetch food an wood fo' da stove, an' help Marsha when she need help, an I keep the garden tidy.'

'And Marsha, what does she do?'

'She cooks an clean.'

'Indeed ... and where do you live?'

'We live in da Township three mile away, we walk here every day.'

'The outside of the house looks in need of painting. Can you paint Mabutu?'

'Yesah, I can paint the house.'

'Good. I'll arrange for some paint as soon as I can. Tell Marsha we will have dinner at seven o'clock.'

At seven, the family sat down to a dinner of quite different food from which they were used to eating and the children took some persuading, but they were hungry and after a little coaxing, they ate in silence. Marsha and Mabutu returned to clear the dishes and after that stood silently by the door.

'Yes, what is it you want?' asked Norman.

'We have finished our work for the day, can we go home?' asked Mabutu.

'Why, yes, of course. What time will you begin work tomorrow?' he asked.

'We be here at seven o'clock in da morning baas.'

'Thank you that will be all for today then, off you go.'

At six thirty, Norman woke from a fitful sleep, worries about the job and their new life weighing heavily upon him. Slipping out of bed he left Lucy sleeping and after peering in on the children made his way quietly downstairs. The small kitchen had only a wood burning stove for cooking and having a less than practical nature he decided against breakfast. He looked out of the window, marvelling for a time at the bright colours of the flowers blooming in the southern summer and was in the process of tying the knot in his tie when he heard Marsha and Mabutu arrive.

'You want us to make breakfast,' asked Marsha, her big, enquiring eyes waiting for his response.

'Er . . . yes, what is there?'

'I make scrambled eggs and coffee.'

Norman nodded leaving Marsha to busy herself filling the kettle from the one tap in the house whilst Mabutu began raking out the fire-box of the cooker and by the time the fire was burning Lucy and the children appeared. They ate breakfast in silence, still a little embarrassed at having servants and at eight thirty, Arthur arrived to collect Norman and take him to the office. As Arthur drove, Norman gazed out of the passenger window, taking in the sights of this new country and wondering what the first day in his new job might bring. As the car pulled up outside an impressive looking building in the centre of the city Arthur turned to Norman and said dryly, 'Welcome to Williamson and Williamson, the best show in town.'

Norman did not hear him at first; he was too busy looking up at the building, impressed by its architecture. Arthur called to him again and this time he did hear, paying attention and following him past a polished brass plate with the legend "Williamson and Williamson, Solicitors and Land Agents". They entered a wide lobby and then Arthur led the new man up a wide staircase to the first floor landing, along a corridor past frosted glass windows to the office door of 'Archibald Williamson'. Arthur knocked curtly on the glass and walked in.

'Good morning Mister Frazer,' he said to a middle-aged man sat at a desk at one side of the spacious room.

'Good morning Mister James.'

'I have Mister Campbell here to see Mister Williamson, he is expecting us.'

'Just a moment,' said the man, rising from behind his desk and walking the few paces across the room to a second door where he knocked twice with the knuckle of his index finger. Norman heard a muffled command from the other side of the door and watched as he opened it and peered into the room.

'Mister Williamson will see you now,' he said, turning to wave them in and Arthur led the way. They walked into a carpeted oak panelled office to see a man with a portly frame standing by the window.

'Good morning Arthur,' he said and then to Norman, 'Campbell, I trust you had a pleasant voyage?'

'Indeed I did sir.'

'Good, good. I would like to welcome you to the firm and for that matter to South Africa. We have seen an increase in business since the Union and we need someone with your background. A lot of our clientèle are first or second generation British. I am hoping that you will be able to engage with our aspiring middle class, make them feel they are still part of the mother country. Some people have become extremely wealthy and they want to move up the social scale, buy bigger houses and we want to sell to them. Mrs. Bingham told me that you are the type of chap we need. Now, if you will excuse me I will bid you good morning and leave you in the capable hands of James here. He will show you round, sort out your office and set you to work.'

'Thank you sir,' said Norman, a little bewildered and unsure of what else to say.

Leaving Williamson's office, they walked back along the corridor, stopping at a door leading into a small room containing nothing more than a desk and chair.

'You've met the top man, and he seems to like you'.

'Mm . . . what happens now?'

'This is your office. I will work with you for a few days, until you find your feet. With some hard work and a little luck a fellow like you could do well here at the Cape.'

'Well, it's what I hope'.

13

'You've certainly got the bearing and manner they want. Mrs. Bingham told me all about you when she returned from Scotland. She is a good judge of character. We deal with farmers and settlers out in the country you know, they're always impressed by someone with a bit of breeding.'

'Breeding?'

'It's a tough country but it's possible to make a lot of money, and often, when people do become wealthy, they want bigger houses, and show off a bit. That is where we come in; help them sell their farms, buy bigger ones or maybe a fancy house in Cape Town. The most lucrative part of the business is land. If we can get hold of land from the blacks, we can sell it on to immigrants flocking out here. Your job will be to get out there, see exactly what the clients want and jolly well find it for them. If you can't find what they are looking for, then talk them into buying something we can sell them, anything, but make the sale, convince them it's best deal they ever had.'

Norman smiled to himself, things were not so different here after all – lawyers and land agents no less greedy than the ones back home.

For almost two years, Norman worked hard at his job, enjoying some success selling properties to the wealthy colonials and just as Williamson had predicted, his Britishness, together with a smart appearance impressed clients. He was surprised how eager they were to hear about the "old country" and before long; he had concocted a simple story describing in glowing terms the country he had left behind and he never failed to be amused at how instrumental it was in closing deals.

During this period, Norman became firm friends with Arthur and the two of them would often call at one bar or another after work and after a few whiskies, Arthur would tell him of his escapades. He had come out from England shortly after the war and had roughed it to begin with, finding odd jobs in the diamond mines of Kimberly before coming to Cape Town to try his luck. At first, he had found work as a runner for a firm of solicitors delivering mail around the city, sometimes taking the train to Bloemfontein or the coastal towns of Port Elizabeth and Durban. 'Johannesburg wasn't the city it is now,' he once told Norman. 'No, it has grown rapidly since the war and now the Boers aren't running things it's a place where a man can make a fortune.'

The bar of the Athenaeum Hall Theatre was their favourite haunt, always busy and exciting, a place where the business people of Cape Town and hangers on met each evening to relax and swap stories. It was also a place to learn of opportunities and it was here Norman's real education about South Africa took shape amongst an atmosphere thick with cigar smoke and constant chatter. The two of them would watch and listen, talk with friends and strangers alike, consider anything they heard that they might turn to their advantage, a new strike in the Witwatersrand, a rich miner looking to retire to the Cape perhaps, anything and everything would interest them.

One night Norman and Arthur were sitting next to a window overlooking the street and discussing nothing in particular when suddenly Arthur jumped to his feet. Without a word, he disappeared outside and a minute later returned accompanied by a shabbily dressed stranger. The man was an inch or two taller than Arthur, a powerful looking individual with broad shoulders and he was wearing a battered bush hat on his head.

'Norman! This is Hans Lockmeyer, Hans, this is Norman, a colleague and a good friend from work.'

Norman reached out to shake the stranger's hand but the man only nodded.

'Hans, you still don't seem to have acquired any manners.' Snapped Arthur and sheepishly the man shook Norman's hand. 'I've known Hans for ten years or more. We met just after the war, just after they let him out of the prisoner of war camp and we have been friends ever since. I won't tell you too much about the scrapes we got ourselves into, but we survived, didn't we, eh, Hans? So what are you up to now old friend?'

'You don't seem to have acquired much in the way of manners either. For instance, where's the drink you promised me?' he said in a thick Afrikaans accent.

Arthur laughed, called a waiter over and ordered four more whiskies, one each for Norman and himself, two for Hans. The Afrikaner managed a half smile, seemed pleased enough; although to Norman, the man seemed to not easily show emotion.

'I've been on a scam here in Cape Town but things are getting a little hot for me so I'm catching the morning train to German West Africa. They've discovered another diamond field and I'm going to see what the prospects are amongst the blockheads.'

'Not much fun there, just desert and a few watering holes. I reckon you can easily fool those Germans though, particularly if they haven't seen a swindle before. Which one are you thinking of?'

Hans looked thoughtful and downed the first glass of whisky.

'Are you still working the clothing scam? That was a good one for us a few years ago wasn't it?'

For the first time the stranger managed a little more than half a smile. His lips twitching upwards and he downed the second whisky..

'Yes, but it can be a bit tricky once the miners become suspicious. Then you have to move on pretty quickly before the police arrive or maybe they run you out of town. It's getting harder to fool them, but I think it'll still work up there.'

Arthur turned to Norman to explain. 'In the early days a prospector would work his claim alone, hard work and isolated. They would be very protective of their claims, and who can blame them, it was not unknown for someone to come along and take advantage, do some digging of their own if a claim is left unattended. The prospectors, often reduced to rags, could not work properly without decent boots so we would show up with some catalogues and sell them all sorts, take a deposit saying that we would return the following week with the goods. But of course, we never did. We could spend weeks in one small area, before the miners swapped stories and realised what we were doing. By then we would be gone and they would have had forgotten what we looked like. It worked well for quite a while until the police got onto our trail and we had to make a run for it. We made some money though didn't we Hans? All gone now, spent mostly on whisky and girls.'

They both laughed at some private joke, Norman was not a party to but he laughed anyway. This was probably the missing piece of Arthur's jigsaw puzzle. If they had made easy money by swindling people, he guessed the police were probably forever on their trail, perhaps a magistrate had jailed them for a while.

For the rest of the evening Arthur and Hans reminisced, delighting in recalling their adventures but looking less pleased when they remembered the fortunes they had lost and Norman listened to it all. He was learning more about the real South Africa and through a whisky haze he saw the possibility of a lucrative future for himself. Then he looked at his pocket watch; it was getting late and time for him to leave. He finished his drink and put on his hat and bade the two men goodnight. Hans raised his hat in acknowledgement and Norman noticed for the first time how white his hair was and, curiously, that the top half of his left ear was missing.

Staggering out into the warm night air he did not hail a cab or a rickshaw as he normally would, instead he decided walk home. It was a pleasant evening and he had enjoyed himself but after he had gone no more than two hundred yards, he realised that he had left his cigarette case on the table. It was solid silver and engraved " *To my darling husband.*" If Lucy found out it was missing she would be devastated and so he turned around and retraced his steps.

Unknown to him, as soon as he had left the bar Hans had turned to Arthur and said, 'I need some money for the train to Windhoek tomorrow, how about helping me get my hands on some right now?'

'The match trick?' replied Arthur.

'Yes, we can work that in a hurry. I need to be on my way and there's a candidate just leaving by the main door and I've seen his wedge, come on.'

As the two men stood up Arthur noticed Norman's cigarette case lying beside his empty glass and with a thief's natural instinct, slipped it surreptitiously into his jacket pocket before catching up with Hans who was leaving by a side exit. Outside he observed their victim's progress from a distance and kept a wary eye out for passers-by, relieved to see that the street was practically deserted. Several yards away their victim was making his way from the main entrance unaware of the two men watching him. They had worked the routine enough times for it to be almost second nature and moving silently along the sidewalk they took up well-rehearsed positions. Arthur quickly made his way ahead of Hans and slipped into the shadows of a doorway at the first opportunity. Hans sauntered slowly along behind, letting their victim overtake him and as the man drew level with Arthur, the silver cigarette case appeared in the moonlight.

'Say friend, would you have a match for my cigarette?' Then Arthur half stepped from the shadows, showing just enough of himself for the man to see where he was but not enough to recognize him later and, taken a little off guard, the man automatically reached into his coat pocket for his matches,

'Sure mister here...' he did not finish his sentence, a vicious blow to the back of his head sent him slumping to the ground and Arthur stepped completely from the shadows to catch hold of him. Dragging the limp form back into the doorway both he and Hans reached over the prostrate form, swiftly feeling for any valuables in his pockets and from the opposite side of the street, Norman watched, recognising Arthur and Hans illuminated by a solitary gas light. Shocked, he retreated into the safety of doorway and strained his eyes to see them rifle through the man's clothing. It was over in seconds and the two assailants disappeared into the night leaving Norman alone.

Taken aback he stood still, wondering what to do when a shout from someone leaving the bar reached him. He looked at the man lying on the sidewalk and realised then that anyone seeing him might accuse him of the crime. He must leave before anyone saw him and hastily he walked away wondering about Arthur and Hans, wondering what kind of a man Arthur really was, all thoughts of the silver cigarette case forgotten.

Chapter 2

Solomon Silongo opened his eyes an hour or so before the dawn, woken by his internal clock, and lying still in the dark he listened. He could hear the light breathing of Mary lying beside him on their bed and the baby asleep not far away. He stared into the blackness his ears picking up the sounds of his cattle moving about outside their tiny hut, hooves scraping on the hard earth and he quietly rose from the bed. Slipping on his trousers and jacket, his bare feet carried him silently through the drape over the doorway and out into the cold morning air. He walked around the primitive corral towards the pile of dried feed and the animals, sensing his presence moved towards him, their steamy breath clouding the air. Solomon gathered an armful of the dried straw, spread it amongst his cattle and reached for his wooden bucket to begin milking.

Dawn was breaking over the distant horizon just as he finished milking the last of the cows and he placed the bucket of warm milk safely near a tree before walking over to a small brushwood hut where his few chickens nested. There was a clucking from disturbed birds as he reached in expecting to find two or three eggs secreted in the dried grass. Gradually his eyes became accustomed to the gloom but instead of finding an egg, he saw one of

21

the chickens lying dead. There were no loose feathers, no apparent injuries to the body, he would certainly have heard had there been an intruder during the night and he was puzzled. Picking up the dead bird, he made his way back to the shack just as the first wisps of smoke began to rise from the cooking fire. Entering, he caught sight of Little Amos leaning against the post where gourds containing their food hung out of reach of marauding ants. The little boy stood unsteadily, his big eyes watching his mother as she busied herself making maize cakes for their breakfast and as Solomon walked through the drape, she looked at him and smiled.

'Solomon, you want your breakfast?'

'Yes, it's a cold morning and I'm hungry.'

'What you got there?'

'A chicken – I found it dead but I don't know why ... maybe you can cook it.'

Mary's eyes narrowed and her body stiffened. 'Bad medicine Solomon, I'm not happy; I will not eat that chicken. Something bad is going to happen.'

Solomon shrugged his shoulders said nothing and took the dead bird back outside to lie it on the ground before returning to squat on the animal skins spread on the floor. He sat beside his wife and together they closed their eyes to pray, 'Thank you God for this food and for another day on your earth, Amen.'

Solomon and Mary were both Christians, taught by Anglican missionaries who had descended upon their villages after the defeat of the Zulu army by the British thirty years earlier. The kingdom of the Zulu had undergone catastrophic upheaval before they were born, partition, civil war and a once proud nation had become nothing more than a reservoir of labour for the

Europeans. Not all white men were avaricious though, the missionaries, in their own way, wanted to help. They had come from Europe and America driven by an overpowering desire to educate the children and convert them to the ways of the Christian church and Solomon's village was no exception. As well as the teachings of the Bible, they taught the children to read and write leaving the witch doctors unimpressed. Before the upheaval a shaman would rule the kraals with fear of the spirit world, administer to the sick a mixture of black magic and potions and they had resisted the change as much as possible. In some villages, they gained support from the elders and eventually the children were educated with a mixture of Christianity and witchcraft. Because Solomon was intelligent and resourceful he had easily learned the basics of reading and writing but Mary had not been so attentive and still more than a little influenced by the old ways.

'Come along Amos,' she said to the little boy, offering her breast.

The small child staggered across to his mother and began suckling as she cuddled him with one hand and fed herself with the other. Solomon smiled, even though they were very poor they had each other, the small-holding they rented from Jan Hendricks was productive enough to feed and clothe them and to pay the hated hut tax. Each year, as part of his rent, he would share some of his produce with Hendricks and during planting and harvest seasons; work on the Boer's farm. Suddenly he stopped eating, the hairs the back of his neck rose, a feeling of foreboding began to engulf him and he jumped to his feet. Slipping outside the hut he looked towards distant hills, his eyes narrowing as he discerned a cloud of dust a half mile or more away and he could feel rather than hear the thud of the horses' hooves. Gradually he was able to make out the figures of two men on horseback, one on a white horse, Hendricks he was sure, but the other, riding a grey he at first did not recognise. The rider was wearing darker clothes and he had a bush hat of the same colour on his head, and as they came nearer he realised that it was the police constable. Why were they here so early in the morning?

He picked up a hayfork and began lifting straw onto the stack, trying to appear casual but in his heart he knew that something was not right.

'Solomon, I want to talk to you,' called out Hendricks as the two riders pulled up alongside the cattle pen.

'Yes Baas,' said Solomon with some deference, as was the way between the Boers and the natives.

'You heard of the Native Land Act that came into force today?'

'No Baas.'

'Then I'll tell you. It means you cannot farm this land as a tenant any longer. You can work for me with your wife and family as indentured labourers and I will pay you thirty-five shillings a month. I will take your cattle for use on the farm and they will help pay your wages.'

Solomon was flabbergasted, this was unwelcome news and his mind spun as he tried to grasp fully the meaning of Hendricks words. Was his wife's prophecy of impending misfortune coming true? He felt the muscles in the pit of his stomach clench and his mouth became dry as he listened.

'I will give you seven days to decide, but, if after seven days you will not agree to my terms I shall ask the constable here to evict you and your cattle from my land.

Where you go after that, I do not know or care. I advise you to accept my offer Solomon, your native way of life is changing and you can do nothing about it.'

The old Boer had no more to say and turned his horse away followed closely by the constable to leave Solomon stunned. The native did not understand and stood in a daze staring after his unwelcome visitors and then Mary emerged from the hut holding their baby to her bosom.

'What has happened Solomon? What did the baas man say? Why the policeman here?' she said with a trembling voice.

Solomon recovered and with some bewilderment tried to explain, but he had not fully grasped the significance of Hendricks's words but Mary, with a female instinct, realised that her family was in trouble.

'Solomon, husband, I knew we had a bad omen! This is the work of evil spirits, go to the kraal, and ask the witch doctor for help. Ask for a potion to help us.'

Solomon did not believe a great deal in the traditional Zulu explanation of things, but he did still believe in the power of the witch doctors and he was beginning to believe that a witch doctor might be their only chance of salvation. Hurriedly he tried to pull himself together, a feeling of anger and fear coursing together through his veins causing his chest to heave, his breathing to quicken and he had to reach out to hold the rail of the cattle pen. After a few seconds, the feeling passed and he looked down at Mary.

'I will go to the village to talk to the chief, ask for his wisdom, seek out my father and ask him. While I am gone will you manage; can you cope with everything there is to do? I will be gone for three or four days and you must tend to the animals and look after Amos on your own?'

Mary looked at Solomon, tears forming in her beautiful brown eyes, she struggled to speak, able only to nod her head and Solomon knew what he had to do. His only course was to go to his home village to seek advice, a 70-mile journey and the sooner he left the better. First, he tended to his animals, spreading dried grass for the cattle and scattering some seed for the chickens, Mary took his leather pouch with the shoulder strap and filled it with mealie cakes and strips of dried meat for the journey. It was a long way on foot but if he could keep up the loping run of the Zulu, he might get there in two days. He was fit and strong, felt sure that he could do it and so when he had completed all his chores, he touched his son's head, held up his hand in farewell to Mary and left them.

For six hours, he managed his long loping run until forced to rest for an hour, to eat some of his biltong and to drink from the flask at his waist. He looked up at the sky, the afternoon was passing the sinking sun told him he must to decide to carry on during the hours of darkness or rest for the night. He was feeling the strain of his ordeal and made the decision to journey until the sun was just above the distant mountains and then he would rest for the night. With some light remaining, he could gather kindling and firewood to make a fire to keep him warm and safe from wild animals. With his mind made up, he resumed his journey until the light turned to the orange of sunset and he found a safe place for the night.

Dropping his sleeping mat from his shoulder he gathered up some dead wood and soon had a fire burning. Tired as he was from his exertions he could not sleep, the sound of wild animals away in the darkness unsettled him and it was some time before he eventually drifted off to sleep. At first, he slept deeply and then more fitfully until the first grey dawn climbed over the eastern horizon, alerting him to the new day. Opening his eyes, he stretched every sinew to throw off the vestiges of sleep before springing to his feet and picking up his bag and gourd of water. Dousing the fire with loose earth he looked towards the path he must take, the sun rising in the east illuminating familiar shapes amongst the hills, he was on the final stretch of his journey and nearly home.

By late afternoon, a circle of huts came into view: his village, the kraal where he had grown up and his mind once more tussled with the questions for which he needed answers. An hour later, he reached the gate and walked into the familiar compound, passing through the entrance and striding purposefully towards the centre of the village. On raised ground at the far side of the central area sat the headman of the village, a fine leopard skn draped over his shoulders and a kilt of furry animal tails about his waist. On his head sat a polished black ring plaited into his hair, in his right hand he held a spear and perched on the grand throne of carved and blackened wood he made an imposing sight. The chief was not alone, surrounding him were his advisors, and together they watched Solomon's approach.

The Chief was fat, his dark eyes piercing and he constantly prodded the ground with his spear, behind

27

him a young boy held a large umbrella to shade him from the sun. Not far away, on the dusty earth, children played games and nearby a witch doctor watched as Solomon reached the throne, sank to his knees out of respect and exhaustion. The chief showed little emotion, clapped his hands and gestured to a servant girl to bring food and water for Solomon.

'Greetings, Solomon, we have not seen you for a long time. You have travelled far . . . we know why you have come, you are not the first son to return to the kraal.'

The chief indicated with his spear that Solomon should sit at his feet and then the girl reappeared carrying a large leaf of mealie and some curdled milk in a small gourd. Solomon held out his hands and took the food and after he had eaten, the chief began to speak.

'Solomon! A great cloud has descended upon us. The Government has made a law that forces us to leave our farms and fields or remain only as the White man's chattel to work the land that once was our own. The White man forces us to leave the land because he needs our labour in his gold mines. It is a tragedy the witch doctors have prophesied for many years and now it is upon us.'

Those surrounding the chief became silent and a gloom seemed to descend upon them, something intangible an unseen force that animated the witch doctor who, standing to his full, impressive six feet, slowly moved towards the group. His broad ebony chest glistened in the sunlight, an ancient black cloak fashioned from the skin of a long dead animal covered his shoulders, it was a sacred robe and its wearer was purported to command mystical powers. In his right hand, the shaman carried a staff of dangling monkey skulls and in the other a vase containing a smouldering substance that gave off a bitter-sweet fragrance that repulsed the senses.

The small crowd gasped as he began to shuffle towards them, one foot before the other and he chanted in a low voice. The air seemed charged with some mysterious potency as he approached the headman. He stopped and shook his staff of skulls, the action visibly affecting the onlookers. Many present had memories going back to the times when the Zulu nation was at its height, a time when the witch doctors possessed immense power and were the only ones to command the attention of the king.

The King's word meant life or death and the older ones remembered the days when he would order his people to assemble in the Royal kraal for the smelling out of evil. That was when the Isangoma, the Witchfinder, was at his most powerful. Dressed in goatskins, adorned with skulls and the dried body parts of various animals, his skin painted with white clay and divining bones in his hands, the Witchfinder would strike terror into mere mortals.

Assembled in peer regiments, standing in tightly formed rows on the parade ground, the male population would await their fate. The Isangoma would gyrate between the assembled warriors, hissing, screeching and making even the bravest warrior's eyes roll in terror. Then he would begin smelling out the evil, passing along row after row of tall, fierce soldiers trembling at his passing until eventually an accusing finger would single out a poor unfortunate. Behind the Isangoma came the slayers, who would rush forward, restrain the one accused of harbouring the evil spirits and drag him off to a painful and lingering death. The man, knowing his fate and too traumatised even to speak, would find himself forced to his knees and then flat on his belly and then several wooden skewers, as long as a man's forearm and as thick as a pencil, would be driven up his rectum and his executioners would leave him to die a lingering death. Even then they were not finished, going to search out the dying man's relatives, to put them to death, to exterminate the whole family, women, children and the elderly, to finally banish the evil spirits.

The Headman remembered well those days well and shuddered at the memory before finally he spoke.

'Solomon, what have you to tell me?'

'Oh great chief, I have travelled far to return to the village of my birth, I have come with a heavy heart to seek guidance.'

The Chief's eyes lowered a little and then he looked at the proud Zulu man before him.

'Solomon, I know why you have come. We Zulus are not the power we once were, we are no longer the feared warriors of my youth and I know you are here because of the White man's law. You are not the first of our sons to return.' The old chief sighed and paused for a moment before continuing. 'If you refuse to turn over your cattle to the land owner and to work as a labourer you must leave, to go to tribal areas set aside for us. The lands will not sustain you and your family and so you must go and work in the mines of iGoli. It is a harsh law but we cannot fight it and so my advice is to leave for the Homelands and work in the mines.'

As he finished speaking and silence descended once more, the witch doctor came back to life, circling the group and shuffling towards Solomon where he stopped and tossed a handful of bones onto the ground at Solomon's feet.

'I see the future, I see great things for our brother Solomon.' The silence was palpable, the onlookers held their breath and Solomon felt afraid.

'Speak,' ordered the chief.

'He will become an important messenger for all the Zulus.'

'When?'

'Many years, many years,' repeated the witch doctor before falling silent.

The tension began to ease and a surprised Solomon looked at the headman, waiting for him to speak again but he had closed his eyes and had no further interest in him. The headman of the village had his mind on other things, the gifts and the praise he would receive from the Government for all the bad advice given to his people. They had visited his village, explained the new law and of what he must do to stay in favour with the White man.

Solomon was aware his audience was over and with a puzzled mind; he looked at the Chief's advisors for help and then at the Witch doctor but each averted his eyes. He felt that he was on his own and that there was only one place left for him to go. With a heavy heart, he turned away from the group surrounding the Chief and walked across the compound. The huts were still familiar, one or two had disappeared but others had taken their place and as he threaded his way between them, he saw what he was looking for.

'*Sawubona*, I see you,' said Solomon.

'*Ngikhona*, I am here,' was the reply.

He had found his father; still inhabiting the same beehive hut and sitting cross-legged in front of his dwelling inhaling snuff. They had not seen each other for more than two years and had a lot of catching up to do and with a grin the old man offered some of his snuff to his favourite son who squatted down beside him.

'My son it is good to see you, how goes it in the land of the White man?'

Before replying Solomon sprinkled some of the snuff from the small horn onto the back of his hand and inhaled, taking time to decide what to say.

'Father a great black cloud is descending upon us, the White man has made a law.'

'I know Solomon, I have heard of this law, others have returned and spoken with the chief, they have visited their fathers as well and I have spoken with them.'

Before Solomon could say more his youngest sister, Sibongile, appeared from inside the hut and smiled broadly at seeing her older brother. She was the only one of Nkosinathi's family still living in the village, spending her time looking after her father. 'Fetch us some biltong and beer my daughter and then you may speak with your brother.'

The girl grinned and turned back, crawling through the narrow tunnel into the hut and the two men began to talk again, small talk to begin with, catching up on family news and when Sibongile returned they talked of one thing only, the Native Land Act, the storm cloud that was about to change native life forever.

'Solomon my son, I have seen the end of the Zulu ways, I was with the Impi at the hill of the cows stomach when we defeated the White man's army but I was at Ulundi also and saw their power. We cannot hope to resist the White man and his laws. You will have to make your own choice between staying on the farm and moving to the homelands set aside for us. There is no other way.

Sibongile, fetch me the snakeskin pouch,' he said to his daughter who once more crawled into their hut.

'I have something for you, a talisman I have carried since the day of the great battle, it something that will bring you luck and keep you safe it is a relic of war taken by the once great Zulu army of Cetshwayo.'

Sibongile returned carrying a soft-skinned pouch and gave it to Nkosinathi who carefully pulled it open and reached inside, his fingers caressing the precious contents, valuable icons of his life and a smile creased his leathery cheeks as he found that for which he was searching.

'Here my son, take this,' he said, placing the object in Solomon's hand.

It was a silvery metal badge adorned with a crown and a ring of leaves surrounding a central disc. There was some writing around the ring Solomon did not understand but in the centre of the disc was the number 24, something he could understand but its significance he could not.

'What is this father?'

'It is from the White man's army, I took it from the battle field, from a redcoat soldier I killed. I do not have much to give you but this is a badge of courage and it will remind you that we Zulu's once defeated a mighty foreign army. One day we will do it again,' he said falling silent, his eyes closing and the memories of those glorious days returned and then he opened them to look straight at his son.

'You will have to fight many battles before you are done Solomon and this will help you through.' Nkosinathi reached out to grasp his son's hand as the soldiers of the

Impi had done before and Solomon felt a lump of emotion grow in his throat.

The journey home was no less tiresome and by the evening of the fourth day, he came in sight of the little hut that was his home. He was exhausted in body and mind, his exertions and the worries that plagued him taking their toll. Ever since leaving his father he had turned over the problem repeatedly, looking for a way out of his dilemma and then he saw a wisp of smoke curling up into the sky from the cooking fire.

All day Mary watched out for him attending to her chores, forever looking towards the distant horizon. She saw him coming and scurried to their hut to light the cooking fire, knowing that he would be hungry from his journey and as he came near, she ran towards him, standing for a while in silence until, in a faltering voice, Solomon began to speak.

'Our choice is not a happy one, my wife; I do not know what to do. We can stay here and work as labourers for the Baas or we can leave for homelands set aside for us to the north. The land there is poor and I will be forced to work in the mines for many months of the year.'

Solomon knew he had only a short time left to decide their future. At least if they remained here and worked for the old Boer farmer they would have enough food to survive. To drive their cattle north to the homelands would be difficult but at least they would be free and so all of the next day Solomon and Mary managed to shrug off their problems. Working hard, they gathered in as much of the ripened crop as they could and in the evening they began to discuss their predicament, decide which path they should take.

'Solomon, do you want us to be slaves, for that is what we will be?'

Mary's words resonated and Solomon's hand went unconsciously to the talisman hanging from his neck and at that moment, he made up his mind. They would not remain as slaves to the old Boer; they would leave the farm to carve out a new life and immediately after finishing their meal he set to work gathering their belongings together, loading them onto their primitive ox drawn cart and then he began making bales of straw to feed his animals. Mary attended to their own food supply, crushing what mealie they had into a coarse flour for the mealie cakes and gathering up all that was edible. The task was still incomplete and so early the next day they began harvesting what they could of their crop, filling two sacks with corn and then, late in the afternoon, they saw a small band of natives with some cattle and a wagon like their own approaching.

They were a native family from a neighbouring farm, people they were acquainted with and Solomon invited them to stay a while and rest. The hut was too small for them all and so they made a fire outside and gathered round to keep warm, Mary and Solomon joined them to talk, the conversation centring on the Land Act. Solomon learned that a great migration was in progress, native families all across the land were leaving their homes to find somewhere free to farm. He heard that many had sold everything to travel to Johannesburg or Kimberley to work in the mines.

'You are fortunate Solomon; you have had seven days to decide, we had only two,' said his guest.

Solomon thought about that, very soon the seven days would be up. 'Tomorrow I must decide to stay or leave.'

'I see that you are prepared to leave this place.'

'Yes, but I can still change my mind.'

Mary looked at her husband, her large brown eyes puzzled that he was considering staying.

'Do not look so worried, we are going to leave. I will not be a slave to the White man.'

At dawn the following day Solomon was loading the last of their belongings onto his cart when Hendricks rode up with a piece of paper in his hand.

'Well Solomon, are you going to give me your livestock and come and work for me? Here, sign this paper and all will be well between us.'

Solomon slowly shook his head. 'No Baas, we are leaving. I will not give you everything we have worked for.'

Hendricks kicked his horse forwards towards Solomon and raised his whip to strike him, hesitating when he saw the second cart and the sorrowful looking family standing next to it.

'Who are these trespassers on my land?' he shouted.

'From the east. They are leaving as well.'

'Are they?' said Hendricks.

Then a thought occurred to the old Boer. He really did not want Solomon and Mary to leave – they were good workers, all he wanted was their animals and for them to work for next to nothing. Perhaps he could convince these other people to work for him instead.

'You, what's your name boy?' he said to the leader of the group.

'Peter, Baas.'

'Peter, I will pay you and your wife 30 shillings a month to work on this farm. You can live here, what do you say, this is a good offer.'

Peter looked at his wife, her sad pleading eyes, and he agreed. The old Boer grinned with satisfaction, taking a perverted pleasure in telling Solomon and Mary to get off his land and never come back.

Solomon felt anger rising in his chest, he wished he could do something but there was no going back and so, with his stick, he began to drive his animals forward. Mary coaxed the lone oxen pulling the cart and Amos sat amongst their chattels not understanding. Solomon and Mary both had tears in their eyes, distraught at leaving yet neither of them looked back.

Chapter 3

After ten days' trek across the endless veldt they had covered well over 100 miles, they were beginning to meet other natives on the move and Solomon had decided to make their way to the north, to the part of Zululand near to the gold mines of iGoli. One night they made camp and a short time later, a family of Zulus stopped alongside them. The group looked as if they had travelled a long way, weary from their journey, sadness in their eyes.

'*Sawubona*', said the head of the family as they made camp. 'I see you have travelled many miles just as we have. You must sit at my fire tonight and tell of your journey.'

'*Ngiyabonga*' – thank you,' said Solomon, introducing himself and finding out that the man was called Joshua, and in the early evening he and Mary joined them at their fire.

Darkness was falling and Joshua threw more wood onto the fire, sending sparks high into the night sky before sitting back on his haunches and calling out a greeting. He was older than Solomon and took great pleasure in telling his new friends all about himself, that his mother was a princess, that he had left his kraal and gone to work in the diamond mines. Then the recession of the early 20th century had swept through the Cape and the mine owners had reduced their wages, making it difficult for him to earn a living. He had used his savings to buy seed for the new season and for the rent on his small-holding but the estate manager, a devious and cruel man had cheated him and the other tenants at every opportunity leaving him with little choice but to make his way to the homelands.

Their journey had been hard, their trek starting almost a month earlier. Half his cattle had perished on the high veldt due to the poor quality of the grass. When he did find decent pasture, white farmers forced them to keep moving, harassing them. On the high veldt of the Orange Free State, the nights had been bitterly cold and together with the lack of feed, several of his cattle had succumbed leaving him with only three skinny animals. Worse than that, a week earlier they had lost their year-old son to sickness and the cold and they had not known what to do with the body. If they buried him on the farmer's land, he would have them fined or thrown into prison, so during the darkest part of the night they had returned to a conspicuous outcrop of rock and buried the child, weeping and whispering a Zulu prayer, hoping one day to return and visit the tiny grave.

'What upsets me most is that the White man considers us beasts of burden with no feelings. The White man does not care what happens to us as long as he has use of our labour, for us to work for nothing. We are a broken people and we have no future,' said Joshua falling silent for a time and then he began to speak of the old times, mesmerising Solomon and in the light of the flickering flames, he reflected on Joshua's words. He thought about the early days of his own life when he was carefree, enjoying life amongst his family, his father, brothers and sisters. He remembered the sights and sounds of the village, the tribal ceremonies when everyone dressed in their finest plumage, the noise of the drums. However, things had changed under the White man's rule and Solomon was learning from his new-found friend about the suffering of the native peoples brought about by unjust reforms and he began to feel a bond of kinship with this proud Zulu.

'Joshua, what will you do when we reach the homelands? Will you work in the mines again?' Solomon asked, his face aglow from the flickering flames.

'I go to Ulundi, the home of our people to find some land to farm, then, yes, I will have to go and work in the mines to support my family. What else can I do? We cannot rise up against the White man; we do not have their guns, there is no other way for our people.'

Joshua fell silent, poking the dying embers with a stick, causing them to crackle and flare up, the smoke making his eyes water as if he were crying, and he was crying.

After a silence Solomon spoke in halting tone, 'Can we come with you to Ulundi? My cows are still giving some milk, we can share it.'

'Thank you Solomon, you are welcome. Your company will lighten my load,' said Joshua, his poise returning.

The following day, as the sun rose over the horizon, they broke camp and resumed their trek across the vast empty landscape and by mid-afternoon they came upon a Zulu kraal, smoke rising from the cooking fires. For them it was a welcome sight and for the villagers who ventured out to watch them pass, a highlight. Mary led their oxen, waving to the Zulu women who asked where they had come from whilst Amos sat in the cart watching, his big round eyes taking it all in. Behind them came Joshua and his family who underwent the same treatment, their sons briefly playing with boys from the village as they passed by. But they could not stop: they must reach Ulundi as soon as possible, negotiate with the tribal elders to find a plot of land on which to build new homes.

Leaving the village behind, they made their way up a gentle slope and onto a plateau of dry barren land with poor pasture and scarce water. The cattle were struggling and by evening they made camp on exposed ground, the only flat area in sight and throughout the night a cold wind blew steadily, forcing them to huddle under their waggons, and then the fires died.

Solomon had become steadily weaker during their trek, their food supply was dwindling and there was little to scavenge. The cold of the night had made him sleep fitfully and the following morning he awoke to find the sun had already risen. He had never slept past the dawn before. Emerging from under the waggon, he went to milk his animals becoming aware that all was not as it should be. Tethered to their stakes his animals stood looking miserable except for the oldest, lying motionless on the barren earth. Despair washed over Solomon, his favourite animal was still warm but she was dead, her black and white skin limp on her emaciated frame.

He went back to the waggon to wake Mary; his resolve returning and after he told her of the loss of the animal he found his sharpest knife, at least he could butcher the animal for its meat and he called to Joshua for help with the carcass.

41

'We will eat like kings for a few days my friend. There is nothing else I can do.'

'We will stay here a while longer Solomon, we need to rest and the women and my sons can cut up some of the carcass and dry the meat for biltong and then we go to Ulundi,' said Joshua

They had not eaten so well for weeks, each of them was close to starvation and very soon, they had consumed their fill of half-cooked half-blackened meat from the spit. At least the food would restore some of their strength for the last few miles to Ulundi and sitting round the campfire wrapped in blankets, Solomon and Joshua speculated on what their arrival in Ulundi would mean. They would need to persuade the chief to allocate them some land and that would not be easy.

'Don't worry Solomon! My mother was a princess. I have many relatives in these parts and I am sure they will help me persuade the elders to give us some land. You have helped me and shared your food as a true Zulu and they will be generous with you – I'm sure.'

And so it proved, the chief and the tribal elders held council, listened as Solomon and Joshua made their case and after a speech from Joshua's uncle, granted each a small area of land adjacent to one another. There was water not far away and some communal grazing rights for their cattle, a satisfactory conclusion under the circumstances. Joshua had only one animal left and only three of Solomon's cattle had survived, barely enough to give them a fresh start. If they were to feed their families, they needed to seek work in the mines of iGoli but before they could consider leaving they had a week of backbreaking work building new homes to shelter their families.

After a week of toil, Solomon stood surveying his work and looked up at Joshua sat astride his new home.

'If it rains tonight my friend we will stay dry,' he said Joshua grinning as he pushed the last of the roofing material into place. We have two fine huts for our families. We can rest easy when we are working in the mines.'

'Two fine homes indeed Joshua. Perhaps tonight we can celebrate a little. We still have meat and it would be fitting indeed to bless our new homes.'

'Perhaps we should find a shaman to protect them from evil spirits,' said Joshua, eyes widening at the possibility of evil spirits invading his new dwelling.

'I do not think we need to do that, we have nothing to pay the shaman with.'

'Ah...I have something.'

Joshua slid to the ground from where he had been working and disappeared towards his rickety waggon. Solomon watched him go and wondered what it was that could attract a witch doctor to come and bless their new huts.

'Look, Solomon, these will pay for a shaman.'

He held his hand out to expose several coloured glass beads, each with a neat hole through the middle.

'I will ask my uncle, he will find a witch doctor to come and ward off any evil spirits that come to harm us.'

Joshua's uncle was a man of some influence and the following day he arranged for a witch doctor to come and protect the huts from evil, a happy occasion. Joshua's relatives came to sing and dance and to eat the last of

Solomon's meat in celebration. The witch doctor performed his ceremony and then, when it was over, Joshua said. 'Solomon, tomorrow I go to iGoli in search of work. Will you come with me?'

'Of course my friend.'

And at first light the following day Solomon and Joshua made ready to leave, packing rations of food and water in their leather shoulder pouches for the journey to the City of Gold. Before leaving, Joshua instructed his sons to help their mother on the land, to be good sons, ones he could be proud of and Solomon held his own son in his arms for the last time in what could be a long time. He kissed Amos on the forehead and Mary threw her arms around them both as they said their farewells and then the two men began the trek westwards to Johannesburg.

For two days they followed the trail eventually coming across a railway track and Joshua stood still for a moment listening and then he turned to Solomon and said, 'Johannesburg is along the path of the sun so we must wait for a train heading in that direction. We should walk along the track until we find a steep bend or an incline, a place where the train will have to slow down, then we will get on it and hitch a ride.'

For the rest of the day they followed the railway track. First westwards and then, in the evening, they came across a sharp bend turning the north as the track negotiated a small, steep sided valley.

'This is the place, the train will have to slow down here or it will come off the rails. We wait here.'

Settling down for the night, they ate some of their small stock of food and listened for the sounds of an approaching engine. As darkness closed in Joshua said that it was unlikely that a train would come until the following day and so they found a comfortable place in which to rest and as the dawn broke, Joshua shook himself free of his slumber. Jumping up he crouched next to the track, his ear tight against the cold steel rail and he listened for a few seconds before finally letting out a grunt.

'Nothing yet, I will keep listening,' he said and for most of the morning, he lay by the track with his ear pressed to the steel rail and then, when the sun was nearing its highest he let out a cry of joy.

'Train comes, train comes! I think maybe soon. Let's get ready and find some cover where the track bends.'

Solomon's heartbeat picked up with excitement and anticipation and he strained his ears but could hear nothing.

'Joshua laughed at him, 'here, put your ear to the track then you will hear it, but be quick, we have to get ready.'

Solomon dropped to all fours and gingerly put his ear to the hot metal and was amazed to hear the faint metallic sounds of the approaching engine. Jumping up with a grin on his face, he followed Joshua to a place where the train would be at its slowest and there they hid themselves in the bushes at the foot of the Kloof. A quarter of an hour later the engine approached and Solomon could hear the "Shush, shush, shush" of escaping steam, louder and louder it sounded and he felt strange new vibrations through the ground and then, suddenly, there it was – steam and smoke rising in a great plume, terrifying him. Solomon's heart was racing; he felt as if his chest would explode but alongside him, Joshua seemed confident and unperturbed.

The metal beast was level with them and Solomon's heart was in his mouth. He had never seen a steam engine before, and at six feet away, the noise was deafening. Passing them, the engine approached the bend in the track at reduced speed and as it traversed the bend, it slowed even further. Joshua watched it pass noted the waggons and carriages, looking for one he considered safe to climb aboard. The first of the carriages were for passengers – no good for them, but behind came goods waggons, at least ten of them and as the second of those drew level he tapped Solomon on the shoulder, broke cover and ran for the gap between it and the one following. Dodging between them, he sprang nimbly up onto the buffer, and then scrambled up the inspection ladder and into the waggon top. Solomon followed and within seconds, both men lay spread-eagled on the curved roof of the waggon, gasping for breath and for a time they felt like the Zulu warriors of old.

The remainder of the journey was uneventful, mostly spent sleeping under the warm sun, one man on watch while the other rested and late in the afternoon, as the train approached Johannesburg they began to wonder how they could get off without injury. The answer came several miles before the city limits as the train slowed and then came to a stop alongside a water tower. Peering over the edge to see what was happening, they saw the engineer transfer from the foot-plate of the engine onto a small platform and began to refill the engine's water tanks.

Joshua whispered to Solomon, 'When it starts again, we'll slip down and lie flat on the track. It'll pass over us and we can get away when it's gone.'

Half an hour later, a roar came from the engine as it let out a great cloud of steam and then it shuddered, the great steel wheels skidding on the rails and slowly it began to gather momentum. Joshua judged that this was the moment and dug Solomon in the ribs, gesturing for him to follow down the ladder to lie flat on the track, allowing the wagons to pass slowly over them until finally, there was nothing above them but the bright sunshine.

The guard in the last carriage was an old man who had been doing the job for many years and one of his favourite pastimes was watching to see how many jumped the train without paying. He saw them lying on the track and smiled to himself, muttering, 'Poor bastards', and shaking his head slowly from side to side. He was supposed to report any train jumpers to the authorities, but he never did. In his younger days, he had known the hardship that drove men to do such things and anyway, they would be long gone by the time he had raised the alarm.

Joshua and Solomon lay still for a few minutes more, letting the sound of the train fade, before attempting to get to their feet. There was not much cover on either side of the track and anyone looking in their direction would easily see them. If the authorities caught them, then it would mean imprisoned as vagrants, so they needed to get away unobserved and quickly.

Joshua stood up first followed closely by Solomon and they both looked around to make sure that the train was well on its way and then they had a shock: they were not alone. Staring at them, not more than 20 yards away, was a White man, a bag over one shoulder, several days' growth of beard on his face and a well-worn bush hat covering his head. His clothes were those of a down and out, patched dark brown trousers with braces over a rough grey cotton shirt and a corduroy jacket of a different shade to the trousers. He saw the two black men but did not acknowledge them, turning sharply away and striding over the line, quickly making off towards the dusty road running alongside the track.

The man was heading the same way they were and so they followed him, keeping several yards behind him and within a short time they approached the first shantytown on the outskirts of Johannesburg. Walking past the ramshackle buildings Solomon's heart began to sink when he saw the squalor the people were living in, their sad faces, and he began to wonder if this would be his fate. Would it have been better after all to work as a farm labourer?

Nearing the city, horse drawn vehicles and pedestrians appeared, white men, black men and hues in between and when they reached the city proper, a motor car appeared. Solomon looked at Joshua with bewilderment and a little panic in his eyes as he stared at the horseless carriage, transfixed.

Joshua laughed, 'have you not seen one of those before Solomon?'

Solomon could not take his eyes of this strange contraption, shaking his head instead. Then Joshua tapped him on the shoulder and pointed to distant mine dumps piled up like man-made anthills and let out a whoop of joy before performing a short war dance.

'Look there, the mines, we have arrived.'

To show his joy Solomon joined him in his dance until the White man they had followed from the train turned around and shouted something unintelligible at them, raised his hat and shook his fist in anger. They stopped their dance and Joshua looked sheepishly at the man who shook his fist once more before putting his hat squarely back on his head and walking away.

'Have we offended him?' asked Solomon.

'I think so. White men sometimes get angry when we dance our native dances, I have seen that same reaction before in the Big Hole. When we find one of the stones, we celebrate with a dance. I think the anger is because they do not find the stone.'

Solomon shrugged his shoulders; his only experience of white men was the old Boer, the constable, and the missionaries. He did not understand, it seemed the man did not like black men and after watching him walk away, his attention was drawn towards the mine dumps and then he saw a large black man in a dishevelled suit approach who spoke to them in their native tongue.

'Hey you boys, you looking for work in the mines?' Joshua nodded; he guessed what the man was and knew that their journey would soon be at an end.

'I am the mine agent and I can get you work in the mines. You come with me and I get you started. Good wages and somewhere to live, come!' He beckoned them to follow.

They followed him for two or three miles to the west of the city until they came to a fenced compound with rectangular huts inside the perimeter. The gate had armed Kaffirs guarding it and after an exchange of words, he beckoned them to follow him towards a large hut at its centre. Entering into the dark interior their eyes slowly became accustomed to the gloom and sitting behind a desk a large White man stared at them. The

49

mine manager, fat, sweaty and with a large unlit, half-smoked cigar protruding from the corner of his mouth.

'You two, you want work?'

'Yas Baas,' said Joshua, looking down at the floor.

'You worked in the mines before?'

'Yas Baas.'

'Where?' asked the man in disbelief.

'Kimberley, Baas, in de big hole.' The man grunted, Joshua was not a gold miner but if he had worked in a diamond mine, then he would be able to do the job here.

'And you?' he asked Solomon.

Solomon's heart was beating at twice its normal speed but he had a quick mind and guessed that the right lie might get him a job. Looking down at the floor like Joshua, he stuttered, 'Y-yas Baas, de big hole.'

The fat man grunted again; it was hot and he did not really care if the pair of them had told the truth or not; they looked strong enough. His instructions were to get as many able-bodied blacks as he could to work in the mine and here were two more.

'All right then boys, put your thumb print on these contracts and you can start work. The pay is one pound ten shillings a month and you get your food free, that is, if you can eat it, and you live in the compound. The work is hard, ten hour shifts and you get Sundays off.' He took two sheets of printed-paper from his desk drawer and passed them across and then he took a tin from the same drawer and removed its lid, revealing a black shiny pad.

They signed their contracts with their thumbprints, and the fat man grunted again before shouting to an old native sat outside. The man rushed into the office to receive instructions and the fat man told him to show Solomon and Joshua to a bunkhouse. The man nodded, he had performed the task many times and beckoned Joshua and Solomon to follow him.

The old man led them across the compound to the dormitory where they were to live for almost a year, an austere place with cramped conditions, the beds simply two rows of cast concrete cots covered with a layer of straw for mattresses. Above the cots, hanging from thin ropes attached to the roof beams, were the belongings of those already employed. It was the only space available. Then the old man allocated them two of the remaining cots and left them to their own devices until the start of work the following morning.

'This place is like a prison,' said Joshua looking round. 'Still we have a job and we can earn money.'

'I did not like the White man we followed from the train Joshua. Are all white men like that?' enquired Solomon.

'A lot of them, some are different, some are kind and do not kick us.'

'And do many of them have pieces cut from an ear like that man, is it a tribal mark?'

Chapter 4

Lucy was sitting at her sewing table mending a small rip in Alistair's school trousers and reflecting on their time in South Africa. After her initial reservations she had to admit she was happy; they had been here for almost three years, moving to Bloemfontein almost a year before. She loved their house and garden and she had begun to make a few friends. Norman had really taken to the life, becoming moderately successful in the land and property business and he had made numerous acquaintances and his salary was far better than he could have expected back home.

Early on Norman's boss had realised that he had the credentials necessary for management and had decided to offer him the position of assistant manager in their Bloemfontein office to begin with, see how he got on. Even she was aware that the diamond mines in nearby Kimberley were thriving, that farm prices were rising and the ostrich feather industry, the main ingredient for the fashion conscious women of Europe, was booming. Economic growth had taken off not long before they had arrived and she was thankful Norman had been lucky enough to land the job he had. They had moved with their servants, Mabutu and Marsha, to Bloemfontein in

52

May to the new house, a larger than the one they had left behind in Cape Town. Built on two floors, just like the old one, it had more rooms and a much bigger garden where Lucy had worked with Mabutu to create the vegetable plot and it was beginning to show results.

On occasion she had felt lonely and more than a little homesick it was true, but the lifestyle and the warm climate made up for a lot, particularly when she could see how healthy and happy her children were. News from home was always a welcome distraction, but for months talk of war with Germany had dominated the correspondence and now that war had finally broken out Lucy, like everyone else, was anxious to know what was happening. The South Africans were deploying men, equipment to Europe, South African troops had opened hostilities in German East Africa with an assault on the Ramansdrift police station and she prayed that this terrible business would not last long, not affect their comfortable lives.

Talk of war had been an important part of her sister's letters but she was a long way from Scotland, her interests and priorities somewhat different. A pretty and intelligent woman she was able to hold an interesting conversation and made friends easily, virtually all of her new friends having been born in Great Britain or in South Africa of British parents and most regarded Britain as their real home, harbouring ambitions to one-day visit 'home'. The more they knew about the ways and customs of the mother country the better and were eager to know every detail and so her letters from home became a useful topic for conversation

Lucy stopped sewing for a moment, placed her left hand flat against her stomach and leaned back. She was almost certain she was pregnant again, having missed her period by more than a week. She would not say anything to Norman quite yet, not until she was sure, perhaps in another month. She looked through the window at Alistair and Rosemary playing a game of quoits, watching for several minutes before putting her sewing down on the small table and going outside to the children.

'Come along children! It is time you were in bed'. The two of them dropped the quoits they were holding and raced laughing and shouting into the house, their feet clattering on the wooden steps as they went. From the kitchen, Marsha heard the children and came to help get them ready for bed.

After washing and putting on their pyjamas, they ran screaming with terror as their mother chased them upstairs to their bedrooms, their little legs a blur in their rush to avoid her clutches. Nevertheless, she did catch them and one at a time, tucked them into their beds and kissed them goodnight. Pulling the mosquito nets over them she left the bedroom doors slightly ajar before making her way quietly back downstairs. The servants had already left and so she pushed the bolts securing the door and then, in the fading light, sat by the window to read a few pages of her book and to wait for Norman to return home, believing that she and the children were alone.

Unknown to her, four shadows were at that moment passing through the gap in a partially open window on the first floor, slipping quietly into the house in search of victims. Two rapidly traversed the hallway, locating Alistair's bedroom, the remaining two making their way into Rosemary's room to circle for a few seconds, locating the faint odour of their victims' exposed flesh. Next, the mosquitoes searched for a way past the nets, finding gaps and squeezing in to anchor their jaws to their victim's skin. Inserting their needle-like mandibles, they sucked out as much of the victims' blood as they could manage and seconds later left the house to fly off into the gloom, unseen, mingling with a million insects going about their business in the African night.

The following morning the children rose from their beds and went downstairs to breakfast complaining of itching. Their mother could see that they had received a number of nasty looking insect bites by the red wealds on their skin and applied vinegar to the inflamed lumps. She spoke softly, reassuring the children that they would feel better during the day and that vinegar was the cure for insect bites. Back home in Scotland vinegar had been a cure all and she expected it would do the trick here. Three days later, within twelve hours of each other, the children began to complain of headaches and feeling tired. Lucy realized straight away that it was a more serious condition than she had at first believed and told Mabutu to fetch the doctor. After an anxious wait, he arrived two hours later in his pony and trap and hurrying to the front door Lucy flung it open to let him in, her face creased with worry.

'Oh, Dr Meadly! It's both the children – they are ill with fever and I am so worried. Please come in and look at them.'

The doctor followed her up the stairs, first into Rosemary's bedroom where he placed his bag on the bedside table and looked down at the little girl. She was constantly twisting and turning, her face covered in sweat. The doctor took her limp wrist gently in one large yet delicate hand finding her pulse weak and irregular. He placed a thermometer in her mouth, her temperature was abnormally high and finally he removed his stethoscope from his bag and tested the little girl's chest. When he finished examining Rosemary, he followed Lucy into Alistair's room only to discover the little boy had all the same symptoms. He was quite sure now; both children were suffering from the early stages of malaria and he must move quickly if they were to have any chance of recovery.

'I am afraid, Mrs Campbell, that your children have malaria.' Lucy looked at the doctor, shocked. 'This is a very serious situation. The children are gravely ill and we should move them to the hospital as soon as we can. Where is your husband? I suggest that you contact him as soon as you can whilst I make arrangements to have them moved to the hospital.'

Lucy was suddenly stricken with fear and did not know what to do, her eyes flicking from side to side as the significance of the doctor's words sank in. Then with the same soft and reassuring voice he said, 'Mrs Campbell, I will drive into town to your husband's office if you will give me the address and I will ask him to come home right away.'

Within the hour, Norman had returned home and almost knocked Marsha over as she opened the front door for him. He rushed past her, taking the stairs two at a time and reached Rosemary's bedroom to find Lucy waiting there for him.

'Lucy, Dr Meadly has told me what has happened. How are they?'

Tears filled Lucy's eyes, 'not very well and I do not know what we can do,' she said holding the back of her hand to her mouth.

Norman quickly explained that the doctor had called in at the old military hospital on his way to the office to tell the nurses to prepare to receive the two sick children and Alan Forbes, Norman's boss, had helped by driving him home and was waiting outside with the car.

'Give me a hand to wrap them in blankets Lucy and we will take them straight to the hospital.

The following days were very hard for Lucy, her children in a critical condition and almost certainly a third was growing in her womb, two lives in the balance and a third just beginning. She was not sleeping or eating properly and beginning to lose weight and the doctor could not stop thinking about her. He saw the strain she was under and aware that she may be pregnant he was concerned for her well-being.

'I want you to be careful during the next few weeks; I believe you could well be pregnant Mrs Campbell and I do not want you taking any unnecessary risks. You can visit the children whenever you wish but when you come to the hospital I want you to see me first.'

The hospital, originally an old colonial house, had two corrugated sheds at the rear used as wards, one for men and the other for women. Children did not have the luxury of a separate ward, only beds in the adult wards and a matron, in her starched white gown, presided over it all. Six full-time nurses and several volunteers assisted her and then there were the two doctors, Dr Roberts, and Dr Ovens. They had seen service in the war on opposing sides but a doctors task was to save life not to destroy it.

Dr Ovens was a Boer, born and bred in the Transvaal. Tall and strong, as most Afrikaner men brought up in the countryside were and he had worked zealously behind the Boer lines in field the hospitals. By the time the peace arrived, he was well aware of the horrors warfare spurned and had learned of the British concentration camps. Thousands of women and children had died in these camps and he had spent time in one after the fighting ended. He was not alone in that task, earning his admiration and respect were many volunteers from England; people appalled at the situation, often just ordinary people come from England to help. One of these volunteers was Dr John Roberts, a slightly built man with a shock of curly black hair and kindly brown eyes and if ever the subject of the camps reared up, his eyes would flash. Those dark orbs betraying an immense inner compassion and strength. It was these attributes that had compelled him to sell most of his possessions and with the money purchase medical instruments, medicines and book passage on the first available ship to Durban.

The two men became firm friends and as a semblance of normality returned to the Orange Free State, they decided to work together. The military had turned the old colonial house into a hospital for the duration of the war but when the fighting was over and they had no further use for it, the two doctors had decided to keep it open for civilian use.

Dr Roberts had brought with him knowledge of some of the most modern medical techniques developed in England and America. Dr Ovens was a quick learner and by expanding the Boer doctor's existing knowledge, the two of them became a formidable team. The most important lesson Dr Roberts could teach was good hygiene the introduction of which dramatically reduced the mortality rate from cholera and associated diseases. Dr Roberts drilled the nurses constantly in hygiene procedures, employing several native women to daily clean the wards and very soon the procedure showed results.

Alistair and Rosemary were put into beds alongside adult patients, the only privacy afforded them a curtain pulled around their beds and within these curtains their parents would sit for hours to keep watch over them. Lucy was able to visit every day, to hold their little hands, dividing her time between Alistair and Rosemary until Norman arrived from work to take over. She would cry inwardly as their little bodies convulsed and shivered with the fever, hoping desperately that they would recover.

The mosquitoes had done their worst. The malaria developed rapidly, the children suffered headaches, bouts of sweating and then sudden coldness and Dr Roberts explained that all they could do was to treat the children with quinine and wait. Lucy's hopes rose when she thought she saw signs of improvement only to have them dashed two days later as the illness began to take a turn for the worse. The convulsions became more severe and Rosemary's skin was so pale and cold that it felt as if the hand of death had already taken hold. Even so it still came as a shock when, the following morning, Dr Ovens came to see them.

'Please come into my office and take a seat,' he said in his calm Afrikaans accent. 'I have consulted with Dr Roberts and we are extremely worried about your children. Rosemary slipped into a coma last night, we

59

have not seen any change and Alistair's illness is following a similar pattern. I am sorry to have to tell you this, but we are afraid that your children might not survive for much longer and you will want to be with them at the end. Doctor Roberts, the hospital staff and I will give you all the support we can. If you want to sleep here to be with them then I can arrange for some camp beds to be set up in my office.'

The tears Lucy had been holding back for days welled up in her eyes and she began to cry, her body shaking as tears poured down her cheeks. Norman put his arms around his wife and pulled her to him, his eyes not entirely dry and Dr Ovens slipped quietly out of his office allowing them some privacy. Lucy sobbed and shook uncontrollably as Norman held her tightly to him, sadness and despair descending over him together with a feeling of guilt; after all, he was the one who had brought them here to start a new life and to make his fortune.

Rosemary died later that day and Alistair survived for a further two days before he too slipped inexorably away. Dr Roberts helped them as much as he could with their grief and Dr Meadly called in at their home early the following day to offer comfort in what was a heart-rending situation. The hospital staff felt it, several of the nurses had tears in their eyes and two attended the funeral under a hot African sun, standing with heads bowed as the priest said a prayer while Lucy sobbed and sobbed. Norman held her arm fighting back his own tears and then the pallbearers lowered the two little coffins into the ground.

Lucy visited the graves of her children every day and the following months were the most unhappy and lonely in her life. Friends rallied round, comforting as much as they were able, but this was a tough land and she had to get over her grief, get on with her life as soon as she could. Her pregnancy seemed to be going well, the doctors were keeping a close eye on her and even Norman thought the sooner the baby was born the better, it would take her mind off their loss and give her something to live for.

The baby was born in August 1915 and Margaret, or Peggy, as they affectionately called her, weighed in at a healthy seven pounds ten ounces. Dr Roberts had insisted that the delivery take place at the hospital and that he personally attended the confinement and after what proved to be an easy birth; he had triumphantly held the baby and smacked her bottom.

For the first time in months, Lucy was happy; she had a family once more, a bouncing baby girl who gurgled from the word go and as soon as the nurses had cleaned up both mother and baby, Dr Roberts came to visit his patients. Looking down at them he smiled, popped his thermometer into Lucy's mouth and noticed how bright her eyes were. She had been through a lot but he felt confident she would cope and as he removed the thermometer from her mouth he said, 'Nothing wrong there'.

Lucy had not really prepared herself for the arrival of her second daughter. She had been too upset over the deaths of Alistair and Rosemary to think about the approaching birth but as soon as she saw Peggy, her maternal instincts took over and she busied herself knitting clothes and decorating the baby's bedroom. This

61

time she would be taking no chances with mosquito nets, or anything else for that matter. A short time later she had another surprise and within the space of a little over eighteen months a second child was born, a little boy bringing untold joy to Lucy.

Prior to the war the South Africa had performed poorly but now things were picking up, the main driver the German submarine menace. Having depleted merchant fleets around the world, local industries had begun to flourish replacing the shortages of imported goods. Activity had increased and Norman was working long hours to make the most of the opportunities and his escape at the end of a hard day's work was the sporting club on the outskirts of town.

One evening he walked into the bar and ordered his usual whiskey, picked up a newspaper lying nearby and settled down to read. The stories were almost all about the war and although South Africa was well away from the battles of the Somme and Ypres there was still the threat of the Germans in their African colonies. The British and Empire armies were pursuing the a German force the length and breadth of East Africa, attempting to secure the railway from the coast at Dar es Salaam to Ujiji in Western Tanzania but Colonel von Lettow-Vorbeck and his column were proving elusive. In Europe the great loss of life and difficulties at the front meant conscription and Norman, who had escaped the call up, began to worry that the authorities might consider increasing the age of conscription to men in their thirties. Depressed by stories of war he folded the newspaper and put it down, his mind turning to his time in Cape Town and his erstwhile pal Arthur. He had not seen him for quite some time and wondered what kind of tricks he might be playing wherever he was. Arthur had occasionally made visits to their Bloemfontein office with the accountant and on his last visit, he had told Norman he was running the accountancy department. That revelation had amazed Norman, how could he manage to acquire such a job? Arthur was a sharp operator though and Norman guessed he had little in the way of formal qualifications for the job, probably using personality and guile to con others into doing the technical work. Norman chuckled to himself at the thought as his friend John Thompson strode in looking round for a familiar face and Norman gave him a wave.

'What will you drink John, whisky?'

'No thanks, a cool beer tonight if you don't mind'.

Norman ordered two more drinks and the two men began to chat about work, swapping stories and information. John was a local lawyer, often working on the same deals as Norman; a little insider knowledge could be useful.

'Say Norman, things have been pretty good and I'm thinking of buying myself a motor car. You have the Buick for work – what's it like?'

The Buick was primarily for his boss's benefit, but Norman's job entailed the most travel and so he had the most use out of it. He had spent two days learning to drive, and soon found out just how much easier it was to visit outlying farms by car rather than in the horse drawn buggy. 'Well I can certainly recommend it. Travelling by car saves hours. I don't know how I managed before.'

'They tell me that the roads are getting better for these motor cars. Seems you can get to all the big towns now,' said the lawyer.

'Yes I think so. I haven't been so far yet, just the outlying farms, I have never really considered Cape Town or Johannesburg. Do you want to go as far as that?'

'I wouldn't mind, I've never been up to Johannesburg and I have only been to Cape Town on the train. Could open up the business a bit I think.'

Norman offered his friend a smoke. 'I think I am close to selling the Du Plessis's old farm out at Fairview. If you are interested there could be some business in it for you.'

'Hmm. I used to do quite a bit of work for old man Du Plessis, thought his sons were going to take it on after he died.'

'They were till they joined up. Poor sods were both killed in France and their sister and mother decided to sell up and move into town.'

The two men fell silent for a few moments, this was not the first bad news from the front and it would not be the last. They ordered more drinks and toasted their good luck in being too old for the draft.

For almost three years, Norman worked the area around Bloemfontein and made a good living. Lucy spent her time with the children, making their clothes and reading to them and not a day passed when she did not think of Alistair, Rosemary, and at least twice a week she visited their graves tending the flowers. She had a hole in her heart that would never heal but life was good, the war seemed a long way off and her children were growing healthy and strong.

One day, in late summer Norman was at the rear of the office preparing the Buick for a short journey to Kleinstradt unaware that Archibald Williamson had arrived from Cape Town in his chauffeur driven Rolls-

Royce. He walked into the office unannounced and accompanied by MacDonald, the Company accountant.

'Forbes make us some coffee and get hold of Campbell will you. It has been a long journey up from the Cape and I could do with a drink. If I didn't know better I would make that a whisky, a double.' He half smiled at Forbes's reaction, enjoying the man's discomfort. 'So why are MacDonald and I are here, you wonder? Get the coffee moving and bring it into your office and I will tell you.'

Alan Forbes was used to running the office in his own way, starting and finishing work when it suited him, getting Norman do the donkey work and so it was with some discomfort he pumped the percolator and lit the methylated spirit fumes. Leaving the machine alone to produce the coffee, he went outside to find Norman who about ready to drive out to his appointment.

'Hey Norman, something's up – Williamson's in the office!'

'What? From Cape Town? I don't believe you. He never comes here.'

'Well you'd better believe me because he's in there,' said Alan, pointing his thumb over his shoulder, 'and he wants us both in my office for a meeting – and McDonald's with him.'

'The accountant!' exclaimed Norman, a perplexed expression crossing his face as he followed his boss into the building. Inside they found the Company President sitting pensively in Forbes's chair. He greeting them with a cursory nod of the head and Norman responded with a rather reserved 'Good morning sir'.

Alan Forbes came into the room carrying a tray with the coffee on it and placed it in front of Williamson who pointed to two chairs in the corner of the room and twiddled his index finger. 'Campbell, bring those two chairs over here, because I think you'll both be better sat down to hear what I have to say. Pour the coffee first will you Forbes.' Norman and his boss glanced at each other with perplexed expressions on their faces and did as they were told.

'I have had some rather disturbing news in the last few days, it seems Arthur James has been embezzling the Company and thanks to MacDonald's vigilance, the problem has come to my notice. James left the Company almost two months ago and last week we discovered a rather strange transaction in our land register. MacDonald here has had a look into it and it appears we have a fictitious client on our books. This 'client' acquired a land holding, illegally, through us. The transaction passed through the hands of Arthur James at some time and he has now disappeared off the face of the earth so we cannot find out what actually went on. We presume that he is involved somehow but it is hard to prove it. The Company seems to have lost no money! On the contrary, we've been paid full value for the work done and so there is no real urgency in tracking James down.'

Alan and Norman looked at each other in amazement, Norman practically choking on his coffee. He did not know that Arthur had left the Company, let alone been guilty of a false transaction but he wasn't surprised. Arthur was capable of anything.

'So I am here today to ask that should you come across Arthur James in the course of your work or otherwise, I want you to inform me immediately and I will ask the police to investigate. Up to now, we have kept things rather low key and we have not involved the police – it would not be good for business if it were to get around that we could not control our employees. I want you all to know that we are tightening up on our procedures to make sure this sort of thing cannot happen again and MacDonald here will be going over previous transactions to see what else he can find. Forbes, he will want to go over all the transaction you have made from this office during the past six months.' He paused and took a drink of coffee. 'Now, all this is confidential and I do not want anything I have said to you to leave these four walls. It is important that as little of this as possible gets out and if I find out any one of you has talked about it, then I will come down on you like a ton of bricks. Understood?' He put his empty cup down on the table in front of him and looked for agreement that was quickly forthcoming.

'Right, good, I have some more pressing business to discuss. We are considering opening an office in Johannesburg. All across the Rand prospectors are finding gold deposits, usually on land owned by Boer farmers and once they get the chance, the farmers are happy to sell. The reef has grown to a hundred miles long and in the middle of it is Johannesburg. I would like Norman here to have a look around Johannesburg for a decent office and run it for us. It will mean you moving from here to be nearer the new office of course Norman, but we'll help with removal costs and there will obviously be a salary increase.' Leaning back in his chair, he regarded the other three men for several seconds before saying, 'Well gentlemen . . . if there are any questions?' There were no questions, only bewilderment. 'In that case I will be in the hotel over there having lunch whilst MacDonald does whatever he thinks necessary.'

Archibald Williamson rose from his seat and sauntered out onto the street leaving the accountant to finish the meeting, to explain how quickly they wanted to open the new office and how much of a budget Norman would have and after a further two hours poring over the books, the accountant announced that he had completed his audit. Collecting his papers together and depositing them in his leather case, he left to join Mr Williamson ready for the journey back to Cape Town leaving a relieved Alan Forbes and a puzzled Norman Campbell in his wake.

Alan turned to Norman. 'Well, it looks like you will be leaving us. You'd better get up to Johannesburg as soon as you can after Kleinstradt and take a look around.'

Norman nodded, wondering how he might break the news to Lucy, how she would react to the news that they were to move to Johannesburg, how was he going to handle the situation? He had to tell Lucy they would be moving again and he knew it would be a wrench. This time though, he felt destiny was drawing him to Johannesburg, a gold rush town where a man could make a fortune and perhaps this was his big chance. Johannesburg had the trappings of civilisation and was a man's town, a place where a smart operator like him could make money.

He could not stop thinking about the move and returning to Bloemfontein later in the afternoon, he felt that he needed a drink. Driving up to the Sporting club, he parked the car, climbed the few wooden steps to the entrance, and walked into the bar. Someone waved a greeting to him but he was oblivious to it and made towards the bar to order a double whisky and water. He sat on the nearest bar stool and sipped at his drink, not intending to stop too long, he had to speak to Lucy and he wanted to be in control of his faculties. However, it was not long before some of his friends arrived and he soon jettisoned that idea, refilling his glass several times over.

The room was thick with cigar smoke, the clink of glass and, as usual, the conversation centred on the war, the news of the day mainly about von Zeppelin's airships spreading fear and destruction over London. The Cape Times ran the story on its front page and most people in the bar had read or heard about the raid. Norman listened to opinions and forwarded one or two of his own and as the evening passed, he drank more than his fair share, eventually finding that his pockets were empty and he no choice but to leave. Swaying a little unsteadily, he put on his hat, made his way towards his car, and set it lurching off down the road.

By now, it was so dark that the dim headlights barely illuminated the road and about a mile from the club, as he rounded a bend obscured by bushes, a movement caught his eye. A man staggered out in front of him and before he could take any evasive action, there was an almighty bump. The man's body rode up onto the bonnet of the car and for a few terrifying moments a pair of glazed eyes stared through the windscreen forcing a shaken Norman to bring the car to a halt.

Less than steadily he climbed from the car to make his way back towards the figure lying in the road and even though intoxicated himself, he could smell liquor as he leaned over the prostrate figure of a native. By the dim light of the half-moon, he could see that the man's left leg had twisted to an unnatural angle and his eyes were staring straight up. It had all happened so quickly, he had killed him, if he reported the accident there would be questions from the police and lots of paperwork. There was no law against killing people with an automobile, but if some police officer wanted to be awkward, he could have a problem – and he did not need that. He looked out into the blackness and listened, nothing except the sound of running water then he saw a faint glint as moonlight reflected off that water, The Bloemspruit River, of course, he had just crossed a bridge two hundred yards back.

Standing up he returned to his car and manoeuvred it off the road, he turned the car's engine and lights off and began to feel his way back to the body. Almost tripping over the lifeless form, he managed to reach down and grab hold of the man's collar to drag the body in the direction of the river. The corpse was not heavy but still Norman struggled to move it, stumbling more than once and tearing his trouser leg on a thorn bush. He stopped for a few moments to let his breathing subside, listened for the sound of the water and realised that he was only a few yards away from the river. With renewed effort, he dragged the body to the water's edge to roll it into the water but the broken leg was an obstruction. Each time he tried to roll the man towards the water the leg got in the way and then he felt the weight of the body lessen as it began to slide down the muddy bank towards the river. Suddenly a hand clutched at his leg with a vice like grip, a grip so strong that it made him scream out in fright and he had to prise the fingers loose one by one. At last, the body was free to fall into the swiftly flowing water and as it disappeared, Norman collapsed onto the riverbank, gasping for breath, his mind in turmoil. Was the man still alive, did he really grip his leg or did he simply imagine it? Confused and exhausted he staggered back to the car to slump into the driver's seat to wonder about the man he had just killed. He was only a native, what did it matter. Norman was no longer a naïve Britisher, he had become a devious and uncaring opportunist.

Chapter 5

Solomon rose shivering from his hard bed and pulled on his clothes ready for the new working day. It was early, still dark and the work he was to do was hard but he was young, fit and having worked at the mine for almost six years, he was used to the routine. It seemed to him that he would spend the rest of his days here, toiling for ten months, returning to his family for only a few brief weeks each year. He missed them terribly, his eldest son Amos had grown tall and his younger brother, Jacob, almost five looked to be going the same way and he worried about Mary, struggling with their tiny small-holding.

Fastening the last of his shirt buttons Solomon looked across the spartan room at some of the other workers queuing for their toilet, a long wooden bench with holes cut into it and washing in a single bucket of freezing cold water. At least at the end of their shift things were a little easier, they had a large concrete trough located near the centre of the compound and half a dozen galvanized metal tubs. Then there was the compound wall, high, watched over by armed guards, the only way in and out through a pair of double gates covered with metal sheets and lockable from the outside. There was little chance of Solomon walking away from this prison until his contract ended although at times the management allowed a few trustworthy native workers out on a weekend pass. The Compound Manager was the only man with the power to issue them, the man at the pinnacle of the harsh system that confined the black labourers to live in the compounds for the duration of their contracts.

White shift bosses and an Induna controlled the system of working. The Induna was a native who had impressed with his work and diligence and who liaised between management and the black labourers. His job was to maintain order, to settle quarrels, and to represent the workers in disputes with management. Joshua had used his influence and guile to rise to the position of Induna, utilising skills acquired during his days in the diamond mines and he soon demonstrated his worth to the native workforce. In his late thirties, an advanced age for mineworkers, this less physical job was important enabling him to work longer to support his family and he was a popular choice.

Solomon was Joshua's closest friend and because Solomon could read and write a little, helped with letters to chiefs and magistrates to complain of the men's working conditions and to write to the newly widowed wives of men killed underground. As a reward for his help, Solomon had old newspapers and the occasional tattered book given to him and from these his reading and writing improved markedly.

Solomon put on his wooden soled shoes and his flowerpot shaped hat and joined the queue to wait his turn. Very few words passed between the workers, still fatigued from the previous day's toil but once they had eaten their breakfast of mealie meal, a form of porridge washed down with a watery beer they would begin to emerge from their shells. Then came the 2,000ft descent into the mine, some were able to walk down the sloping passages but most went down in mechanical lifts and then had to climb down ladders for a further 1,000ft to the working faces.

Solomon worked in the deepest part of the mine, the fifth level, and he needed to descend the central shaft in the cage and then walk on down a sloping tunnel for another 700 feet to the working face to join the gang setting up the heavy drills cutting deep into the shale for the explosive charges. Conditions were difficult, the air hot and humid, often filled with choking dust, especially after the dynamiting of the rock. The incessant noise of the hammers and drills numbed their senses and anyone not used to these extreme conditions could stand only an hour or two without having to leave for the surface.

Solomon was young and strong and worked hard during his first year in the mine. The shift boss had moved him from shovelling the ore into the skips to working as a "boy" for the White man operating the steam machine that provided power to the rock drill. Sometimes they would work perched along the side of the stope, excavating between levels equipped with hand drills and hammers to cut the ore, letting it fall to the level below. They worked completely naked, sweat running down their bodies and to pass the time, the black workers would sing tribal songs in step with the striking of the hammers.

One day, after drilling for an hour or so, Solomon noticed two white men making their way along the stope with small hammers in their hands. He had seen them before, the surveyor and his assistant, climbing over the broken shale towards the end of the shaft. Out of the corner of his eye he watched them pick their way to the very end of the workings when suddenly the ground began to shake violently. At first only a cloud of dust appeared and some small pieces of rock fell from the roof and then, without warning, a second tremor shook a section of roof free and it collapsed into the tunnel. The men working in the area froze, staring fearfully towards the rock fall, mesmerised by the dust cloud rolling towards them. No one panicked, but many of the men had worried looks upon their faces, were braced for further upheaval and then a scream pierced the gloom.

'What was that?' queried the driller looking along the tunnel to where the cry had come from, trying to see what had happened.

'The two men boss, those two who just passed, the roof has landed on them.'

'Bloody hell, come on let's see if we can help them.'

The white miner and Solomon stumbled over fallen rock and shale, making their way towards the sound of the screams and behind them, shouts echoed off the walls of the tunnel. The dust was thick and blinding to begin with but cleared enough for Solomon to make out the shape of a man lying on the ground, a roof timber lying across him. Without thinking, he lifted one end of the great balk of timber, rested it on his shoulder, and then straightened his legs to push the wooden trap just high enough for him to reach out and grab hold of the screaming man. With super human effort, Solomon used his free hand to pull on the man's shirt and drag him free just as others arrived to complete the task and with their help, he managed to discard his heavy load. He looked round and saw the injured man, saw plainly the relief on his blood soaked face and the man's thankful eyes met his.

By now, more miners were beginning to appear, scrambling over the debris blocking the tunnel, shovelling it away from the stricken men. Two burly labourers stepped forward and managed to pull the surveyor away to safety while others worked feverishly to remove obstacles and pull out the second white man and then came a shout.

'There is someone else here boss.'

Half-an-hour later they reached the third man, a Zulu, working alone at the very end of the tunnel who looked in a bad way when they finally dug him out. The man's thighbone was broken and Solomon saw that it was protruding hideously through torn skin as he was dragged clear of the fall. Someone wrapped his injured leg in rags and the shift boss carried out some rudimentary first aid, fitting a splint and binding the wound tightly. Solomon watched from a distance and marvelled at the proud Zulu who was obviously in pain and yet not a sound passed his lips. His work mates carried him along the tunnel and as soon as the cage returned to the bottom of the shaft, they laid him on its floor and sent him to the surface.

After the shift had ended, Solomon sat in his cot mulling over the events of the day and was surprised to see Joshua come into the dormitory. He jumped up from his bed and strode over to the door, following Joshua out into the open air.

'Solomon my friend how goes it?'

'You have heard of the roof collapse.'

'Yes, and I have come to see how you are. They told me earlier, when the shift returned to the surface that you were all right and now I have come to see for myself.'

'Two white men were injured and one of our own. How is he, do you know?'

Joshua said quietly, 'He died, Solomon. The doctor did not come for four hours and he died by losing his blood. The doctor was seeing the white men, of course, and he came too late for Siyanda. I am sad for his family – you will have to write another letter for me.'

Solomon felt sad too; they all knew that the mine work was dangerous and that any day a roof fall or gas explosion could claim their lives but to be so near to a fatal accident had shaken Solomon, made him realize just how close he had come to his own death. A few feet closer and it could have been him lying dead in the hospital and now he had to write the letter to tell the man's family of their loss.

Some distance away, inside the Company's whites only enclosure, Dennis Atkinson lay on his bed covered in cuts and bruises from the rock fall. His assistant, Joe Entwhistle, had regained consciousness during the journey up the central shaft to the surface and now he lay in the next room. The mine management, had sent to Johannesburg for a doctor as soon as they heard of the accident and after his inspection of the men's injuries, the doctor anounced that Joe had sustained a fractured skull along with his broken arm. The doctor set the broken arm and left his patient as comfortable as he could and then cleaned stitched the more severe of Dennis's wounds. After giving him a sleeping draught he left him and 12 hours later, the chief surveyor awoke to

77

the smell of beef broth. His appetite had returned and after consuming a bowl of food, he lay back on his bed, revisiting the horror of the rock fall.

Normally the shift boss provided the samples, sending them to his laboratory for testing and analysis, but occasionally he was required to make the descent to take samples himself. He remembered their descent in the cage to level five and the scramble down the steep slope to the bottom of the mine. He re-lived the scene in his mind, the dim electric lights, the ghostly shapes of workers hacking away at the shale and the incessant roar of the rock drills, he remembered sweating profusely and wondering if this was how Dante's Inferno must have looked. Then the rock fall that had been so sudden he remembered little, only that he had experienced a lucky escape: they both had. He thought about his mother back home in England – how would he write and tell her of his accident without alarming her. He had come out to work on the Rand six years before and reckoned that in another year or two, he would have acquired enough capital to return home and with Germany defeated, he could spend the rest of his life in peace fishing the Trent river near his home. Slowly his eyes closed and he drifted off into sleep . . .

He saw again the roof of the tunnel crashing down again on him, earth and dust blinding his vision, clogging his airways and he was unable to move. He felt himself trapped between the beam and the floor of level five and his arms reached out for a purchase to pull him free, but there was nothing, he was trapped. From behind, Joe screamed as the falling roof engulfed him, then silence and darkness for what seemed an eternity until the release of the beam pinning him to the floor. A big Zulu worker crouched with one end of the beam on his shoulder, heaving it off him, the black man's hand grasping at his clothing. Sweating profusely and his body shaking, he was re-living the experience and somehow knew he had to claw his way out of the nightmare and gasping for breath, he shouted into the blackness for someone to help him.

The bedroom door opened and a voice asked, 'Are you all right sir? You shouted out and seem to be in some distress.'

'Ahh..., yes I'm all right . . . th-thank you . . . j-just a dream. Th-thank you, nurse,' he stammered. The door closed and he was alone again, seeing nothing but the face, the face of a black man – his rescuer was a black man, a black man had lifted the beam and pulled him clear of his trap. A black man had saved his life and he was grateful. He understood the native workers situation of course – paid a pittance, and beaten into the bargain for trivial offences but he had never really thought of them as human beings, just a means for the mine owners and their financiers to get rich. As a mining surveyor he was well aware of the riches buried beneath the Witwatersrand reef, but it was of poor quality, the average amount of gold recovered from a ton of shale a mere third of an ounce. This was not the Klondike; the only way to make mining profitable was cheap labour; masses of cheap black labour and one of these faceless black men had saved his life and after such a close encounter with death, he found time to reflect, the system did seem very unfair, but what could he do? He had come to South Africa to seek his fortune, as had many others; it was not his place to change the order of things. The system was at least workable if not perfect.

Nevertheless, he felt he owed a debt: he was sure he would have perished if his saviour had not lifted that beam off his chest so promptly.

Solomon finished his breakfast and joined his workmates shuffling into the cage for the descent down the central shaft to begin another gruelling shift. Not far away, in a different world, the surveyor was recovering, sitting up in bed tucking into a plate of bacon and eggs. He had not slept well after his nightmare, was still sore and stiff from his ordeal, but he felt better. In the next room, the doctor had returned to have a look at Joe, change his dressings and then the doctor called in to see him.

'How is Joe now? I know he was quite badly injured and concussed.'

'A little more severe than concussed I would say. He may have a fractured skull and will need several weeks of rest to help it to heal. He also has a fracture to his right arm, routine in this industry and it should heal satisfactorily.'

'What about the labourer in there with us? I heard there was a black labourer with us when the roof collapsed – is he all right?' asked Dennis.

'I'm afraid he died from loss of blood, poor fellow. They got him out all right and took him to the cook house in the compound. I suppose it was warmer there, but I was unable to attend to him until I had fixed you and Joe up. You two are a bit more valuable than a Kaffir, plenty more where he came from,' replied the doctor taking off his stethoscope.

'You seem to be recovering well enough Dennis. I recommend you stay in bed for a day or so then take it easy. I will call in most days,' he said, closing his medical bag and reaching for the door handle.

'Well, good day doctor, thank you.'

As the door closed behind the doctor, Dennis began to wonder a little more about the lot of the native workers. To show any sort of compassion for the native labourers would not go down well with his fellow whites, still he felt he must do something and so decided to have a word with the mine manager.

Several days later Solomon's gang was hard at work, enveloped in the usual cacophony of drilling, when the shift boss signalled a break to allow the men to relax for a few minutes. They downed tools and sat about on the bare rock eating some bread and drinking water, but best of all was a chance to smoke some dagga. They regularly smoked the drug as an antidote to the constant hunger pangs and as an escape from the drudgery of their lives, the management believed it made them more productive and soon a thin, sweet smelling haze drifted through the mine.

After a while, one man began to sing in deep sorrowful voice, a song about the loneliness of the miner's lives and soon the whole shift joined in, their resonant tones echoing off the walls, a counterpoint to the raw sounds of the machinery still working further along the tunnel. Then, too soon, the call came to return to their labour and as they began hacking at the shale a white man, a big Afrikaner, appeared to speak with the ganger. They conversed for a few seconds and the ganger pointed across to Solomon. More often than not if a white ganger singled someone out it meant trouble, maybe even a beating and Solomon prepared himself as the man approached. He was a powerful looking individual with a sjambok hanging from a leather belt around his waist and he carried a heavy stick in his left hand. As the man crossed the open space towards him, Solomon began to feel uneasy.

'You Solomon Silongo, boy?' asked the man.

'Yas Baas.'

'Get your things together and follow me. We got another job for you to do, come on follow me.'

'Yas Baas,' said Solomon. To do anything else would invite trouble and so he followed the man obediently up the sloping tunnel to the cage at the base of the central shaft. It already contained four skips of shale ready to go to the surface and so they had to squeeze in before the Afrikaner could give Solomon the order to shut the gates ready to begin the hoist.

Minutes later, they stepped out of the dimly lit cage and into bright sunlight where Solomon struggled to adjust his eyes. They were heading towards a part of the mine installation where he had never been before, an area of increasing racket where the stamp mills crushed the ore to a dust. The rumble from the mills was so overpowering at close quarters that Solomon instinctively covered his ears with the palms of his hands and the Afrikaner grinned, nodding his head in the direction of the mill manager's office.

Inside the small office the noise reduced but it was still essential to talk in raised voices and the Afrikaner was almost shouting at the manager.

'Herman, this is the boy. They say he works well and is obedient. I'll leave him with you to instruct,' said the man opening the door to leave. The manager nodded and as the Afrikaner disappeared he kicked the side of the office with his boot, a signal, and a moment later a short, bearded White man appeared at the doorway dressed in dirty blue overalls.

'Phil, this is your new boy. Take him away and show him what you want him to do will you. And any funny business – kick his arse!'

Philip laughed and waved at Solomon, directing him to follow towards a small lean-to shed where the maintenance crew worked.

'You must have done somethin' right to be put in here away from the drillin' underground. Well, your new job is with me, to carry my tools and do as I say. And if you don't, then I kick your arse just like the man said. Here boy – stick this cotton wool in your ears before you go deaf.'

Solomon took the small white bundle, stuffed half in each ear, and then looked around, puzzled by his new surroundings and still not knowing why he was here. No one had told him that his new job was to clear the conscience of the head surveyor and probably no one ever would. Nearby, a maintenance man and his boy were working on a piece of equipment, the black man doing the work whilst the White man stood over him giving instruction.

After his first introduction to the maintenance crew Solomon carried out simple, menial tasks: carrying tools, cleaning machine parts with an oily rag, and sweeping the floors. He rejoiced in the fresh air and warm sunshine, a long way from the dark, hot, and humid world underground and he quietly acknowledged his good fortune by touching his good luck charm.

Although he did not realise it, Solomon was an intelligent man, and soon learned the techniques needed to perform the work assigned him. His white baas was fair, and when he saw Solomon was such a good labourer he refrained from bullying him too much and Solomon soon slipped into a routine.

Several weeks later after he had finished his shift, Solomon returned to the dormitory to find Joshua waiting for him.

"*Sawubona* Solomon, how are you? You are looking well in your new job, it must suit you.'

Solomon returned the greeting and smiled, 'I am well my friend, but I look forward to visiting my family soon. I have been here nearly ten months now. I'm weary of the mine.'

'I have news for you, good news: I can get us passes to go to Sophiatown at the end of the week. We can leave on Saturday after work but we must be back before work begins on Monday,' said Joshua, a grin spreading across his face. Solomon matched his grin, he knew very well of Sophiatown, a district on the edge of Johannesburg, the nearest township to the mine.

Saturday's shift finally ended and the two of them eagerly hitched a ride in the direction of the township and for over an hour, the lorry bumped along over the uneven dirt road. Eventually, over the noise of the engine they heard the driver shout for them to get off and walk and the vehicle slowed just enough for Joshua and Solomon to clamber over the tailgate. Landing in the dust, they picked themselves up and looked around and to their delight, not more than three or four hundred yards away, stood the shanties of Sophiatown.

Without so much as a word Joshua began to walk at pace in the direction of the township and approaching the first of the buildings they caught the sights and sounds of a vibrant neighbourhood. They heard voices and the clatter of hammers from a gang of men constructing a new shack, children calling to each other as they played in the street. It was in stark contrast to the grey existence of the compound, Solomon watched children running along the street in bare feet, groups of men standing idly on street corners and women in brightly coloured dresses sitting outside their shacks and Joshua stopped to speak to one of them in his native tongue.

'On the next street is a shebeen where we can drink cheap beer. Come on Solomon, let's go there.'

The shebeen was a corrugated iron clad building, strings of beads hanging loosely from the doorway and it was with some trepidation that Solomon followed Joshua inside. The room was small, furnished with several rough wooden benches for customer seating and in the middle of the far wall was an opening with yet more strings of coloured beads hanging to the floor. In one corner of the room sat six or seven natives sharing a pot of beer and smoking dagga and on a stool next to the opening in the wall sat a large woman with a brightly coloured headscarf, a formidable looking woman. As they became accustomed to the gloomy interior, they saw a woman watching them and after a few seconds, she pointed towards an empty table. Joshua and Solomon meekly went to sit at the table and as they did, the Shebeen Queen slid off her stool and came across to welcome them to her establishment.

'Hello boys, you come for a good time at Mama Portia's?'

Joshua released a contagious laugh and clapped his hands. 'You right their mama, how about two beers for me and my friend.'

She catered mainly for miners, knew exactly what they required and disappeared through the bead curtain for two pots of her homemade beer. She returned a short time later to place them on the table in front of Joshua and Solomon and held out her hand for payment. 'Four pence each for the beer boys – and if you are hungry, then there is food: stew with beans, fresh vegetables, buffalo meat, very tasty and filling for two strong men like you.'

Joshua gave the woman a wide grin and handed over the money for the beer. 'You're a fine host, woman; we'll drink some of your beer first and then maybe eat. But I hope you have plenty of beer.'

The woman threw her head back and laughed heartily, her ample bosom heaving in her dress. 'Plenty of beer? Well you come to the right place today my friends, because I have just finished brewing a whole barrel, and this a good brew, very tasty beer, very happy beer, you will have a good time here in my shebeen, the best shebeen in all Sophiatown!' Laughing loudly she left them and went across the room to attend to her other customers.

Joshua and Solomon lifted the pots to their mouths in unison and quenched a thirst built up over months in the dusty confines of the mine. At last they had some respite from their toil, a release, and as the evening wore on the shebeen filled up and they relaxed amidst their fellow natives. Men from the township came and went, for others who had finished their contracts and with money in their pockets, it was their first chance to enjoy themselves.

After Portia had served her newly arrived customers she came across to Joshua and asked if they wanted more beer.

'I think we are ready to try some of your food as well, how about two platefuls of that stew you were telling us about?'

The woman laughed heartily as she was prone to do and disappeared through the doorway, returning minutes later with two plates piled high with her home cooked stew and flat bread. The two men looked greedily at the plates and soon devoured the food, washing it down with beer. It had been a long time since either of them had eaten so well or been able to forget the hardships of the mine. Then, from across the room somebody began to sing and others soon joined in, deep melodic voices resonating round the room and before long, Joshua and Solomon joined them and for a time all thoughts of the mine and the compound were banished to the back of their minds.

The shebeen was a male preserve but at intervals during the evening women had come in to lead away some of the drunken men. Solomon was aware of this to-ing, fro-ing although he did not understand the significance, until a beautiful girl, tall and slender with tight curly hair caught his eye and Joshua laughed at him.

'You like the girl Solomon?'

'Yes she is pretty.'

'Do you want to sleep with her?'

Solomon was astounded at Joshua's comment and felt too shy to answer, yet still he could not tear his eyes away from her. Joshua did not pursue the question; instead, he turned his mind to the problem of where they were to sleep for the night and the next time the Queen brought their drinks, he asked her how much for a woman for the night. She gave him a knowing look and bent down to whisper something in his ear causing Joshua's face to break into a broad grin. He stuck two fingers up in front of her face and then stabbed his index finger in Solomon's direction. Solomon gazed blankly back at Joshua who was whispering again into the woman's ear.

'What was all that about Joshua?' slurred Solomon, through reddened, tired eyes.

'My young friend, I have found somewhere for us to sleep tonight. We are in very good luck, because the Shebeen Queen will look after me. She knows I am of royal Zulu blood and I have told her it will be an honour for her to sleep with me.'

'So what about me?'

'Ha!' replied Joshua. 'You will sleep with her daughter tonight.'

Solomon's heart skipped a beat, aghast: he had only ever been with Mary but as the last of the drunken natives left the shebeen, the woman closed the door, pushed a chair up against it, and blew out most of the remaining candles. The sound of drapes parting at the back of the room drew Solomon's attention and he turned to see the girl he had admired so much walk into the room and after a brief, whispered conversation with her mother she crossed the room towards him.

'You come with me,' was all she said.

Solomon stood a little shakily to his feet, unsure of what to do until the girl took hold of his hand and guided him through the doorway and across a small yard towards a long low shack. Solomon had not appreciated how much he had drunk and feeling his head spin, he felt unsteady on his feet and then the call of nature beckoned. Gesturing to the girl that he needed to relieve himself he looked round for some private place, finding nothing until she pointed to a hole in the ground at the far end of the yard and pushed him in that direction and afterwards he staggered back to see the girl grinning from ear to ear.

They entered a sparsely furnished room containing no more than a straw bed on the floor but still it was a welcome sight for an exhausted Solomon. The girl turned to face him, reached out with both hands and, with some fascination, Solomon watched her as she began to undress him. First, she undid the buttons on his shirt, slipping her cool, soft hands expertly across his chest, and then she undid his belt and let his trousers fall to the ground. Her actions had the desired effect, his tiredness temporarily forgotten he began pulling at her clothing, but she was more dexterous than he was and quickly slipped out of her dress, letting it fall to the ground to stand naked before him. The bright moonlight streaming through the glassless window silhouetted her fine figure and tearing off the rest of his clothes, he took hold of her, and together they collapsed onto the bed. He felt her breasts pushing against his chest, his hands explored her and he experienced sensations he had not felt for months.

Sweating with their exertions, their shiny black bodies intertwined, she arched her back and spread her legs wide apart ready for him, but Solomon did not move. Her hands clasped behind his neck, pulling him down to her, she bent her knees and wrapped her legs around him, pressing her heels into his buttocks, forcing him inexorably towards her, but Solomon still did not respond, his mind deep in turmoil.

His physical feelings for this woman were almost overpowering, but he had only ever been with Mary, only ever with his wife and a powerful force took control. A strong feeling of guilt swept over him, he was betraying Mary and she sensed it, her frenetic clawing suddenly stopping.

'Why do you stop, do you not like me, am I not beautiful enough?'

'I have a wife and children many miles from here and I cannot do this thing. You are a beautiful woman and I want you, but I keep thinking about them,' Solomon whispered.

The girl tried to slide from under him and Solomon rolled onto his side to set her free, but as their bodies parted, she reached out with her strong soft hands and grasped him, slowly working him to a climax.

The morning light was bright, the sun's rays easily piercing the ragged curtains and falling on Solomon's eyelids. Stirring from his slumber, he felt the sleeping girl's warm body pressing against him and for an instant thought that it was Mary, and then she turned towards him. Her hand slid across his chest, Solomon stiffened, wondering what to do, and then, slowly, he managed to move away, roll off the bed and stand up.

'Where are you going?' said the girl startling him.

Solomon froze and turned his head to look down at her. She still had her eyes closed and he wondered if he was hearing things but then those eyes opened and she looked straight up at him, her face creasing into a beautiful smile and then she yawned. She took a deep breath and stretched her body, throwing off the last vestiges of sleep and then she watched him before reaching out a naked arm to grab hold of her dress. Still holding his gaze, she pulled it under the single rough woollen blanket and dressed herself in a far more modest fashion than when she had undressed.

'Good morning Solomon,' she finally said. 'I see you have lost your tongue. Would you like me to get you some breakfast?'

'You know my name?'

'Of course, you told me last night.'

Solomon could not remember and blinked as he attempted to piece together the events of the previous evening. The girl threw off the single blanket and stood up, kissed him gently on the lips and spoke softly to him.

'Did I make you happy last night? Your wife will not mind because you have been apart so long and I know a man's needs. What is her name? Is she Zulu?'

Surprised by her questioning Solomon replied, 'her name is Mary and yes, she is Zulu and we have been married since I was 15 and she was 13. What is your name?'

'Mbali, you have forgotten already,' she said pouting her lips'

'Flower,' he said, 'you are Zulu as well. You don't look Zulu – you look more like Ndebele.'

91

'My mother is Ndebele, but my father was Zulu. I have family in Zululand but I never have seen them,' she said in her soft lilting voice.

Mbali looked into the eyes of this handsome, gentle man, a man far different to the four men she had been with during the previous evening, earning money with her body whilst she was still able. They were not like this man; coarse and aggressive whereas he was gentle and caring, she liked him. Solomon caught the look in her eyes in the clear light of the sun's rays and something within him stirred. She smiled and turned away, slipping through the drapes to return a minute later.

'Come, my mother has prepared breakfast and your father is already eating his.'

Solomon laughed aloud and she gave him a puzzled look. 'Joshua is not my father, he is my friend, and I will have some sport with him when I tell him what you have said.'

Mbali giggled. She had met Joshua only briefly the night before and had assumed, wrongly, that he was Solomon's father.

'What are you doing today Solomon?' she asked, 'I am going to the church soon, do you want to come with me?'

Without hesitation Solomon nodded, he had not been to church in a long time, perhaps he could repent his sin he thought as he followed her her into the main room and found Joshua sitting at one of the tables eating eggs his breakfast and he looked up as he and Mbali entered.

'Solomon, you slept well?' he asked with a glint in his eye.

'Yes I slept very well. Mbali is taking me to church this morning,' he said, with a self-conscious look on his face.

Joshua laughed. 'Don't forget we must return to the mine today. If we are not at work tomorrow morning, then we will be in trouble and we will not have another pass for a long time. Be back before five o'clock this afternoon, we will leave then. In the meantime, I will ask around to see if we can get a ride back. I will ask my new friend if she knows of anyone who can take us, and we must pay her for her hospitality. Give me your money and I will take care of it.'

After giving Joshua his few coins Solomon followed Mbali into the street and towards a corrugated iron building that served as the American missionary church. They had arrived with the aim of converting the population to the way of their church, to educate the children and eventually they became involved in the general health of the diverse community. The ending of the Great War caused such an influx of migrants looking for work that there was a desperate need for voluntary organisations such as theirs. The missionaries provided as much comfort as they could to the poor both physical and spiritual and for many people the church had become the centre of their lives.

Mbali led Solomon inside the church and after finding seats amongst the congregation, they waited for the service to begin. Solomon had enjoyed going to the little church in his village, a lean too shed with a roof of dried grass, but this was his first time in a real church. He cautiously took in the surroundings, the people around him, the airiness of the place and he began to feel at home. He knew the hymns, joining in with his rich baritone voice, attracting one or two admiring glances and after the service Mbali encouraged him to join the congregation filing past the priest.

'It is good to see you this morning Mbali, how is your mother? We haven't seen her here at the church for some time; tell her we miss her wonderful singing voice.' Mbali nodded and said that she would tell her. The missionary held out his hand to Solomon. 'Your friend is new to us Mbali.' And to Solomon he asked, 'what is your name my son?'

'Solomon.'

The priest's eyes lit up. 'A good biblical name – who gave you such a name?'

'The missionaries in our village taught us the Bible and my mother liked the name Solomon. She gave us all biblical names as well as our Zulu names.'

'Ah, so you are well versed in the Christian church, that is good and I must say that you are very welcome here, as is anyone who needs us. Would you stay a while and meet our congregation? Mbali is one of our children; she always stops behind after the service to help serve tea. It will be pleasant to get to know you a little more and perhaps you will join us more often.' The priest smiled at them before turning away to acknowledge the next person in line.

'I help here every Sunday Solomon,' said Mbali proudly, 'I help with the refreshments for the people who stay, they talk with one another and it is very interesting for me. We enjoy Sunday mornings, we discuss the Bible and catch up on the gossip.'

Solomon was not sure he would stay, but once Mbali had prodded him in the ribs and looked at him with pleading eyes, he felt he had no choice. 'I have not been to church for many years, this morning brought back many memories, memories of happier times in our village. Yes Mbali, I will stay with you for a while'.

Mbali's face showed obvious pleasure, she had not known him very long but she felt very much at ease in his company and would do anything to prolong their time together.

'Come Solomon, we will go outside and meet everyone.' She pulled him unceremoniously out of the church and towards the shade of an acacia tree. Here volunteers had set up a wooden table and were busy with Cups and saucers, laying them in two neat rows. A woman with a brightly coloured turban on her head appeared with the largest teapot Solomon had ever seen and began proudly to pour the tea. Those of the congregation who had remained behind after the service filed past her, picked up a cup of tea and went to sit on a bench or to stand in the shade and chatter and to Solomon everyone seemed to be talking at once.

He remained politely silent, listening, and then Mbali brought him a cup of tea and stood beside him. She seemed to know everyone and gradually she drew Solomon into the conversation. Shy to begin with, he eventually found the confidence to speak and with Mbali egging him on, he was soon the centre of attention. Some of those present had only heard of the conditions in the mines, never seeing for themselves and were inquisitive to know more.

Solomon answered questions where he could and as the afternoon wore on a change seemed to come over him. Until the present time he had never found himself involved in discussion of any kind, never expressed his opinion and although he had read the newspapers and books Joshua had managed to beg, steal and borrow for him, he had never discussed their contents with anyone else. Suddenly he was aware that he could hold a conversation and these new and interesting people were helping his confidence grow.

On the fringes of the crowd, a tall, elegant looking native man wearing a suit and tie was listening and he overheard Solomon talking. The man knew very well the conditions the native labourers worked under and was impressed by Solomon's clear descriptions. He came closer and after listening some more, finally introduced himself. 'Good morning, my name is Alfred Mdinga and I could not help but overhear you. Your portrayal of the conditions in the mines is very interesting.'

Solomon looked at him, a little overawed by this tall, well-dressed man who was nothing like the other people of Sophiatown he had met.

'Thank you, I am Solomon and I am only telling how it is.'

'I know and I must say you put it across very well, it is as if I am there when I listen to you. Where do you come from Solomon?'

Solomon explained how the law had forced him from his smallholding, that he had come to iGoli in search of work and Alfred nodded understanding. For a time, the two men talked about the problem of the native peoples and Alfred explained that he was a lawyer, acting mostly for the poor and dispossessed of the townships. He said he sympathised, he had met a great many people who had undergone similar experiences and that he had many friends concerned for the plight of the.

'Not just the black workers, whites as well, the mine owners are greedy and together with the Government it is they who have formulated the hated Land Act and the Pass Laws. Something needs to be done about it, the workers need organising and to have some sort of representation if they are to fight for their rights. Solomon, I have friends who are not happy with the oppression of the black man. They want to do something about it. Do you know of the South African Native National Congress?'

'Yes, I have read about the Native Congress in *Abantu Batho*, in the *Indian Opinion* and *Llanga Lase Natal* as well. My friend Joshua finds old newspapers for me.'

Alfred was surprised to learn that Solomon had acquired the skill to read and write, and he learned then of the letters Joshua had asked him to write and was impressed. Solomon's head dropped a little as he recalled some of those letters to newly widowed wives and others to the tribal chiefs pleading for help to improve the miners' lot and Alfred looked at him with some respect. Here was a man who had suffered, seen the suffering of others and had offered solace in a way few others could.

For a minute, neither spoke until Alfred broke the silence in a voice touched with feeling. 'Solomon, I have friends who are associated with the *Abantu Batho,* the voice of our people. Our circulation is growing, and we need good people who understand the plight of Africans, who can tell the story of inequality. We need accounts of what goes on from people like you who are involved, who know first-hand the hardships and poverty our people endure. You impress me Solomon! You have seen a lot in the mines, and you can read and write. Could you write an article for us? Try, Solomon, and if it is good enough, I will show it to the editor of *Abantu Batho* and see if he will publish it. Will you do that for me, friend?'

'But what can I write about?' asked Solomon.

'Anything! Something about the plight of our people, a first-hand narrative with which we can tell the world.

Here is my address in Johannesburg. If you do decide to try and write something, then send it to me to read will you.' Alfred turned to Mbali, 'How is your mother? I hope she is well.'

'Very well.'

'I hope that you are getting proper work now, young lady. You should not be earning a living looking after the men in your mother's shebeen,' he said sternly, and then he was gone.

Mbali looked a little awkward.

'What's the matter, is it because Alfred mentioned what you do to earn money?'`

'Yes,' she said, some embarrassment showing.

'Well I don't mind.' He smiled at her and she smiled back. 'I have worked in the mines for six years, I do not see my family for many months at a time, and I know how hard life can be, how loneliness eats away at your soul – you have helped me with that'. He paused for a moment taking stock and then he spoke with conviction. 'I know now what I shall write about.'

Chapter 6

Peggy looked out of car the window to see her father standing on the pavement holding her little brother's hand. Her mother sat by the open car door, her arms outstretched to receive the little boy and take him into the car to sit beside his sister. Peggy watched her little brother snuggle up to their mother and then she looked at her father walking away to start the car's engine.

'Are we leaving our house now Mummy?'

'Yes Peggy, we're off to a new house in Johannesburg,' said her mother putting her free hand around her to drawing her close.

'Jo-anbug!' mouthed Peggy.

Lucy smiled at her and the three of them settled back in the seat as Norman wound the starting handle and the engine roared into life. She was sad to leave her little house and its lovely garden but Norman's promotion meant a higher salary, more responsibility and she felt she had to support him as much as she could.

Since Williamson had informed Norman of his new status, he had made the trip several times looking for suitable office space and accommodation for his family. Eventually he found a building on Fox Street at the heart of the city, office space with living quarters above and with almost everything in place, it was time to leave Bloemfontein. He would take his family together with a few essential belongings in the Buick, their furniture and the servants following the next day by lorry.

Lucy had become fond of her little house with its memories, good and bad, and she glanced back at it one last time as the car pulled away. She would miss the light airy rooms and the garden with its stunningly beautiful flowers, a place where she would sit watching her children playing and then she wondered what Alistair and Rosemary might look like if they had survived. She felt a twinge of sadness that almost made her cry and vowed one day to return to visit their graves.

Leaving the town limits the car headed north through fertile grasslands until, in the early evening, they reached Kroonstad and the small lodging house Norman used on his trips to Johannesburg. Resuming their journey the following morning the Buick laboured as it climbed the escarpment to the Highveld where the rolling, fertile countryside changed to a landscape of brush and solitary bushes.

'I'm glad that bit is over Lucy, I really thought we might have to stop and let the engine cool down. How are the children managing?'

'They are fine, the have both fallen asleep.'

Norman looked in his rear view mirror and saw his children lying against their mother, he smiled to himself, and then he noticed dark clouds gathering in the distance, storm clouds. He had seen those dark foreboding shapes heralding the arrival of rainstorms on previous trips and he began to wonder if they were heading his way. The storms on the Highveld could be fierce and frightening and he decided to stop the car to take a better look.

'What's the matter Norman, why have we stopped?'

'Those storm clouds over there, do you see them? I want to see where they're heading.' He whetted his finger and held it aloft to feel the wind. 'Hmm' looks like it's blowing towards the hills – over there,' he said, pointing to a range of low-lying hills in the distance. 'Should miss us I think. Better to be safe than sorry Lucy, storms up here can be pretty nasty.'

He climbed back in the car and set off at a slower pace, allowing him time to monitor the storm but in his calculations, he had not allowed for the effect of the African landscape. Alarmingly the storm seemed to change direction, beginning to head straight for them. Soon the first bolts of lightning traced their zigzag paths to earth and the low rumbling noise of thunder reached their ears. Although the storm was still a long way off Norman and Lucy could see that it was increasing in intensity. Above them, the sky was darkening rapidly and soon it began to release a deluge. Norman struggled to drive the car at speed as lightning flashes became more frequent, the thunder deafening and grey streaks of rain lashed the Buick as it careered along the road.

'Norman, can't we stop for a while and let it pass?' she said Lucy in a trembling voice.

Norman considered his options. They were isolated their only shelter was in the car so he could either stop to ride it out or he could try to outrun it. Lightning was striking with alarming regularity, the road was filling rapidly with water, and he feared disaster. If the car sustained damage then they would be completely isolated until someone came along, and that could be

101

days, and then, quite suddenly, the storm was overhead. Lightning flashed repeatedly lighting up the darkened landscape, Lucy shrieked in fright, and in unison the children began to scream. The rain intensified to such a pitch that Norman could hardly see where he was going but the road was straight and surely, if he kept control, they would be safe enough.

The rain became an almost solid sheet of water, the windscreen was awash and Norman could see nothing of the road, the torrent running down the windows completely obscuring his view and forcing him to slow to a snail's pace. Spray came in through the ill-fitting door and up through holes in the floor, the engine coughed and the car began to buck and lurch. Even with the pedal pressed hard to the floorboards the power just drained away – and then, to his relief, the next bolt of lightning struck the ground well behind them. The worst of the storm had passed, and then the engine finally spluttered to a stop.

In the back of the car, Lucy was unaware of Norman's problems, only interested in comforting the children, trying to keep them warm and dry.

'Norman!'

'What?'

'Give me your jacket,'

'What?'

'Give me your jacket,' she commanded, her only thought to protect the children.

With a sigh of resignation, Norman stripped off his jacket and passed it over and then he turned his attention to their predicament. The engine had stopped, probably flooded with water and he had little idea of what to do.

'So now what Norman, stuck are we?' she said seeing his forlorn face.

'No, we're not stuck yet,' he snapped, frightened to think they really might be and he peered out through the windscreen. He was relieved to see at least the storm was passing over and the sky was beginning to clear, the thunder only a distant rumble. He sat back in his seat, concerned by the pool of water he could see surrounding the car and wondered what to do. They had come to a halt in a small depression filled with storm water making their predicament appear worse than it really was. A few feet in front of the car the ground was already beginning to dry in the heat of the sun, the little lake surrounding the Buick was beginning to drain away and within an hour, the water level had dropped enough for Norman to venture outside and inspect the engine. He lifted the bonnet and looked it over, it seemed dry enough and he reached for the starting handle.

'There! We're off!' he shouted, mightily relieved as the engine started and when he engaged the gears the little car pulled itself out of the hollow and for a time Norman was able to forget the discomfort of soaking wet shoes.

The Buick entered the outskirts of Johannesburg just before eight o'clock in the evening, three hours later than expected and came to a stop outside the Carlton Hotel. Norman had arranged for them to stay in the hotel until they could move into the house on Fox Street and the following morning he took them to see their new home. Lucy gripped her daughter's hand to keep her from straying as they walked and Norman carried Henry astride his shoulders. The crowds of people fascinated Lucy, it was her first time in Johannesburg and the sights and sounds fascinated her. Black native people, Indians from the sub-continent, a smattering of Orientals with yellowish skin sitting behind shop counters decked out with rich and colourful fabrics, ivory, wooden carvings and her nose twitched at the strange exotic aromas drifting from them and there were the white people going about their business as if in any European city.

Finally they reached Fox street, a wide thoroughfare with four storey buildings on each side, houses set in terraces of six, with shops or office fronts at ground level, living accommodation above and Lucy cast her critical eye over them.

'Which one are we to live in Norman?'

'The next block, there look the one with the double wooden doors. We have a yard where the children can play and where I will keep the car.'

They walked a little further and then Norman set Henry down on the ground, took a key out of his jacket pocket and opened the front door. Lucy held hands with each child as he walked in and then she followed with the children.

'Come on let us have a look at our living quarters, these are the offices down here.'

Norman led the way up the creaking staircase, his footsteps amplified by bare the wooden flooring, the sound too much of a temptation for the children who stamped their feet as well. They broke free of their parents to clatter noisily along the floor and Lucy followed them, not sure she liked the house very much, it was so very different from the one in Bloemfontein with its garden.

'Norman, it's a nice big house but I can't see what Mabutu will do when we move in.'

'It's not such a problem Lucy. We have to keep the office clean and tidy, and the car needs regularly maintenance. I will find him plenty to do so don't worry.'

The following day Norman and Lucy returned to Fox street to meet the vehicle bringing their furniture. It was piled high with their accumulated possessions and in amongst them, Marsha and Mabutu had found a comfortable space to journey and true to his word, Norman found plenty for Mabutu to do. First of all keeping him busy carrying furniture and carpets, hanging pictures, sweeping up dust and debris, washing windows, fetching water, and a host of other duties. Norman had hired tradesmen to start work on the offices, they appeared the day after to build a partition, paint the walls, and he acquired desks, chairs, and other office furniture before making a visit to the offices of *The Star* newspaper. Archibald Williamson had instructed him to take out a series of advertisements to announce the arrival of "Williamson and Williamson, Estate Agents Extraordinaire" and because it was a fledgling venture, he would need as many properties on his books as he could get.

The real money though would be in land – that was the real business, land, the boss had stressed that they must become involved in dealing in land. The Witwatersrand was the largest, richest goldfield in the world, with enormous potential. Within two weeks the advertising bore fruit, Norman had properties for sale on his books in Jeppestown, Fordsburg and the fashionable district of Parktown, a place of sumptuous mansions and super-bungalows and he knew that he could earn fat profits selling them.

By the end of the second week the offices were complete, a telephone installed, and Archibald Williamson lost little time in ringing, calling almost every day from Cape Town. He had a large network of friends and business associates throughout South Africa and now that it was so easy to contact Johannesburg, he would ring Norman to advise him of potential clients, though it seemed telephoning was not enough. Not long after Norman had the business up and running he journeyed from Cape Town to see first-hand how it was developing. Ernest Grey, a mine owner invited him to stay for a while and he jumped at the chance and a few days later Norman was waiting patiently at the railway station for him.

'Well Campbell, how d'you like it here?'

'Very well, thank you sir.'

'You seem to have done some decent business already. I must say so far I am pleased with your progress, but I think we need to up the tempo on the industrial side. I'll have a chat with Grey to see what I can find out. I am keen to get in on any land deals happening up here and he knows what is going on. Useful fella Grey.'

Eventually the Buick reached the wide boulevards of Doornfontein, a suburb of beautiful houses set in their own well-tended gardens. Norman sighed; his home in Bloemfontein had been pleasant enough, but nowhere near the scale of these mansions. He looked at each house as they passed, wondering how he might make his fortune and live like this. His concentration returned and he turned the car into a wide, gravelled drive pulling up outside a sumptuous porch. Grey came out to meet his guest, instructing a pair of servant boys to take care of Williamson's luggage, and without a word to Norman the two of them disappeared inside the house, leaving him to make his way back to the city.

So easily dismissed by the two rich men, Norman felt somewhat dejected and decided that perhaps he needed a drink. He knew just the place, a little bar on Joubert Street he frequented, where he might find one or two acquaintances hanging out. The Silver Star had been a popular watering hole for almost 25 years, a witness to both the good times and the bad and an Italian immigrant named Alessandro had run the place ever since the Boer war. Alessandro had shrewdly grabbed the place at a knock down price when the original owner had wanted to get out of town with his capital intact. Because Alessandro was neither an Englishman nor a Dutchman it was of no interest to him who won the war, he would simply make sure that he was on the winning side and at the end of it all his English improved, his Afrikaans did not, and his bar thrived.

Norman walked in and slid onto a bar stool. 'Give me a beer Alessandro, will you.'

'For ahew Mr. Norman, no problem!' said Alessandro in his comical English. 'Hew want I give you some to heat?' he said as he polished the copper topped bar to a brilliant sheen.

'Naw, just a couple of beers tonight. My boss is in town and I have to be presentable tomorrow.'

'Aw, I thought you the boss man!' replied Alessandro.

'No, not yet, but I'm working on it,' Norman said, glancing around the room.

Illuminating the bar were three dim electric light bulbs, enough to see by and yet just dim enough not to be seen easily by others if a man wanted to remain in the shadows. Looking over Alessandro's shoulder towards the back room Norman could see a number of black natives, some already slumped over the tables and he knew that within a few hours all of them would be blind drunk. They were some of the most profitable of Alessandro's patrons, spending almost all of their wages on alcohol. A few white men sat around a table against the back wall drinking, smoking, and playing cards and the atmosphere was thick with the smell of their burning tobacco. Norman viewed them with only a passing interest before he took a drink from his glass and leaned back slightly to look round the rest of the bar, his eyes coming to rest upon a slightly built man with a thin moustache and he almost choked on his drink. Arthur James – his erstwhile friend from Cape Town.

Shiny beer pumps separated him from Arthur's direct line of vision and he pulled his head back a little to make sure he was not recognised and hoped Arthur would remain seated. He decided that under the present circumstances it would be best to avoid him and then Alessandro began grumbling to Norman about the new city taxes, how they would cost him dearly. Norman replied with uninterested nods and grunts, his attention focused purely on Arthur who he now knew had been up to no good in Cape Town. He did not know exactly what Arthur had done but with Williamson in town for the next two days, he felt it best to keep clear of Arthur.

Chapter 7

The autumn of 1919 saw Sophiatown growing rapidly, it was more than a year since the end of The Great War, the army had returned from overseas and the ex-soldiers were looking to pick up their lives where they had left off – but things had changed. The British Government had abandoned the fixed price of gold in order to pay for the war, a premium had evolved and the price of gold was rising steadily, a benefit for the Rand Lords but equally, their wage bills had reached astronomical proportions. During the war, capable black workers, had taken on the jobs of the white miners at a fraction of the cost and when the soldiers returned home to look for work, reclaim their old jobs, they found black workers had taken them and the situation was becoming unpleasant, an air militancy spreading across the Witwatersrand.

Alfred Mdinga was well aware of the growing industrial unrest amongst the white population and the threat to the native workforce and deep in thought, he considered the problem. The city of Johannesburg had grown; African townships like Sophiatown were bursting with poor and destitute people struggling to survive. These people depended upon the work the mines provided. He saw children playing in the street as he passed, patched-up clothing covering their little bodies and not a shoe between them. In the streets in front of their ramshackle homes, women washed clothes and preparing food. From the doorways of illegal drinking houses, he picked up the sweet smell of brewing beer. Shebeens were the few places where the men could go to forget their troubles. He had grown up in Sophiatown and attended a school run by the American missionaries and as a promising student; they helped him complete his education and funded his law degree studies in the United States. On his return, he had at first lived in the township and then set up as a lawyer in Johannesburg, often offering his services for free to the underprivileged.

He turned a corner and a smile came to his lips as he recognised an old man sitting in a bamboo chair beside an open door.

'Manqoba my old friend, how are you and how is Nomathemba?

'Good,' replied the man. 'We are very well thank you.'

Alfred lifted his arm in a brief wave and carried on walking, his mind drifting back to those early days when he had returned from America, when he had become a political activist. In 1912 he had been at the inaugural meeting of the South African Native National Congress in Bloemfontein where he met Pixley Seme, also a practising lawyer in Johannesburg and the two of them had become firm friends. Pixley told Alfred that he had the backing of the Queen Regent of Swaziland who was keen to start a newspaper and would he, Alfred, take on the task, create an African newspaper for circulation amongst the native population.

Alfred had felt honoured and soon the *Abantu Batho*, newspaper was born, the voice of the Congress and not long after its launch circulation increased so much that they began printing in English, Zulu, Xhosa, and Sotho. Alfred was completely engrossed in the newspaper, contributing articles on the law and practises of the land. He travelled as much as the Pass Law would allow him, writing articles about the native people, the injustices imposed upon them and his articles proved increasingly popular with the downtrodden masses.

As he walked, he considered his latest writings about some sanitary workers. They had downed their buckets demanding sixpence a day extra to lift them above the poverty line but the authorities had reacted aggressively. Scab labour was brought in, the strikers arrested and sentenced to two months' imprisonment under the Master and Servants Act. The instigators of the strike were charged with incitement to violence and Alfred knew that if found guilty, which was inevitable, the men faced long prison sentences. He had made it his business to help and after making some enquiries, he had discovered that the police criminal investigation department had infiltrated a section of the workers' union. Publishing an embarrassing series of articles, he showed that it was entrapment and it now appeared that the Attorney-General was refusing to prosecute. He was glad his articles had made the establishment reconsider.

Reaching an alleyway between a solid wooden building and a corrugated shack, he turned and walked into a cramped yard. In front of him was a lean too shed and in it, he could see a man sitting at a small table and scribbling away with a pencil.

'Good morning Solomon, how are you today?'

'I am very well,' replied Solomon looking up from his work.

111

'How are Mary and the boys settling in to their new home?'

'They are well, Mary has just taken Amos to his new school and will return soon with Benjamin,' said Solomon, with more than a little pride in his voice.

The conversation with Alfred on that Sunday morning had inspired Solomon, he had taken up the challenge and spent the remainder of his contract thinking about the subject matter: loneliness, the loneliness of men separated from their families for many months. Most of the men in the compound suffered unbearably from it and with very little to occupy them during the small amount of free time they were allowed, many would sink into depression. Sometimes their mood could leave them open to carelessness underground which could be fatal and Solomon knew a lot about that for he was the one who wrote to their families informing them of their loss.

He had begun his article with a short introduction about the backbreaking work, the men's spare time when they had little else to do but sleep or play a traditional pitch and toss stone game. Many of them simply lay on their beds, thinking of loved ones far away and he had rewritten his article twice before he was satisfied, and only then had he delivered it with a letter to Alfred Mdinga. Alfred had not really believed Solomon would write the article and when it had arrived, he had read with interest. Moved by the subject matter he knew instinctively that Solomon's style of writing would appeal to the newspaper's readership. Though unsophisticated, Alfred's editing had made it presentable enough for the next issue and after publication, many readers had asked whom Solomon was. Alfred was impressed and wrote to Solomon asking him for more articles and six months later, the editor offered Solomon a place on the newspaper staff. Solomon was overwhelmed and could think of nothing else until the end of his contract when he would be free to move his family to Sophiatown.

'iGoli, the city of gold?' Mary had exclaimed when he had returned home and told her the news.

'Yes, Mary, iGoli. I have seen so much since I left here to work in the mines. – I met a good man who makes a newspaper and he has told me that he wants me to write for him. He says they need someone like me who has worked underground and can tell the readers what it is really like. The chiefs do not like their young men working in the mines because so many die there and he says that if I write about the problems, tell others what to expect, then maybe it will save some lives.'

After that, Mary spent some time thinking about her husband's words . . . were they really leaving for iGoli, for a new life in the city. Then she began to tidy up in a haphazard sort of way and to sing in a soft voice, not having the vaguest idea of what it would be like but they would all be together and that made her very happy.

'What are you writing about today?' asked Alfred as he entered the shack.

'A boy at the mission school has done well, and the missionaries are paying for him to go to the Christian industrial school. His parents are so proud of him and I wanted to follow his progress and encourage more youngsters to work hard at school.'

'What a good idea Solomon. We must encourage the brighter children to do well in their education. After all, they are our main hope for the future! If we can't fight the White man on his own terms, then what chance do we have?'

The two men fell silent for a moment until Alfred spoke again, slowly, 'Solomon, there's a campaign against the Pass Laws about to begin and the miners are mobilising for strike action. You have improved markedly since you came here, and you have experienced the miners' situation, so we want you to go out and cover the story. This time The South African Native National Congress is helping the miners to manage the strike. We need to report it so the people know what is happening, so that they can follow events closely, and prevent the mine owners from hijacking public opinion. Normally it would be difficult for you to move about but we have obtained some passes for you to travel. We will leave for Johannesburg soon and I will introduce you to some people who will help you.'

Solomon looked at Alfred, excited yet apprehensive; this was a chance to help his people, not by subterfuge or strike action, but by writing. He would travel wherever the passes allowed him, talk to the miners and find out as much as he could before telling their stories. Was this his mission in life, to shed light on the issues affecting the native, illuminate their hardships and give them some sort of voice? His mind drifted back to that fateful day when he had left his village, and he remembered his conversation with his father, instinctively touching the talisman around his neck. The words of the Isangoma came back to him, clear and strong, 'I see the future; I see great things for our brother Solomon, he will become an important messenger for all the Zulus.' Solomon shuddered at the witch doctor's insight, a powerful force for the old ways and for a few moments, he felt his Christian beliefs displaced by the world of the spirits.

Alfred noticed something in Solomon's eyes, something immeasurable, but before he could comment Mary appeared in the yard with Benjamin and she greeted Alfred with a big smile.

'Hello Mary. Are you well?'

'Very well, Mr Alfred,' she replied with some respect.

'Mary, I have come to see Solomon, to ask him to come to work in Johannesburg for a short while.'

Solomon stood up from the table, 'I must go with Alfred but I don't know when I will be back. One or two weeks at least I think,' He looked at Alfred and then back at Mary, 'you will need to manage alone for a while'.

Mary looked down at the ground and said nothing, her eyes clouding at the thought of Solomon leaving her again. She had spent so long alone with her sons when he worked in the mine and she dreaded returning to that life.

'Do not worry Mary – I will not go to the mines again. I am going to write for the newspaper and I will not be away for long so please do not be sad,' he said reaching down to pat his son on his head. Alfred smiled at the gesture for he was not married and had no children of his own and he was happy to have helped this family to come together.

After a brief goodbye, the two men made their way back along the passage and into the street where Alfred hailed a passing rickshaw to take them into the city. It was a rare treat for Solomon not to have to walk, a pleasure he was unaccustomed to and he made the most of it taking in all the sights. Finally, they arrived in the city, paid the rickshaw driver, walked between two tall buildings towards the entrance of a corrugated iron shed squashed between them and from the interior a large black man appeared, Walter Ndumby the newspaper's editor.

'Welcome to the office of the *Abantu Batho*, the most important native newspaper in the country,' he laughed, his deep, sonorous voice echoing off the surrounding walls. He reached out with his left hand to greet his visitors and although he was a big man, physically strong and active, he had a weakened right arm, deformed since birth and it had prevented him from working in the mines. However, he had a sharp and active mind and because he could not undertake manual employment he had acquired literary and numeracy skills to work first as a clerk and then as the editor of the newspaper.

'Come inside my friends, I will make you some tea and then we can talk.'

The two visitors trooped into the little office crammed full of papers, books, and on a table at the centre of the room sat a battered old typewriter, a machine Solomon hoped that one day he might possess. Walter gestured for them to sit down whilst he went out to make some tea, returning several minutes later he found a chair and joined his two guests to listen as Alfred explained what it was he wanted them to do.

'There is a lot of unrest around the country, not just here on the Witwatersrand, the dock workers in Durban are considering strike action and so are those workers in the factories, but this time the strikes will be better organised and better led. Two years ago, I attended a meeting of the Industrial Workers of Africa behind the general store on McLaren Street. Reuben Cetiwe outlined a plan of action to those present, which, by the way, included some white radicals. He said they would organise the union of Industrial Workers to fight for rights and benefits for the natives, try to withstand the worst of the capitalist exploitation. Since then, together with the International Socialist League they have organised an Indian workers' industrial union in the port of Durban, founded the clothing workers' union here in Johannesburg and the horse drivers' union in Kimberley. As you know, almost all of the strikes over the past few years eventually collapsed, but they showed what we could achieve. This year we will campaign against the Pass Laws, and you Solomon will report as much as you can to Walter. And you Walter, you must give prominence to industrial action in the paper with your editorials.'

Walter pursed his lips in thought, the importance of the newspaper's task plain to see and he turned to Solomon. 'We will follow events closely, get the stories and give support to the cause. You Solomon, will be at the forefront, you must meet with the workers and the union officials, find out the root causes of our people's grievances.'

Solomon nodded his head slowly, becoming aware of the burden suddenly placed upon his shoulders and it made him feel proud.

Chapter 8

Mabutu leaned on his brush and watched the two men leave the office before continuing to sweep the pavement. It was the end of the working day for the white men but he still had a further two hours of toil before both he and Marsha could leave for their single room in the township. He heard the men bid each other goodnight and watched as they parted company, one of them, Brian Alders, was Norman's stockbroker assistant, the other the secretary and Mabutu wondered where his boss was.

Norman was sat at his desk going through forthcoming deals and planning the following day's work and was feeling pleased with himself. Business was picking up, he had made enough sales to show a decent profit, Brian was building up the trade in mining stocks and he had made quite a few useful friends in the city. In the time he had been here, he had become something of an expert on the Johannesburg property scene and it was beginning to pay off. One benefit of this networking was his nomination for membership of the Rand Club, the foremost business club in the city.

He reached for the knot in his tie, undid it walked across the room to the filing cabinet, lifted out a glass and a bottle of whiskey and returned to his desk. He took the occasional drink at work and today he felt he was entitled to a small reward for all the work he had put in. Letting the first flush of the fiery liquid slide down his throat he considered just how much money he was making for Archibald Williamson and felt a twinge of regret that he was not making it for himself. He looked out of the window to see Mabutu slowly pushing his brush back and forth and feeling benevolent; he went to the office door and called to him.

'Hey Mabutu, you can finish early today. Go and see if Marsha has prepared dinner and If she has then you can both leave early.'

Mabutu gave a toothy grin and Norman decided to have a second drink before locking the office door and making his way to an adjoining door leading to their living quarters. He made his way up the stairs, the noise of his shoes on the wooded staircase attracting the attention of Peggy and Henry who came rushing out of the lounge to meet him. Each child grabbed hold of one of his legs, their little arms clasped tight and both feet standing on one of his. Norman had to walk the full length of the hall and back with them clinging on, their laughter ringing throughout the house. In the dining room, Lucy and Marsha were laying the table for the evening meal and Lucy smiled as she heard them coming.

'I hear you are letting Marsha and Mabutu off early today.'

'Yes, it's not much but I am feeling pleased with myself and thought it was a good thing to do.'

'Well we had better eat, and soon because we are holding them up.'

119

After dinner, Norman picked up *The Star* newspaper, walked over to the big armchair by the window and sat down to read by the light of the setting sun. The leader was all about the price of gold on world markets, the increase beginning to show hansom profits for the mining companies and these companies were investing in land and machinery, drawing more people into the area. Just what Norman wanted; the demand for property would pick up, Brian would sell more stock, and he would earn more bonuses. He read on, there was unrest in one of the mines, the management had called out the police to deal with it and it seemed they had stopped any real trouble. He turned to the sports page, noticing that on Saturday, there was a race meeting out at Turffontein and he decided that he could do with some relaxation.

'Lucy! How do you fancy a day at the races on Saturday? A day out will be fun for the children.'

'Oh yes I have not been to the races for years. Did you hear that, children, we are going to watch the horses on Saturday?

The children squealed with delight, though they had no idea what they were going to see. If their mother was pleased, then so were they. They saw horses all day long, pulling waggons and trams but they knew nothing of racing.

When Saturday finally arrived, Lucy helped the children wash and dress in their best clothes ready for the day out.

'There children, you do look nice, stand over there and let me look at you.'

The two children obeyed, standing by the window so their mother could inspect them. Lucy thought Peggy looked pretty in her new white dress, a bright red ribbon in her auburn hair; her brother wore a pair of grey shorts and a crisp white shirt, his hair brushed flat across his head. She was so proud of them and sighed to herself just as Norman came into the room and broke the spell.

'Come on you lot, we don't want to be late and miss the first race. D'you know, I think it might be my lucky day today, Lucy – how do you feel?'

Lucy laughed. Lucky day! When had Norman ever had a lucky day? He worked hard but he never had any real luck. Other people in Johannesburg get the lucky days she thought, swanning about and hardly lifting a finger, yet possessing all the things they could ever want. She sighed again and took hold of the children's hands to help them down the stairs to the waiting car.

'We're ready Norman; I hope you have everything, the tartan blanket for us to sit on and the picnic hamper. We don't want to go hungry do we?'

Smartly dressed in his dark business suit, his Homburg squarely on his head Norman waited patiently for his family to climb into the car on a perfect day for horseracing and he felt confident that he would win something.

'Shit,' he murmured as he swung the starting handle for a third time. 'This bloody car has been playing me up too often and I'm getting a bit fed up with it.' He swung the starting handle again, more vigorously cranking the engine over and over breaking out into a sweat. Pausing for breath, he looked up to see a black man peering at him from the other side of the street. 'What are you looking at?' he said in temper. 'Bugger off!'

121

Solomon ignored the irate white man's abuse; he was learning how arrogant some of them could be. He had seen the woman and two children emerge from the house dressed in fine clothes and thought for a moment of his own family, living in the one-roomed shed and dressed in patched clothing. The white race seemed to live such a good life on the back of the black man's labour, the position Alfred and his friends were taking became clearer and he was glad that he could play his part.

Norman soon forgot the native watching him and swore under his breath again as he swung the starting handle and this time, to his relief, the engine burst into life. The exertion had made him sweat, he had a small streak of dirt on his shirt and as he climbed into the driving seat, his face contorted from his ordeal he looked in the rear view mirror. Lucy looked back, gave him an encouraging smile and thought to herself, not a good start to his 'lucky day'.

The drive to the Turffontein racecourse was a little tense to begin with as Norman regained some composure and Lucy kept the children quiet. She held their attention by asking them to name trees and dogs, anything that they could see out of the window and both responded with enthusiasm. They passed horse drawn vehicles with bells and ribbons heading towards the racecourse and once Norman had relaxed, he began to amuse the children by blowing the car's horn. Finally, they arrived at the racecourse, the car came to a stop on some rough ground, Norman jumped out, opening the rear door for Lucy and the children and then reached for the picnic basket before walking towards the family enclosure.

Lucy took charge, finding a space for them and spreading the blanket on the ground whilst Norman lit a cigarette and looked across at the crowds gathering near the start. He would have been a lot happier in the thick of the action with some of his drinking friends but today he had promised to be with his family. Lucy placed the picnic basket at the centre of the blanket and kept a watchful eye on the children, telling them to listen to the sound of the army band playing in the distance.

Norman gripped his cigarette between his teeth, felt inside his jacket pocket for the racing page from the previous day's newspaper, took it out and studied the list of runners and riders and Lucy looked up at him wondering if, at the end of the day, they would have any money left.

'So what horses shall we back? I fancy The Dandy for the first race. What do you think?'

'Norman, I haven't the faintest idea. If you really want me to pick a horse then it will need to have a nice name. Let me have a look.'

He folded the newspaper and passed it to her, letting her study the runners and riders for a minute or two.

'Bay Prince, put five shillings on Bay Prince for me will you?'

Norman smiled, there was just about as much chance of her winning as the man in the moon, he thought. Five shillings was a bit more than he really wanted to let her spend, but today, he decided, they were going to have a little fun.

'Half-an-hour until the first race, I think. I will put the bets on now. You look after the children,' he said leaving them to walk the short distance towards the bookmaker's stands.

123

On the way, he passed a crowd of people, talking, shouting and as he made his way towards the row of Tic-tac men waving their arms about he passed the members enclosure. Gawping with envy at the wealth on parade, the men resplendent in top hats and tails, the ladies a cornucopia of colourful dresses and bonnets he wondered if he might one day be able to join them. Then he reached the parade ring, stood for a few moments looking at the horses with a practised eye, and scanned the area for a familiar face. He had briefly met several racehorse owners at the Rand club and felt a little social climbing would not hurt. He thought he recognised Sir Abe Bailey and Alex Campbell, probably the two most successful racehorse owners in South Africa but there was no one he was even on nodding terms with.

Reaching the bookmaker's stalls, he pulled the racing page from his pocket for one final check and, after a cursory glance, placed the bets. He was in the thick of the action, excited, felt a buzz and a visit to the beer tent was a tempting proposition, deciding instead to return to his family. Perhaps he would find time for a drink later.

The crowd in the family enclosure was full of anticipation when he returned; the adults had spotted the horses lining up for the start of the first race and were lifting up the children for a better view. He strained his eyes and saw the starter in his white coat and bowler hat standing on stepladders and within seconds he was bringing his flag down sharply and they were off.

Norman lifted Peggy onto his shoulders for a better view and Lucy picked up Henry – smaller and lighter than his sister, but still too heavy for her to hold for long. The galloping horse soon neared the family enclosure and as they rounded the bend the thunder of their hooves causing the crowd to let out a great roar. Lucy struggled to hold onto Henry and had to lower him to the ground but the boy felt he was missing out and started to whine so she gripped him by the arm and pulled him through the crowd towards the rail for a better view.

The horses were almost level, their hooves thundering loudly as they pounded the ground, alarming Henry. He gripped his mother's hand in terror, and then, in a flash, they were gone. Relieved, he thrust his arm straight out in front of him, pointing his finger and shouting, 'Horsey, ma.' Lucy's heart missed a beat; Alistair had made exactly the same gesture when they had first arrived in Cape Town. For an instant, tears welled up in her eyes at the memory of her two lost children; she could not help herself and gathered Henry up into her arms. She squeezed him close and he squirmed and laughed, expecting her to tickle him, his obvious delight breaking the spell.

'What happened to you two?' enquired Norman. 'Did you see the horses, Henry?'

Henry grinned and pointed again in the direction of the finishing line and this time Lucy missed the gesture. Her attention had moved to Peggy and she gave her daughter a hug, asking what she had seen. Peggy recounted everything and that the winning jockey was wearing a yellow top.

'Yellow!' exclaimed Lucy. 'Why, wasn't the jockey on Bay Prince wearing yellow Norman?'

'I do believe he was, but Peggy couldn't have seen it,' retorted Norman.

'Do go and see,' said Lucy, her momentary lapse forgotten in the excitement. 'I'll get the picnic ready. Go on! And put something on Freewheeler in the next one.'

Norman left his family, set off for the bookmakers and passing through the crowd gathering near the winner's enclosure he managed to catch a glimpse of the horses. To his amazement the winning colours were indeed yellow and Bay Prince was the winner at the hefty price of 12/1, but his horse, The Dandy, had not come anywhere. Collecting Lucy's winnings, he wagered ten shillings of it on her selection for the next race, Freewheeler, and a further ten on his choice, Native Commander before passing back through the throng of race goers to return to Lucy and the children.

'Well? Did I win Norman, did I?'

'Yes you lucky thing. You did, and at a good price too.'

'How much?' she asked with glee.

He showed her the money and she laughed with a schoolgirl's delight as he counted it into her outstretched palm.

'Did you put a bet on Freewheeler like I asked?'

'Of course.'

'Give me the paper again I need to know the jockey's colours.

Norman handed over the folded paper. 'I put ten shillings on it for you and ten shillings on Native Commander for me. We'll see who wins this time.'

Lucy hardly heard his last words, too engrossed in the newspaper, searching for her Jockey's colours.

They were a little more prepared for the second race, wrapping up the blanket and moving to a better position before the majority of the crowd blocked their view. There were fourteen horses, a novice race for two-year-olds, and even though they had a good vantage point they still had to crane their necks. From such a distance the horses were just a mass of browns and blacks with one grey horse standing out,

'Yours is the grey Lucy.'

'I know,' she said, handing him back his paper.

A roar drifted across the course as the distant crowd announced the start of the race and around them people jostled for a better view of the horses. They appeared a mass of charging bodies with the jockey's colours the only distinguishing marks, apart from one grey horse.

'My luck is in this time,' Norman shouted above the roar of the cheering crowd, perceiving his horse to be amongst the leaders.

As the stampede rounded the bend and headed towards them, Lucy lost sight of the grey and then she saw it again, second to last and felt a twinge of disappointment. Then, as the horses drew level, Freewheeler reappeared; passing first one and then a second horse and she could not help herself. At the top of her voice, she cheered, shouted its name until the horses and riders disappeared in a cloud of dust. She guessed that Freewheeler was maybe fifth or sixth and going well but they were too far away for her to be sure.

Norman had drifted a few yards away to watch and returned looking none too pleased, almost positive that his horse was not in the frame and it was with a long face he set off towards the bookmakers. Passing the winner's enclosure, he suddenly stopped and stared in disbelief. A grey horse was leading, the grey and two black horses and he almost stopped breathing, Lucy had done it again. Shaking his head in disbelief, he walked towards the bookmakers stalls and was astonished to see that this time the odds were 20/1.

Norman collected Lucy's winnings and placed bets on the next race, Kingmaker for Lucy, Sweet Charity for himself, and then, as he pocketed the money he felt a hand on his shoulder. Alarmed he spun round, surprised to find Arthur James looking at him, a wistful smile spread across his face.

'Steady on Norman, mate! I'm not out to rob you, though you do seem to be cleaning up today. I saw you collecting your winnings after the first race and now you've done it again. You must be in luck my old friend.'

'It might look like that to you Arthur, but I haven't won a damn thing. This is all Lucy's; she's won twice in a row and at pretty good odds.'

'I don't suppose she's such a good judge of horse flesh is she?' asked Arthur.

'No, she really hasn't a clue. She bets on nice names or if they look pretty.'

'I thought so. You know the wealthy mine owners sail to England for the winter to look at two and three-year-olds to race over here. They might buy ten or 20 horses and ship 'em back as unknown quantities. They need a few races to acquire their handicaps, so in the meantime, if you know what you are doing, you can make a profit. In Lucy's case though, it seems it's the horse's looks that are working for her.'

Norman put on a false smile, piqued that his wife knew more of horse racing than he did. 'Yes, anyway, what are you doing here? I thought you were out of the country.'

'Out of the country? What makes you think that? You saw me playing cards at the Silver Star not so long back.'

Norman's eyes narrowed as he recalled the night. He had not wanted to become involved with Arthur, had slinked off believing Arthur had not seen him but now it looked as if he had.

'Yes I did see you but you were engrossed in a card game. I know you like to have all your wits about you when you're taking some poor bastard's money off him so I kept out of the way.'

Arthur looked straight at Norman, his face serious and then he grinned and they both burst out laughing.

'Listen Norman, I don't know why you tried to avoid me but I have a proposition for you. We can't talk here, where can we meet – how about the Silver Star one night?'

'I might have a better idea. We can meet in the Silver Star but I have recently joined the Rand Club, we can go there and you can be my guest, as long as Williamson doesn't find out. If he does, I will tell him I was trying to discover what you got up to in Cape Town. And what did you get up to, Arthur?'

'I can't tell you that here, but I like the idea of the Rand Club, old boy. Fits in wonderfully with my proposition, shall we say Tuesday next?'

Norman thought for a few seconds. 'Yes, I can arrange that.'

Arthur nodded, 'good, how is the business working out in Jo-burg, you must be well entrenched by now,' queried Arthur.

'Not bad, not bad, we had a tough time of it not so long back but things have picked up recently. What about you Arthur, what are you doing?

'Ah...perhaps we should leave that for our next meeting,' said Arthur tipping his trilby and winking at Norman. 'Until next Tuesday,' he said before disappearing into the crowd towards a tough looking man wearing a bush hat.

Grinning, Norman pulled out a handful of coins and banknotes and watched Lucy's eyes when he returned to his family

'How much did I win?'

Norman counted her winnings into her hand and could not help but feel pleased for her.

'Oh Norman, how wonderful, I can buy a new dress for Peggy and a new suit for Henry. I think there may even be a little left for me.'

'This plus the winnings you already have is quite a sum. What about the next race, I put five shillings on Kingmaker as you asked, I thought about putting ten shillings on it.

'No, five shillings is quite enough; I'm risking no more than that. I would be horrified if I lost it all now,' she replied.

'But what about the South African Derby, that's the big one. We must have a decent bet on that race Lucy.'

'Well perhaps I will, ten shillings maybe though we should have our picnic first, the children are hungry. I will unpack the food and I can pick another horse – the winner, whilst we have lunch,' she said with a laugh.

The meeting was finally working its way towards its climax, the South African Derby, and Norman had decided to bet on a British horse this time, Moscato, a fancied five year old. Lucy said she liked the look of Grenade because she liked the jockey's colours and for once took she took note of the horses form. It was joint favourite, owned by one of the foremost breeders in South Africa and she had already decided to play safe,

130

satisfied with a small win to complete her day, she was far shrewder than Norman would ever realise.

After their picnic, Lucy wiped the children's mouths with her handkerchief; Norman stood up and watched as a large group of horses and riders slowly made its way past. The South African Derby was a longer race than the previous ones and the start for this longer course was near to his position. He could see the horses clearly, their colourful jockeys sitting high in their saddles and then the starter walked out onto the course to the cheers of the watching crowd. Waving his arms he began marshalling the runners for the race, a race of over one and a half miles and with the starting line not far away the crowd on the embankment would have a good view.

After milling around for a time, the runners eventually managed to form an uneven line, the white coated starter lowered his flag, the crowd roared and the horses charged forward. Eyes wild with exertion, nostrils flaring they headed for the bend nearest to Norman and Lucy and all around them the crowd's cheering reverberated louder and louder. Even the children joined in, shouting at the top of their voices, though Lucy was unusually quiet. She was concentrating on the red and green cap of Grenade as the horses approached, sure hers' was amongst the leaders. As they turned into the grandstand straight for the first time, she clenched her fists tightly with excitement and a roar of encouragement drifted across the course. By now, the jockey's colours were barely discernible from the spectators in the family enclosure and she had to strain their eyes to see them.

The pack was beginning to string out once they hit the bend and then they galloped and Lucy past for a second time and could not restrain herself. As the leaders passed for the last time, she shouted encouragement, stretching on tiptoe to see the horses and was sure she could see the red and green of Grenade leading. She reached down and picked Peggy up, telling her that they were winning and the little girl clapped her hands in delight and together they shouted 'Grenade Grenade'.

Very soon, after the race Norman walked over to the winner's enclosure and discovered his wife was still on a winning streak. How had she managed three winners in a row he wondered and then he allowed himself a smile. Moscato had come a respectable second and with his each-way bet, he would collect at least some winnings for himself.

A few days after the race meeting, Norman was getting ready to leave for the Silver Star, slipping on his suit jacket and briefly admiring himself in the hallway mirror. As he tightened the knot in his tie he wondered about his short conversation with Arthur, what was the proposal he had mentioned all about? With that thought still in his head he looked in on Lucy to tell her he was going and left for the Silver Star.

He found Arthur standing against the bar, one foot on the brass rest and a glass of whisky in his hand. He looked relaxed and Norman could see he was itching to join in a card game. Arthur was an expert in these situations, noting the players who drank too much, became careless and creating chances for him to take their money off them. Tonight though, Arthur was simply an onlooker and as Norman approached, he tore his eyes away from the game he was observing.

'Good evening Norman, what will you have?'

'A whisky and water will be just fine'.

'How is your family? Lucy made a pot of money at the races last week I hear.'

'Yes, beginner's luck you could say. She took the children shopping today to spend most of it on new outfits. All I got was a new tie for work.'

Arthur chuckled, 'Well that's the ladies for you. If they can get their hands on your money then do not expect to see it again. Not had a lot to do with women lately, but you have just reminded me of what I am missing. I must say Williamsons have done the right thing opening an office here in Joburg. Don't know why they left it so long. They were operating at the Cape when the Langlaagte farm was still just that, a farm and look at it now. If they had been here from the beginning, they could have made millions from dealing in land; I would have moved the whole operation here long ago. Enough of Williamsons, I expect you are wondering why I wanted to see you tonight? Well, I've been working on a little idea to make us all rich.'

'All?' asked Norman, 'who is all?'

'Me you and Hans, no one else, and I don't intend to involve anyone else,' he lied. 'The less people that know about what's really going on the better and I want you to promise now that you won't divulge anything I tell you tonight, to anyone, not even your wife.'

A little too cockily Norman said, 'And if I do, then what?'

'Hans is in on this, and you have seen what he's like if he's crossed.'

Norman forced a smile. 'Well it had better be good then. I don't want to be keeping a secret about nonsense.'

Arthur's voice was not much more than a whisper. 'Nonsense! Is a half a million pound sterling nonsense

133

Norman?' Norman almost choked on his drink. Five hundred thousand pounds was a lot of money and the thought left him speechless.

'We can't talk here,' said Arthur, 'there are too many ears listening. Are you going to introduce me to the famous Rand Club?'

Norman nodded dumbly, finished off his drink and together they left the Silver Star for the more elegant setting of the Rand Club and as they walked, Arthur began to talk in a more earnest tone.

'You know, Johannesburg revolves around gold. People have made fortunes here almost overnight.' He paused for a few seconds and in a more measured tone, 'you're probably curious as to what happened at Williamsons, what caused me to depart in such a hurry.'

'More than curious,' said Norman.

'Well, the two questions are connected. Williamsons had one or two deals involving farmland, purchased by the mining companies for their expansion. The British have always been here, but now American and Australian companies, particularly Americans, are looking for ways onto the Rand. They have a lot of experience, technology and believe they can extract gold better than local companies can. Even I can see the advantage of better equipment and technical knowledge, but today the problem is one of securing the land to work'.

'How does all this affect you Arthur?' asked Norman. 'I can't quite see your point.'

'Ah, be patient my young friend, this little enterprise would not be worth doing if it were transparent. We need a few mirrors and some smoke to cloud things up a little if we are to make some money. Let me explain a bit more: I was put in charge of a land sale to an American company, and as the ownership papers were being prepared and registered, a new Company appeared. This new company acquired ownership of some of the land, about half a square mile in size, plenty for a small mining operation.' He looked at Norman with a twinkle in his eye. 'You haven't figured it out yet, have you?'

'Afraid not,' said Norman, a puzzled look on his face. 'Should I have?'

'As I said, it wouldn't do for anyone to figure it out too easily'.

The penny had not still dropped and Norman's face remained blank until they reached the Rand Club, an imposing four-storey building with a grand entrance of oak and glass. An attendant dressed in a top hat and tails saw them approach and opened the door.

'Good evening gentlemen. Is there anything with which I can help you? Do you require a reservation for the dining room?'

'No thank you Harold. We are just here for a quiet drink tonight,' said Norman.

They passed through the double doors into the entrance foyer where a large painting of Cecil Rhodes hung and to their left was the imposing sweep of the grand staircase. A black servant boy took their hats and coats and left them to make their way along the corridor to the main bar. Paintings of the Great and the Good of Johannesburg adorned both walls, and Arthur showed some excitement when he recognised one of them.

'See him there, Norman.'

'Yes,' replied Norman, slightly puzzled.

'Barney Barnato, one of my heroes.'

'I have heard of him, one of the richest men on the Rand wasn't he.'

'Oh yes – he was certainly a rich man, but he came from humble beginnings, from the east end of London, not far from my old stomping grounds. He was just a music hall turn and pavement entertainer before he came here. He started off working in the diamond trade in Kimberley for his uncle – or maybe his cousin, I'm not sure.'

They reached the entrance to the main bar, a room furnished with large leather armchairs and a polished bar top stretching half way round the room. It was a quiet evening; most seats were unoccupied and that suited Arthur, he did not wanting anyone to overhear their conversation.

'Quite a man Barney. I remember now, he worked for his cousin David Harris who I met in the early days in Kimberley. He told me how Barney got started; said he was alone in the office one afternoon, when a digger came in with a diamond for sale. The digger believed that Barney was the proprietor of the establishment and let the diamond go for a knock-down price to Barney who managed to turn a profit of almost £100 for just a few minutes' work and, as they say, the rest is history.'

'How on earth can we be like Barney Barnato? We don't have any capital and the mining industry is not as it was in his day. Big corporations now, industrial mining, the days of the small prospector have gone.'

'Hang on Norman! I didn't finish telling you about selling the farmland to the American Company. I mentioned that a new company acquired some land at the same time as the Americans. Well, that new company is called The Transgold Mining and Exploration Company and it belongs to me. I happen to be the sole director of the Company.'

Norman stared a little bewildered at Arthur, still not grasping the significance of what he was hearing.

'The land is on the reef,' continued Arthur, 'and there will certainly be some gold, how much and how deep we don't really know, or care for that matter.'

'What! You need to know how rich the reef is if you're going to mine for gold. If it's not very rich then you'll be wasting money,' said Norman.

'Who says we're actually going to mine gold? Difficult and expensive operation, old chaps. No, what we do is sell shares in the Company.' He lowered his voice and glanced around before continuing. 'If we can get it right we can sell maybe half a million pounds worth of shares before we have to close down the operation due to, shall we say, unsafe ground, flooding, anything we can think of to fool the investors.'

'Sounds illegal to me,' said Norman. 'And where will you get your investors from?'

'That's where you come in my friend. You are good at persuading people to part with their money. I've seen you operate, and I must say you have always impressed me by the way you can convince people that what you are selling is just what they want. I would like you to front the operation, Hans will be our surveyor and produce a positive survey to make it look as if there really is a rich deposit of gold. I still have a lot of detail to work out but as soon as you come in with us, Norman, I can start the ball rolling.'

Arthur put his hand into his jacket pocket and drew out a sheet of paper, spreading it on the table in front of them. It was a share certificate for 'The Transgold Mining and Exploration Company' and staring up at Norman was the legend 'Capital of £500,000 in 500,000

137

shares of £1 each'. It had a share sequence number, registered office, and stockbroker's address in London, a very impressive piece of paper. Norman was beginning to understand.

'It seems to me a wee bit more difficult than you might think. For instance, where will you get the investors from and how will you convince them that it's a genuine gold mining company?'

'Advertising Norman, I will take out adverts in American magazines – there are many weekly and monthly publications in America and it is a wealthy country. I do believe that they will leave the gold standard quite soon and then the price will begin to rise. People are greedy, and if they think that they are investing their money on a sure fire winner, then they will invest.' Arthur fell silent for a minute, draining his glass and allowing Norman a few moments to digest his proposition.

Continuing, he said, 'you have the use of a car and you're a good front man, a natural salesman. If we can get investors to show an interest and visit the workings and you can convince them that everything is genuine, then I feel sure we can sell shares. We will have a surveyor's report from Hans showing how much gold there is in the ground. Your job is simply to convince investors that it will require capital to continue the mining operations, and that they will get a fantastic return on their investment'.

Norman sat for a moment simply staring at Arthur, saying nothing. He had come to South Africa to make his fortune, and although he was making a decent living, it was hardly a fortune; could this be his big chance?

'I just can't give up my job Arthur, although it sounds very tempting. The house is the Company's, and I have a family to support. If I haven't a job and there's no money coming in, then where will I be?'

Arthur looked him in the eye. 'Norman, my son! Can't you see? We don't want you to give up your job. We want you to keep use of the car and even sell shares through the office. Your man, what is his name, he could sell some of the shares to your existing clients couldn't he?'

'Brian is a capable young man, but if he got wind of it, I don't know what he would do. He might tell Williamson, and then I am dead. You know very well that Archibald Williamson can be a vindictive man when he wants to be. What puzzles me though is that if you swindled his firm, why he didn't come after you?'

'Quite simple old chap. When I sold the land to Denver Mining and Investments, they paid handsomely for it. What they did not know was that they also paid for the land that went to The Transgold Mining and Exploration Company. All the money went through Williamson's books so they did not lose a penny. In fact, they made a little more than they would have – I simple ascribed the title to my own Company and the Williamsons had to keep quiet unless prospective clients got wind of their incompetence,' said Arthur with satisfaction.

'Well I'll be blowed, old man Williamson knows everything and is more or less powerless to do anything about it?'

'Exactly.'

The two of them lifted their glasses in mock salute, Arthur pulled out a tin of cigars, offered one to Norman and lit them. Inhaling a little of the smoke Norman summoned the waiter for their next round of drinks and sitting back he remembered the last time Arthur had played with matches.

Not long after their evening in the Rand Club, Norman entered the Silver Star, ordered his usual whisky from Alessandro and looked round for Arthur with who had said he needed to discuss his proposition a little more. Norman could see no sign of Arthur in the sparsely populated bar and so, to pass some time, he sidled up to one of the tables to watch a game of cards and wait.

'Norman, how are you?' said Arthur, taking Norman by surprise.

'Fine,' said Norman swivelling round in his seat 'why don't you join me.'

Arthur had Hans with him, both men sat down at the table, and Arthur signalled to Alessandro to bring some whiskey.

'How are you feeling about my idea Norman?'

'I have thought of nothing else since I last saw you. Not too sure about some of it though.'

'Well I thought it would be a good idea to bring Hans along tonight so that we can really get down to business, try to sort out any problems. I'm not too happy talking in here, I'll have a word with Alessandro and see if he'll open up one of the back rooms for us.'

A bottle of whisky and two more glasses appeared and after a few words between Arthur and Alessandro, the three of them moved into a small room at the rear of the bar. Arthur poured the drinks and leaned forward.

'Hans, the survey will need to be professional enough to hold water. If a potential investor challenges it, then we could have a problem. We do not want anyone questioning too much too soon, it's important we appear

140

to be a company with adequate assets and a realistic plan to cover the share price. Investors are a greedy lot, and if we can offer a big enough carrot I don't believe they will look too closely, but we need to cover our arses just in case.'

Hans grunted, 'dat's okay by me. I can get an assay report on the workings, no trouble. It will look like the richest mine on the Witwatersrand when I have finished.'

'I don't think we need to go that far Hans. If it looks too good someone might smell a rat. And you Norman, I've explained how we try to get investors to take an interest, so it'll be up to you to make sure they take up the shares. I have not decided on the price just yet but I'm hoping you can help me on that once we see what interest we can stir up!'

'Good idea, I like that! It leaves our options open.'

'I have already started advertising in America.'

Norman looked at Arthur, his eyebrows rising in surprise. 'So soon?'

'I'm serious about this. The first advert is just a fishing expedition to see what interest we can generate then we can tailor the next ones for a good catch.'

Arthur went on to detail the percentages each of them could expect once the money started to roll in. He argued that it was his idea and his capital that was funding the swindle and so he would take the lion's share. Norman briefly wondered how Arthur could have got hold of that kind of money; it must be thousands of pounds, something did not seem quite right. Arthur could see what he was thinking and suggested that if he was not happy with the arrangements then he need not become involved and at that moment, when it appeared that the chance might pass him by, any misgivings he had slipped from his mind.

Hans remained silent for most of the meeting but now he spoke up: 'I think it would be a good idea to get hold of some proven shale or even some gold dust to seed the ground in case anyone wants a sample for their own analysis. Will your funds stretch to dat Arthur?'

'Good idea Hans. I'm hoping we sell most of the shares to Americans and I have wondered whether the big investors might send someone over to have a closer look at what we are up to. That would help and might assist Norman in selling shares; a rich sample will convince them I am sure. So, let's drink to our success,' he said filling their glasses.

Chapter 9

The morning after his meeting, Norman woke with a headache, the result of one too many whiskeys and after struggling from his bed, he dressed and made his way down to breakfast. Walking into the dining room, he kissed each of his children. Henry hardly noticed, more interested in his breakfast, but when it was Peggy's turn she could smell her father's breath, it made her nose turn up and she refused his greeting. Lucy forced a smile and pulled Peggy away from her father, her smile beginning to disappear. Norman had been drinking much more lately, his attention was always on something other than his family and she was becoming worried, nothing tangible, but she had a strong feeling that things were not as they should be.

Henry broke the spell, tripping over the coal bucket as he climbed from his chair, falling face down into the hearth and letting out a scream of anguish. Lucy managed to grab him before he could do too much damage, but his shriek still managed to shatter his father's peace. Staring blankly at the domestic scene Norman drank some of his coffee, trying to recover his senses, foremost in his mind the substance of Arthur's proposal. One question stuck out from all the rest: where had the money to finance the land come from? Thousands of pounds surely, and out of character, Arthur always spent every penny he had in watering holes and gambling dens. His head began to thump with the hangover as more questions without answers filtered through his brain.

At the same time as Norman was nursing his hangover, Arthur James, unaffected by the alcohol, was speaking on the telephone in his hotel lobby.

'Don't worry about Norman. We had a meeting last night. I told him and Hans most of the plan and how we should work it, and I'm sure we have him on board. I have promised them each five per cent of the proceeds as you suggested and they seem happy with that. Norman's biggest worry is that he will lose his job before he has made any money, so I just need to reassure him that he would be safe enough as long as he keeps his mouth shut. Hans is happy enough following me, we have known each other long enough and he trusts me to make this thing work. Incidentally, Hans made a good suggestion last night; we should get some gold dust to salt the ground in case anyone wants to carry out their own analysis. What do you think?'

The voice at the other end of the phone, fell silent for a moment and Arthur felt he could hear the man thinking.

'I will make enquiries about gold dust. It may take a day or two but I don't think we have any visitors just yet, have we?' said the voice.

'Not yet, but soon, I think. I got a cable from a stockbroker in New York suggesting he may want to visit us, but nothing is finalised. I haven't replied because I thought you might want to decide how we should handle it,' said Arthur.

'Get 'em over! As soon as possible. The market is rising and shares in South African gold mines are popular. The British have done us a favour in abandoning the gold standard. Letting the pound float against the dollar is working in our favour, it's already about ten per cent up on a month ago. I know the Americans are looking to invest their profits from the war and where better than South African gold? If you believe that Norman can handle it, send your telegram, get the share certificates printed. I'll make money available in the account at the Cape of Good Hope Bank but we need to be careful about releasing any shares on the Johannesburg market in case someone starts asking questions. We may be able to sell in Johannesburg for a short while before we close down, but I don't want the police involved – my name must be kept out of this Arthur. You can make a substantial sum of money out of this venture, and then you will have to leave the country for a while in case things become too hot.'

The man at the other end of the line replaced his receiver and clasped his hands together as if praying before letting out a long sigh. They were playing a dangerous game and he knew it, but if they could get it right, then he would make some real money and no one would know that he was involved. His only worry was Arthur, so long as he could keep him under control everything would be fine and his hold over Arthur was strong, solid evidence in his safe linking Arthur to past crimes his guarantee.

Arthur's advertisements had shown results, an American stockbroker had made contact and insisted upon visiting them. Arthur decided there and then that it would be prudent to get hold of some gold dust and mulling things over, he remembered an acquaintance, Jimmy McBride. He would know how to get hold of the gold, the price might be a little high but so what, the rewards would far exceed the outlay. He leafed through his notebook and picked up the telephone, asking the switchboard to connect him to Germiston 876. After a conversation of no more than a few minutes, Arthur pressed the receiver button several times and asked the switchboard to connect him to the number in Cape Town.

The following day Arthur received cables confirming the visit of the New York stockbroker and that the account at Cape Bank had seen a sum of money deposited. This was the news he had been waiting for. The stockbroker, Lewis N Rosenberg, was arriving by steamer in Durban on November 24 with a surveyor named James Brand. His heart began to beat a little faster, normally cool, he began to fret because if this thing worked, he would be a rich man, a very rich man but the risks were beginning to weigh heavily. He opened a bottle of whisky and took a drink, letting the fluid burn its way down his throat, steadying his nerves. It did the trick; he was back in control and he made a second telephone call to Jimmy McBride, anxious to know when he could get his hands on the gold dust and he was worried that Hans, their so-called geologist, was no expert. Could he really fool the Americans into believing the mine was rich in gold? If it did become a problem then Norman's powers of persuasion and his presentation would have to deflect any awkward questions. What really mattered was the potential of the mine to deliver and a sure way of convincing them was to present them with some of that

146

gold. After a wait of several minutes, the operator connected him.

'Jimmy, how are things?'

'Arthur, good to hear from you, all is arranged. Do you have a pencil and paper...?'

Two hours later, Arthur accompanied Hans to the railway station and handed him a bundle of banknotes telling him to travel to the small town of Petrusburg on the road between Kimberley and Bloemfontein and there to meet a courier at an outlying farm.

'This is important Hans, we will be rich if we can pull this off. The parcel you are bringing back is the key to our success, and when you do return I will explain what we have to do.'

Oblivious to the goings on across town, Norman carried on with his day-to-day routine. The end of hostilities with Germany and the return of the soldiers fighting overseas had seen the real estate business pick up. Today though was uncomplicated; a morning meeting with a client to look at a bungalow in the Bez Valley and an afternoon set aside to catch up with his paperwork. There was never a great deal of paperwork because he didn't keep meticulous records, but he did have to write an in-depth weekly report for head office to keep them informed of bank deposits, withdrawals and expectations of future business.

One of his jobs was to pay himself and his staff. He earned £20 a month, the other two slightly less and driving back from his meeting, he mulled over his salary. Compared to five per cent of £500,000 it did not seem very much and would take him most of the rest of his working life to earn so much and he told himself that the

147

chance he had been waiting for had arrived. He parked the Buick outside the office and walked in to find both of his colleagues at their desks, Brian leafing through a sheaf of papers and Jeremy bashing away on his clumsy typewriter.

'Anything to report.'

'There's been a bit of a drop in mining shares this morning. To me it looks like a good time to buy,' said Brian

'Why not,' said Norman, 'if you have the money to buy some shares. You can see what's happening so why not make a few pounds yourself?'

'Well, I'm not supposed to use my knowledge for myself. If I were found out I could lose my licence.'

Norman looked at him for a moment. 'I suppose you're right.'

Brian smiled back and turned to gaze out of the window.

'Why do you think it's a good time to buy if the price is dropping?'

'Because I know the market, the fundamentals are sound enough and the mine owners are cutting their costs, employing more cheap labour. Mark my words the market in mining shares will pick up.'

'I hope so,' muttered Norman under his breath as he went into his office and straight to the filing cabinet. He filed whisky under whisky and was soon pouring himself a glassful. Sitting at his desk he picked up a pencil, took a scrap of paper from his in-tray and wrote on it the number five, following it with three noughts and then he wrote twenty five thousand pounds sterling beneath it. He liked the look of the numbers. Could he really make that kind of money from Arthur's scheme?

Another sip of whisky and more daydreams. If he could get the money out of the country easily enough, then why not return to Scotland, maybe he could afford a small country estate, retire and occupy his days with hunting and fishing. Now that was a tempting prospect – but first he had to persuade investors to buy the shares.

Hans climbed down from the railway carriage and onto the tiny Bloemfontein platform, sad memories returning as he knew they would. He had come here on his release from the prisoner of war camp to search for his wife and child only to find that they had perished in the concentration camp. It had been hard, all his hopes and dreams had evaporated in an instant and left him to spiral downwards into a life of petty crime and alcoholism. That was until he met Arthur James.

Arthur was in no better shape, drinking, scratching a living from card games and petty swindles. They were two of a kind; both men had touched the bottom rung of society's ladder and were living off their wits but they had teamed up, watched out for each other and a bond had formed. Eventually, Arthur got himself a job as a clerk in one of the mines, found a room to rent and after he was back on his feet, he found Hans some labouring work.

Then, one day, Arthur had announced that he had packed in his job. It came as a shock to Hans to learn that Arthur had decided to seek his fortune elsewhere and he asked Hans to come with him. Hans did not take long to make up his mind, becoming a miner was not his destiny, to roam the country again was a chance not to be missed. He respected Arthur, one of the few people to have shown him kindness when he needed it most so if

Arthur wanted him along, then that was a good enough reason to go.

Hans left the platform and walked onto the street, there was not much in the way of traffic and he wondered how was to make the journey to Petrusburg 80 miles away? His instinct told him to steal a horse and ride out there, but if he fell foul of the law then he would jeopardise everything so instead, he made his way on foot through the town looking for the road to Kimberley. He saw several ox drawn carts rumbling in the right direction but they made slow progress and he could not afford the time. Contemplating his next move he did not notice a motor car pull up at the opposite side of the street until a voice called to him in a thick Afrikaner accent.

'What are you doing soldier? Keep a sharp look-out tonight; British soldiers roaming around out there. It wouldn't do for them to surprise us would it?'

Hans reeled around to face the car. The sun was in his eyes and he was unable to recognise the owner of the voice, but the voice seemed familiar. His mind raced as he attempted to match it with dormant memories and had just about figured it out when the man said, 'What are you doing here Hans? I haven't seen you since the fight at Elandslaagte. Do you remember, a British sniper shot me and you got me out of the line and down to the field hospital.'

'Caas, I should have known you would've come at me from out of the sun.'

'Yes it's me,' said the man, stepping out of the car. 'How are you my friend? That last battle was almost 20 years ago. I have often wondered how you might be, if you had survived. How has life treated you?'

'I manage. It was not particularly easy to begin with, but I manage,' Hans said, sighing, the memories of those times never very far away.

'Where are you going? This is the road to Kimberley, it will take you six weeks' walking to get there.'

'Well, not quite Kimberley. I'm making for Petrusburg. I have to meet a man and collect something for a friend in Johannesburg.'

'Johannesburg, I live there now. I run a small engineering Company supplying and repairing the stamps for crushing the ore. My cousin in Holland makes them and I am his agent out here. It is not as profitable as mining but it gives me a good living. I have 6 whites and 14 blacks working for me and we keep busy with all the expansion going on. I install more stamps each year and that means more spares to sell and more breakdowns to repair,' said Caas laughing.

He looked Hans over, it was obvious to him that he had not prospered, and though he smiled a little, Hans did not seem able to laugh aloud. The battle still loomed large in his own mind and he subconsciously rubbed his thigh where the bullet had entered his leg and remembered how desperate they were trying to escape the advancing British. He had lain helpless in the mud awaiting his fate, expecting the British to shoot him and then he had felt those strong arms lifting him up. Hans had managed to half carry half drag him to the last waggon taking wounded soldiers to Pretoria and had saved him. He owed his life to this man and if he could help, he would.

'Hans, I'm heading for Kimberley and I'll take you to Petrusburg. Your company will be a bonus and I expect

I'll get at least one puncture along the way, so you can help with the repairs. What do you say?'

'Kind of you Caas. I'll take it,' replied Hans, just a little embarrassed.

Throwing his carpetbag on the back seat, he jumped in alongside Caas and together they began to follow the road to Kimberley. It took nearly four hours of bumping along over the dusty and potholed road to reach the settlement and along the way they talked non-stop. Mostly they talked of the old days, a real feat for Hans who found it hard to hold a conversation for so long but shared memories of the war and their time in the Johannesburg Commando seemed to release him from his inner prison. They recounted skirmishes and battles with the British, their orders not to fight but to harass constantly, disrupt lines of supply, steal horses and kill soldiers with as little loss as possible to themselves and it had worked well until Elandslaagte.

They advanced into Natal, a force of 17,000 men formed from several commandos, the plan to invade from various directions and meet at Newcastle to destroy the railway line and prevent the British from supporting the beleaguered garrison at Dundee. Eight hundred men of the Johannesburg commando were part of that force and when they finally became involved in the fighting, they managed to destroyed a British supply train and cut communications and then the men of the commando occupied, what seemed at the time to be strong positions around Elandslaagte.

The following morning the British force attacked with mounted squadrons and batteries of field guns and a short time later reinforcement arrived to tip the balance. Fighting continued all day as the enemy forced the commando into retreat to where Hans and Caas waited and then a thunderstorm broke, making conditions desperate. It was then that a sniper's bullet embedded itself in Caas's left thigh and Hans had found him screaming in pain. Slinging his rifle across his shoulder and with both arms wrapped around Caas's chest, he had managed to get him to the medical orderlies who were helping the wounded onto the waggons.

After leaving him with the orderlies, Hans had made his way through the rain and the mud to re-join his unit when a British cavalry trooper emerged from cover taking him by surprise and slashing at him with his sabre. Hans tried to fire his gun but the cartridge jammed in the breech and all he could manage to do to defend himself was to jab at the oncoming horse and rider with his rifle barrel and attempt to throw the trooper off balance. He stood his ground as the horse charged towards him, losing its footing and slipping on the treacherous mud. It gave Hans a half chance as the trooper lost his concentration and he was able to side step away from the falling horse but he did not manage to get completely out of range and the trooper's razor-sharp sabre caught him a glancing blow across his left ear, slicing off the top with a surgical precision.

By now, the Boers were in disarray, the survivors running and sliding through the mud to regain their horses and some did manage to escape but Hans was not so lucky. A British soldier took him prisoner within minutes of him receiving his wound and marched him away at bayonet point. At least he had survived and he received prompt medical treatment from an army doctor and then they sent him on a troopship bound for a prisoner of war camp in Ceylon. He languished in that camp until the war ended and returning to South Africa he went in search of his wife and his young son, discovering eventually that the British had interned them near Bloemfontein.

With some difficulty he managed to tell Caas his story, how after this loss he felt that he had nothing to live for and had wandered aimlessly from job to job, drowning his sorrows in alcohol. Caas was sympathetic; an Afrikaner like Hans and somehow managed to get Hans to talk about the loss of his wife and son, gaining some release from his torment and it was almost dark when they arrived at the outskirts of Petrusburg. Caas said that he knew the whereabouts of the only lodging house in town.

'It is run by a Boer family. They are good people and I am sure they will find us a bed for the night. They are our people Hans; they will make you feel at home for a while.'

After breakfast, Caas left to drive towards Kimberley leaving Hans to find some form of transport to take him to the Coppach farm. He did not know the exact whereabouts of the farm and asked the innkeeper how he might get there. The Boer innkeeper told him that the farm was about twelve miles away to the north and his best method of getting there would be on horseback, offering his own horse for the trip so long as Hans looked after it and paid for the privilege. Hans relished the idea of riding again; he had not been in the saddle for a long time and soon he was following a bridal path winding its way up onto a low, fertile plateau and just before noon came across the small homestead. Here a man named Harry Endicott was to give him a parcel; he was to hand over the banknotes and Harry was at the window watching him approach.

'You are Hans?'

'I am.'

'Lift your hat.' Hans did so and Harry was convinced that this was his contact, disappearing into the house and returning a short time later with a small parcel.

'Have you the money?'

Hans pulled the bank notes from his pocket and Harry proceeded to count them, grunting with satisfaction before handing the parcel over, a package deceptively heavy for its size.

The telephone on Norman's desk rang, disturbing his concentration and he reached out to pick up the receiver, it was Arthur.

'I want to meet in my hotel room Norman, there have been developments and we need to talk urgently and I don't want to risk anyone overhearing us.'

'When?'

'In an hour, can you make it?'

'I'll be there.'

Puzzled as to why Arthur would want such an urgent meeting, Norman replaced the receiver, checked over his papers and then told Brian he was going out for a time.

He went straight across the city to Arthur's hotel and as Norman entered the room, he saw that Hans was already there. The gangly Boer was standing by the window with his hands clasped behind his back and looking down at the street.

'Here, Norman. What do you think of this?' said Arthur pointing to the table.

Norman picked up the parcel and literally weighed it in his hand. 'Doesn't take a genius to know what's in there, does it? What's going on Arthur, I haven't heard from you for a while, and now this meeting with you, Hans, and a bag of what...gold?'

'Patience Norman, we've been working on our part of the plan and soon it will be your turn. That is the reason I have called you here, to explain. An American stockbroker will be arriving on a steamer quite soon He will be landing in Durban, he is bringing a surveyor with him and he wants to take some samples. I expected that it might happen and I have taken precautions, no one in their right mind would simply take our word for it, though it would make things a lot easier if they did. This parcel contains a quantity of gold dust for us to salt the claim.'

'And what do you want of me?'

'You Norman are to meet the Americans when their ship arrives and bring them here. I have already booked them a room at the Carlton, now, this is what I want you both to do. . .'

Chapter 10

Norman felt compelled to tip his homburg over his forehead and shield his eyes from the midday sun as he strolled along the Durban waterfront watching the *SS Clan Macquarie*. He had observed her for almost half an hour as she slowly slid across the still blue waters of the Indian Ocean and now she was finally entering the dock.

Feeling for the cigarette case in his pocket, he leaned against a wall and lit a cigarette guessing that it would be an hour or more before his visitors disembarked. He decided to wait, sit on the low wall and pick out Lewis Rosenberg and James Brand from amongst the crowd. Customs formalities would be minimal and he did not expect much in the way of delay but if he could find an official, proffer a few pounds, it might be possible to get them ashore more rapidly. It would certainly make his task easier and demonstrate his capabilities, perhaps gain their confidence from the outset. Decision made, he stood up and walked towards the customs shed, catching sight of a man in naval uniform giving orders.

'Excuse me sir, I'm looking for the customs and immigration people, you wouldn't be able to help me would you?'

'Yes, I'm the assistant harbour master. Perhaps if you tell me your problem I might be able to help,' replied the man in a strong Afrikaans accent.

Fighting back his nerves Norman carried on, 'I am here to meet two gentlemen from the United States, to accompany them to Pretoria on business important to the Transvaal.' Norman guessed the man was more likely to help him if he thought he was taking them up into the Transvaal, Afrikaner country. If he could convince him into believing the Americans were here to conduct business with Afrikaners he might be more amenable. He continued in a low voice, 'Their business here is with some farmers, I cannot tell you any more than that, but certain people in Pretoria would appreciate it if I can get them and their baggage ashore as quickly as possible. Perhaps you can help. The Transvaal Chamber of Commerce would be most grateful,' said Norman, briefly touching the seat pocket of his trousers.

The man understood, he would not have been the assistant harbour master for 20 years if he did not know a bribe when he saw one and if he could help the Afrikaner cause then he would.

'Leave it to me,' he said, unconsciously straightening his tie. 'I expect your guests are arriving on the *Clan Macquarie*,' give me £5 and their names and wait at that gate there.'

Norman slipped his hand into his pocket retrieved a five-pound note and then scribbled 'Lewis Rosenberg, James Brand, first class passengers' onto a scrap of paper handing both to the assistant harbour master. The man seemed satisfied and turned to walk along the dock towards a group of men mooring the ship. Norman watched him go and then turned his attention to their transportation to the railway station. Not sure of the exact time of the ship's arrival, he had daydreamed in the warm sun and not planned sufficiently. So, for the next half-hour he searched the dock area for a decent taxicab, eventually finding one and asking the driver to wait by the dock gates.

When he finally returned to his vantage point, the ship was alongside; a gang of men were busy manoeuvring the gangplanks into position and a loudspeaker was booming out information for the passengers. It was difficult to hear the metallic diction from where he was sitting but he was sure he heard the name 'Rosenberg' and ten minutes later an officer of the ship's company walked down the gangplank followed by two white men. Behind them came two African porters carrying their luggage and on seeing Norman the officer made straight for him holding the piece of paper he had given to the assistant harbour master.

'Are you the gentleman waiting for Mr Rosenberg and Mr Brand?'

'I am indeed.' Norman said stepping forward.

The officer saluted and turned away, leaving the two Americans with Norman. One looked to be about 50 years of age, not quite six feet tall, of slight build with a pale complexion and wearing a well-tailored double-breasted dark suit. To Norman's mind, the man looked every inch a stockbroker and with him was a younger man of medium build and not quite as tall. The younger of the two had shock of dark curly hair in need of trimming and together with his healthy complexion he had the appearance of a man used to being outdoors. He must be the surveyor thought Norman.

'Good morning gentlemen! I presume you are Mr Rosenberg and you, sir, must be Mr Brand.'

Rosenberg nodded and reached out to shake Norman's hand, casting an inquisitive eye over him.

'Welcome to South Africa gentlemen. My name is Norman Campbell and I am here to escort you to Johannesburg and look after you during your stay. I hope your journey was a pleasant one.'

'Thank you it was. Two weeks of relaxation is a rare commodity these days,' retorted Rosenberg.

Norman forced a smile and turned to give the waiting porters instructions before the three of them left the dock area for the sleeper train.

At 10 minutes past seven the following morning, the train passed through the suburbs of Johannesburg and the Americans were already standing in the passageway to catch their first glimpse of the famous city of gold.

'Good morning Mister Rosenberg, Mister Brand, I trust you slept well,' said Norman joining them.

'Not bad, the bunk was a little hard but after two weeks at sea a train ride is no problem,' he said turning away to look back out of the window.

The train began to slow noticeably as it made its final approach into the station and Norman pulled down the carriage door window. He called to two porters running alongside the train looking for customers and within a few minutes they were leaving the station behind to emerge into the early morning sunshine and load the company car parked only a few yards away.

'Say Norman, this is a fine American auto you are driving,' said Rosenberg. 'I know only a little about automobiles, but I did meet David Buick once when I sold some stock for him.'

Norman was impressed; Rosenberg had connections, he looked to be just the man they needed to move the stock and as he began to drive away from the railway station, he glanced briefly in his rear view mirror. Rosenberg was certainly the self-assured, successful businessman, a man used to calling the shots. On the other hand, Brand had said very little, appearing in awe of his boss and Norman began to consider that he might have his work cut out with Mister Rosenberg, a thought that occupied his mind on the short drive to the hotel.

'Well gentlemen, this is your hotel. I hope it lives up to your expectations and they make you feel at home,' said Norman bringing the car to a halt outside the entrance to the Carlton Hotel.

'I'm sure it will Mister Campbell. Not quite New York but it will have to do.'

'Er...no, not quite New York I'm sure, but this is a young town,' he said, his confidence returning, realising that his selling point needed to focus on future potential. 'It is a young town with an expanding industry that will create opportunities for those who invest early. The Rand is growing, gold deposits are being discovered every day and I firmly believe that investing early will bring the greatest rewards.'

'Perhaps Mister Campbell and that is why I am here, to see for myself.'

Before they could carry on the conversation the hotel porters arrived to take their luggage and after depositing his guests Norman said, 'I will leave you here to settle in for a few hours and return at noon to take you to meet the principal of the company, Mister Arthur James,'

At twelve 'o' clock Norman returned to the hotel to find Rosenberg and Brand in the lobby looking refreshed after their journey and he greeted them with enthusiasm.

'Hello gentlemen. I hope your accommodation is to your liking?'

'The hotel is fine,' said Rosenberg, 'and the service is as good as back home. I must say, so far, I am pleasantly surprised with Johannesburg. For a mining town it looks remarkably permanent. Back home in the States a mining town grows up out of nothing and then, within only a few years, they turn into ghost towns.'

For once James Brand joined in the conversation. 'I've been involved in the mining industry back home for almost twenty years, and I've seen many ghost towns. The gold runs out, the miners pack up and leave to go look for the next strike and then the hotel owners, the shopkeepers have no more business so they leave too. Here though, buildings are as fine and as permanent as in any of our great cities. I know that the reef here on the Witwatersrand is something special, more than 60 miles long I think, and mined to great depths. Some say they will extract gold here for the rest of the century. My guess is Johannesburg will never be a ghost town.'

'Yes,' said Norman, 'the whole area is growing and changing constantly. There has been a need for proper investment in mining ever since the Union back in 1910. Up until then the mining companies were small affairs but as it became necessary to sink deeper shafts, it also became evident that the companies needed to grow and they needed serious finance to do so. And I might add, the reef is nearer one hundred miles long.'

Norman felt pleased with himself. Until only a few days before he had known very little of the mining industry but he had done his homework, spent time in the Silver Star talking to miners, buying them drinks, playing cards and they had told him all he needed to know. He had gained a basic knowledge of gold mining and the machinery involved and was able to briefly describe how the rock crushing stamps worked, how their numbers had increased and how the output of the mines had grown, painting as rosy a picture as he could and hoping that the Americans were swallowing his story.

'You will be aware, I am sure, of the benefits to South Africa that have accrued since the British government decided to drop the gold standard. The profitability of the mines has increased and it is a good time to invest.'

Lewis Rosenberg pursed his lips and nodded his face blank and unreadable. Norman led them out of the hotel and back into the sunshine, opening the rear passenger door for Lewis Rosenberg. James Brand sat in the front passenger seat and spent a few seconds looking at the dashboard, running his hand over the polished wood as if he were enjoying a fine wine.

'This is a Buick B25 isn't it Norman? Do you find it easy to drive?

'Yes, it's easy enough. Sometimes a bit hard to start though and it can be a pain to change the tyres. The roads out here are not great, I must get at least one puncture a week, but having a car makes my job so much easier.' He bit his tongue – the last few words spilling from his mouth. He could not let them know he was really an estate agent. They had to believe that he was working full time for the mining Company. He must be careful he thought as he began the drive across town to the building where Arthur had rented an office.

163

The day was hot and humid and when Norman opened the passenger door for the Americans he noticed that Rosenberg seemed to be suffering from the heat. The man was perspiring freely and seemed a little unsteady as he stepped out onto the pavement.

'Are you feeling all right, Mr Rosenberg?'

'Phew . . . rather hot. I hope I haven't contracted one of your African diseases already,' he said reaching out to grasp the open door and steady himself. Norman was unsure of what to do until Arthur appeared at the office door to welcome them and saw that Rosenberg was unwell.

'Our guest seems to be suffering a little from the heat. Take him inside and I will go and fetch a pitcher of iced water from the bar next-door. Sit him down and let him cool of a bit Norman.'

The three men went into the small office, James Brand to one side of Rosenberg, Norman to the other and between them they sat him on a chair. Moments later Arthur reappeared with the jug and four glasses and then he pulled down one of the sash windows to let in some air.

'Excuse me sir, but I think you might be wearing too many clothes for today,' he said. 'Perhaps it would help if you removed your jacket and tie.

Rosenberg took Arthur's advice and after a drink of cooling water colour began to return to his cheeks and he began to recover.

'Thank you gentlemen, I admit I felt a little dizzy for a few moments. I guess I am having trouble shaking off the New York winter wearing all these clothes. I should have realised yesterday when we landed.'

Arthur glanced at Norman, they had made a favourable impression on the American, a good start, but now they had to sell him a gold mine. Norman took the initiative and cleared his throat.

'Gentlemen, perhaps we can get down to business. You are aware we are in the process of capitalising a project to extract gold from the mine we are developing out on the Western Rand. We are looking for investors and I can tell you that to date we have received interest from all over the world, particularly from Great Britain and Australia and now yourselves from the United States.'

He went on to describe briefly the process of recovering gold, the projected reserves and the need for investors' money to purchase the equipment. This was to ensure a successful operation and then he lied about the amount of the dividends they might expect, told them that it had become necessary to sink shafts to depths of 4,000 feet or more because of the sloping nature of the reef. Because it lay so deep beneath the surface, they needed modern, sophisticated equipment such as winding rigs, jackhammers and stamping machines. Producing gold had become a cash intensive industry and hence the need for investors he explained.

'To date we have used our own money. A secret survey of the gold content of the reef, carried out last year, suggests to us that the mine will be extremely productive when working at full capacity. I have here a copy of the surveyor's report and assay results for the samples tested.' He passed a copy of the fictitious assay report across the table to Rosenberg.

'So far, we believe that the reef under our land will produce around 12 ounces of gold per ton and we expect to be able to recover almost 100 per cent of the gold from the ore giving us a return on capital in excess of 25 per cent. We expect our start-up costs and the slower rate of recovery in the first year or two, to produce lower profits than in later years and initially we will reinvest any profits. It is during the third year when profits are expected and those profits will be available in full for the shareholders. Here is a prospectus outlining the figures.' He passed a second sheet of paper across to Rosenberg, pausing for a few moments to give him time to study the numbers.

'The projected profits you see are derived from the price of gold several weeks ago, four pounds and five shillings Sterling per fine ounce. Since the suspension of the gold standard, the price has risen steadily, today standing at four pounds eleven shillings. We believe that the price will keep on rising to who knows what. My own view is that it will double within two years. Now sir,' he said, addressing Rosenberg directly, 'you have come here with a view to investing in gold shares and I can say with confidence it will be a wise decision to put money into the Transgold Mining and Exploration Company. You will be able to buy into the operation early with the potential for your shares to reap fabulous rewards in both capital appreciation and dividends well into double figures.'

For all his poker faced exterior Lewis Rosenberg did seem captivated by the proposition and Norman thought that he appeared an almost comic figure sitting there in only his shirtsleeves. If it were not for the fact that he was one of the most influential men in New York financial circles Norman could easily believe he had come to take away the garbage. He glanced at Arthur, noting he had a faint look of admiration on his face and that gave him a confidence boost. He knew he was a good salesman, well aware that the art of effective selling depended largely upon the punter's greed and although he had a comic look about him he knew Rosenberg was a hard-headed businessman and in the cold light of day his enthusiasm might well wane.

Norman's fears were soon realised when Rosenberg began to ask one or two searching questions. He wanted to know production figures, how much the increase in production was expected to be year on year and the net profits his clients might expect long term. If South African gold was to keep on growing at the same pace, he did not want himself or his clients left behind. His clientèle relied upon his knowledge and judgement to give them sound advice on where to invest their money and his sole reason for visiting South Africa was to gain an insight into the industry.

Very soon, Lewis Rosenberg's recovery was complete. He sat with both elbows on the table, his hands clasped together and with a stern look on his face as he listened to Norman and studied intently the figures in front of him.

'I like what I am hearing Norman, the figures are interesting. However, before I can make any judgement I think a visit to the mine is in order. I want Brand here to have a good look round to be able to offer me his technical advice. After all, that's why I've brought him with me.'

Brand nodded his agreement. 'I'm sure you will not mind if I take a sample. It is my job to assess the content and quality of the ore for Mr Rosenberg.'

Arthur spoke directly to Brand, beginning to see him as the crux of their scheme, the one man Rosenberg would listen to, the one man he would not suspect of pulling wool over his eyes. They had to make Brand think that any sample he obtained was not only rich in gold but also genuine and then they would have a good chance of duping Rosenberg.

'I think we would be disappointed if, after travelling so far, you did not wish to have a closer look at the operation. Well, if we have concluded this part of our discussion, please allow me to take you all to lunch, and afterwards perhaps we can talk more about the financial side of things. Tomorrow, mister Brand, we will take you out to the mine and you may take your sample and now lunch. I have booked us a table at the Weil building on Market Street and after that, I have a little surprise for you all. Norman, you can drive us there, gentlemen, if you will follow me please.'

Norman felt annoyed, Arthur had not informed him about any lunch arrangements and this 'surprise' he had in store, what was it? He shrugged his shoulders: it was Arthur's style, and there wasn't much hope of changing him now and what about Hans, where was he? He had expected him to be at the meeting, but there was no sign of him. He really must have words with Arthur about his 'surprise' plans. If he did not handle things properly, he could unwittingly jeopardise the whole enterprise.

Still fuming under the surface, Norman turned the car onto Market Street and towards the Weil building, home to an arcade of expensive shops, offices and a very good restaurant decorated in the style of a Greek temple with marble pillars and fountains of running water to keep the customers cool. Fortuitous for Rosenberg, he would be comfortable and in an agreeable atmosphere and maybe receptive to some of their proposals.

168

Arthur led them into the lobby where the maître d'hôtel greeted them and escorted them to a table close to one of the fountains. Arthur ordered drinks while their American guests scrutinised the menu and Norman felt that he could down a large whisky, the stress of the past 24 hours beginning to take its toll but he knew it was not a good idea. Their little scheme was progressing as well as could be expected but even so, a misplaced comment or some unexpected news from the goldfields could still spoil their chances. There was also the possibility that the Americans might be stringing them along, finding out as much as possible before they entered into negotiations with a third party – a ploy not unheard of. He just did not know, and getting drunk wouldn't help.

The drinks arrived and they ordered the food, sitting back to make small talk until it arrived.

'Say Arthur, what's the proportion of whites to blacks in the mines. I see there is some problem with the different pay rates. Bit like home I guess.'

'Erm... Norman can answer that can't you Norman.'

Norman almost burst with frustration; Arthur was doing it again, putting him on the spot without warning. He had no idea of the numbers; the miners at the Silver Star had made no mention of that.

'The er..., proportion of whites to blacks is somewhere in the region of ten to one, blacks to whites that is. They are cheaper to employ so it makes good sense to have more of them working in the mine.'

'And the Transgold mining and exploration company, how many of each do you employ?'

Norman felt sick; he had no idea, Arthur could see he was struggling and came to his rescue.

169

'We are at the early stages of extraction; we haven't fully crewed up yet but we expect to employ over two hundred blacks within two years. As for white miners, I would say we should peak at about fifty but our long-term plan is to use modern machinery, displace the expensive labour and that is why we are looking for investors. As we have already said it is a new venture with a lot of potential for those lucky enough to invest early.'

Norman felt he could kill Arthur, but as he carried on speaking, he felt his anger abate, admiring such a slick sales pitch and then, before Rosenberg could answer any more questions, lunch arrived.

'Arthur that was a fine meal you treated us to,' said Rosenberg when he finished eating, 'I am not so sure I have had any better in New York. This city seems to be going places and I must say I am mightily impressed by what I've seen so far.'

'Why thank you Lewis,' said Arthur, feeling he could be on first name terms. 'I have a little treat in store for you, I am going to take you to our famous stock market. It is just down the street from here.'

'I like the sound of that. I have heard a lot about the rough and tumble of your stock market. Do they still trade out in the street?'

Arthur laughed, 'You've heard about trading between the chains haven't you? They used to put chains across the street in front of the old exchange building to keep out the traffic so that the brokers could spill onto the street to trade when the building became too small. Oh yes, those must have been exciting days, they would trade until it was too dark to see, and Sundays too. Things have changed, it's more sober now and even so I thought you might like to see just how dynamic things still are here in Joburg.'

After settling the bill, Arthur led them away from the Weil building towards the stock exchange. Rosenberg kept pace with Arthur and asked more questions whilst his assistant fell back to walk alongside Norman.

'You know Norman I've long wanted to visit South Africa and the Witwatersrand. I have been in this industry for quite a time and I have worked on some of the major strikes in the States, mostly Colorado and Utah. Problem is that it takes only a few years to exhaust the seams back home and then there is no option but to close down and start looking for another strike. They have plugged away for 30 years over here and yet the reef just gets bigger. A friend of mine from college days came over here just after the war between the British and the Boers and did very well for himself. From the money he earned, he could afford to retire after only ten years. How about that? I guess I might look for a job here myself.'

'Well I can recommend it. I came out with my family nine years ago and I would say that without doubt we have lived better than we could have done back home. The air is good; if you suffer from of asthma the climate here is very kind and I know that quite a few people have come here just for that.'

'Interesting, I'm looking forward to tomorrow, having a look round your mine. It will be fascinating to see how you reclaim such small quantities of gold from the shale. Back home you can often pick nuggets up off the ground.'

Eventually they entered Hollard Street and Arthur led them up the steps of the stock exchange building and after a brief conversation with a uniformed door attendant, led them inside. Immediately, they became aware of a hubbub, the sounds of traders feverishly buying and selling and Lewis Rosenberg's expression showed he was in his element. Although a stockbroker, he informed them that he was never involved in day-to-day trading and to see the market in action fascinated him.

Arthur began climbing a wide staircase to the spectator's balcony surrounding almost the whole room and facilitating a bird's eye view of the trading floor. It was an impressive building, constructed from polished marble, dark African wood panelling and with tall, arched windows reaching almost to the roof. On the wall facing were two rows of trophy heads mounted on polished wooden shields: gazelles, antelopes, and springboks and below these grisly artefacts, a large blackboard covered the wall where a clerk continually climbed up and down a stepladder to chalk stock prices against the names of the mines.

Arthur leaned over the balustrade and waved to the men below as if he knew them but no one returned the gesture. Norman guessed it was purely for show, to impress Rosenberg, but his attention was elsewhere, enthralled by the activity going on below, mesmerised by the ever-rising prices. Lewis Rosenberg was making mental calculations as he watched fortunes of the whole of the South African gold mining industry change before his eyes. Norman could see his interest; felt encouraged by his enthusiasm, wondered if greed was Rosenberg's driving force. If it was then he felt confident he could convince him to buy into the scam.

Chapter 11

Breakfast the following morning was a studious affair for Norman, hardly touching his scrambled eggs he considered the various scenarios that might unfold during the day. They had left the Stock Exchange and returned to Arthur's makeshift office for a final meeting before he had driven the Americans back to their hotel. As he drank his second cup of tea, he mulled over their conversations. Rosenberg had wanted to know more about the techniques used to extract the gold, the kind of returns the mines were making.

'The industry here seems advanced, your stock market is vibrant and seems well organised,' said Lewis.

'Well we have been engaged in gold mining over here for quite some years now and it has been established beyond doubt that the reserves of the Witwatersrand will last a hundred years or more. The problem is one of extraction, mining here in South Africa is labour intensive and we need a lot of machinery.'

He remembered glancing towards Brand who had said very little so far but it had dawned on him then that the young American surveyor was crucial to the deception. It could well be his advice that tipped Lewis Rosenberg's scales in their favour. Mining was his field and too many wrong answers to his technical questions might expose them. but so far the young American seemed happy with what he had heard and then the conversation had turned to the mine and the visit to the site.

'I expect you are looking forward to seeing the mine tomorrow mister Brand,

'Yes, I am interested in seeing your operation. I hope tomorrow will be as informative as we expect and I look forward to obtaining a sample for Mister Rosenberg's examination.'

'Of course,' Arthur had said, a weasel smile spreading across his face and Norman remembered wondering how they were going to salt the ground that was only a tiny fraction of the mine's total area. How could Brand possibly take a sample from the right place without some conjuring trick?

He put a forkful of food in his mouth, chewed slowly as he went over the plan and then his concentration evaporated as the children began to squabble.

'Quiet children,' said there mother. 'Where are you going today Norman?'

'I . . . have a client to see in Roodepoort today. I think I might be a little late home tonight dear,' the lie coming automatically to his lips.

'What happened to the men you were picking up from Durban the other night, are they who you're going to see?'

Norman hesitated just long enough for Lucy's suspicions to be aroused, long enough for her to pluck up enough courage to confront him.

'What exactly is going on? You are very secretive these days, always working late or out drinking, coming home in the small hours. I have had to put up with it for long enough. So tell me – what is going on, is there a problem I should know about?'

Lucy had changed, no longer a quiet little housewife, a mousewife, the experiences of the past few years had toughened her. Even so, she felt unsure confronting her husband like this but she was convinced something was troubling him. It suddenly occurred to her that perhaps Norman was seeing another woman and picking up her teacup she eyed him closely from across the breakfast table. Norman realised instinctively that he had aroused his wife's suspicions and he tried to conceal his guilt by slowly pouring a third cup of tea to secure a few seconds of thinking time, but his silence only served to raise the tension. He did not want to become involved in a row; he had a very important day ahead of him and domestic trivia was the last thing he needed.

'Lucy, these men are important. They work for an American mining Company about to move several senior managers here from the United States. They asked me some time ago to find suitable properties for them to live in. Roodepoort is a good area I think, not too far from their mine and it was arranged that I would pick them up and show them around the properties so that they can report to their headquarters in . . . Cincinnati,' he lied.

Not true – Lucy knew it, but all right she would leave it be for now. Her best option was to accept her husband's story and try to find out for herself exactly what he was doing. She had made new friends in Johannesburg, particularly a ladies' circle where she mixed with some strong characters. Several spoke with particular passion about the growing suffragist movement, following avidly the reports in the newspapers of their exploits, ladies who had no intention of bowing down to men. Yes, her

175

new friends would give her good advice and help her find the best course of action.

At nine 'o' clock Norman brought the Buick to a halt outside the Americans' hotel and after a few minutes he spotted Arthur and the two Americans coming through the entrance. He waited until they were in their seats before he slipped the car into gear with a shaky hand and the Buick lurched towards the outskirts of the city.

They travelling dusty roads for almost 30 miles until Arthur finally spotted the small ravine that signalled the turn off to the mine and after driving along a twisting dirt track for a further mile the car climbed onto a flat expanse of scrub. Norman expected to see an empty landscape, the place where he would have to convince the Americans that there really was a mine, but to his surprise, instead of empty veldt he saw several ox drawn waggons and a gang of native labourers digging away at the earth. He could see Hans amongst the labourers gesticulating, waving to the men in the waggons. The heavy ox drawn transports began to move towards him carrying loads of what looked like mining equipment. He brought the Buick to a halt alongside Hans and as Arthur ushered the two Americans out of the car the wily Boer turned towards him with a grin on his face and winked.

Hans had arranged all this without him even knowing and the look on Arthur's face showed that he was just as surprised. Norman's main worry had always been that the Americans would be difficult to convince of the existence of a real mine. However, he had to admit that the site looked every bit a mining operation and his admiration for the lonesome Boer grew. On the desolate high veldt surrounded by nothing but boulders and brushwood Hans had established something that had the appearance of a genuine gold mine.

Norman felt a weight lift from his shoulders, it was obvious that the stage was set for him to perform. Nervously he began his sales pitch: 'Lewis, may I introduce you to Hans, our geologist and mining engineer. As you can see, we have started digging the main shaft. The winding gear is expected to be delivered shortly and it will not be long before we are extracting the ore in large quantities.'

He looked at the two Americans with the practised eye of a first class salesman, the expression on his face saying: "you should believe everything I tell you". 'Hans is supervising the digging of the main shaft here because our analysis suggests that we will recover the highest quality ore at a depth of less than 1,000ft. We need to mine the high quality ore as soon as we can to generate cash for wages and more equipment and as the operation expands, we will be in a position to declare dividends for the shareholders.'

Hans pointed his thumb over his shoulder to the four large ox-drawn waggons that were moving slowly towards them. 'These waggons here are carrying the first of the stamps. I expect we will begin crushing the first shale before the month is out.'

Rosenberg and James Brand looked at each other, then at the four white painted waggons carrying the stamps and Norman noted their expressions. They seemed impressed and he began to speak with increasing confidence.

'The money from the first share offering will pay for more stamps like these. We can employ native workers to dig out the ore but the stamps are the potential bottleneck and so the more we have the better. Other waggons will soon head here from Johannesburg with materials to build the sheds for the machinery and the accommodation for the miners. We will be building a compound for the native labourers over there.' He pointed in a general direction and the two American turned to follow his gaze, none the wiser yet becoming convinced a real project was under way.

Norman took a sideways glance at Hans and their eyes met briefly. The fish were taking the bait, Hans had proved good at organising the charade and now he would complete the illusion with a short lecture.

'We have been surveying the area for nearly a year. Our first observations led us to believe that the site would produce some gold but after further analysis we were astounded at the richness of the shale.' He paused for a few moments, took a look at the two Americans, waiting for his words to sink in. 'Arthur, Hans and I have put all out savings into the project and with the help of a bank loan we have brought the project this far. Arthur can explain the finance of the operation better than I can but let me assure you, this mine will produce gold – a lot of gold,' he lied.

'Mister Rosenberg you will notice that the gang of men over there to your right are clearing the scrub. That is for our main road onto the site. The ground is dry and firm now and will easily support traffic, but when the rains come, it is a different story. We have to get a base laid to form an all-weather road. The stamps you see on those waggons are here to enable us initially to crush rock for this purpose and to train the operators for full production.'

Norman felt pleased with himself, surprised that his limited knowledge of mining could sound so convincing and he was encouraged further by Rosenberg's attention. He went on.

'The shaft will eventually sink to half a mile deep, perhaps even deeper, depending on what we discover. Make no mistake Mister Rosenberg the main reef lies just here, under our feet.'

Arthur stood back, amused at Norman's sales pitch. He had known that Norman was good at selling property and now he could see he was just as good at selling an idea. He followed the little group around, listening to Norman's 'expert' account until they neared the Buick where Norman said 'Gentlemen, I imagine you are feeling hungry, well you will be pleased to know that I have brought some food for you. If you would like to follow me to the car we can have lunch.'

He looked across at Arthur who slowly nodded approval and felt things were going well but at the back of his mind, he knew there was still a vital hurdle to clear: the sample. Where would Brand decide to dig for it?

Norman ate his sandwich, downed a bottle of Pale Ale and began to wonder how they could possibly know the place Brand would choose to take his sample from. He did not have a clue where Hans had planted the gold dust and if it all went wrong; at least he had the grim satisfaction of knowing that it was not his fault if the Americans took a dud sample. They would simply walk away, the whole scheme would collapse, his mood became a little sombre, and then some of his earlier confidence began to evaporate until Rosenberg spoke again.

'Say, Norm, the Company name. Where did you get that from?'

'Ah yes, Lewis, the Company name. Where did the name come from?'

'Yeah, Transgold Mining Exploration Company. Where does the exploration come in? You never mentioned anything about exploration.'

'Well,' Norman's mind was racing again. 'Because of its very nature exploration can be successful or unsuccessful depending upon where you're exploring.' How was he going to get out of this one? 'Here on the Rand it is far easier to be successful than in many other parts of the world. It only takes a few years to exhaust goldfields in Australia and the United States, but here in South Africa the reef will last the rest of the century. Once we get this mine running properly and the engineers take over, I will look for Boer farmers who want to sell up. Many Afrikaners are farming land that is literally sitting on a goldmine and if I can get to them first, it is certain that there will be gold under the ground somewhere and we will find it. The reef is enormous, stretches for a hundred miles or more with pockets of shale, in places, quite near the surface. These pockets are much easier to exploit and we intend to explore for them.'

Judging by Lewis's nodding head he felt that must have sounded convincing and he sighed quietly with relief.

'A novel approach to prospecting, Norman, not quite what I am used to. Anyway, we need to take a sample for analysis – if you have no objection. I could be making a considerable investment and I do not want to be betting on a loser do I Mister Campbell. Let's get this sample Brand. You have had a good look around, so where do think is the best place for it?'

Brand walked past several scattered heaps of brown earth and then he went over to the drilling rig. Norman followed a few paces behind, looking at the heaps of earth, finding it hard to believe that Hans had managed to drill so many test bores. To drill just one to the depths required to reach the reef must have taken days to complete and yet he counted six more. It seemed as if Hans was reading his mind, a crafty twinkle coming into the Afrikaner's eyes and Norman could see that something had changed in Hans; he was more dynamic, more animated but it still did not answer the nagging question of the sample.

The four of them followed James Brand to his chosen borehole where he began to move lose rock with his hands until Hans handed him a shovel and a container for his sample. Brand dug deeper into the heap until he was satisfied, lifted some of the material with his bare hand and placed it in the container. As he did so, Hans began to ask questions.

'Have you ever seen any Indian wigwams James? Norman's head snapped towards him. Why should he suddenly be so interested in American Indians?

'No, I have never actually seen any wigwams out on the prairies if that's what you mean, only in wild west shows like most other people,' answered Brand.

'I've heard lots of stories about your natives and I've wondered how they made their shelters'

Brand paused for a few moments to listen to Hans and then he resumed his task, filling the container with the broken shale before stowing it safely in his holdall. When he had finished Rosenberg pulled him to one side to speak for several minutes out of earshot before eventually returning.

'Gentlemen, it seems mister Brand here has completed his survey and I guess I have seen all I need to for the time being.'

'Good, Norman here can take us back to town, can't you Norman.'

Norman nodded and turned to walk across to the Buick with the Americans and Arthur took the opportunity to engage in a hurried conversation with Hans before joining them.

The ride back to Johannesburg was uneventful, Norman's three passengers sat quietly looking out of the window and he could not help wondering how Hans and Arthur could possibly have known where to sprinkle the gold dust. He glanced in the rear view mirror and saw that Arthur seemed relaxed and unconcerned and then his eyes turned to Lewis Rosenberg. He saw that he had drifted off to sleep and next to him, James Brand was alert, looking at everything they passed. Eventually they reached the city and Norman left the Americans at their hotel.

'Well, how do you think it went Norman?' said Arthur as soon as the Buick set off.

'I think the day went well, Hans did a great job of making it look as if a real mining operation was in progress. But tell me Arthur, how could he possibly have known where to seed the ground for Brand to take a sample? That's what I don't understand.'

'Don't worry Norman. It's all under control. First, the sample – let me put you straight. We never salted the ground.

'What? You're telling me there's no gold?' yelled Norman. 'If there's no gold, it's a useless sample and we're done for! Rosenberg won't want to advise his clients to invest in a pile of useless dirt.'

Arthur laughed. 'Nothing to worry about, Norman, the sample will be top class. Hans has a second sample, the best ore around, and tonight, when we are entertaining our guests to dinner, he will get into their room, switch samples and when they finally get the assay results, they will be top class. With a little luck, it will not be long before American investors are falling all over each other to buy stock in Transgold. Hans knows one of the door attendants at the Carlton who will let him into their room to switch the samples. You heard him questioning Brand about American Indians like a little boy didn't you? Well he was distracting Brand so as he would not look too closely at the sample he had taken. Each piece of rock has a unique shape and if Brand has a good memory he might notice a difference when he takes it for analysis.'

'What about the gold dust?' enquired Norman, still exasperated, 'What happened to that?'

'It's our first pay day my son. Tomorrow, when they've caught the train to Cape Town, we'll meet in the office and share it out between the three of us.'

Miles away out on the Veldt, Hans was riding at a steady trot towards Johannesburg. Not along the poor, rutted road, but taking a more direct route overland to cut at least five miles from the journey. As soon as the Buick had left, he had told the labourers to stop work and paid them off. Then he had walked over to a big, familiar man standing with his back to him, rearranging the traces on one of the waggons.

'Thanks Caas! You and your men did a great job for me, so here's your money,' he said, passing a bundle of bank notes between them.

'Thank you Hans; it's a pleasure to do business with you. Lucky we were making a delivery out this way. We will be a day late delivering the stamps but what does it matter, you have more than compensated me for my lost time and it has been good to help an old friend. I won't ask what you are up to; I have been living around here long enough not to ask too many questions.'

They were both, tough men in a tough world and felt a bond as they shook hands and then Hans had mounted his horse, lifted his bush hat in salute before spurring the animal towards the city. That had been two hours ago and he still had more than 12 miles to go.

Rosenberg and Brand were standing outside their hotel taking some air when the Buick arrived to collect them.

'Good evening gentlemen,' said Arthur leaning out of the car window. 'I hope you are ready for dinner at The Rand club, a fitting place to take you I think.'

'Really,' mused Rosenberg,

'Oh yes, it's the centre of the gold mining industry, a place where many a fortune has been made.'

'And lost, I expect?'

'Quite so,' said Arthur, a hint of uncertainty creeping into his voice. The pressure must be getting to him as well, thought Norman.

'I say, Brand, what do you think about driving us to the Rand Club? You said you are a fan of Buick motor cars. I don't think there will be anyone around to stop you tonight. Here, jump in and I will get in the passenger seat to give directions. How about it?' said Norman in an attempt to take their minds off gold mines for a while.

Brand's eyes lit up at the prospect but he hesitated for a few seconds, took a sideways glance at his employer, wondering if he was overstepping the mark. Norman noticed the hesitation, guessed why and with his best persuasive voice turned in his seat to sound out Rosenberg.

'Sir, Mr Brand is interested in my car and I think it would round off his day admirably if he were allowed to drive us the short distance to the Rand club. What do you say?'

Rosenberg smiled as much as it was possible for him to smile. 'Go ahead Brand,' he said, 'I'm too old to learn to drive one myself, but you youngsters seem to thrive on it. It baffles me how you can operate those pedals at the same time as steering the damn thing.'

With a happy look on his face, Brand slipped into the driving seat, gripped the steering wheel tightly with both hands and a little jerkily to begin with, set the car in motion. It was a simple ploy to take Brand's mind off the day's events, relax him and with luck, cloud his memory of the shale sample even more. Tonight was a turning point, from just being an idea and a few transatlantic telegrams the swindle now had the potential to deliver real rewards and the enormity of what they were doing came home to Norman. He was relatively unconcerned as to the legality, but he did worry that a fortune might slip from his grasp.

Alone on the veldt, Hans was making good progress, his horse was moving at a steady trot and he reckoned he had less than eight miles to go. He would have plenty of

185

time to make the switch and as he let the horse make its own way, his mind began to drift. The three of them had discussed the swindle many times, the logistics, the potential rewards and during these conversations, one thing had become clear; Arthur could not be bankrolling them. Arthur did not have the kind of money they were spending; someone in the background controlled the purse strings. Who was that someone he wondered?

Another hour and the sun had slipped low in the sky, the horse picked its way over the uneven ground and Hans' thoughts moved on to the money he could make and the farm he might buy. He half closed his eyes and then, suddenly, his dead wife and child appeared before him, his mind was playing tricks and for a moment, he saw them in the shadows looking up, trying to talk to him and then the images dissolved back into the shadows. He would give anything to have them back. What is money compared to losing the woman you loved and your only child? He took a deep breath, exhaling with a sigh and closed his eyes tightly for a second or too.

The horse sensed an instruction, she pulled forward trying to break into a trot, and Hans instinctively reined her in and causing her to stumble, catch a hoof on a rock and lose her footing. Her head dropped as she tried to regain her balance, taking Hans by surprise and he lost his grip on the reigns. Sliding uncontrollably over her neck he grasped wildly at the horses mane but his feet came out of the stirrups and he could not stop himself falling. Hitting the earth awkwardly he was stunned for a time and when his head finally cleared he could see his horse was some way off and heading in the direction of Johannesburg.

'Damn horse,' he said to himself scrambling to his feet, 'I will never catch her now. She will head straight for the stables and . . . bastard horse.' Dismayed, he realised that not only would he struggle to get to the hotel room in time for the swap, the 'good' sample was in the saddlebag.

'Shit and double shit,' he muttered in his thick Afrikaans accent. How much money was he going to make now? Nothing at this rate, he thought as he watched his horse disappear. He was in a predicament, it was at least five more miles to town and maybe he could do it in less than two hours but the track was rough and he was wearing riding boots.

It was beginning to get dark when Norman and his guests entered the comfort of the Rand Club and straight away, he could see that the colonial grandeur impressed the Americans and he took the initiative.

'Shall we make our way to the dining room gentlemen?'

'After you Norman,' said Rosenberg, 'I am ready for dinner after today's exertions. The air out here seems to make you hungry don't you think so Brand.'

James Brand smiled his agreement; he was certainly ready for dinner and felt he had earned it. He knew from their visit to the mine that it was still a long way from producing gold in profitable quantities but it did seem to have potential and he had told his employer so. The sample would determine Mr Rosenberg's course of action more than his opinion he was sure and tonight he felt his work done. He had enjoyed driving the Buick, looked forward to a good dinner and decided that tonight he would relax and enjoy himself as much as he dare.

As they made their way along the corridor towards the staircase, James Brand and Lewis Rosenberg fell back momentarily examining portraits hanging on the wall and Norman took the opportunity to whisper into Arthur's ear.

'D'you suppose we should hold back on the alcohol tonight. Rosenberg is interested I know but it will be too easy to make a slip up and we don't want that at this stage.'

Arthur looked casually round at Rosenberg and Brand who were catching them up and out of the corner of his mouth said.

'You're right just a couple.'

The strain of maintaining the myth was getting to them both but at least they were astute enough to realise that a combination of stress and alcohol could ruin everything. Arthur was especially aware of how a heady mix of emotions, tiredness and drink could dull the senses. After all, hadn't he and Hans taken advantage of miners at the card tables in just such a condition, relieving them of their hard-earned pay?

'You know, I was impressed by your operation out there in the back of beyond,' said Rosenberg as they finished eating. 'If the sample lives up to what you have told me I think we can do business. I have had a look at the figures you gave me and they make for interesting reading. I have already cabled my office in New York to find somewhere here in South Africa to test the sample. I do not want to miss an opportunity like this, but until I have completed my research, I cannot give you any undertaking. Gentlemen, let me propose a toast.' He lifted his glass and the others followed suit. 'To the

Transgold Mining and Exploration Company: may we all taste some of the Witwatersrand's success.'

'Hear hear!' was the chorus from around the table.

'Well gentlemen,' he continued, 'I have enjoyed my short stay here in Johannesburg and I would like to continue the enjoyment but we have a busy day tomorrow and my bed awaits me. If you'll excuse Brand and myself, we should like to go back to our hotel right now.'

Arthur gulped in astonishment, and Norman's stomach turned over at this unexpected request. It was not yet eleven and they had promised to keep the Americans out of the hotel until midnight.

Norman had no choice but to call the waiter, sign the chit for dinner and wonder what he could do to delay things and then his alarm spread even further as Rosenberg prematurely rose from the table. Inwardly, he groaned and noticed that Arthur was looking decidedly pale but they just had to go along with him, the least sign that they were manipulating the situation could set off alarm bells and finish everything.

Leaving the three of them in the lobby to wait, Norman walked out of the club towards the Buick wondering how he might spin things out. Perhaps he could let a tyre down or pull a wire off one of the ignition plugs. No, that would not work; he was starting to get amateurish. The least suspicion from Rosenberg or Brand, and the plot was dead. Reluctantly he swung the starting handle before driving the car as slowly as he could towards the entrance to the club to find Arthur and the Americans waiting for him and as he drove them back across town, he recited a prayer for Hans under his breath.

For the umpteenth time that night, Hans cursed his riding boots, slid out of the saddle and dropped gingerly to the ground. As he tied the horse's reins to a post at the rear of the Carlton Hotel, he shifted his weight to relieve the pain in his feet. He had found the runaway happily chewing on some hay in the stable when he finally hobbled in, his feet blistered from the riding boots and he had immediately checked the saddlebags for the sample, greatly relieved to find it undisturbed. However, time was running out – he had until midnight to complete the switch and it was gone ten 'o' clock. He had unsaddled her, found another horse and made his way to the hotel as fast as he could and now he was ready to complete the switch.

Entering the Carlton's back rooms, he made his way through the darkened kitchens and the deserted dining room to the front entrance where he came across Jacob Muller, an ex-soldier from the Johannesburg commando who was waiting for him. Jacob was a good man, it was he who had found Hans scraps of food and a warm cubby hole for the night during those desperate times after his release as a prisoner of war and they had remained friends ever since.

'You're a bit late Hans. I should have been off half-an-hour ago. Anyway, I told the night man that he could get a quick drink if he wanted. Here, take this,' he said, pressing a key into his hand, exchanging it for the five-pound note already there. 'They are in a suite of rooms on the second floor to the right of the lift, with 207 on the door. The lift is noisy, so use the stairs – over there.'

Hans turned, and without a word hobbled towards the staircase, wincing all the way, the pain in his feet making walking difficult. He climbed the stairs to the second floor and emerged into a carpeted hallway and peering round the corner he scanned the corridor for any sign of life, but it was deserted. He quickly made his way towards room 207, inserted the key and opened the door. Closing it behind him, he re-locked it and stood perfectly still holding his breath and listening for anything that might suggest he was not alone. There was nothing, only the distant barking of a dog and the sound of a passing car. He deliberated for a few seconds: where should he search first for the container. It was too dark to see properly and he was unfamiliar with the suite's layout so he decided to throw caution to the wind, taking the risk of putting on a light.

He searched one of the bedrooms first and found nothing; he switched out the light and moved to the smaller room guessing that this would be Brand's bedroom, turned on the light and scanned for any sign of the container. He swept the room with his eyes and quickly located a large leather case lying open beside the window and taking two paces towards it was relieved to see the container tucked away in one corner. His heart leapt as he fumbled in his jacket for its twin, congratulating himself on how easy his task had been, all he had to do now was substitute them and they were home and dry. He could already envisage his little farm up near Pretoria as he reached out to make the switch until, suddenly, the hairs on the back of his neck stood up.

He had heard a scraping noise, the faint hum of the lift motor running and then it stopped. He concentrated; trying to work out on which floor it had stopped and after several seconds of silence, heard the sound of the gate opening. Remaining motionless, he strained his

191

ears, listening, aware that the carpets would deaden footsteps and so he remained motionless for a few more minutes to be sure that any threat had passed him by. Silence returned and he let out a slow sigh and was about to reach towards James Brand's leather case when the unmistakable sound of a key entering a lock cut through the night. Cursing under his breath he sprang into action, he had but seconds to substitute the sample and escape. In one rapid movement he threw the duplicate container into the open case, grabbed the original and reached back to switch out the light. He was just in time, as darkness descended the door to the suite opened and the hall light came on, trapping him. To try to escape would be futile, they would see him; there was nowhere to go, the game was up and his heart began to sink.

Furtively he looked round the room, the window and then the door but it was hopeless. He was two stories up and there was no chance of escape but quick thinking and a strong will had always been amongst his attributes and they did not fail him now. Dropping to the floor, he rolled into the tight space under the bed, grasping the container tightly to his body as he went. He closed his eyes tightly as his chest heaved, his heart felt as if it would explode and he considered his predicament. He had been in dangerous situations before, life or death situations; this was not one of those. Clearing his mind, he took stock of the situation, the Americans were just outside the bedroom door, their distinctive drawls percolating through the thin wall, but they did not know he was here. He felt that there was a good chance he could remain undiscovered as long as he remained where he was.

'If that sample you took proves as positive as those guys tell us, then I think I will recommend the Company to some of my clients. They are way off producing any gold – I can see that – but at least they have made a start. How long d'you reckon before we see some gold, Brand?'

Brand must have had his back to the door because Hans could not make out his answer. Did he say only a few weeks? He wasn't sure, but it was evident the sample was crucial to the whole enterprise and if they discovered him, all their scheming and hard work would have been in vain. Then Brand pushed the bedroom door open and came in, took off his jacket and dropped it on a chair before he sat on the bed, his feet not six inches away from Hans' face. Kicking off his shoes and socks, he stood up to remove the rest of his clothes and put on a pair of pyjamas and from where he lay, Hans watched Brand's bare feet wander back and forth before he gathered up his clothes and went to the bathroom. A few minutes later, he returned and the light went out, Hans felt the mattress above him sink, reducing the space he had to move in and lying flat on his back, he was unable to turn. The room descended into silence and then James Brand fell asleep, his rhythmic breathing the only sound and Hans was alone with his thoughts.

An hour passed and Hans began to feel stiffness creeping into his body, his feet were hurting, he wanted to shift his position but could not. What if he got cramp, he wondered, if he did then he must surely wake the sleeping Brand less than six inches above him. He considered sliding out from under the bed and creeping across the two rooms into the corridor but decided that the chance of discovery was too great, and then he considered climbing through the bedroom window to crawl along the ledge to the fire escape, but that would be just as difficult to accomplish. No, the only realistic option was to wait until morning and the Americans left.

Steeling himself for a long night, the memory of the war began to loom large in his mind, those long lonely nights on guard duty staring into the black night. He knew this would be a long night just like the ones before and he remembered again those days. They had lived off the land, sleeping where they could, shadowing the British in their khaki uniforms, striking wherever and whenever they could before slipping away.

The British were brave soldiers, but did not seem to possess much in the way of field craft. It amused him that they allowed the commando to creep up on them and get as close as they did. Together with the other Boer soldiers, he would settle on safe ground and one by one, pick off the enemy with carefully placed shots. Ultimately, they had lost, the British had built up a far stronger force and he could see once again his friends falling all around him; hear the chatter of the dreaded machine guns and the roar of the British artillery. For him though, it had not lasted long, missing most of the fighting as a prisoner of war, languishing in a Ceylonese prisoner of war camp. On his release he had found he could not return to his old way of life and worst of all, he had lost his wife and child. The deaths of Ute and Hans junior had been a body blow from which he never fully recovered the root cause of his alcoholism and despair.

As he lay motionless, more thoughts filtered through his mind, the hours passed and stiffness gripped his body, forcing him to try to twist his body and relieve the numbness. It was an impossible task and so, to take his mind off his predicament, he slowly tensed and relaxed his muscle groups, reliving his memories of Ute and Hans, precious memories that circumstances had forced deep into his subconscious. Nevertheless, tonight she came to him. A strikingly beautiful woman, Ute had long blond hair down to her shoulders and the clearest of blue eyes, a good wife who worked tirelessly from morning to night. She cleaned and cooked, looked after him and their son and yet still had energy to satisfy his manly desires.

She seemed so real and he could not hold back the tears welling up in his eyes, it was as if she were there. Then Brand coughed and turned over, muttered something incomprehensible, enough to snap Hans out of his thoughts and concentrate his mind. The dog was barking again and he returned to reality, comforted in the knowledge he was at last able to think of Ute and little Hans and it left him feeling less alone.

Another hour and he was feeling very tired, finding it a struggle to stop himself from falling asleep and he screwed his eyes shut, concentrating hard on keeping awake and then it was Arthur's turn to dominate his thoughts. He had met him in his darkest hour, not long after arriving in Bloemfontein. They were both down on their luck, living as down and outs on the streets but somehow Arthur had managed to lift them both back up. An enigma, a cheat, a liar and a swindler who would sell his own grandmother if he could yet he had shown fortitude and kindness when it mattered, helping him to climb from the pit in which he was floundering. Perhaps it was because neither had any family, both friendless, lonely men and maybe that is how Arthur saw it: they had no one but each other.

195

At last, the light in the room changed from blackness to a barely perceptible grey, then the dull orange of the new dawn broke and to his relief, the birds began to sing. He hoped the men would rise early; allow him some respite because it had been a long day and a longer night. He was weary, numb and hungry, but he was determined to stay undiscovered. Then he heard a quiet knock on the door, Brand moved in the bed above him and from the next room Lewis called out.

'Who is it?'

'Bellhop sir, it is seven 'o' clock and I have left a tray with coffee outside your door as ordered.'

'Thank you,' said Lewis Rosenberg, his bed creaking as he rose.

'Brand, are you up yet.'

'Y...yes sir, wide awake and getting dressed sir,' said Brand barely moving.

Twenty minutes later James Brand *had* moved, washed, dressed, and just finished his coffee when Rosenberg called to him to leave for breakfast. As the door closed behind them a much-relieved Hans struggled out from under the bed, rubbed his legs to get his circulation going again and wiggled his toes to relieve the pain in his feet and then he reached back under the bed to retrieve the sample, kissed it and made a speedy exit.

Later that morning, after cabling his associates in New York and Cape Town, Lewis Rosenberg and James Brand boarded the Cape Town train. Settling into his seat the American stockbroker watched the city of gold slide past, impressed and intrigued by its vibrant, brash culture. From the little he had seen of the place he had soon realised that there were opportunities to exploit, the mine dumps sliding past the carriage window testament to its potential and he wanted to be involved and if the sample lived up to expectations he felt sure the returns would be more than satisfactory.

At about the same time, unaware of the drama played out in the hotel a few hours earlier, Arthur sat reading the financial pages of his newspaper pleased that the increase in value of gold in the early months of 1920 had brought South African mining stocks to prominence in the United States. Rosenberg had believed himself to be ahead of the market and as soon as he could, he had contacted Arthur to buy shares in Transgold.

Arthur believed they had reached a cross roads, they had listed on the Johannesburg stock market but he feared discovery of the scam and it was too costly and time consuming to expand the site. It would be much easier to keep the illusion alive in the financial newssheets of the United States and as long as gold fever spread, he was confident of selling more shares. If investors insisted upon visiting Johannesburg, then Norman would have to take care of them and there was no need to worry about samples, word had spread from New York that Rosenberg had invested heavily.

Across town In the Campbell household, Lucy noticed even more the change in Norman and worried that she could not understand why. He had a spring in his step, often he did not come home until late in the evening and he always had money in his pocket. Lucky at the card tables, he said, but she knew he was not that lucky. Could there be another woman? She put that idea to the back of her mind, not wanting to believe it, busying herself with her chores until one morning when she decided to tidy her wardrobe. Marsha was looking after the children and

197

she had some time to herself and decided to re-arrange her clothes, taking all of them from the wardrobe to brush them free of dust. She held each garment up to examine it for any signs of insect damage and seeing that everything was fine, returned them to the wardrobe. Feeling a little bored she decided that she would do the same with Norman's clothes.

She started with his shirts, brushing off specks of dust with her hand and putting them straight on their hangers and then she took out his best suit and laid it on their bed. Insect damage was her main worry but it seemed in good condition and then she noticed curious lump in one of the pockets. Wondering what it could be she reached inside and grasped hold of a small cylindrical object. It was metallic, cold to her touch and strikingly heavy for its size.

It was about three inches long and an inch or so in diameter with a cap too tight for her to unscrew which only added to her curiosity and she looked around for some means of opening it. There was nothing to hand so she hurried downstairs to the kitchen, returning with a knife and set to work prising the lid from its body. Slowly it began to move as she worked the knife back and forth until without warning, the lid sprang off and a stream of yellow metallic dust cascaded onto the floor. For almost two minutes, she could do nothing but stand and stare at the bright yellow grains sprinkled over the floorboards and her shoes.

Gold! This is gold and a valuable amount for sure, she thought. A mild panic took hold of her when she realised what she had done and wondered how Norman could have come to possess it. She took a deep breath and tried to make sense of what she was looking at. Where did he get so much gold from, why had he never mentioned it? She looked down at the yellow grains sprinkled across the floor and stooped down for a closer look. Touching the tiny grains with her finger, she felt that her first job must be to reclaim as much of it as possible, cover her tracks and so, for half hour, she knelt down and painstakingly collected every grain she could find, sighing with relief as she replaced the container cap with a quivering hand.

After putting the container of gold back in Norman's suit pocket, she went and made herself a cup of tea. sitting at the kitchen table she spooned extra sugar into her tea and began to wonder in what kind of an escapade her husband was involved. She lifted the cup with both hands and she began to consider the situation, wondering if Arthur James was involved. He was her prime suspect, him and that good-looking no-good friend of his, the one with the deformed ear. She suspected Norman was with them on his late nights and although she had only met them once or twice, her instinct told her they meant trouble. Now for the truth, but how was she going to find out that truth? She did not want a confrontation; they had quarrelled more in the past six months than in the whole of their previous time together. No, that was not the way; she would remain silent about the gold, keep her suspicions to herself and watch his every move until she could learn the truth.

Norman walked into Arthur's rented office to find him sitting back in his chair, hands clasped behind his head and in front of him, on the table, stood an empty glass and a half full bottle of whisky.

'Come in, take a seat, have a drink'

'I need half a dozen I think; it's been so bloody hot today, even the Buick has struggled a bit. I think she needs a drink as much as me'.

'Listen, Hans will be coming here in a few minutes. We need to talk,' Arthur released his hands and let his seat tip back onto all four legs. 'I want to talk about the finances and something else, something important.' He pointed to the bottom drawer of the filing cabinet, 'Glasses in there – look, get one and pour yourself a drink.'

Norman found the glasses, took one, filled it with a shot of whisky, and took the seat opposite Arthur before lifting the glass to his lips and savouring the power of the fluid sliding down his gullet.

'Ah, that's better,' he said, almost choking. Then the door opened, Hans walked in looking relaxed and he had a smile on his face.

'That's good timing my friend, get a glass and pull up a chair, let's have another drink,' said Arthur obviously pleased by his friend's cheery manner.

Hans took little persuading, joining the others round the table to toast their success, then Arthur began to speak. He could not help boasting, telling how he had bribed an American investment periodical to print articles written by himself about the South African gold mining industry and how positive the result had been.

'Of course,' he laughed, 'I made sure prominence was given to Transgold and we are starting to see some interest. Only today, I received two cables from Americans, so that makes more than a dozen in the past two weeks and means we are generating a lot of interest in the stock. Lewis Rosenberg has let me know that he has sold shares with a face value amounting to almost

£100,000 in the United States and a further £50,000 or so elsewhere. A payment of £5,000 arrived from him today so that's nearly £15,000 in total,' Arthur lied. 'There is more to come over the next few months and so I have a little present for you both'

Arthur reached into his jacket pocket and retrieved two envelopes, sliding them across the table, one to Norman and one to Hans. 'Five hundred pounds each to keep you going and once I get the next payment there will be more.'

Norman's eyes narrowed slightly as he gazed at the envelope and then he took a lead from Hans who nonchalantly stuffed his into his trouser pocket. Norman had opened an account at the Cape Bank, depositing £300 from his first payment and since then had managed to save well over £1,000, this latest amount would put him on the way to his second thousand, and for a while, he pondered about what he might achieve with such a large sum of money. However, his daydreams did not last long; Arthur's tone changed to a more serious note and obliged him to pay attention.

'I needed to talk to you both because we're running into a little problem. The costs of keeping the mine going are a lot more than I anticipated. The machines we have had to buy and wages for labourers are more than I expected. I'm afraid that we're all going to have to take a smaller percentage until things settle down, me included.'

Norman frowned. 'Why is it a problem all of a sudden? You must have known what it would cost.'

Hans said nothing, just listened as Arthur looked Norman in the eye and told him a pack of lies. He had known Arthur for a long time and saw signs of a double-

201

cross. Norman, on the other hand was taken in, intimidated by Arthur's gaze and he looked away for a fraction of a second, deciding that maybe he should agree to this new arrangement. He had hoped for more money, but he was afraid that he might lose what he had already earned. It would do no good to confront Arthur, he and Hans worked together and if an argument developed, then he was sure that he would be the loser.

'All right, all right, fair enough,' he conceded. He was in too deep now and if they did fall out, Arthur could make things difficult for him. He might even let Williamson know what he was doing with the Buick in Company time and he could not afford to lose his job.

'I wouldn't get too concerned just yet Norman; the shares are still selling and we might soon have to think about issuing more. The *Colorado Mining Gazette* will print anything for money and the false reports I have been feeding them are generating interest. With luck, we could see more Americans wanting shares.'

He smiled at Norman, a friendly enough smile but in reality, he was mocking the Scotsman, content at how easy it had been to deceive him, but there was tension in the air and he had to do something to ease it. 'The bottle is empty; I suggest we adjourn to the Silver Star where we can get another drink and have a little fun – we deserve it.'

Chapter 12

Alfred kept a close eye on his protégé during the months Solomon spent working for the *Abantu Batho*, noting how well his writing improved and how widely his articles were read. Alfred had connections and through his powers of persuasion, he had obtained the necessary passes to enable Solomon to move his family to the outskirts of Johannesburg. No more than a shack at the rear of a drapery shop in Ferreiras Town, it was home, they were happy and from there Solomon frequented the townships, catching up on gossip, looking for those personal stories.

One fine spring day he looked up from his work to stare out of the window for a few moments, clearing his mind, until a voice tore him away from those thoughts.

'Solomon, please will you come with me to the editor's office?'

'Sorry Alfred, I was in a different place. What is it you want?'

'Please will you come with me to the editor's office. We have a new assignment for you, and we need to talk to you.'

'Good morning, Solomon,' said Walter Ndumby, as the two men entered the tiny room he called an office. 'Are you going to do the talking Alfred?'

'Certainly, Solomon we have a job for you, but first you will need some background information. You know there is to be a general election soon and our readership will want to know how it will affect them, whatever the outcome. Most of our people don't have the vote, but if the Nationalists defeat Smuts and the South African party, things could change for the worse, and goodness knows, life is hard enough already. Hertzog and the Nationalists are gaining ground; the Afrikaner party is itching to take power and wants to displace the pro-British movement in the Cape. They represent poor, unskilled Boers, many of whom have come to Johannesburg looking for work and are taking jobs from our people. If the nationalists win, it will mean problems for us and so we want you to write some articles to try to explain what is happening. We need those natives eligible to vote to use their votes for the good of Africans, not whites. Walter has obtained some of the white newspapers from Cape Town and Pretoria to help. Read them and then I want to run through a list of political and union meetings that you can attend. Have you anything to add Walter?'

Walter spread his good hand towards the pile of newspapers on the edge of his desk. 'These papers go back six months and contain information about the parties and their leaders. Find out as much as you can about the International Socialist League, they are the only party that see us as equals and we should help them if we can. Now, the article you are working on about the industrial workers – can you finish it today?

204

'Almost done,' said Solomon, 'I can let you have the copy this afternoon. What about the work I was about to start writing on the Indian workers.'

'Leave that for now and then you will be free to concentrate your mind on these,' he said, picking up the pile of newspapers to give to Solomon.

Walter Ndumby was a kindly quick-witted man with a remarkable understanding of the way South Africa worked. The natives had minimal rights and he felt it his duty to speak out for the oppressed black people. He looked at Solomon and his smile faded, replaced by an altogether more sombre guise.

'Solomon, we have watched you develop, noted how your writing has matured and we know what potential you have. We think you are ready to write political articles, important articles that will shed light on the coming elections and what it will mean to the black population. Only a few of us have the right to vote and we are unlikely to change much on our own. The British mean well, but never carry things through, the Afrikaners are our biggest threat and with political power, they will be able to write laws excluding us from everything. They make laws to keep us out of whole areas, and they use guns to do it – you know that! We can only fight with words and you have shown us your mastery of the written word, let's try and turn the vote against the Nationalist Party. There is a meeting tonight of the Industrial Workers in Ferreiras town hall, we would like you to start there.'

Until late in the afternoon Solomon immersed himself in the newspapers, reading everything relating to politics and labour relations, learning as much as he could. He realised that because most Africans were without voting rights they were not particularly interested in politics, rather industrial and work matters. Perhaps through reporting industrial disputes he might find a way to stimulate them. Since the end of the Great War there had been almost constant unrest in the mines, a truce brokered between workers and mine owners during the war had not lasted long once the peace had returned. Afrikaners forced to leave the land were taking the jobs of Black workers leaving more and more Africans close to starvation and trouble was brewing.

The hall was already filling up as Solomon approached; Blacks, Whites and a sprinkling of Indians from the textile industry, all come to listen to the main speaker, David Ivon Jones of the International Socialist League. Solomon understood a little of the party's politics, and with unrest fermenting throughout the Witwatersrand, he could not fail to realise how involved the Socialist League would be. The League was the only white political party to advocate rights for Africans and as the election looked like a fight between Prime Minister Smuts and Hertzog it seemed unlikely to leave either with a majority. One of the smaller parties could hold a balance of power and Solomon wondered then if the meeting tonight might hold some importance, a pointer perhaps to coming events.

A native boy handed a pamphlet to Solomon as he made his way into the dimly lit hall toward rows of rickety wooden benches already full of people. On the small stage at the front of the hall sat four men, two black and two white and one of them raised his hand. The hubbub died away, the doors to the hall closed and the meeting began.

A tall, thin black man dressed in a loosely hanging suit rose to his feet and banged the table with the book he was holding.

'I would like to bring this meeting to order if I may,' he said, calmly looking around the room. 'I welcome you all to this meeting of the Industrial Workers of Africa. It is good to see so many of you here tonight, so let me begin by introducing my fellow speakers and myself. My name is Hamilton Kraai. I am the union organiser here on the Western Rand. On my left is Colin Dantu, the union representative for the native miners of Ferreiras Town and the surrounding district, next to him is the Reverend Phillips from the American Reform Church, and on my right is David Ivon Jones of the International Socialist League. Tonight we are here to talk about the rights of our native workers and their exploitation by the mine owners . . .'

For more than 20 minutes, Hamilton Kraai spoke, informing the audience of the background to the union, what it represented and about its fight against injustices suffered by native workers. He told how the strikes of the past few years had secured better wages and conditions, how the mine owners had called in the police to force workers back down the mineshafts at bayonet point.

'But, you will remember when, last year, the white miners were given pay increases of eight shillings a week? We only threatened to strike and yet we won three pennies a shift extra. We threatened to bring out at least 40,000 men on any one day – the organisation we showed then demonstrated what we can do.'

A ripple of applause erupted as he sat down Colin Dantu, the union official, rose to his feet to give a short lecture about the need of everyone to become members

207

of the union. He encouraged everyone in the hall to join, told them of the benefits of solidarity and then it was the turn of the Reverend Phillips to speak. Originally from the United States, he had worked in and around Johannesburg for almost 20 years and he spoke mainly about his work educating the children and converting Africans to Christianity.

Solomon listened with interest, took notes and remembered the time he had spent at the missionary school. He listened as the Reverend went on to speak of the townships and their many problems, gradually coming to the point of his speech.

'All this talk of strike action is worrying; we have seen strikes before and we have seen the results. We have seen how the mine owners, hand in hand with the authorities have crushed strikes with violence. We have seen men die because of strike action.'

There was a murmur of disapproval and he held up his hand to silence the audience. 'Please do not think for one minute I am against industrial action, something needs to be done to improve the lot of the vast majority of workers. The mine owners I know are hard to convince and they have the backing of the police but there is another way, a way to avoid bloodshed. My friends, passive action has to be the best way forward, peaceful protest on the streets, petitions sent to the centre of power in Pretoria and the word of God.'

The mood in the hall became more subdued and as the clergyman finished speaking and sat down, he received only polite applause. There was mumbling amongst the listeners and Solomon noted most opinion suggested that passive protest stood little or no chance against a white government determined to subdue them by force of arms. The workers had neither the resources nor the organisation to fight but as he listened, it became clear to Solomon that passive resistance really was all they had and he scratched his chin deep in thought as the final speaker rose to his feet.

The man was a strange sight to native eyes, a stocky Welshman with copper coloured hair, pale skin covered in freckles and a singsong Welsh accent that at times proved difficult to comprehend. He began slowly, having learned already that his African audiences sometimes could not understand him. 'Lis-ten, workers, lis-ten!' he said, pausing for a second or two. A few of the more knowledgeable ones clapped but most remained silent not understanding that the Welshman had just quoted the title of the manifesto of the Industrial Workers of Africa. 'I am here this evening to speak about our common strug-gle against the bosses; they exploit white workers just as much as black. Mine owners can and do sack white workers at any time just as easily as black ones and turn them out onto the street. So I tell you brothers and sisters, we must work together to fight the common enemy, we must rid the country of this most divisive colour bar.' Loud applause filled the room as the audience warmed to him. 'Comrades, our society comprises two classes: we, the working class who toil in the fields, who toil in the factories and who toil in the mines, and the landowners, factory owners, and the mine owners, who benefit from our labours. They exploit the colour bar for their own ends, driving a wedge between the white and black workers with their newspaper stories, frightening us with the threat of imported cheap labour from India and China. Cheap labour, brothers and sisters, cheap labour which will take over our jobs and throw us all on the scrap heap. These threats undermine our solidarity and our ability to fight them. Instead, we should be standing shoulder to shoulder as the true working class and resist them. The means of production and wealth creation should be in the hands of the ones who toil day in and day out to satisfy the greed of this unoccupied class, living in luxury, whilst we live in poverty and deprivation. Our children will have no future if we do not stand up to them now!' he said, banging the table to accentuate his words.

A roar of approval erupted, a vigorous clapping of hands, stamping of feet and whistling drowned out his next words and from the stage, Ivon Jones looked serenely at his audience. His words never failed to impress workers looking towards a better life, for a way out of the drudgery and he seemed to offer them just that. Beside him, Hamilton Kraai and Colin Dantu were smiling broadly, joining with the applause. The Reverend Phillips seemed unimpressed, his face expressionless.

Jones held up his hand for silence before continuing: 'We must work together for the abolition of native indenture and the compound systems. We must work together to lift native workers to the political and industrial status of the white workers. Native workers should have the right to vote, only then can all the people of the Union of South Africa feel free to build a future for themselves and their children. The injustices of the Pass Laws and the compound system must be swept aside and our children educated properly for a better and happier future.' He paused, gripping the table, his bright eyes scanning the audience as applause rippled round the room and then, more quietly. 'My reason for being here tonight is to tell you about the International Socialist

League, formed to achieve the aims of emancipation from wage slavery and to unite in the common cause alongside our native brethren and we look forwards to working with you.'

In less passionate tones he spelt out the structure and aims of the League and after a further ten minutes he sat down to tumultuous applause leaving Hamilton Kraai unable to speak for at least five minutes after rising from his chair. Smiling broadly he eventually raised his hands for silence, thanked the speakers and the meeting came to a close. The doors of the hall opened and people began to leave, chatting, discussing the agenda and catching up on local gossip. Solomon listened to them and began to wonder, could native workers really reach the same levels of employment and wages as white workers, could the workers really take over factories and mines and run them? He did not know, but he would try to find out – it was his job. He had to speak with Kraai or Jones but so many eager admirers surrounded them that he found he could not get close. The Reverend Phillips, however, was standing apart from his fellow speakers, a lack of interest in his point of view leaving him isolated and Solomon thought it a good opportunity to introduce himself and perhaps get some answers.

'Excuse me sir, my name is Solomon. I am a reporter for the *Abantu Batho* newspaper. I would like to speak with to you.'

Reverend Phillips looked at Solomon with kindly eyes. 'Of course, young man, that is why I am here, to try to answer any questions you may have.'

A little unsure of himself, Solomon asked naïvely. 'Mr Jones has told us we will live like the white population. How soon, do you think that will be?'

The Reverend Phillips' smile waned. 'My son, these things do not happen overnight. You must not expect any dramatic changes in the near future. The white Government is very powerful and will always look after the interests of white people first.'

'Oh...you said that passive resistance is the way forward but you did not really tell us how that might be achieved. Could you tell me more?'

'Why, yes I can. First, you must understand that the authorities have little trouble in calling out the police with their guns to break up the strikes. You have heard of striking miners being clubbed or shot.'

Solomon nodded.

'Withholding labour is the real strength of the native miners. As Mister Jones has already said and one of the other speakers too, strike action is your greatest weapon but you need be mindful of the reaction. Better to lobby those in power, state your case with some eloquence so that they cannot deny your arguments. If you are a reporter like you say then you must write about the injustices, bring them to the attention of the wider population and only then will we see real change.'

Solomon listened intently, beginning to understand the Reverend's point of view, his argument becoming clear. He understood why nobody was interested in talking with Reverend Phillips; Jones was offering a quick solution to the problems, a better way of life, better living, and better working conditions – but at a price. Militancy could well achieve those aims but it could bring with it violence and danger to innocent people. The path encouraged by the Reverend Phillips could take a generation to achieve its aims but the benefits would be far-reaching and more permanent. The black miners must achieve change politically, not by an uprising that would cause many African deaths and might lead to a far worse situation than the one existing. He considered the paradox. How could they achieve anything politically without the right to vote? The answer seemed beyond him. His job was to write about what he witnessed, report and inform people, but he realised that he could contribute through the newspaper and he would start tonight.

Chapter 13

The newspaper proclaimed victory for the South African party, Hertzog and the Nationalists had failed to win the General Election, Norman felt a mild relief, and for a moment longer, he studied the front page. If the Nationalists had won, it was a consensus of his British friends that the party would instigate dramatic changes, fitting them all into a Boer straitjacket and the article he had just read seemed to bear out that point of view.

At the opposite side of the table, Lucy spread some jam onto a piece of toast and gave it to Henry. The little boy swung his short legs back and forth, humming an unintelligible tune and normally these antics would be an annoyance to his father but today was different. The 1920 election results were in and Norman was too engrossed in his newspaper to notice Henry. Peggy, on the other hand, quietly munched on her toast and peered over her father's arm. She was six years old and able to read a little but the newspaper text was too difficult for her, so instead, she looked at the pictures and recognised simple words from the headlines.

'How many seats did Smuts win?' asked Lucy.

'Forty-two.'

'How many seats did Hertzog win?'

'Forty-four.'

'Does that mean the Nationalists will form the next Government?'

Norman looked up from his paper; he had never known her show interest in politics before.

'No, the Unionists and Independents will sit with the South African party giving them 70 seats against Hertzog's 44. The Labour party hold the balance of power with 21 seats. Labour will not go against Smuts because of their pro-British standpoint. We will not have Afrikaners running the country thank God. Who wants Boers in charge? They don't like the British.' He turned the page over and Peggy leant over him, following the picture of general Smuts as it disappeared.

'Daddy, will you have whiskers on your chin like that when you're old?' she said.

'I might grow some today sweetheart, if you want me to,' said Norman, smiling down at his pretty daughter. She smiled back at him, a puzzled look in her eyes.

Norman's thoughts moved on from the election to the evening when he was to meet Arthur at the Silver Star for a drink and a game of cards. The conversation would eventually turn to Transgold and the Company's shares, the main point of their meeting. He had felt for some time that the money he received did not match the effort he put in and that it was time to confront Arthur. But Arthur held all the aces it was he alone who dealt with the shares, received all the payments and Norman felt at a distinct disadvantage.

Drumming his fingers on the table, he wondered what he might say when they met and then he glanced at his watch, eight thirty; he must be on his way. Folding the paper, he slipped it into his jacket pocket, took one last drink of tea and made his way downstairs to the office where Mabutu was sweeping dust and windblown debris away from the doorway.

'Mabutu, give my car a wash when you finish will you, I am travelling out to Benoni today and I would like it to look its best.'

'Yaas Bass,' said Mabutu picking up his bucket and making his way to the water tub in the yard while Norman entered the office and went towards his desk. A minute later Brian Alders walked into the office.

'Good morning Brian. How is the share dealing doing? I haven't had time to talk to you recently,' Norman asked, fishing for information.

Brian's face took on a self-satisfied look. 'I must say that things are looking extremely buoyant at the moment. Gold has risen to an all-time high, even the lowest quality mines can make a profit and shares in gold mines are doing particularly well.'

'Good, good,' said Norman, a little miffed at Brian's self-confidence. If mining stocks were in such demand then where was his cut from Transgold? 'I shall be out of the office all day today. I am meeting a client in Benoni and it is quite a drive. If there are messages for me just make notes and leave them on my desk will you. I don't expect to be back before six o'clock this evening and I suppose that you and Jeremy will have gone home by then? And, when he does eventually turn up, give him these papers to type. Right, I'm off then, I'll see you tomorrow. Good morning.'

The road to Benoni was dustier than usual and Norman thought what a waste of time it had been getting Mabutu to clean the car. Two hours later the Buick came to a halt outside an impressive looking bungalow. The owner was a director of the Dunswart Deep mine a man who had arrived in South Africa just as the Witwatersrand began its rapid growth and now he was about to retire, sell his house and return to Britain. The day was difficult for Norman having to listen politely as the man relate his life's story. He had built up a small fortune and was looking forward to spending his retirement back in Great Britain leaving Norman feeling a little gloomy. As he drove back to the city he turned over the problem of the payments from Arthur and wondered if he was ever going to make his own fortune.

Later that evening, still smarting from his humbling experience with his rich client, he stood at the kitchen sink shaving. His face was lathered and he was about to pick up his razor when the door to the kitchen slowly opened and in peeked an inquisitive face. Peggy stood watching her father beside the sink dressed in a vest and trousers, shaving foam covering his face, her bright eyes opened wide as she began to giggle, her infectious laugh filling the room.

'What's so funny sweetheart?' he asked.

'You said you would grow whiskers like the man in the picture, and you have,' she said turning away and running off to the living room, shouting out to her mother, 'Daddy's got whiskers! Daddy's got whiskers!'

Norman smiled to himself as he looked in the mirror and carefully ran the cutthroat razor across his cheek. She will have a surprise when I kiss her goodnight, he thought as the white beard disappeared and he wiped his face clean. He left the kitchen and went into the bedroom to dress, slipped on his jacket and took his newly acquired service revolver from a drawer to stuff into his waistband. Alessandro had advised him to get hold of it because he had seen many things from behind his bar, arguments, fights and the occasional stabbing and told him he ought to have at least some form of protection at night.

Walking towards the Silver Star, he began to think about Arthur, a man who had spent most of his life swindling other people out of their money and felt he was becoming his latest victim. On the drive back from Benoni, he had resolved to confront Arthur head on but as he neared the bar, he began to have second thoughts. Although he was bigger and stronger than Arthur but the smaller man had an inherent ability to dominate, to control. He was difficult to beat in an argument and for the first time Norman realised he did not like Arthur very much.

He turned the corner onto Marshal Street and the Silver Star, the sound of conversation and clinking glasses drawing him in. The interior was dim, smoke-filled, and it took several seconds for his eyes to adjust. It was full of the usual complement, several card games taking place and at the far side of the room, two black labourers waited patiently for their jug of cheap beer. Through the smoky haze, he saw Arthur sitting on the edge of a table weighing up the players of a card school; he looked up and signalled that he wanted a drink.

Norman nodded and went to the bar, irritated that Arthur was already exerting some control and tonight he decided that he would try a different approach.

'Here's your drink,' he said handing over the glass.

'Your good health, come and watch this,' said Arthur pointing to the card school in operation at the nearby table.

218

There were four players, each smoking and drinking and in the centre of the table was a pile of banknotes, the ante. The dealer began to deal, flicking the cards to the players and when he had finished, each player pulled his cards towards him, studying them with a expressionless face.

Through the haze of tobacco smoke, Norman detected some tension on the dealer's face; he was looking miserably at his cards, his stake lying on the table, far smaller than that of the other the players. The betting began, the man's colour appeared to drain away as he matched the stake of each of the other players and then two of them withdrew, leaving only himself and one other in the game. With an unsteady hand, the man bet everything he had left and, as the cards turned, it became apparent that he had lost. His body sagged visibly, he was broke and it was time to go. Pushing back his chair, he reached down to the wooden floor to retrieve his hat and without a word made his way unsteadily towards the doorway.

'Mind if I join in, gentlemen?' asked Arthur.

The winner of the last game, a burly Afrikaner with the stubby end of a fat Havana cigar clenched between his teeth turned his head.

'Help yourself, my friend, what's your name? I am Frank, this is Joe and Ed Bird – Dickey to his friends,' he said, introducing the remaining players.

The man called Joe smiled a welcome whilst the other simply nodded and watched Arthur, a deadpan expression on his face. Frank slid cards across the table to the one called Joe and Arthur pulled up the vacant ladder-back chair before producing a bundle of banknotes from his jacket pocket.

Norman moved closer to the action, watching with interest as Joe expertly dealt the cards. Just how good was the player he wondered? He considered himself a decent player who could normally hold his own but this man made the cards skim across the table like wildfire. He won the next two games and surprisingly, picked up his money.

'Gentlemen, I hope you will excuse me. I have work to do tomorrow and it will not do to stay any later.'

The big Afrikaner, Frank, grunted and looked less than pleased.

'You could stay a little longer; give us chance to win some of our money back.'

'Maybe tomorrow, you have won plenty from me in the past Frank, tonight I am taking my money home, goodnight.'

Norman smiled to himself, glad that such a good player was leaving the table and made a gesture towards the empty seat, asking if he could join the game. Frank looked at the unsmiling Dickey, back at Norman and nodded a tacit invitation to join them. It soon became evident that these two men were also competent card players and Norman realised that he needed to be at the top of his game if he were not to lose his money.

The first two games went to the unsmiling Dickey, one game through simple bluff and the other with a very good hand and Norman managed to lose a quarter of his stake. Opposite Arthur played a cautious game, folding before the betting started, not wanting to risk his stake. The third game was better and after several more rounds, Norman found himself in a winning position. He was beginning to enjoy himself and for the moment, all thoughts of the Transgold Mining Company and a confrontation with Arthur banished to the back of his mind.

Then something changed, Arthur's caution faded, he bluffed, played his hand with more confidence than it deserved and won with only a pair of fives. It left the players all square and they agreed to up the ante. Within half-an-hour Norman found that his stake had reduced once more, a quick tally showed he had lost almost £5 and he guessed by the grim expression on Arthur's face that he was also down; but the big Afrikaner's stake had grown considerably.

Arthur dealt the next round, his eyes flitting from one opponent to the other as he tried to gauge their moods. His style of play served him well against drunken miners but not necessarily against competent players, and these people were competent. Norman cast glances at both Frank and Dickey beginning to wonder if they were playing together; it was not unknown for two players to work in consort, to signal one another secretly to relieve other players of their money. Well, if they were cheating he could not see it, but they were winning too easily. Something must have happened – marked cards or perhaps some covert signal was passing between them.

He watched more closely as Frank picked his cards face up from the table and placed them in sequence face down on the pack before dealing the next hand. Could that be it, perhaps he was remembering the sequence as the cards returned to the pack. Shuffling took place only after three of a kind, a prile had been dealt and if he had been memorising the sequence then he might be able to predict with some accuracy how the cards would re-emerge later in the game. The buggers, he would have to watch them carefully.

He lifted his cards from the table: five, six, seven, and all clubs – not a bad hand. Then, holding his cards higher than normal, using them as a partial shield, he glanced at each of the other players in turn. His eyes met those of Arthur who winked and turned his cards imperceptibly towards himself and Norman realised that Arthur had come to a similar conclusion, a marked deck. He raised his head a little in unspoken agreement: they *were* a pair of cheats, but what else should he expect? Perhaps Joe was better than a good player; perhaps he had seen their ploy and decided to leave with his winnings intact.

Unsurprisingly Frank won the next few hands and then it was Arthur's turn to deal and talking about nothing in particular he began deal, drawing the other men's attention and Norman was able to lift his cards unnoticed from the table and shield them from prying eyes. Frank Van Seters glanced sideways at Norman's hand but he was too late and began to study his own hand. With a grunt of annoyance he placed a maximum bet of £2 at the centre of the table, Arthur matched it, Dickey folded. Norman matched the bet, after all, this was his best hand of the evening so far and he knew he was in with a good chance of winning. Frank placed £2 more on the pile and Arthur followed. Norman hesitated for a second; just long enough to fool Frank into believing that his hand was not so good before placing another £2 squarely on the growing pile of notes and coins. Arthur was next, but instead of following the betting, he folded, leaving only Frank to match the bet when his turn came. Frank's eyes narrowed and he placed another £2 on the pile at the centre of the table. Norman decided he would see the round out, matching

Frank's £2 with his own, then it seemed Frank felt it was time to take the money. He tossed four more notes into the pot and asked to see Norman's cards. Relieved that he did not have to risk more, Norman began to lay out his cards on the table, first the five of clubs then the six and finally, with his heart thumping in his chest, the seven of clubs.

Arthur watched, eyes deadpan and emotionless as the Afrikaner laid out his own cards in a fan – the five, six, and seven of hearts, exactly the same value as Norman's – but, because he had asked to see Norman's hand, he had lost and Norman's heart thumped with joy. With both hands, he scooped his winnings towards him and for once, some emotion appeared on Frank's face, his eyes narrowing and his top lip curling imperceptibly but Norman did not notice, too busy straightening the crumpled banknotes and placing them in a neat pile in front of him. He felt a slap on his back and a voice from the shadows said, 'Well done, Norman.' The entertainment had attracted a small group of drinkers who were congregating around the table to watch.

The next game was Arthur's and then Frank returned to his winning ways. His confidence returned and he took out one of his cigars, his dark eyes scrutinising Norman leaving him with a feeling of uneasiness. It was Norman's deal and as he reached over to collect the cards Arthur clumsily knocked over his drink.

'Oh damn it that was a full glass. Hey Alessandro have you got a cloth?' he called out across the room and for a moment or two all eyes turned towards the bar and in those few seconds Norman dared to push the cards together in as random a fashion as he could. He had broken the sequence.

'Pressure getting to you, is it Arthur?' said Norman, in a matter-of-fact voice.

'Don't be stupid, I just didn't see it.'

Norman began to deal the cards watched closely by Frank and he guessed by the Afrikaner's air of confidence that he still believed he knew the card sequence. Frank was so confident that he elected to go blind, not looking at his cards, forcing everyone betting against him to pay double.

One by one, Norman lifted his cards from the table, first the jack of hearts, then the king of diamonds. His heart rate picked up, he turned the third card towards him, the queen of hearts, a royal straight, a good hand, a very good hand. Frank might have noticed the confidence in his face and spoilt things had he not been so convinced that he himself had the winning hand. Calming his nerves, Norman tossed his pound into the ante and waited for the others to start the betting.

Arthur decided to play along for a while with his pair of twos, perhaps he could encourage Frank to become reckless betting more than he should. He put a pound in the ante and bet a further pound, Dickey Bird followed without hesitation, and then it was Norman's turn. He matched the bet and sat back trying to appear relaxed, wait and see what Frank's reaction might be. The Afrikaner expected to win easily and matched the bet, forcing the others to pay double against his unseen hand. Arthur looked pensive for a moment, folded his cards and sat back in his chair with an air of resignation and Frank's lip curled in a minor triumph. Dickey looking puzzled, Frank had given him the signal that it was time to clean up but Arthur had folded earlier than expected and his own hand was nothing special – a pair of kings.

Frank said, 'I raise another pound to £2,' adding his wager to the growing pile. Dickey knew he would have to double his bet to £4 but he was feeling uneasy; something was wrong. Why had Arthur folded so early and why did he have only a pair when he expected better? Norman saw Dickey's confusion and knew then that he had spiked their guns. He put £4 in the kitty and waited for Frank's reaction, noticing how he seemed unaware of Dickey's confusion but Arthur was out of the game and now Dickey lost his nerve. Folding his cards he left only Norman in the game and Frank suddenly realised he was on his own. His face clouded over, Dickey should have been the only one left in by now and it should have been a simple formality to scoop the pot. He stared at his cards, still face down and then at Norman who was placing his bet and knew that he must go on or risk losing by default.

'I see you,' he said pushing more money onto the pile.

All around the table the onlookers fell silent in anticipation and Norman began to lay out his cards. The big man took a drag from his half-smoked cigar and slowly began to turn his cards, raising the tension. First, he revealed the ace of spades, and then the queen of spades. The next card would be the king of spades and he would have a royal straight flush and take a pot standing at over £30. The silence became overpowering as he turned the final card, revealing . . . the eight of clubs.

Time seemed to stand still for Frank as he stared incredulously at his hand, ace high, not the royal flush he had expected. Norman looked across at Arthur and then at the pile of money at the centre of the table. Perhaps now was a good time to leave.

'You're not going anywhere just yet, mister,' said Frank reading his mind. 'We want a chance to get our money back.'

'We,' thought Norman. So they were working together and he had spoilt their little party. He glanced again at Arthur for guidance, receiving only a fixed and noncommittal stare in return, a sure sign that Arthur was not happy. Perhaps it would be prudent to go along with the Afrikaner for the time being.

'All right,' he heard himself saying, 'I will play one more game, then I will go – win or lose.'

'Win or lose,' chortled the big man. 'My deal and we will see. One more game, one more game,' he repeated.

As he began to deal, each player put his pound in the ante and picked up his cards, no one was risking going blind this time.

Norman turned his cards towards him and froze; his hand consisted of a three of clubs, a three of diamonds, and a three of spades, the best possible hand in brag. It was a winning hand no question and to give anything away now was to risk losing a great chance to win more. It depended very much on what his opponents were holding; a low hand and they might fold early, but with decent hands, the betting could be heavy, but whatever happened, he would win.

The betting started with Norman who tossed a pound note into the centre of the table, not daring to go with more. It proved a wise move and for two more rounds, each player matched the bet until Frank's impatience got the better of him and he raised the stake to £2. Arthur matched him, as did Dickey and then Norman for a further two rounds until Dickey lost confidence and folded his hand; Arthur followed leaving only Norman and Frank once more in the game. Frank leaned back and lit another cigar, blowing his customary cloud towards the ceiling and glowered at Norman. The crowd of onlookers grew larger as word spread that they were playing for the biggest pot the Silver Star had seen in months and the tension in the room increased.

Frank placed £2 onto the pile of money, Norman matched it and so it went on for a further three rounds, neither man conceding. Norman felt the sweat running down his forehead and wiped it away nervously with the sleeve of his shirt. Frank watched him and guessed, wrongly, that he was playing a bluffing game.

Norman realised he had a dilemma, if he ran out of money he would be unable to match Frank's bet and would surely lose. He needed to see his opponent's cards before he reached that point.

'I will see you,' he said, placing the last of his money onto the pile of notes. A look of triumph spread across Frank's face, having no doubt that Norman was bluffing. In triumph, he laid his cards on the table, three aces, and reached out to scoop the pot and one or two of the Afrikaners in the crowd began to cheer seeing one of their own as the winner.

'Hold on just a moment,' intervened Arthur, 'we haven't seen Norman's hand yet.'

Frank looked Norman straight in his eyes and sneered saying, 'all right then Scotty, like the man said, show us your hand.'

Nervously Norman began to place his cards one by one face up on the table. The pot was big all right, he knew for sure that he had won a substantial amount of money and subconsciously thanked God for the crowd of onlookers. If Frank decided to cut up rough then he would think twice with so many witnesses and as the cards turned, Frank's jaw dropped and his face turned crimson, defeat sank sink in and his cigar fell from his mouth. He looked stunned as he pushed his chair back, staring in disbelief at the pile of banknotes that should have been his.

Averting the watching eyes, he stood up and stuck his cigar back in his mouth before walking across the room, pushing violently through the crowd towards the bar. In a dry and bewildered voice, he ordered a whisky and Alessandro, sensing trouble, poured him a large one. The big Afrikaner lifted the glass and downed the fiery drink in one great gulp, turned away from the bar and pushed his way back through the crowd to disappear into the blackness of the night.

Elated by his success, Norman scooped his winnings and looked at Arthur watching from the other side of the table. He had a broad grin on his face and seemed unconcerned that a portion of Norman's winnings had once belonged to him. They were enjoying the moment and neither noticed Dickey leave to follow Frank.

'You have done well Norman, congratulations.'

Norman stuffed the banknotes into his pocket and it was then he realised that Arthur's smile was not as friendly as it had at first appeared; his eyes were cold and hard and Norman felt intimidated, not understanding.

'Yes, a bit of luck came my way for a change.' He looked straight at Arthur and fuelled with alcohol and confidence from his win said at last. 'Transgold shares have sold well I understand?'

Arthur pursed his lips and held Norman's gaze, remaining silent and then Norman understood Arthur's recalcitrance.

'I said the shares in Transgold are selling, we should be due some more money. What is happening to the money Arthur?'

'Yes we have sold a few it is true, but the money doesn't arrive for months. Don't worry, you will get your share. Talking of money, you have won a decent amount tonight.' He leaned forward and lowered his voice. 'I think I am due a drink to replace the one I knocked over, don't you.'

Norman nodded, placated to a small degree yet realising Arthur had outfoxed him yet again and he was not prepared to escalate the situation. Winning the money from the card game would have to satisfy him for the time being.

'Well Norman, the gods were with you tonight,' said Arthur raising his arm to signal Alessandro to fetch two more whiskies. 'Looks like you can keep it for the time being, Frank doesn't seem to want to try and win back his losses. He must have run out of money and I guess we spoilt his little game, the cheating bastard.'

That was rich, thought Norman; Arthur was one of the biggest cheats and swindlers he had ever met. Then, as the flush of success at cards receded, his mind returned to the pressing problem of how to get his hands on the money from the mine swindle.

'Your good health,' said Arthur lifting his glass in a toast.

'Cheers!' said Norman, plucking up courage to tackle Arthur again. 'Arthur, tell me . . . what's happening with the mine?'

Arthur's eyes narrowed. 'Not here my friend, we can't talk here.'

'And what's happened to Hans? I haven't seen him for quite a while.'

'Looking for a farm, he has decided to go back to farming, reckons he has had enough of the nomadic life and I am expecting him back in town any day now.'

Arthur had managed to cut Norman off without a proper answer and then he moved from the table, breaking their connection further. Arthur knew that one day Norman's patience would run out, but he was not the man in control, the money from America went straight into a bank account in Cape Town leaving him just enough to run the operation, pay both Hans and Norman and leave some over as his reward, a reward he was less than satisfied with. He was being blackmailed and if he did not play ball, the police would become involved and that could mean years in prison. Arthur was not a young man anymore and, like Hans, he had had enough of the nomadic life, grown soft in his hotel room, sleeping in a warm bed and without the worry of where the next meal was coming from. As long as he could keep the swindle going, he would have a roof over his head, but like Norman, he wanted more than that.

'Are you playing some more Norman? Arthur asked, trying to distance himself from the immediate topic of conversation. 'There's a school over there with a spare place.'

'I have had enough excitement for one night. It's late and I should really be heading home'.

'Then you won't mind if I join those boys. A word of advice: be careful on your way home tonight, I have heard of Frank Van Seters before, a vindictive and violent man. He just might be hanging around waiting for you.'

Norman nodded his mind still on the situation at Transgold, the quantity of whisky he had consumed leaving him less alert than perhaps he should be. He left the warm, smoky confines bar to walk home along Joubert Street where there were still one or two people heading home. He reached the junction with Marshal Street and decided that tonight he would turn into Eloff Street to avoid a stretch of open ground. It was dark, the night air cool and he realised being alone with such a large amount of money in his pocket was a dangerous proposition. Coming to his senses, he heeded Arthur's warning, pausing for a moment to take stock of his surroundings, fumbling in his pocket for his cigarette case and box of matches.

'Say mate, can you give me a light?' said a voice from a darkened doorway. Taken off guard, Norman turned and held out the matchbox, offering it to the stranger and then an insight, a sixth sense, warned him. In a flash he saw himself back on a deserted street in Cape Town and the figure in the shadows striking a match.

It was that warning that saved him. Without thinking, he sidestepped away from the voice and avoided the full force of the heavy blow that landed on his shoulder. It missed the back of his head by a fraction and forced him to stumble forwards. From the shadows came a second blow aimed at the side of his head but his forward momentum had put him out of reach and he turned to face his attacker. A street light illuminated a face, Dickey Bird and in some shock he realised that the other man must be Frank Van Seters and panic overtook him. With his emotions running high and without thinking, he lashed out wildly catching Dickey full in the face and sending him reeling. From the doorway, Frank Van Seters joined in the fracas, moving forward to grab the lapel of Norman's jacket with a solid grip. He managed to hold Frank off with one hand, grasping wildly for his gun with the other and struggling, squealing like a cornered pig he managed to grip hold of the gun. With a single movement, he pulled it from his waistband and fired at point blank range. Frank screamed and let go of him, stumbling backwards clutching his shoulder before falling to the ground. Norman felt physically sick as they disengaged; believing he had killed the man, but short-barrelled revolvers were notoriously inaccurate and the bullet had just grazed Frank's shoulder.

'A bluty gun, he has a bluty gun!' shouted Frank recovering and reaching out to grip Norman's trouser leg. Yes, it was Frank all right and still very much alive, still a frightening proposition and with energy draining away, Norman managed to twist away from the Afrikaner. Thank goodness for the gun, he thought as he dodged into a darkened alley and his self-control returned. He began to run, stumbling along in the darkness of the confined space until he reached the corner and stop. With his chest heaving, he managed to peer into the next street, straining his eyes, motionless in the shadows and then he became aware of pain in his shoulder and across his forehead. Touching his temple he felt blood from an open wound and his legs felt weak, he found it difficult to walk but he had to keep going. If his assailants came returned he did not believe he could escape so easily a second time.

Slowly, quietly, he emerged from the passageway, glanced both ways along the street and then he saw a man about a hundred yards away on the opposite side heading in his general direction. He took a few paces forward and then recoiled in shock as Frank Van Seters appeared from nowhere blocking his path.

'Well Scotty, I have you now. You might have a gun, but I have this. He turned his right wrist over exposing a six-inch hunting knife. 'Give me back my money and I won't be hurting you too much. If you do not play the game, Scotty, then this is it for you. I slash you,' he said in a calm and chilling voice.

Norman's mouth was too dry with fear for him to answer, but he pulled out his gun once more and faced the fat Afrikaner with trembling hand. Then he managed to croak, 'Bugger off you bastard – or I shoot.' But, he had forgotten Dickey.

From the shadows, a short sharp blow from some metallic object spun the gun from his grasp, his knees gave way and he stumbled to the ground. He was defenceless and kneeling before the victors, he hung his head in defeat and began to pull banknotes from his pocket – then suddenly the world exploded above him.

Solomon was returning from a meeting of the Communist Party, turning over in his mind some of the rhetoric he had heard. The speaker had denounced the mine owners, called for armed revolt against the unfair tactics of using strikebreakers and here, not more than a few yards away, were two bullying white men. It was more than he could take and dropping his bag, he stepped towards Frank Van Seters and gave him a short sharp punch to his stomach, sending him crashing to the floor for a second time and then Dickey appeared armed with an iron bar. Solomon was on the attack and at that moment nothing could stop him, he swung his arm and caught Dickey full on the chest, sending him staggering backwards but he quickly recovered and, mouthing obscenities, stepped forward with a knife in his hand but the sight of such a large and powerful looking man forced him to reconsider his actions. For a split second, each eyed the other until Dickey realised his mistake and turned on his heels to disappear into the darkness, leaving Frank to his fate.

Solomon did not dwell, his experiences in the mine told him to leave well alone. He looked down at the big Afrikaner's contorted face and then at his victim who was recovering from his ordeal. He retrieved his bag, neither white man speaking and there was little in the way of thanks from Norman. He looked each of them in the eye for a split second before he melted away into the darkness, his opinion of white men re-enforced.

Chapter 14

Solomon threaded a sheet of paper into his battered typewriter, and closed his eyes for a moment to gather his thoughts. The situation on the Witwatersrand was beginning to spiral out of control, he had witnessed the mobilisation of the strikers, listened to speakers at the mass meetings and he worried about his people. The first of his articles had not been of great interest to the readership; well written but too complicated advised Alfred, perhaps he had been running before he could walk said Walter. After an hour of discussion the three of them were of one mind, perhaps Solomon's next article should lay some sort of foundation, explain the reasons for the unrest, bring the concerns of their readership to the fore.

'How about a bit of history, let everyone know the recent history of the mining industry and perhaps then people will understand better what is happening today and why,' Walter had said.

Solomon listened, thought about their advice, perhaps Walter was right and he should write about the background history of the mining industry. Most of the native labourers he knew had little or no idea about it, more interested in trying to make a living, but if trouble did erupt, then the native workforce would become involved in some shape or form and the more informed they were, the better their chances of riding the storm.

In only 30 years, Johannesburg had grown up from a rough mining camp to one of the greatest cities in Africa. It boasted some of the best buildings and shops had a fine racecourse, well-maintained parks and the largest concentration of millionaires on the continent. Most of these men had grown rich from the toil of tens of thousands of labourers clawing the gold-bearing rock from the bowels of the earth. Native miners endured abysmal conditions, low wages, long days and many had given up their lives to make these white men rich. They lived in compounds patrolled by armed guards and were separated from their families for months on end, a harsh and cruel existence as Solomon well knew.

The white miners, on the other hand, had strong craft and trades unions to state their case and he had already seen white miners discontented with their lot. The price of gold had begun to drop from its highpoint, the agreements made between the mine owners and the workers at the end of the war were becoming increasingly untenable. Management and workers had agreed to put on hold their differences during the fighting but a shortage of skills had materialised and in the absence of whites, blacks and coloureds had filled the semi-skilled jobs. Compounding the problem were the thousands of Afrikaner men unable to make a living from the land and forced to seek work in the mines. Unrest in the goldfields during 1917 had led to a period of protracted negotiation and the creation of the Status Quo Agreement. The employers had agreed to freeze the labour mix to help prevent whites losing additional jobs to the black and coloured workforce. There would be no more displacement of workers, effectively drawing a line in the sand but with the price of gold starting to fall, the economics favoured employing more black workers, the majority of his readers, and he was concerned for the future.

Not very far away, Norman sat at his own desk sipping a cup of coffee and reading *The Star*, its front page full of mining industry woes. The stock exchange in the city was witnessing a vacillating market as the spectre of a vanishing gold premium created uncertainty. Should Great Britain return to the gold standard, the price of gold would revert to its pre-war level and if it did, then many of the low-grade mines would go out of business, and investors would lose their money. However, Norman was not reading any of it, simply staring at the page, concerned that the real estate business was stagnating and his profits were fast disappearing, but more than that, after finding it almost impossible to get a suitable answer from Arthur he had finally pinned him down. The previous day he had managed a confrontation of sorts and for once Arthur was not evasive, curiously forthcoming, and he had told Norman a few truths that had shocked him to the core.

'What, shutting up shop, closing the whole thing down, why?' he had pleaded.

'The shares are no longer selling; overheads are just too much. I am afraid you will have to be satisfied with what you have had out of it so far. There will be no more money from America because the Americans were the main buyers of stock and they have stopped buying. Look I know this must come as a shock to you but it isn't me that controls things, it's out of my hands.'

237

'What do you mean you don't control things?

'I did not have the money to set this thing up but I knew someone who could.'

'Who?

Arthur looked at Norman, pausing long enough for him to realise that he was not going to tell him. 'Me and Hans are leaving Joburg and going up into the Transvaal to look for silver. Maybe we can work it again with a silver mine, if we do, then I will let you know and you can be the front man again.'

The news had stunned Norman and left him speechless but what could he do, he had no control over anything. Arthur organized the selling of the shares and he collected the money. His job was to convince prospective investors of the merits of the enterprise and now it seemed Arthur had decided that it was time to get out. He had expected to make a small fortune but instead he had received not much more than a couple of thousand pounds. it was a decent amount that would have taken several years to earn but it fell far short of expectations. At least he had managed to keep his activities secret from Lucy, if she ever did find out she would be incensed; he had risked jail and the family's security.

'Mind if I sit down?' asked Brian, disturbing his thoughts.

'Take a seat and help yourself to some coffee. Not much point in looking busy today is there. What have you got on your books, Brian?'

'No, that's what I want to talk about. Share prices are falling, there is very little buying activity, and I believe that the only way now is down. If you ask me, there could even be a depression.'

'Depression!' Norman put down his paper and Brian casually lifted the coffee pot from the stove to fill his cup. It was a reflection of the times, a lack of money, growing unrest and Norman felt as if events were conspiring against him personally. He had some capital to ride out any storm, far less than he had hoped, it might last them a year or two if they were careful, but without a job, his options would be limited and the prospect appalled him. The success he craved seemed to be drifting away.

'So what do you propose to do to get us out of this mess?' asked Norman with a touch of sarcasm in his voice.

'Nothing,' replied Brian, 'At least, not for Johannesburg, I have a solution for myself though.'

'And what's that?'

'Well, I've come to give you this,' he said, producing an envelope from his pocket. 'I'm giving you the required one month's notice that I want to quit.'

After a few moments' shocked silence Norman said, 'Well, this is a surprise. Have you found a better job then? If you have, then you deserve my admiration.'

'No, I haven't, and I don't see any prospects here in South Africa. So – I have decided to give you a month's notice and then spend a few weeks travelling around the Cape before returning home to England. I think job prospects might be better back home so I am going there.'

'Well, I wish you luck, then. I wish I could up sticks and push off as easily. I have my family to consider and it's not easy to move, even to the next street never mind back home,' said a pretty fed up Norman.

After a cursory shaking of hands, Brian returned to his desk and Norman to his thoughts. He gazed aimlessly through the window at the black clouds of a gathering storm and in his mind's eye; he saw Arthur's face grinning at him. It seemed that everyone else was getting their share of the spoils and he was not.

Unlike Norman, Hans had little trouble in confronting Arthur and had done so late on the same evening Frank van Seters had attacked Norman. He had come across Arthur leaning nonchalantly against the bar of the Silver Star. Arthur had laughed when questioned about the money, inviting him for a drink, saying he would tell everything over a few whiskeys and he had.

Hans had listened patiently to the story unfolding, learning to his surprise that an influential man was the power behind it all, someone aware of Arthur's dubious activities, someone who had blackmailed him into running the fraud.

'It was never my money used to set up this scam; you know as well as anyone I've never had that kind of money. He bankrolled everything and he has taken most of the profits.'

It all fell into place, Norman's involvement was also clear; he was certainly a good front man and having the use of an automobile was a masterstroke that fooled the Americans, into believing that Transgold had some substance.

'This man in Cape Town, he must have worried you, having something on you like that. I guess that's why you did what he wanted?'

Arthur laughed, 'He can't prove anything. There is circumstantial evidence – I will concede that, but he won't do anything, not now. I have kept a record of everything so if he tries to pin anything on me he will soon realise that I have enough evidence to drag him down with me and he has a lot farther to fall than I have. Anyway my friend, we've lived like kings for the last eighteen months and we have made some money – haven't we?'

'How much have you made?' asked Hans, looking Arthur straight in the eye. They knew each other too well.

'A little bit more than you, but come on, enough of your questions. Let me buy you another drink.'

It was gone midnight before Hans finally left the Silver Star, expectations lowered and the dream of owning a farm still only a dream.

It was a good half mile to the stables he called home and in the peace and quiet of the night, he reflected on changed circumstances. Then it occurred to him that with Farm prices actually dropping because so many Boers were leaving the land, maybe he could manage to buy a small farm after all, two thousand pounds was a lot of money to some. If he could only find something, at least he would be amongst his own people and maybe live the settled existence that had eluded him for so long. Then there was the prospect of travelling back to his Boer homelands to the north if Arthur's idea of a silver mine became reality. It was half a lifetime since he had, breathed the clear air of the Transvaal. He had known his happiest times there, growing up with his brothers and then he thought of Uti and Hans Junior. Their memory was still painful but at least he was coming to terms with his loss and for the first time in a long time, he felt he had a future.

A week later, his spat with Arthur forgotten and ninety miles to the north of Johannesburg, Hans rode alongside his delinquent friend. Rumours of silver discoveries had drawn them high into the Transvaal after two days in Pretoria, drinking and mixing with miners. They had learned of the location of a silver discovery and were following the dusty trail north to the Rhodesian border. Stopping at mining camps along the way, their disappointment increased at each one. The pickings were paltry, the mines primitive and unproductive and the miners as poor as any they had ever come across. Affairs had come to a head when they stayed over at the Shimwell silver mine and joined in a game of cards. For the first time in years they could not win anything, no one seemed to have much money so the stakes were low and they dare not cheat amongst such tough men. They were never going to get rich here and so for most of that morning they had ridden in silence until Arthur finally spoke.

'Doesn't look good, does it? This place is certainly not another Witwatersrand. What d'you reckon old friend?'

Hans sighed, bit on his bottom lip in sombre mood, and looked across at Arthur sitting awkwardly on his horse and then he broke into a smile. He reached up and tipped his hat back on his head thinking that the East End of London had not really prepared Arthur for the wilds of South Africa; anyone could tell he had not grown up with horses. He looked again and his smile faded, he noticed for the first time how old Arthur was looking. At around 50 years of age his friend looked tired and haggard and at ten years younger, he felt that he was passing his prime and then it struck him that if he was going to get that farm, it had to be now. Suddenly the future flashed up before his eyes and he knew what he had to do.

'I'm going back to Joburg right now. I will go and see Norman and get him to find me a farm that I can afford and if I can't afford it then I'm going to borrow some money from the bank so I damn well can.'

Arthur looked at Hans in astonishment and began to laugh aloud. 'You! Borrow money from a bank? My, how the world has changed! Not so long ago you would only have considered stealing from a bank. Ha, ha! Come on, let's go, I've had enough of this bastard country. Joburg here we come.'

They wheeled their horses round and headed south, their spirits rising by the minute.

'What will you do Arthur?' asked Hans.

'Me? Well, I have a nest egg stashed away and I guess it is time I thought about retirement. A room in a cheap hotel drink myself to death and enjoy doing it.'

The horse's ears twitched at the sound of the two men laughing and by the vigorous swishing of their tails, they seemed glad to be heading home too.

At precisely the same moment, eight thousand miles away in an office on the twenty-first floor of the Park Row building overlooking Broadway, New York City, Lewis Rosenberg was sitting behind his walnut desk. In his hand, he held a gold-nib Schaeffer fountain pen poised and ready and when he had finished reading the document he pushed his horn-rimmed spectacles a little further along the bridge of his nose. Sniffing, as he always did before signing anything to do with money, he scribbled his signature and sat back in his chair. Looking out of the window across Wall Street he mentally totalled up the profit from the deal and then his concentration dissolved as the new-fangled loudspeaker at the edge of his desk crackled into life.

'Mr Rosenberg, your two o'clock appointment is here. Shall I show him in?'

'Yes,' he replied, but there was silence. 'Damn thing,' he muttered and then he remembered to throw the switch to transmit. 'Yes, er, show him in,' he said. 'Damn thing,' he muttered for a second time.

The door opened and his secretary of 20 years ushered in a tall well-built man of late middle age his features partially obscured by a great bushy moustache that hung like a yard brush beneath his strong hooked nose and steely blue eyes.

'Good afternoon, Mr Sheraton,' said Rosenberg, 'please take a seat.'

'Call me Tom, sir. Pleased to make your acquaintance. What can I do for you?' He said in a strong southern drawl.

'You've had a long journey up from Texas Tom. I hope it wasn't too much for you so soon after retiring?'

'Naw, I've spent most of my life travelling this country. It's easy by train, a lot easier than when I used to travel most places on horseback. Now let's git to it: why am I here?'

'Tom, you've been recommended to me by a good friend of mine, the Governor of Texas.' Tom's eyebrow lifted almost imperceptibly. The Governor of Texas, he was impressed. 'You are one of the best US Marshals to come out of Texas and you have all the credentials I require for a little job I need doing. As you probably already know, I am a stockbroker and I run a very successful business – some of my clients are amongst the richest and most powerful men in the United States. A couple of years ago several of my more important clients asked me to look into the possibility of investing money in South African gold mines. That country is now the world's largest producer of gold so I made the decision that the best way forwards, in the interests of my clients, was to go there myself and have a look. I noticed an advertisement in one of the trade papers for a 'Transgold Mining and Exploration Company of Johannesburg', a new Company with excellent prospects – so the editorial said. I hired a mining engineer and we paid a visit to the Witwatersrand where most of the mines operate.

'I liked what I saw. The Company's mine was just starting operations and after looking round we took a sample of the ore from one of their test bores. Damn me if it did not prove to be one of the highest quality samples our assayer in Cape Town had ever seen. We bought stock on behalf of our clients and watched as the price rose. It looked a good investment, and in general, it was, some clients sold their stock and made a lot of money, others hung on for the dividends. The problem is that this Transgold Mining and Exploration Company has not paid any dividends, nor have we seen any accounts and I am going to look a little foolish if I have allowed my clients to be duped. I cannot afford to have my reputation tarnished. I want you and Brand, the surveyor I took with me on the trip some time ago, to go back to Johannesburg and find out what the hell is going on. Find out if those South Africans have defrauded us and if they have, I want that bastard Campbell and the other fella, James, put behind bars – do you understand? You will be well paid and all your expenses taken care of. If you can bring this to a successful conclusion, then there is a bonus of ten thousand dollars in it for you.'

The Texan's eyebrows nearly disappeared into his hairline. 'Waall, your offer sure sounds tempting and I fancy a trip abroad. Count me in. And where is this Brand fella?'

'This Brand fella' was waiting out in the lobby, his meeting with Rosenberg scheduled for half-an-hour after Tom Sheraton's and he had already arrived and was wondering what the summons was all about, he had neither seen nor spoken with Rosenberg since they had returned from South Africa. Then a voice crackled through the contraption on the secretary's desk.

'Send Brand in Marjory,'

Chapter 15

In the troubled city of Johannesburg, an industrial workers' meeting was taking place outside the Trades Hall in Rissik Street, the headquarters of the trade union movement. The mood of the miners was becoming confrontational and a large crowd had gathered to express their grievances. The first to climb onto the makeshift stage was a balding red-faced man in a shabby suit and trilby hat. He raised his arms above his head and signalled the crowd to be silent and at the back, standing on tiptoe, Solomon strained his ears.

'Brothers, we are meeting here today to decide what to do about the outrageous actions of the mine owners and the chamber of mines. They are threatening to tear up the Status Quo Agreement signed by them and us not more than three years ago. They want to reduce our member's wages and worse, replace the white semi-skilled workers with cheaper blacks. Brothers, we cannot allow this to happen.'

A murmur of agreement rose from the crowd, someone shouted encouragement, propelling the speaker into his stride. 'How can our members progress to skilled jobs if they are being pushed out by the blacks? How can they hope to feed their families, pay their rent?'

Roars of approval grew louder and Solomon, one of only a handful of blacks attending the meeting, began to feel uncomfortable. This was not like the meetings of the Socialist League; they did not speak angrily of the blacks as this man did. He stopped taking notes, put his notebook back in his pocket and looked around, feeling that trouble could break out at any moment.

'Four thousand white miners will lose their jobs if the Status Quo Agreement is abolished,' said the man, thumping the makeshift lectern in front of him. More shouting and booing erupted from sections of the crowd. 'If the chamber of mines gets their way, it will lead towards the complete elimination of the white worker, and you men here will all lose your jobs. Fine thanks that is for all the efforts of our members, the ones who make those mine owners rich through their sweat and let us not forget those who have lost their lives underground. We made this industry what it is today, our sweat and sacrifice have built this industry and we are not about to stand idly by while our members are throw out onto the scrap heap.'

Another barrage of shouts and booing echoed around the street and Solomon could see speaker's oratory was stirring up the crowd and he decided that he had better try to leave before things turned violent. Looking round for an escape route, he saw a troop of mounted police moving slowly towards the crowd from the far end of the street and carefully he disengaged himself, moving in the direction of an alleyway to the front of the approaching police. He slipped between the buildings and made his way towards the next street and at half way along the passage, he could still hear the noise of the crowd. Then he heard the whinny of several horses as the police began to break up the assembly and he decided to turn back to see what was happening, try to get a story.

Retracing his steps, he gingerly looked out to see people scattering as a policeman on a white horse waded into the crowd with a sjambok in his hand, lashing out at anyone in his way. Another police officer on a big grey came crashing through the mêlée to send people screaming in all directions and then some of them headed towards Solomon and he had no option but to turn and run before the panicking crowd.

Emerging into the street, he found shelter, pressing himself tightly in a doorway as the fleeing crowd passed him by. He could still hear the commotion in the next street as the police broke up the meeting and he understood well enough what was happening. Earlier in the year 70,000 black mine workers had come out on strike against the Pass Laws only to be put down by the brutality of these same police. On that occasion the police had used fixed bayonets to force the men back to work and the confrontation he was witnessing had all those same hallmarks. He guessed that things must be getting quite serious for the police to be out in such numbers, something big was happening for events to move so fast and as a reporter he had to try to keep up with them.

Leaving his sanctuary, he ran towards the newspaper office to write his story whilst it was still fresh in his mind. He had travelled as much as the rigid pass law would allow, attending similar meetings and it had become apparent that a major strike was brewing and it worried him.

During December, the call for strike action by white miners gathered momentum, sweeping through Johannesburg and the surrounding districts. The workers had battled long and hard to secure better conditions and earn a decent wage but if the mine owners replaced them with native labour that would push the movement back years and they felt that they had no alternative but to make a stand and at police headquarters, Commissioner Coetzee studied the paper on his desk. It was a report from a detective assigned to work undercover and it had just arrived. Informants had alerted him to the trouble brewing in the mining districts and he had assigned detectives to find out more, talk to the miners and see what they could turn up. The report in front of him was one of many making him aware of the developing situation and he realised that his police would struggle to cope on their own. A knock on his door disturbed his thoughts and made him look up.

'Come,' he uttered in a strong Afrikaner accent.

The door opened and in walked an impeccably dressed soldier, Brigadier Albert Smyth of the Rand Light Infantry. He snapped smartly to attention and saluted the commissioner.

'Brigadier Smyth?'

'Commissioner.'

'Pleased to meet you,' said Coetzee rising from his seat and reaching to shake hands with his visitor.

'You know why I'm here Commissioner Coetzee?'

'Yes, of course' said the commissioner, a frown creasing his brow. 'I sent a report to the Internal Security Minister in Pretoria last week informing him that my detectives were becoming aware of more and more militancy. It looks as if the workers are forming and drilling their own commandos and I considered it a serious development and I do not think my police force will be able to cope if things get out of hand.'

'Quite,' said the brigadier. 'I have been ordered by the army department to come and talk with you, see what we can do to prepare for an emergency. I believe that the original order came from Smuts himself.'

The brigadier leant forward and in a serious voice said, 'You know, I was in France with our troops for two years and I saw how capable they were. We had some damn fine soldiers in the South African army and now here we are, four years later, with many of those same men forming commandos. They know how to drill and how to fight and I dread the thought of a full-scale insurrection! Most of my troops are just boys who have never seen any action and with large numbers of these veterans opposing us, I worry about our ability to contain them'.

'Hmm, I hadn't thought of it quite like that. What can we do to stop them if they do mobilise?'

'First thing is to call up the reserves and if things get really bad we'll need to call on the burgher commandos. The mounted volunteer forces will be particularly useful to take control of the outlying districts.'

'What about any support for my police officers? What can you do in an emergency?'

'I've already begun training ten special machine gun detachments to rapidly re-enforce your officers when and where you might require them. I also have it on good authority that we have received the first of the aircraft for the new air corps. Smuts had a hand in forming the Royal Flying Corps; he's a big believer in air power, says they'll be good for reconnaissance.'

The Commissioner looked startled. 'Aircraft? You don't think we will need aircraft do you? Sounds a bit like overkill to me.'

The brigadier smiled, 'They are the future. Saw them almost every day in France. If they are not firing their guns or dropping bombs, they really are good for observation. Should your strike get out of hand we will know where their forces are and in what strength, a big advantage. What about your police force, can they be trusted to be loyal?'

'Yes, I think so,' answered the Commissioner. 'They are paid regularly and with things so bad outside the force, what with the recession and lack of jobs they will remain loyal. I've got some good officers and they know how to crack heads, so let's hope we can control things on our own.'

The two men discussed the unfolding situation for a further hour, discussing troop dispositions, the enemy's capabilities, and various logistical issues, finally agreeing to meet the following week to discuss progress, to bring their aides into those discussions and to formulate a strategy.

'Well, thank you for your time commissioner. I am sure that we can work together and overcome this little problem. They don't like the bayonets you know!' said the brigadier saluting. He turned and marched smartly out of the office, leaving a worried Commissioner reaching for a cigarette.

Chapter 16

Christmas of 1921 was not a happy affair in the Campbell household, at least not for the grown-ups. The children waded into their Christmas presents with gusto, Peggy finally managing to lay her hands on the doll she had wanted ever since seeing it in the shop window. Henry received a wooden horse mounted on four hardwood wheels and by noon, he had ridden it almost to Pretoria and back. For Norman and Lucy though, Christmas day was not as carefree as it might be, not with the future looking so uncertain.

After the fourth general election back in February, Smuts had won a clear majority on hopes that he would secure a prosperous future for the country, but the recession did not go away. The price of gold had dropped by a third, house sales had tailed off dramatically since the winter and Norman had been unable to replace his erstwhile stockbroker.

Christmas dinner lifted their spirits a little, a goose with all the trimmings and a generous helping of plum pudding cemented a traditional Christmas day and after clearing the dishes, Lucy let Marsha leave early and watched as the children squeezed a last few ounces of fun out of their Christmas gifts. Afterwards she picked up her sewing and Norman became engrossed his paper spending the next hour reading about the woes of the world.

'Lucy,' Norman said quietly after he finished reading. 'Lucy, what do you think about going home?'

She looked up from her sewing. 'Home? To Edinburgh, do you mean?'

'Aye, ah do. Things are looking a bit bleak out here and I can see Williamson sacking me if things don't pick up soon. The paper says there will be a long and damaging strike in the New Year and many people will be without work. House sales have been going from bad to worse you know and I have not done a land deal in six months. I can't see much of a future here anymore.'

Lucy looked back at her sewing, not sure what to say. The thought of going back home was certainly tempting, she remembered when they had first arrived in the country how homesick she had felt but those feelings had receded as she had adapted to their new life. The loss of her children had hit her hard but with the help of Peggy and Henry she had survived. Now though, after Norman's suggestion, those feelings of homesickness were rekindled, she would see her mother and sisters for the first time in almost ten years, feel the cool Edinburgh rain on her face – but balanced against that was the knowledge that she would be leaving Alistair and Rosemary behind.

'Here, I haven't given you your Christmas present yet have I,' said Norman, holding a small gift-wrapped parcel in his hand.

'Oh, thank you,' said Lucy, her eyes lighting up. 'And I have something for you.'

After exchanging their presents, they began to unwrap them and Lucy was first to reveal hers, a pair of gold earrings she held to her ears, smiling with pleasure.

'Norman, they are beautiful, thank you.'

Norman opened the small box he had uncovered and looked inside, his smile fading. It was a silver cigarette case, identical to the case he had lost in Cape Town, and he began to feel a little embarrassed. He had never mentioned it to Lucy but she had obviously noticed it was missing.

'Er...it's lovely, thank you,' he said reaching across to kiss her and wondering why she had given him such a present.

'I noticed that the one I gave you on your twenty first birthday has disappeared. What exactly happened to it Norman?'

'Oh...I don't really know, I may have had my pocket picked at some time, didn't notice it myself for a day or two.'

'Well you had better look after this one a little better.'

'Oh, yes, I will, certainly.'

The moment of embarrassment passed and Norman relaxed, stood up and went to the cupboard by the window for his bottle of whiskey.

'Would you like a drink?'

Lucy shook her head, she never drank whiskey and Norman knew it. What had really happened to the silver cigarette case and why had he never mentioned that it was missing? She had decided to buy the new one and to watch his reaction when she gave it to him. He was becoming distant, evasive and now he was talking of returning home to Scotland, something *was* going on.

Chapter 17

The storm broke on 10 January 1922, twenty thousand white miners downed tools and left only a handful of mine managers and strike-breakers to control a black labour force of nearly 200,000. Somehow, most mines managed to carry on producing, albeit at a much-reduced rate and in general, the strike proceeded peacefully. However, by mid-February, the hardships the strikers were enduring became overwhelming and then things took a decidedly different turn. The local commandos moved away from passive protest, ex-soldiers and militant strikers were rising to prominence and pushing aside the elected union leaders. The twin effect of Government intervention on the employer's side and the deprivations of the strikers and their families on the other had persuaded them to take control and the situation was beginning to turn ugly.

The man ultimately responsible for policing the unrest, Police Commissioner Coetzee, was at his desk deep in thought, as he had tended to be on most days since the strike began. Sitting opposite him was an equally pensive Brigadier Smyth who had just entered the room, invited to the commissioner's office several days earlier than their planned meeting. The commissioner seemed to draw a conclusion from his thoughts and leaned forward, looking straight at the brigadier to place emphasise on his words.

'Brigadier, it's the commandos, they are our greatest problem, particularly out on the Eastern Rand, Benoni and Brakpan. The strikers in general have been a peaceful lot but some hot heads are taking over and starting to run things on a military footing. The commandos can be five or six hundred strong and my local police forces of twenty or so officers cannot control them. Some are mounted or have bicycles, mobile and a threat to security but I do not believe that they are particularly well armed. They have a few shotguns and old service revolvers as far as we can tell but we have had reports of break ins to several mine stores and it seems a quantity of dynamite has gone missing. Now, if they can get their hands on service rifles as well then we will have a problem. What plans do you have to support my men, Brigadier?'

Sitting rather stiffly on the high backed chair the Brigadier spoke, 'A dilemma at the moment! The commandos do have plenty of energetic members, but as you comment, they do not have much in the way of arms - not yet. You are right; if they get their hands on service weapons then the situation could very well develop into something rather more grave. The army command has ordered me to take any developments very seriously, to bring the Transvaal horse artillery and Transvaal Scottish regiments up to strength and deploy them on the Eastern Rand ready to move as soon as needed. For the moment, I have the Rand light infantry, the Witwatersrand rifles and the Durban light infantry in reserve, but I can bring them forward at very short notice. My ADC, Captain Lawrence, is talking to the Burgher Commandos, getting them up to strength and we have our fledgling air force in Pretoria covering the whole of the reef as forward observers.'

'Well,' the Commissioner mused, 'plenty of fire-power available if we need it. I just hope we do not. Information from my detectives suggests that the communists are at the root of the trouble. They think these communists will try to rouse the strikers and push them over the limit. If they do, we could well have our very own red revolution here in South Africa.'

Silence descended for a time as each man scribbled a few notes and then the Police Commissioner passed a piece of paper across his desk.

'I have numerous detectives, informers, and regular police dotted about Johannesburg and the outlying districts. They are my main source of intelligence and the information I am receiving is building into a grim picture. This is a map of Johannesburg and the surrounding townships and shows my police stations, I would appreciate it if you would draw up plans to protect them should we need you to.'

For the second time two years James Brand looked down from a ship's deck at a gang of black dockworkers heaving mooring warps to secure the ship just arrived from New York. It had been an uneventful voyage, the ship had made steady progress and he had whiled away his time reading, sleeping, or playing deck quoits with some of the other passengers. Tom Sheraton, on the other hand had hated every minute he spent on the ship, more used to the rolling prairies than the rolling seas.

On the few occasions the Texan sat at the dinner table with James they had struck up a conversation and the Marshall had a shared a little of his chequered history. Growing up when Indian tribes were still a threat to settlers, when many smaller towns in the vast open spaces of Texas were still beyond the reach of the law. He told how, as a young boy, he had watched a gang of outlaws ride into town and rob the local bank. Everyone for miles around knew the teller, Charlie Bains, a friendly, rotund little man who always had a smile on his face and who never did any harm to anybody. But those outlaws shot him down in cold blood and right in front of the young Tom Sheraton's eyes. Shocked and powerless to help he had burst with anger and frustration and when a United States Marshal rode in to town ready to form a posse, he had volunteered. The Marshal said he was too young and asked the boy questions about the incident instead. Tom had given such a good description of the men and their horses that the Marshal was soon on their trail and four days later the posse rode returned with one of the gang tied securely to his horse and the others lying dead somewhere out on the prairie.

The event had left an indelible mark on Tom, he knew then that his destiny lay in becoming a US Marshal and when the chance came, he took it. Over the years his reputation as a hard-nosed lawman grew, everyone within a hundred miles of Pecos knew and respected his name. However, being at sea was something else; Tom had begun to feel seasick almost as soon as the ship had left the Hudson River and he never quite got over it. He spent most of his time lying on his bunk being looked after by a diminutive Indian steward named Koru who would bring him something to eat each day he was confined and looked after the big Texan like a mother. It was an arrangement that amused Brand who was well aware of the Marshal's reputation and seeing him looked after by an Indian half his size proved comical.

Once back on dry land, the Marshal recovered quickly and was able to enjoy the February sun of the southern continent and on the first morning ashore, James Brand wandered down to the dining room, picked up a local newspaper in the hotel lobby and scanned the headlines as he waited for his breakfast. There was only one story, the unrest on the Witwatersrand, the strike, the increasing violence and the more he read the more his brow creased. He began to wonder what was going on for he had heard nothing of any trouble in the goldfields, no talk of trouble when they had disembarked and none in the hotel the previous evening.

'Have you read this, Tom?' asked Brand as the Marshal joined him.

'What is it son?

'This here,' said Brand showing the paper to Sheraton. 'We're heading into this. I wonder if we can still do what we've come here for.'

'Betsy here can handle any trouble,' said Sheraton, patting the Smith & Wesson triple-lock pistol tucked into his waistband, an improved version of the .44 Russian, one of the best Smith & Wesson guns ever made. The Marshals' had an ivory handle and an eight-inch barrel for increased accuracy and James Brand began to wonder if perhaps he should start to carry a gun.

Eight hundred miles away in Johannesburg Norman was reading a similar story in the *Johannesburg Star*. Even before the miners had gone out on strike, business had been bad but now, with the increasing violence, the situation was becoming far worse. Sat at his desk across the office, Jeremy, Norman's secretary was reading his own newspaper and gasped with disbelief as he read a detailed report of killings on the Eastern Rand.

'Blimey Norman! Looks bad doesn't it. I knew there would be some trouble but this is cold-blooded murder.'

Norman took a drink from his cup and was about to reply when a movement outside in the street caught his eye. He turned his head just as the office door burst open and in walked a police Sergeant and constable. The Sergeant was so big he almost filled the space where the door had been and he wondered what it was they wanted and then his heart missed a beat. Had they found out about the mine swindle?

'You two look busy, is that your automobile outside in the street?' said the Sergeant, his thumb pointing over his shoulder.

'Yes, it probably is,' said Norman looking in the general direction of the thumb and feeling decidedly uneasy at the sight of two burly police officers. 'Why do you ask?'

The Sergeant looked at Norman, 'Would you care to accompany us to the police station, and bring your automobile with you? The Captain would like to see you.'

Norman's stomach turned. Had the three of them finally run out of luck – perhaps it was about that big Dutchman he had shot several weeks ago? He knew he had wounded him, not seriously he believed, but what if he was wrong and Frank van Seters was dead? His mind raced over previous events and then he remembered the native he had thrown into the river just before they had moved to Johannesburg. 'Oh God,' the thought, could that be the reason, how could anybody possibly know that he was the one that had killed him?

From the look on the Sergeant's face he could see that it would do no good to argue and so he stood up and dropped his paper on the table.

'What do you want?'

'Never mind that, It's the Captain you need to see, he is the one who sent us here.'

Norman's throat felt dry and he tried to swallow as he walked a little unsteadily past the officers towards the door.

'Look after things here for me until I get back, will you Jeremy?'

'Yes boss, see you later,' said Jeremy returning to his paper quite unconcerned.

Norman walked out onto the street and made straight for the car followed closely by the Sergeant and the constable. Uninvited they both jumped in and sat watching through the windows with expressionless faces as Norman swung the starting handle. After some exertion, he finally got the engine to fire and with a reddened face, climbed into the driving seat.

At the police headquarters, the sergeant climbed out first and straightened his tunic, rotating his index finger and indicating to Norman where he should go and the three of them walked towards the building's entrance.

'Good morning, are you the gentleman with the car?' enquired a voice from behind the reception desk. Norman turned and nodded to the policeman, still unsure of what was going on and he felt worried. Had something gone wrong with Arthur's scheme, why he was here, were they going to question him about the mine scam? Sweat began to form on his brow as he considered the possibility of going to jail.

'Follow me will you please,' said the Captain of police, leading the way into the small office a few yards along the corridor. 'Take a seat. Have my men explained why you are here?'

'N-no,' stammered Norman trying hard to remain as calm as the tension gripping his body would allow.

'You'll have read the morning papers and will be aware of yesterday's trouble out at Germiston I presume?' Norman nodded. But what did that have to do with him? 'Well, the situation is getting serious and I've been ordered to round up as many cars and drivers as I can get hold of to assist us. The Transvaal Motor Club are organising their members and vehicles and I am bringing in as much motorised transport as I can lay my hands on. Before long I should have a decent fleet assembled for ferrying troops and police to where we need them. I presume you are volunteering your automobile and your services as driver for as long as we need?'

Norman swallowed hard and the Captain passed a piece of paper across the desk to him. 'Sign this to say that you are volunteering your services and we can slot you into our plan. You are not too far from our headquarters here, so the Commissioner will more than likely use you for driving him around. You can pop off home or back to work and sort yourself out, but I want you back here in an hour – and make sure you have a full tank of petrol. Good morning Mr er – '

'Campbell.'

'Okay Mr Campbell,' smiled the Captain.

A very relieved Norman left the office and walked out into the sunshine not knowing whether to laugh or cry.

In spite of everything, it seemed that he was not in any trouble; he was simply required to put the Buick at the disposal of the Police Commissioner. With a more settled mind, he hurried to his car thinking that Jeremy would have to run things for a day or two. He would tell him first about the new situation and then he would find Lucy, explain it to her and then it occurred to him that he had better bring his revolver with him.

Not long after Norman left the police headquarters the train from Cape Town was passing through the suburbs on its way to the Johannesburg railway Station. Leaning out of the carriage door window, Tom Sheraton was getting his first sight of the city. The journey from the Cape had been tedious, passing through mile after mile of flat scrubland, strange wild African animals providing occasional highlights. He had found the zebras especially enchanting, believing them to be the strangest horses he had ever seen until James Brand put him right.

'Certainly looks as if trouble is brewing,' said the Marshal spotting a group of armed men at the side of the track. 'Didn't your paper say some of 'em had attacked a mine?'

'Yes, they killed a few black labourers; I can't remember the exact details.'

The Marshal remained silent as he watched the group, eyes narrowing until they were out of sight and when the train slowed markedly, the Americans knew that they had almost reached their destination.

'James, when we get to the hotel can you sort out the rooms? I want to get onto this case as soon as I can. I'm going to take a walk to the police headquarters and see if I can enlist the help of the local police force.'

264

'Don't you think they might be a busy with their own difficulties?' said Brand, surprised at Sheraton's haste.

'Well I ain't hanging about. I gotta keep busy in case I start thinkin' about the return journey on that darn ship.'

Brand allowed himself a smile as he thought that he was probably the only person in the world who knew that Tom Sheraton had a weakness, oh, and Koru – he had forgotten the little Indian steward.

The strike was beginning to take its toll, the gambling and drinking fraternity were feeling the squeeze just as much as everyone else. With the mines hardly working, the suppliers, waggon builders and transport companies were laying men off, there was little money about and in the Silver Star Hans and Arthur could see the difference. A morose looking Alessandro was feeling the pressure too, his face creased with worry as he surveyed an almost empty bar. His few customers were clustered together watching the one card game, Arthur was dealing and he waited until each player had picked up his cards and then the betting started.

'Two shillings,' said the man to Arthur's left, deciding it was worth a gamble.

Hans was next and he matched the wager, as did the fourth man and each time they placed their bets, Arthur's eyes glanced furtively at their faces and from the bar Alessandro could almost see his mind at work.

The betting returned to Arthur, he tossed two more coins onto the centre of the table. The man next to him folded his hand, exclaiming, 'I've 'ad enough. I can't match that, I'm cleaned out,' and sat back in his chair, drained his glass and out a short sigh.

'Me too,' said his companion, mimicking his friend's movements. 'I reckon that will be our last game for a while Arthur, we will be laid off at the end of the week.'

With glum looking faces, the two men stood up and walked towards the door. They were waggon builders from the north of England and even they were feeling the effects of the strike. Arthur watched them go and began gathering up the cards. 'Let me buy you a drink with my winnings, Hans,' he said shuffling the pack.

The lack of punters was taking its toll on him too, the excitement the cards generated had evaporated. He spread the cards face down in a perfect arc and then, with one hand flicked the over first card of the fan and the rest followed as if physically attached. He repeated the trick, flicking them back over before using the same hand to tidy the pack. Hans watched him for a while before letting out a grunt, he had seen it all before and knew that when Arthur started showing off with the cards it was a sure sign he was getting bored.

Hans held up his glass for Alessandro to refill but before the Italian could make a move the sound of running feet and men shouting interrupted them. Hans and Arthur rose from their seats and went to look out of the window and Alessandro stood near the open door. Three black men were running down the street as fast as they could go closely followed by a mob of about 20 whites carrying pick handles. The mob was yelling, 'Get the Kaffirs! Don't let them get away. Come on, kill them!'

To the onlookers it seemed the black men would escape from their pursuers until suddenly a shot rang out, one of them stumbled a few paces and fell to the ground. Within seconds, the pack was on him, beating him senseless with bloodthirsty pleasure and only when they realised that their victim was dead did their murderous lust abate.

It was too late to catch the remaining natives they were escaping down an alleyway, so the mob gave up the chase and three of their number came inside the Silver Star.

'What was that all about boys?' Arthur asked a big man with a shock of black hair and a livid scar across his right temple.

'We've chased these buggers for miles; we have been clearing them out of *Ferreiras Town* all day. The blacks will not be taking our jobs now, will they boys?'

The other men nodded agreement and broke into a chorus of 'Workers of the world unite and fight for a white South Africa.'

Arthur had heard the slogan before, chanted by a crowd gathered in Ellis Park. It had not particularly concerned him then, but if the strikers were going after blacks and killing them, it looked as if real trouble was brewing and he didn't want to be anywhere near it.

'What do you say to that, eh?' said the first man.

It was not Arthur's fight and he chose to answer only with a nod, a tacit agreement. He returned to the card table, picked up the cards, began to shuffle, this time with much less flamboyance and watched as the three strikers drank up and left the bar.

'There's going to be more serious trouble I think, said Hans 'I hear the Burgher Commandos are forming up and maybe I will volunteer tomorrow. Nothing better to do and it will be good to be amongst soldiers again. What about you Arthur, will you volunteer?'

Arthur took a drink from his glass, his face deadpan. 'Me, fight for the Government, risk my life for a bunch of worthless blacks. I don't think so. How am I going to

267

survive without taking the pay packets off the white miners? Natives don't play cards, do they?'

Hans could not argue with Arthur's logic.

There was a more peaceful air in Sophiatown where Solomon was, talking to his old friend Thembisile a wizened old Zulu who knew of all the gossip and goings-on in the township. He was a mine of information, a good source of material for Solomon and when he was looking for a story he could rely on Thembisile.

'This strike is trouble Solomon, I see with my own eyes, trouble.'

'I know, I have seen violence against our people, I have seen the police attack us and I have heard the white man's words. I too am worried Thembisile.'

Suddenly the hairs on the back of Solomon's neck stood on end and his senses sharpened as a gunshot echoed through the street. Straight away, he told the old man to go inside and hide for his own safety and then he set off to investigate. Keeping as close to the buildings as he could, he made his way towards the end of the row of shacks and as he reached the junction, he heard the sound of people screaming and before he could do anything a mass of people came careering round the corner in a blind panic. He stepped back into a doorway for fear of them trampling him, he tried to make sense of what was going on, and then he felt a hand grasp his arm.

'Come Solomon, we must run,' it was Mbali.

'Mbali, beautiful flower . . . what is happening?'

'White men with sjamboks trying to kill us. Come, we must run.' She held Solomon's hand, pulling him after the fleeing crowd and Solomon began to realise the gravity of the situation. He was bigger and stronger than the girl and took the lead, managing a quick glance over his shoulder as they ran and saw the first of the Europeans turn the street corner and then from behind him came a terrifying scream. The mob had caught one of the laggards and Solomon could not help but turn again and look back. Several big white men were beating a man, knocking him to the ground and hitting him repeatedly. He could see that the man had little chance of survival and his fate served to drive Solomon on. He began to move with more urgency, dragging Mbali after him but then she pulled back, dragging him sideways into a dark passageway. Now she took the lead, guiding him between the shanties and into an enclosed space deep in the midst of the buildings, a place known only to locals.

They pressed their bodies up against the corrugated iron wall of a structure, their chests heaving from fear and exertion. Solomon felt Mbali's strong warm body pressing against him for protection, her thin cotton dress no disguise for her heaving chest and for half-an-hour they waited.

Finally, the commotion abated, there was silence and Solomon ventured to look along the narrow space leading to their hideaway. It was deserted and so he cautiously took Mbali by the hand and they retraced their steps. At the end of the alleyway, he peered round a corner into a deserted street, then he turned to look in the opposite direction and his heart stopped as he stared at a lone white man stood not six feet away. It was Frank van Seters who had dropped back from the mob, smashed a shop window and was about to help himself when Solomon appeared.

'Got you, you bastard,' he snarled, pulling his hunting knife from his belt, the shop's contents suddenly subordinate to his desire to kill a black.

Menacingly he moved forward, eyes wild, his knife ready and it was then Solomon caught the brief flash of sunlight reflecting off the blade, a warning that came just in time. Turning on the balls of his feet, he came face to face with his foe ready to defend himself but he was not quick enough and the knife arced towards him. He tried to avoid the flashing blade but he could not and it sliced straight into his chest, knocking him backwards into the passageway and forcing him to his knees. He screamed in pain, clutching at the wound as he collapsed and Mbali stood wide-eyed in shock. Frank Van Seters did not press home his advantage, instead he staggered backwards clutching at his forearm and then Mbali leapt like a lioness, arms flailing, her nails clawing at his eyes and after a few seconds of frantic struggle he managed to push her away and escape.

Mbali turned back to Solomon to see his shirt covered in blood, his eyes rolling in shock and then he coughed and she was convinced that he was dying. She knew then that she loved him and could not let him die and so with both hands on his shoulders, managed to sit him up against the wall. Blood was everywhere. She tore away at his blood-soaked shirt, ripping it from his torso, exposing the wound so that she might stem the flow of blood but she could not find it. At first, she was puzzled and then she gasped in disbelief.

Solomon looked up at her, a painful grin spreading across his face as his fingers felt for the rawhide lacing around his neck. Mbali's eyes followed them as they traced a path down the rawhide to a battered metal disc, deformed by the force of the knife, hanging across his chest. The blade had not pierced Solomon's skin, his talisman, the twisted remains of a British soldier's cap badge, had saved him and Mbali squealed with relief. She stood back, offered her hand to help him to his feet, and guide him to her mother's shebeen a few streets away.

'Here, lie on my bed while I clean the blood from you.'

Solomon did as she said, lying down on Mbali's straw bed for a second time. His mind was in turmoil as he thought about the mob, the killings and the events of the recent past. He ran his fingers gingerly across his chest searching for damage but there was none save the bruising caused by the vicious blow from the knife. And the blood, where had all the blood come from? It must be the Afrikaner's blood; his hand must have slipped along the blade when it unexpectedly hit the solid object that was the cap badge. He must have sliced into his own artery judging by the amount of blood thought Solomon.

He lay back on the bed and closed his eyes for a few seconds. He had not escaped completely, the bruising to his chest was painful and he must have banged his leg as he fell. Then Mbali returned through the string-bead curtain, knelt beside him, and began to wipe the drying blood from his body. She smiled down at him, a beautiful engaging smile and he could not help but smile back.

'You are hurt more than you show Solomon. Is something broken inside?'

'No, it is only bruising I think, the knife struck me with such force. I was lucky.'

'Very lucky. Where did this come from?' she said holding the cap badge between finger and thumb.

'My father, he fought in Cetshwayo's great army and took it from a soldier he killed.'

'And now it has saved your life. It must have strong powers.'

Solomon laughed and then his eyes softened. She cared for him, he liked that and then she began to sing. Her soft voice filling the room, then she reached over him to grasp the deformed talisman once more, leaning closer and then she kissed his lips. It was too much for Solomon, her sweet aroma affected him and he could not help but reach up and pull her towards him.

Waking from a deep sleep, Solomon became conscious of the throbbing in his chest. The pain had lessened and he closed his eyes again for a few moments, exploring his body for damage, twisting and arching his back, remembering those exquisite moments when Mbali had helped to banish the pain. Then, suddenly, he sat up. What about Thembisile, what had happened to the old man? During the excitement of the riot and his time alone with Mbali, he had completely forgotten about his old friend. Staggering unsteadily to his feet he made a noise loud enough to alert Mbali who rushed through the curtain to peer anxiously at him.

'Solomon, what are you doing? You should stay there a while longer, at least until I have made you some food.'

'I am fine, but Thembisile . . . I was with him when the trouble started and told him to hide. I have forgotten him, I must go and find him.'

'Then I will come with you but first though, I will find you a shirt to wear.'

She disappeared back through the drapes, returning a minute later with a bright red blouse, embroidered with a yellow and green flower. Solomon half smiled, but the situation with Thembisile might be serious, he would have to wear it, wincing from the pain as he hurriedly put it on.

The old man's front door was wide-open, hanging from one flimsy hinge and it seemed as if his hovel was deserted. The mob must have forced the door and ransacked the place judging by the old man's few meagre possessions lying on the floor. In trepidation, Solomon entered the gloomy interior of the tiny room, looking here and there but could see no trace of Thembisile. Apart from the wreckage, there was nothing.

'Thembisile, it is me Solomon,' he called out but there was no answer. He called out the old man's name once more but still there was no answer and Solomon's heart began to sink.

'Thembisile, it is me your daughter, Mbali, the daughter you never had. Where are you?'

Then a noise attracted their attention, the sound of scraping and both looked towards the far wall. A wooden panel moved, falling forward onto the earthen floor with a dull thud and then, from out of the darkened recess appeared Thembisile, a huge grin spread across his face.

Chapter 18

The early morning sun streamed in through the flimsy lace curtains of Arthur's cheap room encouraging him to rise from his bed sooner than usual and after a meagre breakfast at a nearby eating-house, he made his way to the stables where Hans slept. He was to collect a horse and small cart and together with Hans, make his way to Germiston.

Two days earlier he had come across Harry Stassen, a sly and dangerous East European, meeting him in a bar in Jeppe. Arthur had heard of a card school that boasted high stakes and he had gone to watch from the sidelines, see if there were any prospects and then he had spotted Harry sat in a corner of the bar. He had sidled towards the table to watch the game and had been less than surprised to see his old acquaintance cheat his way towards a decent pile of winnings. Harry was a master of prestidigitation and Arthur watched with admiration as he manipulated the cards.

'Arthur my old friend, you are looking well,' said Harry. 'This game over, let me buy you a drink. Is Hans still knocking around with you?'

'Yes, we've just come down from the Transvaal. Nothing much doing up there though.'

'So, what you up to now then? I see the Transgold mining is no more.'

Arthur's eyebrows rose in surprise, then his face creased in a sly smile, 'How did you know about that, you crafty bastard?'

'Me, crafty bastard? Come Arthur – I have ways of knowing things. Some of the people you employ to make mine appear genuine are not so thick you know. It does not take too much brain power to put two and two together. It is amazing vot you can find out over a game of cards and a few whiskies, gratis, but you know dat, Arthur.'

They laughed and were soon deep in conversation reminiscing about the old days, exaggerating the stunts they had pulled and then the talk turned to the strike and curiously Harry asked, 'What do you think of the whisky, Arthur?'

Arthur took a sip and said, 'Not bad, but it's not the real McCoy. Might pass for real Scotch in certain quarters.'

'Certain quarters! The Silver Star perhaps? Is Alessandro still running the place?'

Arthur's ears pricked up.

'I can get 20 cases of the stuff, perhaps. That's 240 bottles at five shillings a bottle and you'll get ten shillings a bottle off Alessandro. Then he will sell it for 15 shillings a bottle, still cheap, and everybody is happy. What do you say?'

'And how much of it will be cold tea?' said Arthur.

Harry laughed. 'Me cheat you? I would not dare! You send Hans after me, and I do not want to be tangling with him. I have seen him operate do not forget.'

'OK Harry. I'm semi-retired now and I guess that this could earn me a few easy pounds, it's definitely my style.' He paused for a few seconds and then said, 'you're on! If Alessandro doesn't want the whisky I know a few people who will.'

He was still thinking about Harry Stassen when he reached the stables and found Hans already hitching the horse to the cart. After a drink or two with Harry, he had agreed a place and a time and more importantly, managed to knock Harry's asking price down and today they were going to collect.

'You can manage to drive?'

Arthur looked at Hans with mock contempt. 'Why, do you think I am incapable of controlling that nag?'

Hans laughed and Arthur smiled. In all the time he had known his friend he could not remember him laughing like that. Something had happened to the tough, solitary Boer, somehow he seemed more at peace with the world, more relaxed and Arthur felt a very rare twinge of compassion.

'Should be a few pounds in it for us Hans, a few more for that farm of yours eh...?'

It was a statement rather than a question, Arthur wondered if Hans would one day manage to live his dream and he hoped he had given him a large enough share of their profits for it to become a reality, but he doubted it.

Hans finished adjusting the tack on the horse, gave it a slap on its buttock, and walked towards the stall where his own horse waited patiently. They were heading for Germiston, a dangerous place since the disturbances at the New Primrose Mine.

'You brought your gun?' he said pulling his horse from the stall.

'Of course,' said Arthur already sitting on the waggon seat. 'It could be risky, the local commando will be active no doubt and the police will probably be around somewhere. We don't want to be caught up in any of that; if we do we need to get out of it and quick.'

Hans nodded, patted the back of his waistband for reassurance and climbed into the saddle.

The journey was uneventful; once they had cleared the city limits, they saw little sign of people, no strikers or police and at about eleven o'clock; they arrived at a disused barn on the outskirts of Germiston where Harry Stassen was waiting for them.

'Arthur, Hans,' he said taking a step towards them. 'Leave your waggon here and I will show you the merchandise.'

A man with Harry pulled the creaking shed door half open and went inside followed by Harry and Arthur leaving Hans to look after the horses. The interior was gloomy, just a little sunlight cutting through gaps in the wooden roof slats to reveal several small wooden boxes stacked one upon the other and Harry walked towards them.

'Johnnie Walker, good whiskey, look,' he said lifting the lid from the topmost box.

Inside were twelve bottles and Arthur pulled one out to examine it.

'This better be the real stuff.'

'Try a taste.'

Arthur unscrewed the top of the bottle, lifted it to his lips, and took a mouthful.

'Pretty good. If it's not the real thing it comes close,' he said taking a closer look at the boxes.

'We have deal then,' said the East European, a half smile on his lips, coldness in his eyes.

'Yes we have a deal. Now let's get moving because I don't want to stay here any longer than I have to.'

'You give me the money and we load you up.'

Arthur pulled a thick wad of banknotes from inside his jacket and handed it to Harry who nodded to his man and together they began to carry the crates out to the waiting buggy.

Watching from the roof of a high building was a Sergeant of police who tapped the shoulder of a constable beside him and said quietly, 'Take a bead on those three; I'm going to challenge them. You know what to do if they resist' and with that he shouted, 'You men stand where you are! This is the police.'

Harry was the first to react, pulling out a gun and firing in the direction of the voice before ducking behind the buggy and scrambling back into the building followed closely by his accomplice. Hans and Arthur pulled out their guns, dodged behind the waggon and up on the roof the Sergeant gave a nod to the sniper. Seconds later a shot rang out and Arthur fell to the ground clutching at his chest, Hans reached down and grabbed his collar, dragging him back into the building. It wasn't the first time he had experienced people shooting at him, and when two more shots rang out, missing them by a hairsbreadth, he knew the police were trying to kill them.

Arthur moaned as Hans propped him up against the inside of the shed and pulled off his jacket, tearing open his shirt to try to stem the bleeding but he soon realised that there was little hope for his long-time friend. Then, without warning, the door at the back of the building burst open. Harry and two men carrying rifles rushed in and positioned themselves near the front door of the shed ready to return fire.

Arthur coughed; a trickle of blood oozed from his mouth and he fell silent, his eyes staring at Hans who was still trying desperately to stop the bleeding. Hans did not want to leave Arthur alone to die, he was fond of this scrawny, cheating, good-for-nothing vagabond who had pulled him out of the gutter because without him he had no one. Arthur began to convulse, coughing up more blood as his life ebbed away and with some effort he managed a barely audible whisper: 'Hans, this is it. It was going to happen sooner or later, so listen.' He coughed again, his voice weakening. 'Hans – go to my room and pull up the floorboards . . . money from the mine, gold dust, take it, buy your farm.' He coughed, closed his eyes for the last time and his head slowly slumped forwards.

'Hans, come on,' said Harry, shaking him. 'Come! There is no reason to stay, I'm sorry, Arthur is dead.' Pulling at his shoulder, he forced him to his feet. 'The police will be here soon; we won't get away unless we go now.'

Hans saw the logic and with one last look at Arthur, he turned and followed the men racing out of the back door and for several seconds they must have been in full view of the sniper yet no shot rang out.

'I'm so sorry Hans,' said Harry when they managed to catch their breath out of sight of the police marksman. 'I had no idea the police were watching us, believe me. We should get out of here as fast as we can; we have horses

279

over there look, take one Hans and get away. I will cover you, now go. Go!' he shouted.

Hans looked at Harry; he did not trust him, he had never trusted him and now Arthur was dead. He glanced one last time towards the shed where Arthur lay and he knew instinctively that something was not right. They had been set up, of that he was almost certain, yet there was nothing he could do. It would be futile to try to retrieve Arthur's money or the whiskey from these armed men and he was in a difficult position, he needed to look to his own survival. Leaving Harry and his men was the first step and so, without thinking, he ran across the street to the waiting horses to unhitch the nearest, mount it and kick hard at its flanks. The horse reacted as he hoped, lurching forward at the gallop and soon he was steering it away from the trouble. He twisted in the saddle for one last look, saluted Arthur's memory and vowed one day to catch up with Harry Stassen.

A week later, Hans rode his horse along a bridal path leading to the sun-bleached farmhouse of Cornelius Van der Merwe. It looked deserted as he dismounted and tied his horse to the rail and for a few moments, he stood with his hands on his hips looking at the house he knew so well. He had not seen Cornelius for more than 20 years, not since he had left to fight the British and now he was back. He took a few steps towards the house, looking for signs of life and then the door flew open and a voice called out to him.

'Who are you and what do you want?' and from inside the darkened room the barrel of a rifle protruded to point straight at him.

'Cornelius, don't you remember me? Hans, Hans Lockmeyer. I used to live on the farm over there,' he said, pointing towards the hills behind him. There was a moment's silence while Cornelius looked him up and down, studying his face, a face he had not seen for 20 years. Hans was no longer a young man and he wore the face of one who had known hardship. The one Cornelius had known as Hans Lockmeyer had left a fresh-faced youngster with meat on his bones, this man was gaunt, his clothes hung loose on his frame, his face creased with lines.

Cornelius stepped forwards into the daylight and the two men looked at each other. 'Remove your hat stranger.' Hans did as he was asked, beginning to feel self-conscious and Cornelius studied his damaged ear.

'Hans, Hans,' murmured Cornelius slowly in bewilderment. 'It really is you! My God, what has happened?' He took another step forward to take a closer look. He knew a little of Hans's history from veterans, the loss of his family and of his disfigurement and the realisation that it was him came as a shock. Propping his gun against the house wall, he reached out with large, gnarled hands and gripped Hans by his shoulders, squeezing him to make sure he was not an apparition. 'Come in, come in my old friend, come in, we have a lot of catching up to do.'

Hans followed Cornelius into the house where the sights and smells he had not experienced for more than half his life engulfed him and a lump came to his throat. His mind began to conjure up memories of the house and the one on the far side of the hill; the one he, Ute, and little Hans had rented from Cornelius and suddenly memories of those happier times came flooding back.

'Who lives there now Cornelius?' he asked looking through the window in the direction of the farm that was once his.

'A couple from up-country took it on, but they struggled to make it pay. They gave me notice that they were quitting six months ago, and no one lives there now. Marius reckoned that he could make a better living by moving to Johannesburg and working in the mines. Probably he can – so many have done the very same thing.'

So, the farm was deserted, news that lifted his spirits and then the soft tread of female feet distracted him. Disturbed by the sound of voices Cornelius's wife, Mattie, had come from the kitchen, sleeves rolled up and her hands covered in white flour. She was inquisitive to know to whom Cornelius was talking because the lonely life they lived out on the farm meant that they rarely had visitors. A visitor could transform her day, give her a chance to catch up on gossip, learn a little about the outside world. She cast her eyes over the stranger, he seemed familiar and then, slowly at first, recognition dawned and then she ran to him. His eyes were still the same and once she had recovered from her initial shock she threw her arms around his neck and hugged him so hard he could hardly breathe.

'Oh Hans, where have you been all these years and look at you, what have you been doing?' she said, bursting into tears.

'You will stay with us tonight?' asked Cornelius. Hans began to protest but Mattie would have none of it, insisting that he stay and tell her everything. They had learned a little of what had happened to him, his wound, internment in the prisoner of war camp and the loss of

282

his family. The war caused hard times for the Afrikaner community in general but for the least fortunate it had been devastating and tonight Mattie and Cornelius would try to rectify some of that.

Cornelius smiled broadly at Mattie as she coaxed and then scolded Hans into unslinging his bedroll, making him take the bedroom vacated by their grown up sons. To the old farmer and his wife it was a kind of homecoming and to celebrate the event Cornelius filled his pipe and went outside for a quiet smoke.

'You are settled in?' he said as Hans appeared on the verandah.

'Er...yes, Mattie has made me comfortable but she says that when I have stabled my horse I am to have a good wash.'

Cornelius chuckled, 'how times have changed, eh, our grandfathers never washed,' and then he drew heavily on his pipe. 'We need to feed and water your horse. Come with me, we will take her to the stable and as you see to her you can tell me a little of what you have been doing all these years.'

Cornelius led the way towards the stables and Hans looked towards the distant mountains, grey and faint in the late afternoon sunlight. His eyes scanned nearby hills and squinting, he picked out familiar peaks, remembered the times he had roamed those same hills with his hunting rifle.

As he began taking off his saddle Cornelius went to rouse one of his African boys to come and see to the animal. Leaving the boy to his task, the two men walked back to the house. Mattie and her kitchen girl were busy preparing the evening meal and before they sat down to eat Cornelius decided that now would be a good time to show Hans the water pump and as the cold water splashed over his naked torso, Hans felt he was washing away more than dirt. A change had come over him, it seemed that he was washing away years of torment, he felt happier than he had for a long time and lying under the American surveyor's bed had been the start of it. In this warm friendly farmhouse, he felt that he had returned home at last and for the first time in years, he felt the joy of living and he wanted more than ever to find a farm, that farm, the one over the nearby hill. He was tired of living off his wits and wanted to spend the rest of his days growing crops and raising animals, farming as he had done all those years before. He had some money of his own, saved from his share of the mining swindle and now the money Arthur had hidden. After returning from Germiston, he had ripped up the floorboards in Arthur's room just as he had told him to, finding almost two thousand pounds and Arthur's share of the gold dust and lying amongst the banknotes, a worn, leather bound notebook. He had stuffed the money into his shirt, slipped the notebook into his pocket and set off to ride to the Van de Merwe farm.

The food was good, just as he remembered: meat pie, potatoes and home-brewed beer, it tasted better with every mouthful and sitting opposite his hosts he told them everything. Cornelius and Mattie sat in silence, hanging onto his every word and when he had finished he finally said, 'look, I have some money and I want to buy the farm.

Cornelius looked up and fiddled in his pocket for his pipe. 'Buy the farm; I don't know, I will need to think about it.'

Mattie interrupted, she had listened to Hans and now that she knew what he had been through, she felt protective of him. 'Cornelius, you don't need to think about it at all.' She was determined that Hans would have the farm, Cornelius knew it and his eyes rolled towards the ceiling as his wife contradicted everything he had said. They had been married a long time and he knew that she was a good woman; she was feeling the pain Hans felt, she would help him all she could and Cornelius knew very well that he would do whatever she wanted him to.

Chapter 19

Normans' commandeered Buick stood in the shade of a row of Jacaranda trees alongside four other vehicles outside police headquarters. For almost an hour he had waited, resting his elbow on the open window as he read the day's newspaper spread across his lap. The headlines made grim reading, the strike had turned markedly violent with deaths reported in Germiston, a train derailment in Alberton, skirmishes between police and striking miners right across the Rand and now the authorities were about to call in the army.

Inside the police headquarters, Commissioner Daniel Coetzee had just fitted the shoulder strap of his holster ready to begin his tour of outlying police stations. He needed to see first-hand how his men were faring under pressure from the strikers, to determine if they needed army support because the situation was rapidly turning into an insurrection and he feared his men could not contain it.

He picked up his peaked cap and placed it squarely on his head, checked his holster once more and left his office. He was worried, very worried, concerned that his men could not keep order. The outlying police stations were generally small affairs staffed with only a few officers and then they were thinly strung out across the Witwatersrand, if the strikers decided to besiege them then he needed to know how he could offer relief, if army intervention would be required.

Initial reports from several outlying stations had ceased that same morning, suggesting the overall strategy of the local commandos was to cut telephone wires and before they had completely cut off his police stations, he wanted to see for himself the situation on the ground. There had been isolated reports of strikers indiscriminately attacking blacks, the facts of the killings at the New Primrose mine were well known and he hoped that this was not the general aim of the strikers. He hoped the blacks would not retaliate with similar force because, although armed only with clubs and sticks, they were so numerous that his men could not hope to contain them. Two hundred thousand physically strong men, each with a pickaxe handle, could cause mayhem.

Making his way along the corridor, he turned the events of the past few days over in his mind. The authorities in Pretoria had prepared for the worst, lessons of the great battles between the authorities and striking miners of 1907 and 1913 were still fresh in the collective mind.

Pausing at the communications room, Commissioner Coetzee opened the door, and went inside

'Pawson, I am leaving the building for a few hours and expect to be back later this afternoon. I want you to locate the Brigadier in Pretoria and ask him to come for a meeting as soon as he can. It is important that he does, and tell him that I am looking to implement Shaka. That should make him move. Are communications still open to the capital?'

The operator nodded and began to re-arrange some of the wires on the panel in front of him as the grim faced commissioner left the room. Daniel Coetzee knew that decisions taken early in the crisis were becoming increasingly significant, decisions he hoped that would lead to a quick and bloodless solution, but he doubted that. Shaka was the code word he and the Brigadier had decided upon for the mobilisation of army units to come to the aid of local police stations. If the police lost control then the army would have to step in and take command and with the backing of such a force, he felt confident of success but he still needed to assess his police force.

Lucy was at home with the children; they had decided that it would be safer to keep them away from school until things settled down. Stories abounded of strikers and their wives randomly attacking anyone they believed to be against the strike. The newspapers were reporting vicious attacks on strikebreakers, houses ransacked by the mob intimidating anyone not joining the strike. Train drivers shot at, railway lines blown up, whole areas brought to a standstill and Lucy was in no mood to expose her children to such danger

'That's a pretty little song Peggy. Do you know what the words mean?' asked Lucy.

Peggy was sitting on the floor playing with her doll and she paused to look up at her mother. 'It's about making mealie,' she said in a matter of fact way. 'Grind, grind, grind the corn, gaya, gaya, gaya ummbila,' she sang again.

Lucy smiled through the thin veil of fear and worry she seemed to wear constantly these days, lifting briefly as she looked at her daughter's innocent eyes. How long would this state of affairs last, she wondered. Suddenly, from the street below came the sound of raised voices and a shrill scream pierced the air. She jumped up in fright and went to look out of the window to see two white women confronting a black. The black woman was Marsha: Lucy had sent her on an errand and she watched as one woman grasped hold of Marsha's tight curly hair, restraining her whilst the other lashed out repeatedly with a leather strap and Lucy's blood boiled.

'Come here quickly,' she called to the children pulling them onto the settee. 'You must sit here until I come back. Do you understand?' Peggy nodded and Henry simply looked at her. 'You are a big girl now Peggy – look after your brother and do not let him wander about.'

'Yes mother, but be careful,' said the child insightfully.

Briefly touching both their faces Lucy ran to the top of the stairs, caught hold of a sweeping broom leaning against the wall before running down the stairs and out into the street, where she found the women had Marsha pinned to the ground and she was screaming for mercy. Without thinking, she went straight on the offensive, scything from side to side with the broom, catching one woman on her shoulder and then the side of head, sending her reeling backwards into a doorway.

The second woman was shorter, stocky and with powerful looking arms and in her hand she carried the leather belt. Raising it above her head, she prepared to counter Lucy's offensive but this time Lucy did not swing the broom instead she jabbed twice, catching the woman in her in the stomach. Lucy's blood was up and she swung the broom around to present its handle towards her enemy, like a bayonet, and after several short sharp jabs, the woman backed away, beaten.

Lucy watched them disappear and then she turned towards the sobbing Marsha trying to get to her feet. She found the strength to pull her up and with one arm around her servant's waist, the broom a makeshift crutch, they hobbled to the safety of the house. Lucy left Marsha sitting on the bottom step and rushed up the stairs to the children to find them sitting together on the settee shaking and crying.

Peggy had gone to the window when her mother had left and seen how she had fought the two women, eventually bursting into tears and her younger brother was crying in sympathy. Lucy swept them into her arms and the three of them clung together, crying and sobbing.

'There, there, children! Everything is all right now. We are all safe and Marsha is back with us,' said Lucy, wiping the tears from the children's eyes. 'Sit here a while longer, I will come back in a few minutes.'

Leaving her children again, she hurried down the stairs to find Marsha sat on the bottom step, hands clasped firmly round her shins and her head touching her knees; her body was a tight little ball rocking back and forth and Lucy thought how vulnerable she looked.

'Marsha, how are you feeling?' asked Lucy, resting her hand gently on the woman's head.

'I am feeling better,' she said in her soft African voice.

'Come, let's get the children, we can clean your wounds and then we will have a nice cup of tea.'

Lucy led them all into their kitchen and after putting the kettle on the stove; she retrieved a small bottle of disinfectant, the one the doctor had told her to use instead of the vinegar and cleaned Marsha's wounds.

'I know it stings, hold still, It will stop the cuts getting worse. Here, hold this bandage and we will cover the worst ones.'

Marsha flinched one more time but she did not squeal out and the frowns on the faces of the watching children melted away.

'Where is Mabutu, Marsha? I thought he was going with you to the store.' Marsha stared at the floor, unable to speak. Lucy repeated the question thinking that she had not heard her properly, finally leaning over her to see her eyes filled with tears.

'Marsha, what's wrong? What's happened to Mabutu?' she asked, feeling her chest tighten.

'He dead missy,' said Marsha, beginning to sob.

Lucy was stunned and for a moment or two, in shocked silence, she was unable to move. 'When, how?' she finally asked.

'In the next street, before you come, I see white men with sjambok beat him round the head and he fall. They kept hitting him. I know he dead and I run, then the white women with the men chase me and try to kill me,' she said, her voice fading to a whisper.

Chapter 20

Tom Sheraton marched into the police headquarters just as Commissioner Coetzee was heading down the corridor to his waiting car. Sheraton was not a top United States Marshal for nothing; a large man, physically powerful and with the ability to get what he wanted out of people no matter how important they thought they were.

'Say, you look to be in charge here mister? My name is Tom Sheraton, and I'm a United States Marshal.'

Commissioner Coetzee looked the man and frowned. 'I'm the Commissioner of Police Mr Sheraton, but I am a busy man. What can I do for you?'

'Waal,' drawled Sheraton, 'we've had our attention drawn to some irregularities here in Johannesburg. There's a lot of American money coming into your country, into the gold mines, and we've noticed that some of these new mining operations are not all that they seem to be.'

'In what respect?'

'Waal, some of 'em ain't proper companies. We think that someone has set up a fake company here and they are selling shares in a mine that don't exist or t'aint worth nothing. A well connected New York businessman asked to come out here to have a look-see, unofficial of course, and I guess you're the man I need to see.'

The American's forthright manner impressed Coetzee and he took an instant liking to him, but today he had an insurrection to take care of. The revelation was nothing new, he was aware unscrupulous people were selling shares in fictitious gold mines to the gullible, they had been doing this sort of thing for as long as he could remember. Back in the 1890's, when Johannesburg was not much more than ten years old and he was still a young constable he patrolled vast areas of country on horseback and had come across countless get-rich-quick schemes. He chuckled to himself as he remembered one old time prospector who had filled a shotgun cartridge with gold dust and fired it into the rock to make the stake appear a good investment. The old man had sold the claim and drunk himself to death on the proceeds. It took six months of backbreaking work for the new owners to realise that they owned a pile of worthless dirt, but by then their money was long gone.

'Tell you what, Mr Sheraton; I'm just about to set off to inspect some outlying police stations. Why don't you have a ride out with me this afternoon and see how we run things here. You can tell me all about your problem as we go and if I can help I will – but I can tell you now, these guys disappear at the slightest hint that you are after them.'

'I'm used to that, Commissioner. I bin chasing outlaws around the badlands most of my life.' The Commissioner raised an eyebrow: so had he. Out on the veldt with a native tracker, he often spent weeks chasing fugitives from justice. They had a lot in common and, although it was highly irregular, the American could be good company.

'I cannot promise you anything, Mr Sheraton, but I will help if I can. I have to leave now, you may come along if you wish and explain to me what it is you want.

'That's mighty civil of you!' said the American.

'Blake, get another two constables and bring rifles and ammunition to the cars,' the commissioner ordered the captain of police waiting patiently for him by the entrance.

The police officer gave a perfunctory salute, turned and disappeared down the corridor leaving the commissioner to write something in the in the desk sergeants logbook.

'If Brigadier Smyth calls please tell him that I am out today inspecting the outlying stations but for him to come here for a meeting as soon as he is able.'

The desk sergeant nodded and at the same time, the captain re-appeared accompanied by two constables each carrying a rifle. The commissioner pursed his lips, looked at Tom Sheraton and then led them towards the line of requisitioned cars. In the first of them, Norman was casually turning the pages of his newspaper and folded it away as he caught sight of approaching police officers,.

'Driver, you can take myself and the captain here, the escort officers will follow in one of the other cars, I want to go out to the Eastern Rand. I'll give you instructions as we go.'

Norman stuffed his newspaper in his jacket pocket, stepped out of the car with his starting handle and became decidedly nervous when he saw the guns and swung on the starting handle wondering what was going on. The engine spluttered into life, he climbed into the driver's seat and soon had the Buick heading out onto the open road and then he took a second or two to turn his eyes towards the rear view mirror and have a better look at his passengers. The commissioner he recognised but the man sitting next to him wearing an unfamiliar wide brimmed hat was a stranger.

For the rest of the morning and well into the afternoon the Buick's powerful engine propelled the car steadily over the dusty and pot holed roads of the Witwatersrand. First, they went north to Parktown and then turned towards the Eastern Rand, stopping for a time at Benoni and Springs before heading towards Brakpan.

The police station in Brakpan already had sandbags piled high around the entrance and as Norman drove up to the entrance, he noticed two armed policemen standing guard. The car following stopped and the two armed constables got out to join their colleagues and he watched them chatting, beginning to wonder just how serious the situation really was. They seemed relaxed enough, but sat behind him in the rear seat Tom Sheraton was not so sure. He had learned from the commissioner something of the trouble in the mining districts and during the morning, he had witnessed groups of armed men in the distance.

'Think I'll stretch my legs a little driver,' he said, opening his door.

Norman said nothing, just watched as his passenger got out of the car and walked slowly towards the station entrance. He had gathered that he was an American, tall and confident and he seemed to have the ear of the Commissioner. Then his thoughts were disturbed as the commissioner and the captain reappeared, the police

295

guards became more alert, covering the two men as they made their way back to the car.

'Boksburg driver, our final stop is Boksburg, do you know the way.'

Norman said he did and set off past the town limits to pick up the road going east. In the rear of the vehicle, Tom Sheraton turned away from the window and spoke directly to the commissioner. 'You gettin' on top of your problems Commissioner?'

'Yes, though things are a little turbulent. Industrial unrest is spreading across the whole of the Eastern Rand and my detectives tell me that the communists are stirring things up. I have meetings with one of the army's top men on a regular basis to monitor the situation, so, if the trouble becomes much worse we can call in the army. By the way, are you working alone Mr Sheraton?'

'No, I have a mining engineer with me from the States. James Brand – he was here a couple of years ago doing a survey on a new mine. He's looking for that mine right now to give us some sort of lead. Quite a few Americans have lost money and we aim to find out what has happened to it and see if we can get some of it back.'

The Commissioner nodded; he had other things on his mind, a few American's losing money was not his top priority.

'When this is all over perhaps I can be of some assistance mister Sheraton, there is a growing problem of fraud and it is something we are aware but then this lot happened. I'm afraid you will have to wait a while.'

In the driver's seat Norman half-heard the conversation over the roar of the engine and picked out the name Brand. From somewhere in his head that name seemed familiar but the road was dusty, potholed and it

296

took all his concentration to keep the car running smoothly and the thought slipped away. Then there was a strange metallic 'thwack' sound from the front of the car, making him recoil, believing that there was a problem with the engine. Then there was another and this time he saw paint flake off the bonnet as the bullet smacked into the engine cover.

'Snipers,' shouted the policeman in the passenger seat, 'keep your heads down.'

Norman accelerated as fast as he could and glanced briefly in his rear view mirror to see the car behind swerve and then accelerate in a cloud of dust. They must have taken a hit as well, then he began to worry, the damage seemed minor and the car was running smoothly enough, but how many more snipers were out there, would the next shot be a better one. His mouth dried at the prospect and his three passengers, of similar mind, braced themselves and produced their revolvers.

'Today could be the start of the trouble we have been expecting,' said the Commissioner. 'Driver put your foot down and let's get away from here. Captain, as soon as we get back to headquarters I want you to contact the volunteer Burgher commandos in the outlying districts and mobilise them.'

'Yes sir,' said the captain busy checking his revolver.

The atmosphere in the car had become tense and to try to calm things down a little the commissioner began asking the Marshal questions 'You were saying, Mr Sheraton, you're investigating a mining fraud here in Johannesburg.'

'Yes, and please call me Tom. What's your name Commissioner?'

'Daniel, but I prefer Dan,' replied Coetzee.

297

In the front passenger seat, the Captain of police raised an eyebrow. Nobody ever, ever, called Daniel Coetzee 'Dan' Perhaps the commissioner's reaction was simply a result of the strain that all of them were experiencing and no doubt when it was all over it would be Commissioner Coetzee again.

'Waal Dan, have you ever heard of the Transgold Mining and Exploration Company?'

That was the trigger. James Brand – of course he knew that name; he was the surveyor who had accompanied Lewis Rosenberg, he was the one who had taken the sample for analysis. It all came back, he remembered picking them up in Durban and bringing them to Johannesburg, the visit to the mine, dinner at the Rand Club and the revelation caused his hands to grip the steering wheel until his knuckles turned white.

What was this all about, why was this American here and why was he asking about Transgold? If only he had being paying more attention to the conversation. Bugger he thought, at least now his attention was absolute, thoughts of snipers and revolutionaries temporarily forgotten. Tom Sheraton had no idea who he was, that at least was clear, but if James Brand ever showed up, he would surely recognise him. Sweat oozed from the palms of his hands as his anxiety increased, worried they might connect him with the fraud. He thought the episode of the Transgold Mining and Exploration Company was history; the only remaining problem to get hold of the money Arthur owed him.

The Commissioner and the American, alert and watchful, eventually fell silent as the Buick roared on towards the small town of Boksburg and its police station. The entrance was barricaded with sandbags just

298

as in Brakpan and the armed policemen standing guard pointed their rifles at the new arrivals. The Commissioner swung his door open and climbed out to salute the guards and put them at their ease. They noted his uniform, returned the salute and visible relaxed. The captain joined the commissioner and as the car carrying the armed escort pulled up behind them, they entered the building.

In the rear of the Buick Tom Sheraton sat quietly for a few moments, looking round and weighing up the situation. Then he opened his door, climbed out turned to Norman and for the first time addressed him directly.

'Not a good idea being caught in here if any more shooting starts, pardner! We'll be like a pair of gophers in a bucket.'

What was he talking about, 'gophers'? Norman had never heard of gophers. He would have felt happier sitting alone but Sheraton was telling him not to stay in the car and the logic finally convinced him that he should take the Marshal's advice. He climbed shakily out and joined the police behind the sandbags wondering how the hell he had managed to get himself into such a mess. He felt for his cigarette case, leaned against the wall of sandbags and lit a cigarette to try to calm his nerves. From the corner of his eye, he watched the American take up a position at the end of the barricade and then listened to the police constables quietly discussing the situation.

Lighting a second cigarette from the glowing butt of the first, he worried that the Commissioner might order him to drive to the more dangerous areas and as he took a drag of his cigarette Tom Sheraton called out.

'Hey, you men, have you seen this?' he said an pointing down the street towards several men on horseback who had rounded a building 300 yards away and were trotting towards them. The police stiffened, raised their guns in readiness and Norman swallowed hard. He did not like the idea of a shootout but to his relief, the actions of the police were enough to deter the riders from attacking and they disappeared down a side street.

'Where does that street lead to?' snapped the Marshal.

'The railway station,' said one of the policemen.

'Can they get around the back of us from there; could they attack us from another position?'

'Well, I suppose they could cross the railway line and get to the back of the station but Mulligan is out back. He'll warn us if he sees any trouble,' said the policeman nearest the Marshal.

'One man back there, and there are five of you here?' exclaimed the American with an accusing glare. 'D'ya think he could do with some back up then? You guys are busy talking yourselves into a bad situation here. What we need is some good lookouts and plenty of ammunition just in case they try to jump us. Could take most of 'em out in open ground I guess. So which one of you is going to help Mulligan?' he demanded.

'It's possible they could attack us from behind, but their leader has told us that as long as we stay in the station they will leave us alone,' said one of the policemen. 'I'll go and see if Mulligan is all right,' he volunteered.

Sheraton watched him go, grunted approval and returned to surveying the street. He knew the men of the commando were weighing them up, watching to see if the police would put up a fight. Then he guessed they

300

probably had another agenda, confine the police to their station to leave them free to have the run of the district. That was more like it he thought slipping his gun's safety catch back on.

Norman stubbed his cigarette out on the step and took a quick glance towards the Marshal, but he was gone. Sheraton was not a man for staying put in a fight, after facing similar situations in his colourful life he knew that the best course of action was to search out cover and move quickly from one position to another, get a bead on the desperados before they could figure out where he was. More than one outlaw who had failed to keep a watchful eye on Tom Sheraton would remain in the Texas badlands for eternity.

Norman stood up and walked towards the police station entrance, almost jumping out of his skin in surprise as the Marshal revealed himself from behind some sandbags.

'Looks like these boy's got sensible don't it?' he said, in his matter-of-fact southern drawl and nodding towards the policemen. Norman could only blink in response to this powerful, formidable man, a man he now knew was after him. He took out a third cigarette with a shaking hand and fumbled for his lighter but before he could locate it a steady hand reached out with a lighted match.

'You all right, driver?' said Sheraton as he lit Norman's cigarette. Norman could only nod again, inhaling deeply, trying to hold himself together, telling himself that he was safe so long as he avoided James Brand.

A minute later Commissioner Coetzee and the captain, returned from their meeting with the Station Commander and walked to the car.

'That's it for today. Take us back to headquarters driver.'

Norman slipped the car into gear and none too steadily set off across town and into open country. The commando they had seen earlier had reappeared and were no more than a hundred yards away.

'Look there Tom, a squad drilling as if they are regular troops. I tell you if this thing kicks off we are in for some real trouble,' said the Commissioner.

The Marshal leaned forward for a better view and grunted agreement. 'Sure looks that way Dan.'

Slowing down, the car entered a suburb and edged down a deserted a street and Norman began to feel distinctly uneasy.

'I don't like this Commissioner,' said the captain, similarly concerned. 'There should be people in the street. There is no one at all. Do you think we are heading into a trap?'

'I certainly do, Blake. Driver – put your foot down and get us out of here,' shouted the Commissioner unclipping his holster cover in readiness.

Norman did not require any second bidding, pushing the accelerator pedal to the floor and forcing the Buick's powerful engine to deliver maximum horsepower. The car began to increase speed, 30 then 40 miles per hour and then the commando sprang their ambush. Volleys of shots came from both sides of the street, the strikers firing wildly, most bullets passing harmlessly overhead. Norman kept his foot hard down, the rear wheels span recklessly and the automobile slid wildly over the dusty earth. Struggling to correct the slide, he over-corrected and the car careered out of control along a serpentine course, its powerful engine forcing the mass of steel and men through the trap to relative safety.

Inside the automobile, the three passengers had wound the windows down to return fire and then a second volley of shots rang out, there was a loud bang as the rear tyre blew and the car began to move even more wildly about and behind the wheel, Norman struggled to control the beast's erratic movements. At least they were out of range of the guns, clearing the ambush and driving into open country and Norman was finally able to slow the car to a standstill.

'Why have you stopped?' shouted the Commissioner, 'If they see we have stopped they will be after us. And where is the other car? No sign of it. We have no back-up. What's the matter, man?'

Norman felt angry. He wanted no part in this conflict, he was neither a miner nor a mine owner and yet here he was risking his life. Why, he asked himself, and now the Buick was full of bullet holes and had a tyre shot to pieces? Who was going to pay for it all? What was he doing here in this bloody country? If he had made some real money perhaps he might feel differently, but he had not, Arthur had swindled him and now an Afrikaner policeman was shouting at him.

Norman knew they had to change the wheel and quickly because the Commissioner was right, the strikers would soon be upon them. From somewhere he found enough strength and calmness to face his tormentor. He dropped his hands from the steering wheel and looked round at the Commissioner.

'Look, without that wheel changed we're all done for, so shut up shouting, and let me get on with it.'

303

The Commissioner said nothing, turning to look out of the rear window for their attackers and then Captain Blake and the Marshal volunteered to take up positions on either side of the road in the event of further trouble.

'All right, let's get out and give you some cover', said Sheraton. 'Can you manage to change the wheel on your own?'

'Get going, you two,' said the Commissioner. 'I will help with the wheel.'

Norman jumped out of his seat, colour draining from his face at the thought of a sniper taking a pot shot. He opened the boot, took out the tools and grasping the wheel brace tightly, crept along the side of the car to begin uncoupling the spare. Luckily, it was still intact, fully inflated, and easy enough to unbolt from its bracket, but jacking the car up and removing the damaged wheel proved more difficult.

Tom Sheraton and the captain had already taken up their covering positions, the Commissioner fetched the jack from the boot of the car, and between him and Norman, and they began to change the wheel. Sweat covered Norman's face and each time he wiped it away his hand became more slippery hampering his efforts to remove the damaged wheel. The commissioner kept glancing sideways at Norman, relieved to see the wheel safely secured. It had taken less than three minutes and now they were ready to go again.

Norman removed the jack and applied a final twist to each nut and as he did so a group of men materialised from the bush and began shooting at them. Sheraton wasted no time in firing back, his aim accurate, forcing the assailants to take cover. They returned Sheraton's fire and from the opposite side of the road, Captain Blake stood up to come to his assistance but he was plainly visible in the late afternoon sun, an easy target, and it wasn't long before the strikers turned their guns on him.

Norman and the Commissioner were ready to go and shouted to Sheraton and Captain Blake to re-join them.

'Have you got a gun?' the Commissioner asked.

This was not a time to be shy: 'Yes!'

'Well use the damn thing!' he replied in a surprisingly matter-of-fact voice. Norman pulled his stubby revolver from his waistband and the two men took cover behind the doors of the Buick, peering through the open windows. A bullet whistled past Norman's ear, so close he could feel the air move and he returned fire, shooting wildly in the general direction of the attackers. The Commissioner, on the other hand, carefully chose his targets firing methodically as he waited for the others to make it back to the car.

The Captain made his move and almost immediately took a hit, dropping to the ground and writhing in pain. Norman ducked low against the car, catching sight of their attackers breaking cover and coming towards them and then Sheraton lifted his revolver, a revolver with the longest barrel Norman had ever seen and took careful aim, picking off the men whose attention had centred on the fallen policeman. The Marshal was in his element, he fired shots in quick succession, downing the man who seemed to be the leader, his second shot wounding the man alongside him and then the other men paused in their advance. It was all Sheraton needed, two more shots and three wounded men lay screaming in the dust alongside their dead leader.

The Commissioner and Norman held their breath; the captain fell silent and all three wondered if this was how

305

they dealt with criminals in the Wild West. Sheraton stood up and walked over to the fallen men, kicked away any weapons he saw and put one final bullet into each of them. With a look of satisfaction, he turned back towards the commissioner and touched the brim of his hat in silent salute.

'You're lucky captain, it's no more than a scratch, bullet went clean through said Sheraton applying pressure to stop the bleeding.'

The captain moaned his reply, less than impressed by the rough handling the marshal was giving him but at least he was still alive and on his way back to the city.

'Can you go any faster driver; I want this man to get proper medical attention as soon as he can,' said the Commissioner.

'I'm going as fast as I can,' snapped Norman in a heightened state of agitation. What his passengers did not know was that Norman was not only wary of the strikers attacking them, but that the Marshal might discover his identity.

The drive back to Johannesburg was a tortuous one, lasting the best part of two hours and with some relief, the men climbed out of the car at police headquarters. The Commissioner hailed a police officer standing guard outside the main entrance and soon two burly constables were assisting Captain Blake from the car.

'Sheraton, I will have to write a report of the incident I'll explain that we were all in danger of being killed. I shall say that what you did was in self-defence and you will hear no more of it. But privately, I do not think it was necessary for you to shoot those men,' said the Commissioner.

The marshal looked pensive, not used to having his methods questioned and watched in silence as the Police Commissioner walked away. Still in the driver's seat, Norman saw and heard everything, feeling distinctly drained after the day's events, a day in which he had almost died and now was under no illusion as to how dangerous Tom Sheraton was. A killer with a deceptive charm and the sooner he could get away from him the better.

Suddenly he froze. The Marshal had walked a short distance away from the car and was leaning against a tree rolling a cheroot when a man appeared heading in his direction his arm raised in greeting. Norman squinted against the sunlight, focusing his eyes, what was left of his colour drained away and he stared with fascination at James Brand.

Chapter 21

James Brand caught up with the Marshal and spoke with some confidence. 'Looks like the ringleader is dead.'

'Which one's that?'

'The Englishman, Arthur, the one with the thin moustache. I forget his other name, oh, James I think, yes Arthur James.'

'Hmm', said the Marshal in his slow drawl, 'that still leaves two and I aim to find 'em.'

Norman could not hear what James Brand was saying but guessed that he might be a subject of the conversation and it made the hairs on the back of his neck stand up. It was then he made the decision to run.

The Buick's engine was still running and Norman took his chance, slipping the gearstick forward he set the car in motion but in his haste he let out the clutch too soon and the wheels skidded in the dry road, squealing and drawing the attention of the two Americans.

The Marshal swivelled round, his steel blue eyes vectoring straight onto the Buick and James Brand, facing the car, looked up, recognition spreading across his face.

'That's one of them!' he blurted out. 'They called him Norman; he was the sales director for Transgold.'

The Buick finally gained traction, accelerating past Brand and Sheraton but not before the marshal had drawn his gun ready to take aim on the disappearing Buick and its occupant. But he hesitated, he had only just avoided trouble with the Commissioner and another incident would not help his case and then the Buick rounded the corner and it was too late.

'Hellfire!' he cried, sucking in his cheeks and firing off a long stream of spittle into the settling dust cloud. 'So I've been driven round by one of 'em all day long and never knew it.'

'How could you know, Tom? But I guess he knows who we are by the way he took off.'

'And he's been listenin' to all I said to Daniel. Well I'll be damned'. He stuffed his gun back in his waistband, straightened his hat, and worked out his next move. 'We need the Commissioner's help on this one,' he drawled. 'Need to know where the fella lives and then we can bring him in. Hmm – Daniel let me know in no uncertain terms that I have no jurisdiction here and I ain't on the US payroll no more so I guess we had better ask him real nice for some help.'

Not waiting for a reply, the marshal strode off in search of Commissioner Coetzee and James Brand meekly followed in the Texan's wake.

'Say, can I have a word with the Commissioner?' drawled the Marshal.

'I'm afraid he is in a meeting with the brigadier at the moment and will not be disturbed.' answered the sergeant staffing the reception desk.

'How long will that take?' asked the Marshal, more than a little impatient.

309

The sergeant looked at him coldly. 'A couple of hours, maybe.'

'Then get a message to him! It's pretty important I speak with him,' said Sheraton.

The desk sergeant was in no mood for the American to cajole him; he was just as tough as the Marshal was. 'I think you perhaps should sit over there,' he said pointing to a bench seat alongside the opposite wall, 'until the Commissioner is free. I think he has more important things to attend to right now,' adding, after a short pause, 'sir'.'

Sheraton was mad inside, but knew when he was beaten, recognising that the sergeant was a good policeman and protecting his boss. He just took a deep breath and walked towards the bench, James Brand joined him and for almost two hours they sat in silence until, eventually, the Commissioner emerged from his office accompanied by the brigadier.

'Well Brigadier, I had hoped it wouldn't come to this but I see no alternative,' said Daniel Coetzee shaking the brigadier's hand.

'I will put our plan into operation as soon as I get approval from the defence committee in Pretoria. I have a conference arranged for when I get back to the capital and within 24 hours I should be in a position to send orders to my command. It is a bad business so the sooner we can bring it to a satisfactory conclusion, the better.'

Their meeting concluded the military man saluted the commissioner, turned smartly on his heels and marched away leaving the Commissioner deep in thought. The desk Sergeant looked across at Tom Sheraton, catching his eye and with a slight nod of his head indicated that perhaps now was the time to approach the Commissioner.

'Scuse me,' called Sheraton after clearing his throat. 'Say Commissioner, could I have a word with you?'

'Still here Marshal, what can I do for you?

'Looks like the ringleader of the gang I am after is dead,' said the Marshal.

'What was his name?'

'Arthur James I think,' said Brand.

The Commissioner's lips tightened as he searched his mind for that name but there was nothing there.

'Never heard of him.'

'We're pretty sure he's dead, killed in a gun fight. But his accomplice has been driving us around all day. Yeah, that driver we were usin' was the front man. Brand here says he was the one who did most of the talking, convinced Mr Rosenberg to purchase those worthless shares.'

'So what do you want me to do about it?'

'Waal,' said the Marshal, 'could do with knowin' his address for a start, then I can maybe bring him in.'

Alarmed at the prospect, the Commissioner raised his hand, 'I don't think so Marshal, you have no jurisdiction here and after today's episode I don't want you bringing the Wild West to Johannesburg – it's wild enough just now.

'Sergeant, get Brunner for me, will you, and ask him to assist these men as much as possible – he is to make any arrests necessary, and,' he said, looking straight at Sheraton, 'no shooting. Is that clear?'

'Sure is Commissioner. Thanks for that,' he said holding out his hand but the Commissioner did not respond in kind, simply saluting and leaving the two Americans to sort out their own problem.

The desk sergeant called a passing constable and gave him instruction to go and find the detective sergeant and five minutes later he reappeared accompanied by a tough looking man in plain clothes.

'Gentlemen, this is Detective Sergeant Brunner,' said the desk sergeant.

The detective introduced himself to the two Americans before speaking briefly with the desk sergeant.

'Sergeant Tompkins here has briefed me on the situation, seems the Commissioner wants me to give you some help'

'Sure thing,' said Sheraton.

'What is it exactly you want me to help you with?'

Sheraton explained why he was in Johannesburg and that they wanted to locate the driver of the car the Commissioner had used.

'Americans, hmm... okay, wait here while I go and have a look and see what I can find out.'

Within ten minutes, Detective Sergeant Brunner returned carrying a slip of paper with Norman's address in Fox Street. 'We don't need any transport to get to this place; it's only about 300 yards away so we can walk.

'Follow me!' he said putting on his trilby.

'Three hundred yards, only 300 yards, we could have been there hours ago. I bet the bird has flown by now, damn it,' said an angry Tom Sheraton.

After a brisk walk, they arrived in Fox Street and Brunner banged on the door. There was no answer so he braced himself and expertly shoulder-charged it, forcing the lock and the three men rushed inside. Racing up the stairs, they searched first one room, and then another only to find the property deserted.

'Seems we have missed your friend Marshal, he didn't hang about by the look of this mess, grabbed what he could and went I would say.'

Next the detective walked over to the table in the living room and glanced down at a newspaper lying spread open, a copy of the day's *Star* newspaper. He scanned the pages and in the middle of the left hand column, amongst the advertisements for furniture, clothing and the like, he saw the word 'Durban' circled. It was an advertisement for the Cape Town to Southampton steamer, listing dates, prices and ports of embarkation.

'I think our suspect has bolted and I have a pretty good idea as to where. Here, look at this,' he said sliding the newspaper across the table to Sheraton.

'Southampton! That's England, ain't it?' exclaimed the Marshal. 'He's had hours to get away. Pity we couldn't have had your services earlier, detective.'

'There's nothing we can do tonight, that's for sure. Let's go back to headquarters and see what I can arrange. You know, he might not have bolted for the coast but headed south to Cape Town or north to Pretoria, though I have to say his best chance of escape would be the steamer. Looks like it leaves Durban tomorrow afternoon and I reckon he has just about enough time to catch it.

Picking up the newspaper, Brunner led the way down the stairs and back into the street where he turned his attention to the office door. Another quick shoulder-shove and they were in the office looking for further clues. The only item of interest was the safe, its heavy door swung wide open and devoid of contents. In his haste to escape, Norman had ransacked the safe and the detective guessed that their quarry was experiencing some degree of panic, deducing that the most likely place he would go was indeed Durban to catch the steamer and leave the country.

'Is the boss still here?' Brunner asked the duty Sergeant as the three men trooped back into police headquarters.

'Yes, but I do not think he should be disturbed.'

Brunner needed permission to go after Norman, he would need a car as well, the train was not really an option as the morning train would arrive too late to catch the steamer, even then they still might not make it before sailing time. He looked at the folded newspaper in his hand. According to the schedule, Lourenço Marques was the next port of call after Durban. He needed to talk to the Commissioner, because not only would he need a car and driver, Lourenço Marques was in Portuguese territory. If he decided to go there rather than Durban, it was a place where the South African police had no jurisdiction.

After a brief tap on his boss's office door Brunner poked his head around it. 'Can I have a word sir?'

'What?' asked the Commissioner, looking decidedly fatigued from the day's efforts.

'Looks like Campbell has absconded and I believe he is heading for Durban to catch the Southampton steamer.'

Daniel Coetzee rubbed his eyes and looked at his Detective, wondering what was coming next. Brunner might look like a street-fighter but he had a sharp and nimble brain and he could see that he had already worked out a plan. 'Go on,' he said

'Sir, we entered the suspect's house and found that he had made a run for it. We found today's newspaper with an advertisement for a steamer leaving Durban

314

tomorrow and I believe that is where he's heading. If you will let me pursue Campbell, then we are going to need a car and driver.'

'What about the train?'

'Arrives too late, anyway we will not be going to Durban.'

'What?'

'There is no time to reach Durban before the ship sails, we need to head for Lourenço Marques to have any chance of catching him. Do I have your permission to attempt a chase?'

Coetzee was feeling the strain and did not feel up to an argument. 'Permission granted, take one of the commandeered cars in the morning. If you cross the border then the responsibility is the Marshal's, tell him that and he is to board the ship and sail with it to . . . to wherever! He will have to arrange with the Captain to arrest Campbell, just don't get involved, keep us out of it! Just get rid of them. Is that clear, detective?'

'Yes sir,' said Brunner, with a twinkle in his eye, pleased that he would be running his own show, quite a novel experience and it made life a little more exciting if nothing else.

'OK then gentlemen, it seems we have a free hand in tracking down your suspect but there are some ground rules,' said Brunner as he emerged from the commissioner's office. 'We will need to take one of the cars out front and head up to Portuguese East Africa, not Durban.' The Marshal looked puzzled but said nothing. 'Quite simply, Marshal, we don't have time to get to Durban before the ship sails, but if we travel overland tonight and tomorrow, we might just catch the ship before it sails for Europe. One more thing: we will be

315

crossing the border into another country and I don't have any jurisdiction in the Portuguese colony. That means that when we get there I can only advise. It's up to you to decide what to do, Marshal.'

That suited Tom Sheraton just fine; he had pursued fugitives over the Mexican border many times and had a smattering of Spanish and he was sure the Portuguese would understand that if they did not speak American.

Chapter 22

The sight of James Brand had galvanised Norman into action, panicking him into blasting the Buick down the street as fast as he could go. He had managed a furtive glance in his rear view mirror and seen the Marshals' gun pointing straight at him, amplifying his fear. Screwing his eyes in the expectation of a bullet in his back, he had only just managed to avoid hitting a tree, wrenching at the steering wheel at the last second.

His mind raced almost as fast as the Buick and by the time he arrived outside his front door, he had worked out an escape plan. He would gather what belongings he could and make for Lourenço Marques. He had noticed the advertisement as he lazed in the car waiting for the police to arrive and had once been as far as Nelspruit for his work and he knew the road. He hoped that they would expect him to head for Durban or Cape Town, not Lourenço Marques and because the steamer would be leaving the Portuguese port in two days, he had enough time to get there. With that thought in mind, he jumped out of the car hurried inside and took the stairs two at a time to find Lucy and Marsha in the living room.

'Lucy! Pack a bag quickly, get the children ready and come down to the car. I'm in trouble and we have to leave the country – now,' he shouted.

'What is going on? Why are we leaving in such a hurry?'

She looked at Norman; he had changed. The man standing in front of her with his unkempt hair, creased and grubby clothes, he had the look of a fugitive. He must have done something terrible to warrant such a performance, had he really just said they were to leave the country?

'Where are we going?'

'Home, we are going home, now hurry we don't have much time. I will tell you on the way.'

Norman disappeared, running down the stairs and outside to the rear of the building where he kept several cans of petrol and a spare wheel. He refilled the car's fuel tank, strapped two spare cans to the running boards and then he rushed into the office to ransack the small safe. Business had not been good, but there was almost £100 inside and with almost £50 he had in the house it would have to do, his money at the bank was forfeit.

In the living room, Lucy and Marsha had just finished packing two suitcases when he burst back in with the newspaper he had been reading and now he opened it at the page with the advert for the Union Castle Line. Cheap and regular passage to Great Britain on a Round Africa service, it said. The ship would be in Durban tomorrow, calling at Lourenço Marques the following day before sailing for the Suez Canal and Southampton. He spread the paper on the table, grabbed a pencil from his jacket pocket and carefully drew a circle around Durban and Southampton and hoped that his pursuers would find

318

the newspaper; presume that they were on their way to Durban but they would be heading for Lourenço Marques.

Lucy paused to watch him, her mind in turmoil. She had suspected her husband was embroiled in some sort of dishonest activity and now she was certain. The upset and disruption to their lives tempered only by the fact that they were going home and as soon as she had readied the children, she knew what she had to do.

After the commotion of packing, ushering everyone into the car, Norman began to reflect and a feeling of anxiety gripping him like a vice. He was up against a ruthless professional, a man who had revealed himself as a killer and so, without a backwards glance, Norman slipped the car into gear and left behind his life in South Africa.

'What's she doing with us?' he said with astonishment.

'Marsha is coming with us for now, Norman. She was nearly killed today, and I'm not leaving her behind.'

'Where's Mabutu?'

'He's dead.'

Norman said nothing, gripping the wheel more tightly and staring out at the road in front, he had seen enough death today to last him a lifetime. The children sensed there was a problem and for once remained quiet, beside them Lucy sat looking at her hands in mild shock, trying to come to terms with their flight. She wanted to know why they were running away, what he had done and as soon as she got the chance she would make him tell her everything – yes, everything.

Africa had made a woman of her – no longer the innocent young mother of ten years earlier, wanting to make a home for her family, trusting in her husband.

319

Her experiences had strengthened her character, made her tough and capable. She was afraid of the future, for herself and her family, but not afraid to confront those fears. She had looked after her husband as would any good wife, but she had come to realise that he had not been a good husband or father. He had spent evenings drinking; mixing with shady characters when he should have been at home with his family and now they were running away and from what. Yes, he would tell her everything as soon as she could squeeze it out of him.

Norman drove as fast as the roads would allow until the sun began its final descent and darkness descended, forcing him to slow down. Three of his four passengers were asleep, all except Lucy who was wide-awake, alert to the fact that her children were in danger and she would not allow her children to perish for a second time. Her husband was under a lot of strain and she felt there was a chance of him losing concentration. He might crash the car and she decided that the best thing was to talk.

'We seem to be well away from Johannesburg Norman. How far do you think we have come?'

'Err, maybe a hundred miles, I'm not sure.'

'And you said you would tell me where it is you are taking us – you said we are going home.'

'Yes.'

'Norman, don't you think it's about time you told me what is going on,' she said in quiet voice, trying not to excite him. 'Well, would you like to fill me in on the details? We have been through a lot together these past few years and if we really are going home, I would like to know a little more. Where are we heading now, Durban?'

'No, Lourenço Marques, in the Portuguese Territories.'

'Lourenço Marques!' exclaimed Lucy in surprise.

'It's our only chance to get away. If we head for Durban they will be on my trail and we may not have enough time to catch the steamer.'

'On your trail, who?'

'The Americans.'

'What Americans? Norman, I think you had better tell me what's going on, I don't want the children caught up in something dangerous.'

'It will be all right when we reach Lourenço Marques and catch the steamer to Southampton.'

Norman paused for breath, thought about what to tell Lucy and decided for once to tell the truth and so, for the next twenty minutes, he explained. He told her how he had met up with Arthur and Hans and how they had set up the fictitious mining venture and taken money from the Americans and now the Americans were chasing him.

'If Arthur hadn't cheated me then we would be going home with a lot more money. He said someone was financing everything and was blackmailing him and then without warning the money stopped arriving. I don't know who it was and now I suppose I never shall.'

'Who are these Americans you are running away from? This Marshal, he sounds out of place in South Africa. Where did he come from and what is he doing here?

'Err, I don't know exactly why.' He could not really answer her question, fell silent and Lucy left him to drive on through the night, confident she had at least calmed him down and then she fell asleep too. She dreamed she was back home with her mother and sisters, felt she could touch them, talk to them and then the car bounced over a rut in the road and shook her out of her slumber. It was cold and she pulled her cardigan tightly to her, leaned over to check on the sleeping children, and then looked at her husband.

'Where are we now Norman?'

'Heading towards Nelspruit, we passed Middleburg an hour ago,' he said, startled by her sudden question. 'I need to stop and sleep for a while Lucy. I just cannot keep my eyes open. Will you keep a look-out and wake me if any other car approaches.'

'Of course.'

He drove on for another hundred yards at slow speed until he found an area of clear ground and brought the car to a standstill, switched off the engine and fell into a deep sleep.

Outside the car a cold grey mist swirled, rising from the ground as the first of the dawn began to make its appearance. Lucy glanced at her watch, almost four o'clock in the morning, she looked over to check on the children and then her eyes turned to Marsha who was staring straight at her.

'Missy, I want to go to the toilet.' Lucy realised that she needed the same; it had been a long and tortuous day. Nodding a tacit approval, she quietly opened her door and beckoned Marsha to do the same and quietly the two women slipped out of the car to disappear into the early morning mist.

'Where you going? You be leaving Africa I think, and you leave me behind?' whispered Marsha as they entered some secluded bushes. Lucy did not know quite how to answer. She had brought Marsha with them because of the danger she felt she would be in if she remained behind in Johannesburg and because of a strong sense of loyalty.

322

'Missy Lucy, this is my homeland here. I not been home for many years and I feel the call of my people. I see the hills,' she said, pointing to distant mountains. 'I know it is my home. I want to go – please let me go.'

Lucy's eyes filled up not for the first time that day and she reached out to take Marsha's hands in hers and said softly, 'of course you can go Marsha. You have been a good and loyal servant and I wish you all the happiness and good fortune in the world. I am so sorry about Mabutu . . .'

The two women returned to the car and Marsha noiselessly opened the passenger door, reached in to grasp her bundle of belongings then she turned to Lucy and whispered. 'Thank you Miss Lucy! And may God be with you.' Then she was gone, swallowed by the mist.

Lucy could only raise her hand in a weak wave of farewell before she climbed wearily back into her seat and then Norman stirred, disturbed by her movement.

'What time is it?'

'Half past five,' said Lucy, glancing down at her watch, he had slept for barely an hour and a half. 'How do you feel?'

'Not too bad, actually, I have a headache, but apart from that not bad. Have any cars passed?'

'No, nothing, there hasn't been a thing, except for Marsha . . .' Hesitantly she explained their servant's departure, wondering at his reaction, but he just shrugged his shoulders and left his seat to stand and stretch his body, throw off his weariness and then he went to start the engine.

The journey to Nelspruit was uneventful and late in the afternoon; the first of the town's buildings began to appear. Norman was in need of a proper rest and a good meal and Lucy noticed a small wooden hotel, the Riverside Hotel, with a painted sign swinging gently in the afternoon breeze announcing 'Bed en Ontbyt'.

'There Norman, that looks like a hotel,' said Lucy pointing to the building. 'I bet that sign means bed and breakfast.

Norman pulled up at the front of the hotel, looked it over for a few seconds, left the car and approached the entrance to the building. A well-rounded, red-cheeked, Boer woman appeared at the window and seconds later opened the front door.

'I see you coming and stop here. You are travellers to the port, you want food and a bed for the night?' she enquired.

Norman said they did and within half an hour, she was serving them a fine dinner of game meat and potatoes, homemade bread and butter and fresh black coffee. The woman fussed about, asking questions her contact with the outside world was only with travellers heading to and from Lourenço Marques and although the news was generally days old when she heard it, she was always interested. She had heard about the trouble in Johannesburg and said she hoped it did not spread as far as Nelspruit.

Norman, weary from his ordeal and the driving left Lucy to talk to the woman and went outside to attend to the Buick. He needed to check the oil and fill the tank with his spare fuel and apart from changing a wheel that was about all he knew of automobile maintenance. As he finished his work and wiped his hands on an old rag, Lucy appeared to say that he should go to bed and catch up on his sleep.

324

'The children are already asleep and it's about time we slept too, we have been travelling for almost 24 hours.'

Norman nodded and followed her to their room, climbed into bed and crashed out even before his head touched the pillow. It seemed only minutes until he was awake again and after a good breakfast he prepared the car, swinging the starting handle just as Lucy and the children emerged from the rest house.

'How far now?' asked Lucy, settling in between the children.

'Just over a hundred miles I think, we can be there before this evening and then we will see if we can buy tickets, find a hotel for the night. According to the advertisement the ship leaves at mid-day tomorrow.'

The Buick made easy work of the roads, dried hard by the sun and before long, they came across a rough wooden shed by the roadside. Two dishevelled looking native guards and a European officer manned the border post and anxious the official might not allow them over the border, Norman made sure he had several banknotes in his hand. He explained they were escaping the troubles on the Rand and heading to the port to meet a ship to take them to Europe. The officer eyed him with some suspicion but after shaking hands, the officer suddenly became more amenable and they were soon on their way.

Two hours later the Buick reached the port and Norman drove along the waterfront past the hustle and bustle of the port, looking for the Union-Castle Mail Company's office.

'Phew, that's a relief Lucy,' said Norman returning to the car, 'I have got the tickets and the man in the office told me the Central Hotel is as good as anywhere. Can you sort out a room if I give you some money? I'm going to leave you there for a while because I have some business I need to attend to.'

Lucy glowered at him. 'And what might that be? Where are you going now and leaving us alone?'

'I am going to find a buyer for the Buick. I might get a £100 for it. Look, you wait here with the children and the suitcase and I will be back as soon as I can. It seems silly not to try and make a few quid.'

At six 'o' clock that same morning Brunner met the Americans outside the police headquarters with their valises packed. Detective Sergeant Brunner had with him a small case containing a change of underwear and some literature relating to farming machinery thinking it a good idea to have a decent cover story. He had briefed the driver about the journey, convincing him that it was an important job for the authorities, that he would probably get a medal once the rebellion was over and by ten 'o' clock that evening they had reached Nelspruit and the Riverside hotel for the nights stop.

'You come a long way?' said the woman bringing out plates of steaming food for her guests.

Brunner, ever the detective, liked to keep conversations alive just in case some tidbit of information came his way and showing little apparent interest he said casually, 'Wouldn't have thought you had many visitors up here this time of year, not from Johannesburg anyway.' He nonchalantly skewered a piece of meat onto his fork and continued in the same matter of fact tone. 'You will have heard of the trouble in Johannesburg I expect. Is it affecting business, been much of a drop in traffic?'

'Yes, these last few weeks have been quiet. Normally we get quite a lot of traffic between the port and the Transvaal, but not much now. We used to see perhaps ten or twenty vehicles passing through each day but only two in two days is quite a drop,' she said

Chewing more slowly now, Brunner asked, 'Two cars in two days? What was the other car like? Do you know much about cars?'

'Not much, but my husband does. He said it was American.'

Tom Sheraton's ears pricked up and he looked across the table at Brunner. Brunner caught his eye for only a fleeting second, but it was enough. They were on to something.

'Say ma'am,' drawled Sheraton, 'I'm an American and I would sure be interested if you could describe that car to me.'

'Well, let me see,' she said, lifting her eyes skywards as she tried to remember. 'It was dark blue and it had a funny round thing on the front and . . .' she paused as she searched her memory, 'well yes, it had a name. I can't remember exactly what, but it began with a B.'

'Wouldn't be Buick would it?'

'Why yes, I do believe it was. I recall the man seemed on edge but his wife was very pleasant. Scottish I think, and the two children were well-behaved,' she smiled, looking towards Sheraton for approval at remembering so much and he forced a smile in return and thanked her.

Children, he had not considered that there might be children, nor a wife for that matter, and they were heading for Lourenço Marques, were they? Norman Campbell was not as stupid as he had first thought. He looked at Brunner's face and saw that that the detective had reached the same conclusion and he knew he would need to be careful. Brunner had already told him that he was under orders not to make any arrests and to avoid a shoot-out once they were in Portuguese territory, that would be his job if it came to it and he hoped there would be no complications, not with children involved.

Norman walked out of the hotel into the bright morning sunshine and leaving his family, drove slowly along the waterfront, coming to a halt amongst some warehouses. He parked the car and went into the nearest building, standing just inside the doorway and looked round for someone in charge, seeing a man with a clipboard giving orders.

'Excuse me,' said Norman, 'could you tell me where the owner of this establishment is?'

The man murmured, 'Is a'me. Why you ask?'

Norman pointed towards the Buick. 'I am leaving Africa for a while and will have no need for a car. Perhaps you might be interested in buying it,' he said. 'At a much-reduced price of course,' he added slowly.

The man looked past Norman and towards the Buick and then back at Norman.

'What I want a car for?'

Norman felt dismayed; he had presumed that a man like him would be interested in a good deal. 'How much you want?' he asked in his broken English.

Norman cheered up. 'One hundred pounds.'

'Is a too much.'

Norman became agitated. 'How about fifty?'

'I geeve you 25 South African pound,' said the man, putting his hand into his pocket. In his time, he had seen enough desperate men running away from Africa to know that he could name his price. The car was easily worth £100 and he could sell it to any number of willing buyers. His hand emerged from his pocket clutching a roll of banknotes and Norman looked at the money, nodded and held out his hand.

'Is a pleasure do business with you,' said the man, a smile spreading across his chubby brown face. 'Here! You 'ave one of my fine Havana cigars, came in dis morning.' He pointed to a small wooden box on the battered writing desk that served as his office and gestured to Norman to help himself to one.

Norman walked back to the hotel not completely disappointed, at least he had done the deal, the cigar was certainly a good one and in a little over three hours the ship would sail. Perhaps he could manage a whiskey or two in the hotel bar before they finally left Africa.

'Did you manage to sell it,' asked Lucy as he entered their room.

'Yes, I got a decent price for it too,' he lied.

Lucy could smell the whiskey on his breath and she could see that Norman was still looking a little worse for wear and decided that her best course was to say no more.

The port was buzzing as Norman led his family up the gangplank of the Kildonan Castle to the sound of cranes loading the ship and the barked orders of the ship's officers. He began to recount his flight from Johannesburg, smiling in the belief his false trail had worked. His foresight in keeping spare cans of petrol ready for just such an emergency had proved fortuitous and then his mood changed. Recounting the loss of the money he had left behind in the Cape bank made him sombre and then a shock wave swept through his body.

The gold! He had forgotten the gold! In his panic to get away from Tom Sheraton and that awful gun, he had completely forgotten the gold dust. He had accepted that he could not withdraw money from the Cape Bank. But the gold he had managed to keep hidden in the closet must be worth at least two or three hundred pounds – and now, you idiot, he cried to himself, you've left it all behind.

The Portuguese officer waved and smiled a 'thank you for the bribe' as the car carrying the four men drove off towards Lourenço Marques. Inside Brunner chuckled to himself at how easy it had been to cross the border, half convincing the Portuguese officer they were bona fide businessmen. Only half convincing him, the bribe the necessary component needed to persuade the officer to let them through and by late morning, the shimmering waters of Delagoa Bay beckoned. Within an hour, they were cruising slowly along the dusty dockside road of the port and looking for the Union Castle steamer.

On board the Kildonan Castle, Norman was not feeling too well. After ten years, he was leaving South Africa with little more than the clothes he stood up in and it was depressing him. He leaned on the ship's rail and stared across to the town but could see nothing, only his own failure. He had come out to South Africa with such high hopes and it had seemed, for a time, he would indeed make his fortune but now he had little hope of that.

He felt in his pocket for the silver case, took out a cigarette, tapped it on the rail, placed it between his lips, and cupped his hands to shield the flame. As he exhaled, his eyes focused unconsciously on a car moving slowly past the ship. It came to a halt not more than 50 yards away and he watched as the rear door opened and a man got out and then he froze. To his horror, the man was wearing a large Stetson hat, not unlike the hat the United States Marshal wore and the shock caused his cigarette to fall from his lips.

The Marshal stood to his full, frightening, six feet four inches and looked up at the ship just as two other men appeared and Norman convulsed in panic. He felt cornered and glanced around furtively for an escape. Aware of his gun still in his waistband, he wondered if he should try to shoot at them, stop them from boarding the ship. A stupid thought: ship's officers were all around making ready for sea and at least one of them would see him. Perhaps he could hide, the ship was large and he could probably secrete himself somewhere until sailing time. But what if they decided to sail with the ship, he couldn't hide forever, and what would happen to Lucy and the children? Certainly, they would report him as 'missing' and then not just Tom Sheraton but the whole of the ship's crew would be looking for him, the prospect making him shudder.

Pulling back between two lifeboats, he kept out of sight of the men below and slowly leaned forward to peer down at the dockside. Sheraton and the other two men stood talking, one he recognised as Brand, and then they began to walk towards a ship's officer at the foot of the gangplank. The one he did not recognise remonstrated for a time and then, to his horror, Sheraton turned and pointed up at the ship, forcing him to squeeze further between the lifeboats. He watched as Sheraton walked towards the gangplank and then disappear from his line of sight. He took a chance, leaned out for a better view

331

and saw that Brand was following but the third man remained with the ship's officer.

'Thanks for that,' said Brunner, offering the officer a cigarette. 'We don't expect any trouble, Campbell isn't known for violence, and after a long hard chase, he'll be glad of a prison cell I think.' The ship's officer grinned and took the cigarette. He had not experienced such excitement in a long time and as first officer was enjoying the responsibility.

Above them, shielded by the lifeboat, Norman watched Sheraton and Brand reach the top of the gangplank and his heart rate picked up, his mouth became dry. With fumbling fingers, he pulled the gun from his waistband and squeezed back into his hiding place.

By now, Sheraton and Brand were on the ship and looking round, deciding where to go when a second officer appeared and spoke to them. The man pointed unwittingly in Norman's direction and then Sheraton and Brand began to walk along the deck in Norman's direction.

Fear rose like a tsunami inside him and he pressed himself even tighter into the confines of the space between the white painted lifeboats. In a few seconds, the Marshal must surely discover him and so, when he was no more than a dozen paces away, Norman made a fateful decision. He lifted his gun and took aim, but he could not hold it still, he would have to expose himself more, lean on something solid for a better aim. Forcing himself forward he was finally able to lean on the lifeboat winding gear and point the gun at the marshal. He felt his grip tighten and almost involuntarily his finger began squeezing the trigger and still the marshal was unaware as Norman made ready to fire when suddenly there was a shout.

'There he is! There he is! He is getting away.' They had seen him and Norman felt he had no time left. Without further argument, he squeezed the trigger. He felt the kick as the bullet left the short barrel and at the exact same time the ship's steam whistle emitted a deafening noise and at the same time muffling the sound of the guns retort. Then the shouting began again.

'It is him look, the Buick, he's getting away!'

James Brand had seen the Buick appear and make its way unsteadily along the dock road and he was convinced that Norman was driving. The two Americans turned and hurried back rushing down the gangplank to meet a puzzled Brunner standing at its foot, each unaware of the drama played out on the ship's deck.

'What's wrong?' asked Brunner.

Brand breathlessly explained: 'It's Campbell; he's just gone past in his car. He pointed over Brunner's shoulder. 'Look over there.'

Brunner turned to catch a glimpse of the Buick jerking round a corner and then it was gone,

'Shit,' he exclaimed, his plan was falling apart, the fugitive looked to be getting away and the Americans were still on dry land. What was he going to tell the Commissioner?

Above them, a bewildered and confused Norman finally ventured out from behind the lifeboat. He had seen Sheraton and Brand running down the gangplank and watched as they jumped in their car and drove off at speed. What was going on, why had they left, why had they not come after him? Then he heard shouting and peering over the side of the ship saw mooring warps

333

leave the dockside, the steam whistle sounded again and he felt a reassuring shudder as the ship began to move.

He stared blankly into space for several minutes, the significance of events finally sinking in and he began to recover his composure. Exhilarated, relieved, he watched in fascination as the gap between the dock and the ship grew wider. He still had the gun in his hand and slowly he looked at it, fascinated, then the truth of what he had almost done dawned. He had come close to being a murderer. He was many things but a murderer was not one of them and without a second thought, he tossed the gun over the rail and into the sea and with what might have passed for a spring in his step, made his way up to the promenade deck to look for Lucy and the children.

'Lucy, we are safe,' he blurted out when he found them.

'What do you mean?'

Norman explained as much as he could, his vocal chords tense and unworkable, speaking in stilted monosyllables, finally managing to say, 'it's been quite a day. I think I could do with a drink.'

Lucy looked at her husband and could not help feeling annoyed. He had not mentioned the gun, only that those chasing them had turned up, that they had now gone away and all he seemed to want to do was drink. He should be with them not in a bar and she knew then for sure that their marriage was over.

'Yes Norman, quite a day. Off you go and have your drink, we will stay here a while and say goodbye to Africa, won't we children?'

The children, thankfully oblivious to all that had gone on, looked at their mother and took hold of her outstretched hands and a subdued Norman walked towards the bar.

He felt like a camel that had just crossed the Sahara, parched and drained and as he ordered his drink, he heard his name called out. Shocked, half expecting to find Sheraton had caught up with him, he turned slowly and felt for the missing gun. To his great relief there was no Tom Sheraton, no James Brand but still he was surprised to see a face he knew. Not more than six feet away, Brian Alders, his erstwhile assistant stood with a grin on his face and his glass lifted in mock salute.

'Hey Norman, how are you?' he said, stepping forward, 'where are you off to, back home for a holiday?'

'No, actually we have decided to return home for good. Had enough of Africa and thought I would try my luck back in Scotland. And you, what are you up to these days?

'I had a look round the Cape for a few weeks after leaving Joburg and now I'm off to a job with a stockbroker in London. I don't really need to work though, I made a packet out of gold mining shares you know, sold the lot at the top of the market.'

Norman was flabbergasted and for a few seconds he could do nothing but stand and stare. How could this unassuming little man tell Norman he had made a fortune – right under his nose.

'N . . . nice to see you Brian,' said Norman, downing his drink in one go and gritting his teeth. 'If you will excuse me . . . m . . .my family are waiting for me . . . see you around no doubt.'

'Yes, you must join me for dinner one night. My treat!' said Brian, with a cheeky smile. A smile of triumph thought Norman who stumbled rather than walked away from the bar. He was devastated, how could Brian have made a lot of money and he had not. It was all too much.

'You're back early Norman, I didn't expect you so soon,' said Lucy sitting with the children on a seat near their cabin.

'I erm, had a drink. Didn't want to get too tipsy you know, not after all that's happened'.

'No, well thank goodness you didn't. Come along children, time for bed,' said Lucy leading the children to the cabin door

Norman could do no more than puff out his cheeks in exasperation and watch them go. He had come to Africa full of hope and expectation, to make a fortune and return home in triumph. Yet here he was, leaving with nothing and wearily he turned to follow his family, catching his foot against something lying on the deck. Surprised he looked down to see Lucy's handbag protruding from under the seat and reached to pick it up. He frowned at its unexpected weight and muttered to himself, "What in heaven's name do women carry around in their handbags?"

Epilogue

Emil Brunner sat deep in thought, hands clasped behind his head and his feet resting on his desk. It was the beginning of the winter of 1922, and the insurrection that had crippled the Witwatersrand for several tempestuous days in March, was well and truly over. The strikers had capitulated at midnight on the 18th but it had still taken several months more to round up the ringleaders, unearth the evidence with which to convict them and Emil reflected on his part in it. He and a team of six detectives had sifted through page after page of evidence, taken statements from eyewitnesses, made arrests and now that work was complete it looked as if he would have another task to occupy his energies. The Commissioner had called him to his office and for a long time he sat and mulled over their conversation.

'Emil, the problem with those Americans, we never got to the bottom of it did we.'

'No not completely sir, the insurrection got in the way.'

'And now that is out of the way, out of our hands anyway, it's for the courts to sort out now; I have had a directive from Pretoria. It seems fraud in fictitious mining operations is more widespread than we thought. A government minister has been stung for a large

337

amount of money, he has pulled a few strings and I have had orders to investigate a little deeper.'

Detective Sergeant Emil Brunner looked at the wall in front of him, eyes fixed in concentration as he pondered the commissioner's words. He had not been completely happy with the investigation either, particularly the chase to Lourenço Marques and the delay that had allowed their quarry to escape and he remembered with some irritation as he had watched the ship disappear into the Indian Ocean. If only he could have questioned the man and then he smiled to himself as he recollected the look on face of the Buick's driver. He was obviously not Campbell, a Portuguese trader who shook like a jelly when Tom had confronted him. As soon as they realised their mistake they had raced back to the dock only to see the ship well on its way. To make matters worse, when he finally returned to Johannesburg he found that the insurrection was kicking off big time. The government had called in the army, the striker's commandoes were setting up roadblocks and killing people and the Burger reservists were on the scene. It was mayhem for several days and at the end of it around 300 people lay dead, several hundred more wounded and any thoughts of solving the fraud case forgotten.

Even though the Americans were none too happy with the outcome and wanted to leave South Africa and its troubles he took consolation in the fact that at least they had discovered one of the culprits. If Lewis Rosenberg wanted to pursue Campbell further, he had ample time to have the British police arrest him when the Kildonan Castle docked at Southampton and now it seemed he was to return to the investigation. The Commissioner had stressed that South Africa needed foreign reserves pay its way and Gold production was the only thing keeping the country afloat. If foreign investors thought that they would lose their money, then they would stay away and the economy would grind to a halt. 'If you think the past few months were bad then consider what it would be like with forty thousand black workers joining the ranks of the unemployed,' he had said.

Emil took his hands from behind his head and folded his arms across his chest. Where to start he wondered, closing his eyes for a moment, going over everything he could think of, trying to find a starting point. What about the office Campbell had worked from, yes, that would do to begin with.

Brunner found the office door on Fox street locked and took a few steps back to look over the property. He tried the door he had forced several months previously only to find it repaired and locked. Feeling in his jacket pocket, he found the bent metal implement he had brought with him and pushed its thin, skewered end into the keyhole. After half a minute, the door sprang open and he went inside. Climbing the stairs, he poked his head into each room, surprised for a few moments that the place appeared lived in and then he reached the kitchen and caught the stench of rotting food.

Campbell had left in a hurry all right, taking his family with him, as he now knew, but most of their belongings were still here and looked to be a source of information. He walked into the bedroom and looked around, opened drawers and cupboards, sifting through anything he could find and then, as he looked at the bottom of a drawer, he spotted some screwed up papers. They were small, about the size of a walnut and he began to unravel them, bar receipts for the Silver Star.

The Silver Star was busy again, the miners had returned to work, money was circulating and the working men were relaxing as they always had. Emil walked past several leaning against and wall talking, others stood at the bar and at the tables card games were in progress.

'Can I help you,' asked Alessandro in his usual friendly manner.

'Yes, I need information, is there somewhere we can talk?'

Alessandro looked puzzled and if it was not for the badge Detective Sergeant Brunner produced, he might have refused.

'I ham a busy; let me find someone to serve. We can talk in the back room.'

The back room was a small storeroom and Brunner found a box to sit on. 'Do you know or have you known a man called Norman Campbell, tall, dark haired.'

'Oh, yes, he comes here many times. He meets his friends here.'

'What friends?'

'Arthur and Hans.'

'Are they here now?'

'No, Arthur die, he was killed six months ago by the police in Germiston.'

'Was he one of the strikers?'

'No, Arthur no work, he never work. I think he was doing a deal when he caught up in something.'

'The other one, Hans, what about him?'

'I not see Hans since Arthur was killed, last I heard was he moved up country, bought a farm. Where would he get money to buy a farm?'

'Good question, what does he look like, this Hans?'

'Tall and good looking, he has light sandy hair and the top of his ear, this one,' said Alessandro pointing to his ear 'is a missing.'

It took several days to locate the whereabouts of Hans but Brunner finally managed it and found himself pushing open a gate leading to the small farm. The gate was rustic, homemade and he found some difficulty in fastening it behind him before following the bumpy track towards the farmhouse, a typical Boer farmhouse, made from sun dried mud bricks and with a roof of thatched twigs and grass. Next to it was a smaller building of similar design and standing in front of it, a flat four-wheeled wagon.

Brunner climbed from the car, told the driver to wait and cautiously approached the larger of the two buildings. He called out, banged on the door, but there was no reply and he decided to look inside. Lifting the catch, he pushed the door, took a step back as a cautionary measure and looked around. The air was thick with silence, it seemed as if the place was deserted but it was too silent, and before entering, he looked around again. Suddenly he froze, a rifle barrel was sticking out of a window and pointing straight at him.

'Don't move mister. Put your hands where I can see them.'

Slowly Brunner raised his arms, 'you must be Hans, I'm Detective Sergeant Brunner o the Johannesburg police and I suggest you put down your gun before

341

anyone gets hurt. If you shoot me you will have the whole of the Police force looking for you.'

'Prove it.'

'I am going to very carefully open my jacket and reach into my pocket.'

'Very carefully, I am watching you.'

Brunner felt the sweat running down his face, pulled his jacket open with an exaggerated movement to allow Hans to see he did not have a weapon and produced his police identity card.

'Come closer, I cannot see it from here.'

Brunner walked slowly towards the window and held out the card.

'What does it say?'

'Detective Sergeant Emil Brunner, Johannesburg Metropolitan Police Force.'

'Wait there,' said Hans quickly relocating from the window to the doorway, his gun still threatening. 'What do you want?'

'I am investigating a case of fraud, the murder of a man called Arthur James and the disappearance of one of his associates, Norman Campbell and I believe that you can help me with my enquiries.'

'What do you know about Arthur?' asked a surprised Hans.

'Well, I have read the police report from Germiston and it seems that he was killed by men purporting to be police officers.'

'I knew it; I knew it, dat murdering bastart Harry Stassen. What do you know?' demanded Hans.

'Hold on mister, don't get excited. Why don't you put down that gun and maybe we can talk.'

Hans looked at Emil for several drawn out seconds, deciding eventually that perhaps he was not the threat he at first believed and rested his gun against the wall of the house.

'That's better. I am here to see what I can find out about the murder of Arthur James,' said the detective in the belief that it was better to pursue this line of enquiry first because as it seemed the Afrikaner was more likely to respond. 'What can you tell me about it, what happened... were you there?'

Hans began to relax and started to relate the events of that fateful day. He told Emil all he could and then the conversation turned to how Hans had managed to afford such a farm.

'I know you were involved in a gold mine scam Hans, I know about the Americans.' Hans looked alarmed and Emil moved quickly on. Listen to me Hans, if you help us I can make sure that you are safe from prosecution, you will be able to carry on with your farming without interference. What can you tell me?'

After a short pause, Hans looked straight at Emil, his mind made up. 'Wait here.' Grabbing his rifle, he disappeared back into the house, returning a short time later carrying a small leather bound notebook in his hand. 'Here, look at this.'

'What is it?'

'I don't know, I found it in Arthur's room, I don't know what it says because I cannot read English.'

Emil half smiled as he took the book from his hand and flicked through the hand written pages, reading selected fragments until, suddenly, the smile on his face disappeared...

Daniel Coetzee read silently for several minutes before placing the notebook slowly down on his desk. 'If this is true it's dynamite.'

Brunner nodded; he knew very well how incriminating the contents of the notebook were.

'We need to keep this quiet, there are people in high places that can protect this man and I don't want anyone else knowing about it just yet – do I make myself clear Emil?'

'Yes sir,' said the detective, eyes narrowing slightly as his detective's brain assimilated his boss's words.

'There is one other thing. You have done some valuable work during the past few months Emil. It has been a difficult time for all of us but due in no small part to you, most of the perpetrators of the trouble are in jail. I recommended you for promotion some time ago and you will be pleased to know that you are now Inspector Brunner. Congratulations Emil.'

The commissioner stood up and held out his hand, Brunner returned the compliment, shaking Daniel Coetzee's hand, a wry, knowing smile appearing on his face.

The telephone on Daniel Coetzee's desk sounded its shrill tone and he reached for the receiver.

'Thank you put the call through.'

In Cape Town, a few minutes later, a similar shrill tone echoed round an expansive office and the man sitting at the desk lifted the receiver to his ear. 'Commissioner Coetzee, to what do I owe this pleasure,' he said, surprised to receive a personal telephone call from the Johannesburg police chief. His tie suddenly felt very tight around his throat and with his free hand he pulled it loose.

'Mister Williamson, we have been experiencing an inordinate amount of fraud here on the Rand and I felt that I should have a quiet word.'

'A quiet word, what has this to do with me? Please explain Commissioner,' said Archibald Williamson, his voice suddenly pitched a semi tone higher.

'I will come to the point mister Williamson; I am in possession of a notebook penned by one Arthur James of whom I believe you are acquainted.'

Williamson groaned inwardly, 'Arthur James, I do not know any Arthur James, why are you telling me all this?'

'Arthur James is dead, you have no need to worry about him anymore but I have his notebook with dates, places and transactions, which I can cross reference with your bank mister Williamson and a certain New York stock broker who I know will be only too happy to discuss his transactions with you. It is damming evidence; I have you cold my friend,'

'I... d...don't believe you.'

'There is one way to find out but I don't think for one minute you are prepared to take the risk.'

'What do you want?' said Williamson, his voice beginning to rasp with unmistakable panic.

Daniel Coetzee smiled, secure in the knowledge that he had Archibald Williamson, a pillar of Cape Town society, firmly in his grip. 'There is an account at the Cape of Good Hope Bank under the name of Abraham Ryker...'

June 1924;

Solomon stared out of the small window overlooking the yard to the rear of the shed the Abantu Batho newspaper called an office and sighed. He had come a long way since the day Jan Hendricks had evicted him and for a time he reflected upon that journey. He was luckier than most of his fellow Africans, he had a job and intellectual stimulation and no longer had to accompany the thousands of black labourers underground. He thanked God almost every day that he could see the sun, feel the breeze and rest when he needed to. He thought of their plight, the hardships most endured on a daily basis and he rejoiced that he had an opportunity to do something about it, no matter how small his voice.

Glancing down, his eyes scanned the sheet of paper in his typewriter and he read the two lines that had taken him most of the morning to compose. Sighing, he considered again the results of the General Election that had taken place not long ago. The two main opposition parties, the National Party and the Labour Party were forming a coalition, the two political parties with the strongest desire to exclude blacks from almost everything. He reached out and took hold of the sheet of paper, dragged it from the machine, screwed it into a ball and threw it against the wall in frustration. He took a fresh sheet of paper but before he could feed it into the machine, a voice called to him.

'Solomon, you seem angry, I have never seen you like this before.' It was Alfred. 'You are writing about the election?'

'Of course, there is nothing else to write about at the moment is there?'

Alfred pushed his way through the hanging bead curtains and stood before Solomon.

'No, and I can understand your frustration, we are going backwards. After all the suffering and strife of the past few years, we are no better off. The new government will strengthen the pass laws to restrict the areas where our people can live. I believe they will bring in laws to protect the jobs of the whites, oppress us in our own country and we can do nothing to prevent it happening. I can understand your frustration Solomon.'

'Do you think the new African National Congress party can do anything?'

'It could have if they had not started to introduce laws preventing the native workers joining a trades union. If we cannot unionise we will not have the power to fight for better conditions. The white strikers fought for the protection of their jobs not so very long ago and lost and now that for which they strived is becoming a reality. The government will bring in protection for white jobs, segregate our society. We are the losers Solomon. I cannot say more, it is up to you to let our people know.'

Alfred turned away and Solomon watched him go before returning to feed the new sheet of paper into his machine. As it disappeared, he could not help thinking that it looked whiter than usual and, engulfed as it was by the larger black typewriter, he began to see it as a metaphor for the oppression of the black population by the white minority. The struggle was going to be long and difficult, of that he was sure, as he began to obliterate the paper's whiteness with the black ink of his words.

Other Books by
Kelvin Robertson

Amsterdam Traffik
Published September 2014

In Ukraine, corruption and criminal activity are rife and the people
have little say in the running of the country. FEMEN is one voice of
opposition, young women prepared to bare all to publicize their cause
at great risk to themselves. Katja is one such protester, the daughter
of an officer of the Ukraine Secret Service. Her mother is negotiating
an agreement with her opposite number from the British Secret
Service, when she learns of her daughter's arrest, only then becoming
aware of Katja's involvement. After rescuing her from the clutches of
the President's men, a fateful telephone call sets in motion a chain of
events that spread far beyond Ukraine.

Pickpockets and Zulus
Published January 2015

The harsh reality of Victorian London leaves Georgie an orphan with
the very real prospect of deportation to the colonies until a friendly
recruiting sergeant rescues him and enlists him as a boy soldier.
Campaigning with the mounted infantry, he fights the Zulu army of
Cetshwayo and discovers his long lost, pickpocketing cousin married
to an officer of the Lancers and their stories intertwine once more.

www.ingramcontent.com/pod-product-compliance
Lightning Source LLC
Chambersburg PA
CBHW061316170626
46817CB00001B/206